HER SILENT SPRING

A Veronica Lee Thriller: Book Four

Melinda Woodhall

Melinda Woodhall
Visit my website at www.melindawoodhall.com

Printed in the United States of America

First Printing: December 2020
Creative Magnolia

For Timmy

CHAPTER ONE

The door to the Frisky Colt Diner swung open and a young woman stepped out onto the dimly lit sidewalk. The clattering of dishes and the smell of stale coffee wafted out into the cool night air behind her as Mack's heart began to race.

Sinking lower behind the wheel of his Ford SUV, he kept his eyes on the server's slim figure, watching as she made her way to the battered bike rack by the curb. Despite the absence of a lock, her secondhand bike was still parked just where she'd left it.

One of the many benefits of living in a small town like Sky Lake. Everyone feels safe. No crime. No need to fear strangers.

The thought brought a cold smile to Mack's face. The night he'd been anticipating had finally arrived, and little Darla Griggs was blissfully unaware of his presence on the dark street behind her.

Starting the Ford's engine, Mack eased away from the curb and circled the block at a leisurely pace. He knew exactly how long it would take for Darla to pedal to the end of Fullerton and turn right onto Hidden Fork Road.

From there it would be a bumpy twenty-minute ride out to old lady Murphy's boarding house. Mack knew the route by heart.

He'd watched Darla every night for the last two weeks, and as a hometown boy, he was well acquainted with the lonely roads she traveled each night after her long shift at the busy diner.

I think it's about time someone offered the poor girl a lift.

Turning onto Hidden Fork Road, Mack sat forward in his seat. Overhanging tree branches cast thick shadows on the two-lanes ahead, but he could make out a dark figure in the distance.

Looks like she's already found my little surprise.

Darla crouched next to her rickety beach cruiser to examine the back tire. The deftly inserted nail had done its slow but steady job.

The Ford's headlights lit up a dogwood tree in full bloom behind Darla, illuminating a cluster of pristine white blossoms that hung heavily on the branches above her head.

Glancing back at the approaching vehicle, Darla lifted a small hand to shield her eyes from the glare as Mack brought the SUV to a stop beside her.

"Everything okay here?"

Darla stood and looked into the SUV's open window with wary eyes. Her mouth softened into a relieved smile when she recognized Mack's concerned face in the vehicle's dark interior. The smile told him she remembered seeing him in the diner just as he'd expected.

"Oh, I'm okay." She raised her delicate eyebrows in a rueful grimace. "Unfortunately, my bike isn't."

"Well, it looks like you could use a ride, young lady." Mack's voice was firm. "Where you headed?"

He arranged his face into a curious frown as if he didn't already know where she was going. Murphy's Boarding House was about two miles ahead, just past the turn off to the popular lake that had given the little town its name.

"I'm staying at Murphy's just up the road."

She looked again at her tire and shrugged her narrow shoulders.

"It's not that far."

Leaving the Ford's engine running, Mack opened the door and jumped down onto the rough asphalt. His pulse quickened as he circled around the back of the SUV and surveyed the deflated tire.

He allowed himself one quick look at the face he'd come to know so well, then dropped his gaze back to the bike, worried she would be spooked by the hunger in his eyes.

"I know the place," Mack confirmed, hefting up the bike and carrying it toward the back of the Ford. "I'll drop you off seeing I'm headed in that direction."

Not giving Darla the chance to protest, he loaded the beach cruiser into the rear and climbed back into the driver's seat. Only then did he look over to see that she was still standing in the same spot, her forehead twisted into an uncertain frown.

"Come on," he called through the open window. "I can't just leave you out here. If anything happened to you, I'd feel responsible."

A rustling in the bushes behind her started Darla's feet moving toward the Ford. She pulled open the door and stood looking into the front seat with wide eyes, then hesitated.

Holding his breath, Mack waited in silence. He didn't dare speak, sensing she could turn and flee at any minute, like a deer who'd just heard the crack of a branch under a careless hunter's boot.

The moment of uncertainty seemed to pass as quickly as it had come, and with a resolute nod of her head, Darla climbed into the passenger seat and pulled the door shut behind her.

"Thanks for the ride."

Her words were accompanied by the shy smile Mack had seen her wear when serving tables at the diner. It was that smile that had drawn his attention. That and her big blue eyes that reminded him of another girl, and another dark night near Sky Lake.

Mack's foot pressed down on the accelerator before Darla had a chance to buckle her seatbelt, his heart galloping like a racehorse in his chest. He'd waited so long to get her alone, to get her far away from the suffocating atmosphere of the diner.

Glancing over at the soft, pale skin of Darla's bare knee, only inches away from his hand on the gear shift, Mack felt lightheaded.

He forced his attention back to the road, knowing the detour he was about to take would raise alarm bells, silently rehearsing his excuse.

Darla settled her purse on her lap, gripping the cheap leather with both of her small hands, and stared out the window even though there was nothing to see but the same dark tangle of trees she rode past every night on her way home.

"So, Darla, how long have you been working at the Frisky Colt?" Mack asked, clearing his throat, which was dry and tight with anticipation.

Darla turned to face him. The uncertain frown was back.

"How'd you know my name?"

He dropped his eyes to her chest. Her face flushed a pretty pink as she looked down to see the plastic name tag pinned to her brown polyester uniform. She giggled and raised a self-conscious hand to brush back a wayward strand of short, dark hair.

"Well, I guess it is pretty obvious," she said, relaxing back against the seat. "And I've seen you at the diner. You're there a lot, too."

"You like working there?' he asked, hoping to keep her talking, wanting to draw her attention away from the road.

"Yes, sir," she said with a nod. "And I sure do like the tips."

"Oh, no need to call me sir."

Mack saw the turn-off to the lake coming up on his left. He took a deep breath and kept talking.

"You can just call me Mack. That's what my daddy always called me." Mack looked in the rearview mirror to make sure the road was clear. "It's kinda like a nickname, I guess."

"Well, my daddy never called me anything," she muttered, her eyes shifting back to the dark night outside her window. "Never met the man actually."

Turning the Ford onto Sky Lake Trail, Mack cleared his throat, sensing her stiffen next to him.

"Just gotta make a quick stop," he murmured before she could ask where they were going. "It'll just take a few minutes. Save me driving back this way later. I'll have you home before you know it."

The lie slipped from his tongue without so much as a stutter. He felt Darla's eyes studying him, but he concentrated on the road ahead. Minutes later he made another left and began to bump the Ford down a rutted dirt road.

No matter how far you go, the road always leads back home, doesn't it?

The Ford crunched to a stop in front of a sagging gate. One of the rusty hinges had come loose, and the wood had split open.

"Where are we?"

Darla's blue eyes widened as she took in the dented sign screwed onto the fence post.

"What's Silent Meadows Farm?"

"It's my family's farm," Mack said, offended by the disdain he heard in her voice. "It used to be a grand place, before...well, before my daddy had to sell off most of the land."

Thrusting open his door, Mack stepped out onto the rocky road and pushed the gate back. The old hinges issued a high-pitched creak that echoed like a scream through the still night air.

Glad there's nobody else around here to be bothered by the noise.

Jumping back in the Ford, he ignored the growing tension in Darla's small shoulders as he steered the big vehicle around the side of a dilapidated farmhouse.

A waxing crescent moon hung over the gabled roof of the old building; its frail light enabled Mack to see that more wooden shingles had fallen off since his last visit. The place was falling apart bit by bit, just as his father had.

He guided the Ford past the back porch and came to a sudden stop on a scruffy patch of grass. The headlights lit up the long, sloping lawn that stretched out before them.

"Is that a...a *graveyard?*"

5

Darla pointed a small finger toward the black, wrought iron fence that ran along the west side of the property. The pale arch of a headstone was clearly visible beyond the fence, as was a weathered sandstone cross which had tilted precariously on its base.

Mack shut off the engine, and a blanket of darkness settled over the yard as he turned to face Darla.

"That's the family cemetery."

He could smell the faint scent of her perfume as he spoke, and he had to swallow hard before he continued.

"Lots of old farms have private cemeteries in Kentucky."

He adopted a confident tour-guide tone as he tried to calculate how long it would be before she tried to run.

"There are more than 13,000 cemeteries in the state. Most of them are privately owned like that one. Come on, I'll show you."

The light from the dashboard revealed an alarmed expression on Darla's pretty face. She shook her head, sinking back against the seat.

"No thanks. I'll just wait here while you get whatever it is you need." Her voice cracked on the last word. "I've got a blister, so I don't feel like walking around."

Mack sighed. A hard edge entered his voice as he stared toward the cemetery.

"You know, that's where my daddy ended up."

Even at a distance, he could see the marker that stood guard over his father's grave. As always, the thought of his father sent a jolt of resentment through him. The old man had ruined his life and tarnished the family's legacy.

"He was a...a weak man," Mack heard himself say. "Too weak."

Clearing his throat, he glanced at Darla's face. He thought he saw pity in her eyes and held her stare, trying to decide if it was time.

"What happened?" Darla murmured. "I mean, how'd he die?"

"He died of shame, I reckon," Mack said, his chest tightening at the thought of his father's disgrace. "Dropped dead not long after leaving the state penitentiary over in Eddyville."

Mack thought he saw surprise in her eyes at his admission, and then the pity was back. He didn't like pity. It was a wasted emotion.

"I don't look like I come from criminal stock, do I?"

Mack's mouth stretched into a sardonic smile.

"But looks can be deceiving. Your daddy would have told you that...if you'd ever had one."

Recoiling at the scorn in his voice, Darla dropped her eyes.

"I've gotta get home," she said, twisting the strap of her purse with nervous fingers. "Mrs. Murphy will...she'll be worried."

"Of course," Mack said, although he doubted old lady Murphy would give little Darla Griggs a second thought.

He figured the woman would likely sell the girl's clothes to the secondhand shop to recoup the rent due and then be done with her. Girls like Darla Griggs came and went without anyone making a fuss.

I'll bet the greedy old bag will have the "Room Available" sign up in the window again within forty-eight hours.

Leaning across Darla's legs to open the glove compartment, Mack felt her shrink away from his touch. He kept his voice light as he reached inside and felt his hand settle over the syringe.

"Just need to get something out of here so we can get you home."

No need to tell her he meant his home. She'd find out soon enough. It was always easier to let them believe everything was okay until the very last minute. No need to make a fuss, even if there wasn't anyone around to hear it.

Mack pulled his hand out and pushed the long needle into the pale flesh of Darla's upper arm in one smooth move. He watched her blue eyes widen with pain, and then horror, as she looked down to see him holding the syringe.

"What are you..."

7

Darla's eyelids drooped and her mouth slackened as the Fentanyl began to work its magic. The opioid would put her to sleep with almost immediate effect, and Mack figured she would be out for at least an hour, if not longer.

There would be plenty of time for him to finish what he'd waited so impatiently to begin. Slipping out of the driver's seat, Mack circled around to open the passenger side door.

Watching him through heavy eyelids, Darla's eyes filled with panic even as they began to close. She opened her mouth to scream, but no sound emerged. Her weak protest faded into a soft moan, and then she was still and quiet.

"It's better this way," Mack muttered, hoisting her over his shoulder and turning toward the house. "Now let's go home."

* * *

The first red streaks of dawn fell over the cemetery just as Mack scooped up the last shovelful of loose dirt and dropped it on the ground in front of the headstone.

Bending over, he smoothed the rocky soil, trying to erase any evidence that the ground had been disturbed. It had taken a lot of work to excavate the grave beneath his feet, and he was still shaken by the unexpected turn of events.

His gritty eyes burned with fatigue as he stared down, barely able to make out the faint inscription engraved on the headstone. It made no difference; he knew the words by heart.

Our Beloved Susannah
Born 1878 – Died 1896
Her virtue and grace were still in bloom
Alas, the fair maid found an early tomb.

As a child, Mack had always been curious about the young woman who had lived and died in the house a century before.

He would stare at the weeping angel on the headstone and wonder what had happened to her. How had she died? Why had she died so young? What would she look like now, after all this time?

But an hour before, when he'd stood over the old pine casket, his body coated with dirt and sweat, he hadn't had the strength or the courage to lift the lid and find out.

Instead, he'd pulled Darla's limp body down onto the splintered wood and scrambled up and out of the hole, anxious to finish his morbid chore and be gone.

Looking down at the finished job, Mack sighed in tired relief.

No one will ever suspect she's here, and I'm sure Susannah won't mind.

While Darla's wasn't the first body he'd hidden in the old cemetery, it wasn't something he made a practice of doing. He preferred to bury his secrets far away from the old farm, which had been in his family for generations.

He had planned to keep Darla around for a few days. He'd hoped to make a tidy profit selling her on to a buyer that would pay top dollar for the fresh young woman.

Unfortunately, he must have mismeasured the Fentanyl. Or maybe mixing it with the oxycodone had made it lethal. Whatever the case, Darla had gone to sleep, and she hadn't woken up. It hadn't taken him long to determine she never would.

Carrying his shovel up to the porch, Mack propped it against the rail and stood on the top step, the wood bowing beneath his boots. He took a deep breath and surveyed the property, or at least what was left of it. The sight wasn't impressive.

Any of the land that had been rich and usable had been sold off long ago to pay legal bills and taxes, leaving only the dilapidated house and the family's private cemetery for Mack to inherit.

The old farm had fallen further into ruin after Mack had moved into town, no longer wanting to be associated with the old place.

He'd been unwilling to waste the money he'd been squireling away to fix it up but hadn't been able to let the old place go.

At least not yet. Especially now that the little family cemetery contained more than just the bones of his mother, father, and other long-dead and forgotten ancestors.

Walking back to the cemetery, Mack took another look around, feeling as if he was leaving something behind. He stepped to a simple marble stone and reached out a big hand to brush the dirt off the name etched across it.

He traced the letters with a calloused finger. He had no real memories of his mother, but he sometimes dreamed of the thin, fragile woman he only recognized from the framed pictures still hanging on the walls of the old farmhouse.

If you hadn't died, maybe things would have been different.

Pushing away the useless thought, Mack forced his mind back to the matter at hand. He couldn't let himself fall into one of his dark moods. Not unless he wanted to screw up his long history of flying under the radar.

He'd broken the golden rule Donnie had taught him, and if he wasn't smart, he might end up paying for it.

Never take a girl from your own town again, Mack. It'll get you caught.

Mack had followed the rule for years. But then Darla had come along. She'd been special, and she'd only been passing through. He was sure no one would blink an eye if she suddenly left town. Most people moved on from Sky Lake eventually.

Of course, if someone did raise an alarm, they might be able to track her back to his property. A fresh sheen of sweat broke out on Mack's forehead despite the cool spring breeze, and he headed for the Ford, suddenly anxious to get away from the old place.

There was always the remote chance that someone would come along and start asking questions. Donnie's deep, rough voice played in his head.

You never know when the feds will show up, so always be ready to run.

Mack climbed back into the Ford and started the engine. He drove east toward Sky Lake, heading into the sun. He decided he'd better heed Donnie's warning; he needed to get ready to run.

CHAPTER TWO

The persistent buzz of her cellphone on the bedside table brought Veronica Lee up and out of a deep sleep. Eyes still shut, she reached a sleepy hand out and silenced the unwelcome noise, then relaxed back into the soft pillow. She'd almost managed to drift off again when movement at the foot of her bed elicited a resigned sigh.

"You aren't going to let me sleep in, are you, Winston?"

She didn't have to look down to know that the big orange tabby cat would be staring at her, eager for her to wake up. He had a routine to keep, and he didn't appreciate her disrupting it.

Forcing one eye open, she squinted at the bright strips of sunlight shining through the slats of her window blinds. The sun was already high in the sky, and she sat upright with a groan, grabbing her phone and staring at the time with bleary eyes.

Veronica groaned again and dropped the phone back on the table, then scooped Winston up into a tired hug.

"I'm glad you were here to wake me up," she murmured, carrying him to the bedroom door. "I have an interview in less than an hour."

She opened the door and dropped the big cat into the hall. He quickly padded toward the stairs as she turned and crossed to her closet. If she dressed quickly, she'd still have time to get into town in time for the interview she'd scheduled.

A new source had come forward with information related to her ongoing series on organized trafficking networks and their victims. Veronica didn't want to miss the opportunity to speak to the young woman and hear her story.

She knew how hard it was for trafficking victims to build up the courage to talk, especially to a reporter, and showing up late to their first meeting was unlikely to inspire the woman's trust.

Scanning the clothes in her closet, Veronica decided the fresh spring weather called for a change from the dark colors she'd been wearing lately. She pulled on an apple green jacket and matching skirt, then turned to face the mirror.

Her long dark hair contrasted nicely with the pale green material, and she suddenly felt a surge of determination.

Spring had come; it was a season of renewal and rebirth, and Veronica was hoping that she, too, might get a chance to start fresh. The last year had been incredibly difficult, but maybe it was possible for her to leave the past behind and focus on the future.

And I can start by focusing on getting to Hope House on time.

Hurrying down the stairs and into the hall, Veronica followed the aroma of freshly brewed coffee into the kitchen. She had just enough time to fill a thermos and let her mother know she was leaving.

Ling Lee stood by the sink, gazing out the kitchen window.

"Morning, Ma," Veronica said, joining her mother at the window, her eyes drawn to the backyard where a small figure knelt over a bed of flowers. "Skylar's in the garden already? Or did she sleep out there?"

Veronica watched the morning sun play off Skylar's silvery blonde hair as the girl worked over the flowers, and her chest filled with sudden gratitude that they'd found each other.

"Your sister's definitely a lark." Ling's voice was full of affection as she watched Skylar. "She's not a night owl like you."

Melinda Woodhall

It was still surreal to hear Ling refer to Skylar as her sister. For twenty-eight years Veronica had been raised as the only child of a single mother. Then over the winter, her father had reappeared, intent on revenge and Veronica had learned who she really was, and that she had a half-sister who needed her help.

Accepting that a violent fugitive like Donovan Locke had been her father was hard, and she didn't like to think about all the people he'd hurt during the years he'd spent hiding on his secluded ranch in Montana's Bitterroot Valley.

Before her father had shown up in Willow Bay, everything Veronica had known about herself and her family had been a carefully constructed façade, intended to hide her and her mother from her father's wrath.

But now that Locke was dead, and Skylar, the daughter he'd hidden away from the world for so long had been found, Veronica was starting to come to terms with her new reality.

Against all odds, they had survived to become a little family, and Veronica wanted to believe that the trauma lay behind them and that now they would all get a chance to heal and move on with their lives.

If only she could shake the sense that they were all still in danger and that the evil that had surrounded her father wasn't finished with her and Skylar yet.

That feeling made her want to keep Skylar safe and tucked away from anything or anyone else that could harm her.

So far, Veronica had only told a few close friends, and Skylar's counselor, Dr. Reggie Horn, that Skylar was Locke's daughter, and that her mother had been one of his victims.

No one else knew that Veronica had a half-sister yet, and she wished she could keep it that way, but she wouldn't be able to hide the fact forever. Eventually, Skylar would be strong enough to stand the scrutiny and the questions. Until then, Veronica was determined to shield her little sister from any more pain.

Pushing back the disturbing thoughts, Veronica grabbed her thermos off the counter, filled it with steaming hot coffee, and added a generous splash of milk. She screwed on the lid as she adjusted her work bag over her shoulder.

"And now for the latest local news from Willow Bay..."

The voice coming from behind her was familiar, and Veronica turned to the little television on the kitchen counter with interest.

Tenley Frost, Channel Ten's new morning anchor, sat behind the news desk. Her shiny auburn hair was perfectly arranged, and her cool blue eyes showed no signs of the traumatic ordeal she'd barely survived only months before.

"She certainly bounced back fast," Ling said, nodding at the small screen. "I guess getting fired by Mayor Hadley was a blessing in disguise for Tenley, although I'd have loved to have her on my team."

"How *is* the recruiting going?" Veronica asked, checking her watch. "Will you have a team ready to go in time?"

Ling Lee had won the heated mayoral election in February by a narrow margin and was scheduled to be sworn in as the new mayor of Willow Bay in less than three weeks.

As the first woman to be elected to the position, Ling was determined to build a talented team to support her as she took on the new role. But it had proven surprisingly hard to find ideal candidates willing to leave the private sector.

"I won't have a media relations officer as talented as Tenley Frost, that's for sure," Ling complained. "I think Mayor Hadley got rid of her just to spite me."

Suppressing a smile, Veronica shook her head.

"I'm pretty sure Tenley's late-night activities with Garth Bixby in City Hall played a part as well," Veronica offered, heading toward the door. "At the very least it gave Hadley the perfect excuse to fire them both after he lost the election."

Her phone buzzed in her pocket before Ling could respond. Seeing the name on the display, Veronica raised wide eyes to Ling.

"It's Deputy Santino," she said, tapping on the speaker icon and holding it out so her mother could hear as well.

"Have you found her?" Veronica asked, too anxious to waste time on pleasantries. "Have you found Skylar's mother?'

"That's why I was calling," Santino said.

The U.S. Marshal already sounded tired, even though it wasn't yet nine o'clock, and she heard frustration in his deep voice.

"We've just gotten back the DNA profiles for the remains found at Locke's ranch. None of the profiles match Skylar's profile."

His words sent Veronica's heart plummeting.

"I'm sorry, I know it's not what you wanted to hear."

Santino sounded as disappointed as she felt. They both knew it would be hard for Skylar to ever find closure if her mother's body wasn't found and laid to rest.

As she disconnected the call, Veronica turned her eyes back to the little window. She'd have to let Skylar know that Santino had called. But that could wait for later. She'd let the girl enjoy the pretty spring day. No need to ruin it for her now.

As she climbed into her Jeep and headed into town, Veronica vowed she wouldn't let her sister down. She was an investigative reporter after all. It was her job to hunt down the truth behind a story, no matter how dark, and bring it to light.

And now my sister needs to know her own story. After everything Skylar's been through, she deserves that much.

* * *

The drive into downtown Willow Bay seemed to take longer than usual as Veronica brooded over Deputy Santino's phone call. She needed to find out who Skylar's mother had been and what had happened to her. The question was where and how to get started.

Arriving at Hope House with only minutes to spare, she pulled into the parking lot and nosed her big red Jeep into a *Visitor's Only* space.

The residential rehabilitation center had opened the year before, quickly becoming a haven for women battling addiction, and Veronica had visited the facility several times during her trafficking investigation.

She'd been surprised the day before when the facility's director and senior counselor, had called to invite her to visit a resident who was nearing the end of her treatment.

It was unusual to get a call from a source's doctor, but Veronica had readily agreed when she heard the information the resident wanted to share involved her trafficking series.

Pushing through the rehab center's big glass door, Veronica approached the reception desk and smiled.

"I'm here to visit Misty Bradshaw," she said to the woman behind the desk. "I'm Veronica Lee. I believe she's expecting me."

"Yes, Dr. Horn told me you'd be coming."

The receptionist handed Veronica a visitor's pass.

"Misty's already waiting in the rec room. You know the way?"

Veronica took the pass and nodded, her thoughts already turning to the woman she was about to meet, already preparing herself to once again witness the devastating toll of addiction.

Most of the women she'd interviewed as part of her trafficking investigation had seemed lost and broken. The pain and shame in their eyes had stayed with Veronica long after the interviews were over, and the trust they placed in her by sharing their stories weighed heavily on her shoulders.

Yet the possibility that she could save other women from such a fate had kept Veronica working the story, in spite of the danger she faced from exposing ruthless predators and trafficking networks.

Inhaling deeply, Veronica braced herself as she neared the rec room. A young woman in a crisp white blouse and knee-length skirt stood by the door. She tucked a file under her arm and smiled as Veronica stepped into the room.

"I'm looking for Misty Bradshaw," Veronica said, returning the woman's smile. "The receptionist said she should be in here."

Veronica looked around the busy room. Sunlight streamed in through wide windows as women watched the morning news or chatted in small groups.

"I'm Misty Bradshaw," the young woman said, sticking out a small hand. "I'm the one who asked Dr. Horn to call you."

Trying to hide her surprise, Veronica took the offered hand.

"It's nice to meet you, Misty. I'm Veronica Lee...but I guess you already knew that."

"Yes, I watch you all the time on Channel Ten News." Misty's shy smile revealed the dimples in her smooth, pale cheeks. "I feel like I already know you. Like I can trust you."

Looking over her shoulder to make sure no one else was listening in to their conversation, Misty lowered her voice.

"That's why I wanted to talk to you."

Veronica studied Misty's big brown eyes. They were clear and bright. And the woman's hands appeared to be steady as she tucked a shiny strand of light-brown hair behind one delicate ear, revealing no signs of withdrawal or distress.

"Well, I'm glad you called." Veronica was suddenly anxious to hear the young woman's story. "Let's find a place to sit down."

Moving to the courtyard outside the rec room, they sat at a small patio table. The sun was warm overhead, but a gentle breeze kept it comfortable as Veronica took out her notepad. She gestured toward the file Misty was holding.

"Is that something you wanted to show me?"

The young woman looked confused, then shook her head.

"No, I'm just working on my resume," she explained. "I need to find a job now that I'm going to be getting out of here."

The composed young woman certainly wasn't what Veronica had been expecting. She cocked her head and raised her eyebrows.

"So, what is it you wanted to tell me?" Veronica asked. "Dr. Horn said it had something to do with my trafficking series. Is that true?"

Misty nodded. A shadow fell over the young woman's eyes and she wrapped her arms around herself, her confident demeanor slipping.

"I just didn't know who I could trust."

Her eyes searched the empty courtyard.

"Trust with what?" Veronica asked, beginning to sense the fear behind the girl's words.

"I have information regarding a...a trafficker...a predator."

Considering Misty's words, Veronica nodded.

"Okay, but why call me?" she asked. "Why not go to the police and file a report?"

A bead of sweat worked its way down the side of Misty's neck and disappeared behind the crisp white collar of her blouse.

"I heard that a policeman was helping the traffickers caught in Willow Bay a few months back." Misty's voice faltered and she cleared her throat. "I'm...scared of the police."

"Does your information have something to do with those same traffickers?" Veronica asked, feeling her own heart start to beat a little faster. "Do you have information about the Diablo Syndicate?"

Misty hesitated, then nodded.

"I know the police killed Diablo, but there are still people out there who were working for him." She inhaled deeply, then squared her small shoulders. "I know who they are. Or at least, I know who one of them is, and I know where she lives."

"She?" Veronica couldn't hide her surprise. "The person you believe is working with the Diablo Syndicate is a woman?"

A glint of anger brightened Misty's eyes as she spoke.

"Yes, and she's worse than any of the men I had to deal with."

Misty clutched the sleeve of Veronica's jacket as if she feared the reporter would turn away.

"She was the one who pulled me in and got me hooked. Once I saw your report on the news it dawned on me what she really is...she's a trafficker. And she's still out there."

Looking down at the hand on her arm, Veronica noticed the phrase *PS 23:4* had been tattooed across Misty's delicate wrist.

"This is what got me through detox," Misty said, catching Veronica's eyes on her wrist. "Psalm 23:4 has always been my favorite. You know it?"

Veronica nodded, but Misty had already closed her eyes and begun to recite the words in a ragged whisper.

"Though I walk through the valley of the shadow of death, I will fear no evil: for thou art with me..."

Voices sounded in the rec room behind them and Misty opened her eyes, blinking into the sun as if she'd woken from a dream.

"Sorry about that," she said, leaning closer. "But it was by the grace of God alone that I was able to get out of that situation alive, and how I managed to get clean."

Staring at Veronica across the table, Misty's eyes filled with tears.

"And now that I'm...*free*, well, I can't just sit by and let that evil woman put anyone else through the hell I've been through."

Questions flooded Veronica's mind, but she knew she needed to take things slowly. Women who had fallen victim to traffickers often suffered from PTSD. Asking them to relive their trauma could trigger unpredictable reactions, and she didn't want to cause the young woman any more pain.

As if sensing Veronica's unease, Misty sat back with a deep sigh.

"Look, I know I sound crazy, but I'm not. I'm sober and ready to move on with my life," she said. "But I can't do that while Amber Sloan is out there looking for me and preying on other women."

"Amber Sloan?"

Veronica wrote the name on her notepad.

"Is she the woman working with the Diablo Syndicate...or whatever's left of the Syndicate?"

"Yes," Misty admitted, absently rubbing a thumb over the tattoo on her wrist. "And I want to tell the police who she is and what she's done, but I'm scared. I mean, what if she really does have a connection there? Or what if they won't believe me?"

Wishing she could assure Misty that there was nothing to worry about, Veronica knew that wasn't quite true.

The Willow Bay Police Department had a history of police misconduct, and even though Nessa Ainsley had taken over as Chief of Police, and was working to clean up the department, Veronica couldn't be sure that Amber Sloan didn't have a connection with someone inside the WBPD.

"Well, I believe you." Veronica's voice was firm. "And if you want to tell the police what you know, I'll go with you to the station so you can file an official report."

She raised a hand to quiet Misty's objection.

"And I'll make sure you talk to someone you can trust."

Sensing the young woman wanted to believe her, Veronica offered a reassuring smile as she continued.

"And after you've filed a report you can tell me your story. That is if you still want to. I may be able to use it in my next report. You could make a difference for other women who may be watching."

"Okay." Misty nodded slowly. "If you think it's safe, I'll do it."

CHAPTER THREE

The air inside the Willow Bay Police Department felt suffocatingly warm as Chief Nessa Ainsley sat at her desk and tried to ignore the queasy feeling in her stomach. She was now well past the dreaded first trimester of pregnancy, but the morning sickness hadn't gotten the notice. Nausea had become her constant companion as she went about her business, determined to hide any sign of weakness from her team.

Pushing away the cup of ginger tea she'd been sipping with a grimace, Nessa brushed a damp red curl off her forehead. She leaned back in her chair and adjusted her jacket. She was still able to fasten the top button, but it was getting harder.

She knew from past experience that it would be at least another month before an obvious bump would appear and she could pull out the old maternity clothes she'd worn during her back-to-back pregnancies with Cole and Cooper. In the meantime, she would have to accept feeling like a stuffed sausage in all of her suits.

A buzz from the phone on her desk provided a welcome distraction, and she jabbed at the intercom button.

"Chief, you've got visitors up in the lobby."

Frowning at the desk sergeant's words, Nessa looked at the calendar and email inbox displayed on her computer screen, then back at the phone on the desk.

"I haven't got anything on my calendar," she said. "And I'm–"

"It's Veronica Lee from Channel Ten," the sergeant interrupted. "She says she needs to speak to you about something urgently."

Nessa hesitated, remembering the last time Veronica Lee had shown up unannounced at the station. She wasn't sure she was ready for the kind of trouble that always seemed to follow the young investigative reporter.

The sergeant spoke again in a lowered voice.

"You want me to tell her you're not in?" he asked. "Or that you're in a meeting?"

"No," Nessa sighed, knowing the persistent reporter wasn't likely to give up and go away. "I'll be right out."

When she stepped into the lobby minutes later, Nessa saw Veronica's familiar figure standing next to a young woman with dark, shoulder-length brown hair and wide, nervous eyes.

"Veronica, how are you?"

Nessa injected a welcoming tone into her southern drawl. The reporter may bring trouble, but she'd also helped save Nessa's butt on more than one occasion.

As Veronica returned her greeting, Nessa thought she saw the reporter's eyes dart down to her midsection for a quick peek.

No use in even trying to keep a secret in this town.

Tugging her jacket tighter around her, Nessa turned her gaze on Veronica's companion, noting that the woman's hands were balled into tight fists by her side.

"This is Misty Bradshaw." Veronica rested a protective hand on the young woman's arm. "Do you have a few minutes to talk? In private?"

Nessa felt the desk sergeant's curious eyes on her and decided any questions could wait.

"Sure, let's talk in the back." She motioned for them to follow her. "But I only have a few minutes."

Leading the two women down a narrow hall, she found an empty interview room and waited for them to take a seat around a square, wooden table.

"Misty needs to file a report," Veronica said without preamble.

"Then I'm not the one she should be talking with." Nessa prepared to stand up. "I can get an officer in here to-"

"No, please."

Veronica put out a hand to stop her.

"She's seen the news...about the connection between the WBPD and the Diablo Syndicate. She's worried the information she has could be shared with certain people who might try to retaliate."

Veronica looked over at Misty, offering a reassuring smile.

"I told her it was safe to speak to you. That she can trust you."

An uneasy ache joined the queasiness in Nessa's stomach at the mention of the Diablo Syndicate. She had hoped that taking down the man running the organization would stop the trafficking activity that had been plaguing South Florida for the last year.

But recent updates from the FBI trafficking task force had dimmed her hopes, and now this young woman was confirming her worst fears. Factions of the Diablo Syndicate were still out there, and they were now working within a wider network that was still operating in Willow Bay.

"The detective mentioned in the press is no longer employed with the WBPD. The team I have now is completely trustworthy."

Nessa avoided Veronica's questioning gaze as she spoke. She knew the reporter would want to hear that Marc Ingram was going to be prosecuted for aiding and abetting the traffickers. But the former detective was denying all charges, and with Judge Eldredge presiding over the case, she couldn't be sure yet what would happen.

Focusing her attention on Misty, Nessa leaned forward.

"Now, Ms. Bradshaw, what is it you want to tell me?"

Misty's eyes dropped to her hands, and for a minute Nessa thought she wasn't going to respond. Then she squared her shoulders and looked up, her eyes bright with sudden emotion.

"I have information about a trafficker," Misty said in a low, bitter voice. "Someone who's been victimizing women in this town for a long time. Someone operating right under your department's nose."

The accusatory tone took Nessa off guard.

"Okay, and just how do you know about this trafficker?"

"I saw everything with my own eyes," Misty said, her cheeks flushing with anger. "I was lured in and ended up at Diablo's camp. I was held there and...well, I was one of the lucky ones, I guess. I got away. But not before they got me hooked on oxy."

Nessa raised her eyebrows. The woman in front of her was clearly upset and angry, but she didn't display any of the telltale signs of an addict.

"I've gone through the detox program at Hope House and I'm trying to get my life back, but...but I need to know I'm safe." Misty's voice cracked on the words. "And I need to know that she's off the street. That she can't hurt anyone else."

"Who's off the street?" Nessa asked. "Is there another woman in danger from this trafficker?"

Misty swallowed hard and nodded.

"Every woman in this town's in danger as long as *she's* out there," Misty said. "She's evil, and she'll do anything to protect herself."

Confused, Nessa looked to Veronica, then back to Misty.

"Who's evil?"

"Amber Sloan," Misty whispered. "You need to stop Amber Sloan before it's too late."

* * *

25

The door to the briefing room was closed, but Nessa could hear Special Agent Clint Marlowe's deep voice as she stood in the hall. It sounded as if the update meeting on Operation Stolen Angels was already in session.

Opening the door and slipping into the room, Nessa motioned for Agent Marlowe to continue as she sank into an empty seat next to Tucker Vanzinger. She ignored the detective's look of concern and tried to focus on what Marlowe was saying.

After the FBI and the WBPD had managed to take out the leaders of the Diablo Syndicate earlier in the year, they were now investigating the wider network of organized criminals trafficking in illegal weapons, illicit drugs, and vulnerable women and children.

Feeling Vanzinger's persistent stare, Nessa looked over to see the big detective raise his eyebrows and lean forward.

"You okay?" he whispered, his gaze dropping to her stomach.

Rolling her eyes, Nessa nodded. The detectives on her team had started treating her like an invalid ever since her condition had become an open secret. She wasn't sure who'd spilled the beans, but she was dying to find out so she could give them a piece of her mind.

"Is there something you two want to share with the rest of us, Chief Ainsley?" Marlowe's voice was dry. "Or is it a...*secret?*"

Looking around the room, Nessa saw that all eyes were on her. The federal agents were openly grinning, while her own detectives struggled to keep their expressions neutral.

"Okay, fine," Nessa said, raising her hands in surrender. "I'm pregnant. There, I've said it. Now can everyone just stop staring at me like I've grown another head and get back to work?"

A gasp sounded behind Nessa, and she turned to see Detective Peyton Bell staring at her with wide eyes.

"You're expecting?" Peyton's face broke into a delighted smile. "That's wonderful. When are you due? Do you know if it's-"

"Not now, Detective," Nessa snapped, feeling another wave of nausea bubble up. "Let's just move on with the meeting."

The room fell quiet for a long beat, and then Nessa spoke again, this time in a calmer tone.

"I'm sorry, but we need to focus on more important things right now." She held up a copy of the statement taken from Misty Bradshaw. "I just talked to a young woman. A victim who claims a trafficker with the Diablo Syndicate is still operating in Willow Bay."

Holding the paper out to Peyton, Nessa tried not to think about the fear she'd seen in Misty's eyes when the young woman had described the ordeal she'd been through.

"The perp is a woman?"

Peyton raised her eyebrows as she scanned the report, then handed it to her new partner. Vanzinger read through the statement and issued a low whistle.

"Sounds like this Amber Sloan is a real piece of work," he said, shaking his head. "But she might have what we've been looking for."

"And what's that?" Nessa asked, worried by the sudden gleam in the brawny detective's eyes.

Vanzinger held up the report.

"It says here that Amber Sloan had been working for Diablo, but now she's starting to work directly with his key suppliers and buyers. If that's true, then she may be our way in."

Plucking the report out of Vanzinger's hand, Marlowe read through it himself, then dropped it on the table in front of Nessa.

"We'd have to get this woman to talk," Marlowe said. "And based on this statement I'd say she's unlikely to be cooperative."

"You never know until you try,' Vanzinger shot back with a grin.

Peyton picked up the report and turned to Nessa.

"Let me and Vanzinger take this one," she said, sounding eager. "I have a good feeling about this."

CHAPTER FOUR

Peyton sat next to Vanzinger in the black Dodge Charger as he drove north on Channel Drive. Nessa hadn't handed them the case until they'd both sworn not to disclose Misty Bradshaw's identity or the details of her complaint once they managed to find and question Amber Sloan.

The police chief had stressed Misty's fear of incurring Amber's wrath, and based on the details she been given, Peyton couldn't blame her. Amber Sloan sounded like an extremely dangerous person to cross.

"Turn left on Huntington," Peyton instructed, checking the map displayed on the laptop mounted between them.

Suddenly worried her new partner might take offense at her barking commands, she looked over at Vanzinger with a grimace.

"Let me know if I'm getting too bossy," she said, studying his profile. "I can get a little intense sometimes."

Vanzinger shrugged his big shoulders and laughed.

"If you think that's going to bug me you must not have met my wife," he teased. "She wrote the book on intense."

It was the first time Peyton had heard Vanzinger refer to state prosecutor Riley Odell as his wife, and she detected more than a hint of pride in his voice.

Her new partner had only been married a few months, and from the lovestruck look on his face, Peyton decided that Vanzinger and Riley were still in the honeymoon phase of their marriage

"We're looking for Fox Hollow Apartments," she said, her tone once again all business. "Should be just past Citrus Drive."

Pointing toward a modest, two-story complex on the right side of the road, Peyton checked her notes again.

"Amber Sloan lives in Unit 124," she said, as Vanzinger turned into the lot. "Let's circle around the back."

"There it is." Vanzinger nodded toward a corner unit on the ground floor. "You know what car she drives?"

He continued past the apartment and backed the Charger into an empty space with a good view of Unit 124. Peyton tapped on the laptop's keyboard, then nodded.

"She's got a 2016 Toyota Camry. White with..."

Peyton trailed off when she saw the door to Unit 124 swing open. A thin woman emerged carrying a bulky backpack that appeared to weigh more than she did. The woman walked in their direction, then stopped beside a white sedan and opened the trunk.

"I'd say that's her," Vanzinger muttered.

He gestured toward the photo displayed on the laptop's screen. Amber Sloan's driver's license showed a young woman with frizzy bangs falling over dark eyes.

"Looks like she's getting ready to make a delivery," Peyton said, feeling her pulse jump. "You want to follow her?"

"Oh, yeah," Vanzinger said, his blue eyes following Amber as she climbed in the Toyota. "I want to see what's in that backpack."

Once the Camry had pulled past them, Vanzinger steered the Charger out of the lot and followed at a distance. They'd only gone a mile down the road when the Camry turned into Bayside Municipal Park. Vanzinger drove past the entrance before making a U-turn at the next light.

By the time they got back to the park, Amber was out of her car and talking to two young girls sitting on a bench.

"Looks like she's already looking for Misty's replacement," Peyton said, leaning forward to get a better look at the girls.

"They can't be more than sixteen."

Vanzinger's voice was incredulous. He ran a big hand through his red crewcut, his forehead creasing into a deep frown as he watched Amber unzip her backpack and reach inside.

When she slipped something into one of the girl's hands, Peyton looked at Vanzinger and raised her eyebrows.

"You ready to do this?" she asked.

"Hell, yeah," Vanzinger agreed, already opening the door.

Jumping out after her partner, Peyton adjusted her jacket over the holster on her belt and followed him across the parking lot.

One of the girls caught sight of the big detective approaching and recoiled, causing Amber to turn around. Her eyes narrowed as she took in Vanzinger's broad shoulders under his jacket and the edge of the holster wrapped around his narrow waist.

Peyton hurried up beside him and held up her badge.

"Willow Bay PD," she said, keeping her eyes on Amber.

Smirking at the badge, Amber lifted her hands in mock surrender.

"I give up, officer. Now, what is it I'm supposed to have done?"

Vanzinger ignored Amber's sarcastic remarks and faced the girls. Up close they looked even younger than they had from a distance. Peyton noticed that one of them still had braces and that the other was fighting a losing battle with acne.

"How old are you two?"

Vanzinger's voice was hard. He nodded at the girl with braces who had something clutched in her hand.

"And what's that you've got there?"

Before Peyton knew what had happened, the girl spun around and ran, dropping whatever she'd been holding behind her. The second girl darted after her friend. Neither Peyton nor Vanzinger made a move to follow as the girls reached the edge of the park and disappeared around the fence.

Bending over to pick up the small baggie the girl had thrown down, Peyton wasn't surprised to see that it held a dozen or so little blue pills.

"Those aren't mine," Amber said automatically when Peyton held the bag up. "I've never seen them before in my life."

"And I suppose you don't have a backpack full of little bags just like this one in your trunk?" Peyton asked, unable to keep the disgust out of her voice. "Little bags of pills you can sell to little girls?"

Vanzinger frowned and shook his head.

"Oh, I don't think she was selling these."

He stepped closer to Amber. His jaw clenched as he met her defiant scowl with his own assessing gaze.

"I think you were giving them away." His voice was low and hard. "Isn't that how you get girls like that hooked? Isn't that your game?"

Not waiting for Amber to respond, Peyton moved toward the white Camry parked by the curb.

"I'd say that baggie gives us probable cause to search her vehicle."

The Toyota was unlocked, and Peyton glanced into the interior, noting a half-empty water bottle in the cup holder and a pack of Juicy Fruit gum. She didn't smell smoke and the ashtray was empty of cigarette butts or drug paraphernalia.

Moving to the trunk, she popped it open. The bulky backpack Amber had been carrying sat on top of the spare tire. Peyton leaned inside and saw that the backpack's main compartment was unzipped. Her heart jumped as she saw the jumble of baggies and pill bottles inside.

She lifted the backpack by one strap and held it up.

"I've never seen that bag before."

Amber's voice was cold.

"And I know my rights. I'm not talking without my lawyer."

Vanzinger ignored the comment. As he pulled out his Miranda card and began to read, Peyton felt a flicker of doubt.

Maybe we should have waited longer to see what she was really up to. We could have seen who else was involved and taken them down as well.

But as they led Amber toward the Charger, Peyton knew it was too late to turn back. They'd have to see what information they could get out of the woman during an interrogation.

Telling herself that Misty Bradshaw would be safe now that Amber Sloan was in custody, Peyton couldn't silence a niggling doubt.

But what'll happen once Amber posts bail and is back on the street?

* * *

Amber sat in stony silence. Her thin face held no sign of emotion as Peyton stared at her across the little wooden table.

"What were you planning to do with the drugs recovered from your vehicle?" she asked again. "Was your intent to sell them?"

"My client has no obligation to answer your questions, Detective."

Eugene Wexler had arrived within an hour of getting Amber's phone call. The lawyer wore a shiny suit and thick glasses, and he'd done all the talking so far.

"Your unwarranted search of my client's car violated her rights, and anything found inside will be inadmissible in court."

The door behind them opened and Peyton turned, expecting to see Vanzinger. Instead, Clint Marlowe stepped into the room. The FBI agent's tall frame towered over the table as he approached.

He ignored Amber, pinning his gaze solely on her lawyer.

"I'm Special Agent Marlowe with the FBI."

His words were accompanied by an accusatory glare, and Peyton saw Wexler shift uncomfortably in his seat.

"I have some questions for your client about her involvement with the Diablo Syndicate. I assume you've read about them in the paper?"

Nodding up at Marlowe, the lawyer appeared to be lost for words.

"What about the Diablo Syndicate?" Amber asked, speaking up for the first time since Wexler had arrived.

"That's what I'm asking you."

Marlowe switched his hard gaze to Amber's thin face.

"Are you now, or have you ever, worked with anyone associated with the criminal organization known as the Diablo Syndicate?"

Wexler finally found his voice. He banged a fist on the table.

"My client doesn't have to-"

"Shut up, Eugene," Amber snapped, keeping her eyes on Marlowe. She spoke slowly as if trying to piece together her words.

"Who said I was working with Diablo? Who told you that?"

"Excuse us just a minute," Peyton said, standing up and turning angry eyes to Marlowe. "We'll be right back."

She crossed to the door and swung it open, then gestured for Marlowe to follow her out into the hall.

"What do you think you're doing?" Peyton hissed. "You know we can't tell her that Misty Bradshaw filed a report."

"I wasn't going to tell her anything," Marlowe said with a raised eyebrow. "But since you and Vanzinger jumped the gun and brought her down here, I figured we might as well try to get something useful out of her before she bails out and goes to ground."

Chiding herself again for acting rashly, Peyton sighed.

"Okay, we should have trailed her for a while to find out who she's been working with, but she was already preying on some teenagers in the park," Peyton protested. "If we waited too long who knows what she would have had them doing."

"That may be," Marlowe said calmly, "but Amber Sloan's just a little fish in a much bigger and more dangerous pond."

"What are you saying?" Peyton asked.

"I'm saying I think we may have to let the little fish go in hopes she'll lead us to the sharks."

Peyton stared up at Marlowe in dismay.

"Now, let's go in there and prepare the bait."

Following Marlowe back into the room, she bit back further words of protest. Marlowe was heading up the task force, and it wasn't her place to argue with him, especially in front of Amber Sloan.

If she had doubts about his decisions, she'd need to take them up with Chief Ainsley. In the meantime, she'd have to be a team player.

"Ms. Sloan, if you know anything about the Diablo Syndicate, I'd advise you to tell us now."

Marlowe lowered his big body into the chair next to Peyton.

"It may help you in the long run."

Amber stared at the agent for a long beat, then shrugged.

"I might know something," she admitted. "But I'd need some assurances before I tell you what that is. I'd need immunity."

"I wouldn't advise you to say anything else before we have a chance to review the charges against you."

Wexler's eyes were wide with alarm as he regarded his client through thick glasses, but Amber didn't seem to hear him.

"If you can deliver us someone high up in the wider operation, we might be able to work something out," Marlow said in a neutral tone.

Leaning back in her chair, Amber studied the agent. Seemingly satisfied with what she saw in his stony face, she nodded.

"I know a guy at the heart of the whole damn network."

Amber ignored Wexler's groan at her words.

"He arranges shipments and plays middleman between buyers and sellers. You get him and you'll disrupt the entire supply chain. Give me immunity and I'll make it happen."

Peyton stared at Amber in disgust. The woman was talking about the trafficking network as if they were selling any old product. The fact that they trafficked in human beings, along with life-destroying drugs and dangerous weapons, didn't seem to register with her.

Standing up from his chair, Marlowe crossed to the door. He looked back at Amber with his big hand on the doorknob.

"I'll talk to the state prosecutor and see what I can do," he said, then turned to Peyton. "In the meantime, let's get Ms. Sloan some lunch. This could take a while."

Peyton's stomach lurched at the thought of food. She followed Marlowe out to the hall, but he was already pushing his way through the door to the lobby. Chasing after him, she caught up to him just before he could exit the building.

"Where are you going, Agent Marlowe?"

"I'm going to talk to Riley Odell and see if we can work out a deal."

A familiar voice spoke behind her, and she turned with a frustrated sigh as Marlowe's tall figure vanished through the door.

"Peyton?"

Frankie Dawson stood in the lobby, a hesitant expression on his clean-shaven face. His shaggy hair had been smoothed down, and he was wearing a neat, button-up shirt instead of his usual baggy hoodie.

"You ready for our lunch date?" he asked, watching the door swing shut behind Marlowe. "Or is this a bad time?"

CHAPTER FIVE

The look of dismay on Peyton's pretty face quickly answered Frankie's question. She didn't appear to be happy to see him, much less eager to join him for a romantic lunch. The thought that Agent Marlowe's abrupt departure may have had something to do with Peyton's distress prompted a familiar pang of jealousy in Frankie's chest.

"I'm sorry, Frankie." Peyton stepped forward to put a hand on his arm. "Something's come up and I can't go to lunch."

Closing his hand around the now wilted rose he'd impulsively picked from his mother's garden on the way out, he pushed the crushed petals into his pocket and felt around for a stick of gum.

"No big deal," he said, shrugging his skinny shoulders. "I had a big breakfast so I'm not really that hungry anyway."

Peyton's face softened as she watched him unwrap the silver foil and push the stick of gum in his mouth. With a sudden smile, she pulled him toward the back.

"Come in here for a minute."

She led him through the door and into a narrow hall, then stopped abruptly. He opened his mouth to ask her what she was doing, but she stopped his words with a kiss. Lifting her hand, she ran a finger down his smooth cheek.

"You shaved and put on this new shirt just for me?"

A warm flush of embarrassment flooded through him.

"What? No...I've got an appointment this afternoon and..."

Smiling up at him, Peyton pulled his head down for another kiss, then stepped back quickly when the door behind them opened and Tucker Vanzinger's bulky figure filled the doorway.

"Hey, Frankie, how's it going?"

Tucker didn't seem to notice the pink flush on Peyton's cheeks as he turned to her with raised eyebrows.

"So, how'd the interview go? You get anything out of her yet?"

"I guess you could say that," Peyton answered stiffly. "She's still in there, and apparently I'm supposed to bring her lunch."

Frankie looked down the narrow hall toward the interview rooms. Memories of his own harrowing interrogations behind those very same doors came crashing back. Although he'd eventually been exonerated, and more than ten years had passed, he'd never forgotten the feelings of helplessness and fear he'd endured. He wasn't sure he ever could forget.

Realizing Peyton was talking to him, Frankie looked up to see a hint of a frown between her big amber eyes.

"Are you okay?"

Frankie snorted.

"I should be asking you that," he said, trying to laugh off his unease. "You're the one who looked like you'd just lost your best friend when I came in."

"Well, I was just saying that I need to get back to work." Peyton's eyes followed Vanzinger as he stopped outside a door down the hall. "But I'll give you a call later, okay?"

She hurried toward her partner, leaving Frankie staring after her. He took a tentative step closer, leaning forward to catch a glimpse into the little room that he'd often revisited in his nightmares.

Spying the same wooden table he remembered from the times he'd been inside the room, Frankie stepped even closer, unable to resist the pull of the past.

He stopped short when he saw the woman sitting in a metal folding chair behind the table. The door swung shut before he could do anything more than gape, but the woman's frizzy brown bangs and hard, thin face were impossible to mistake.

What the hell is Amber Sloan doing in there?

* * *

The fresh spring air went unnoticed as Frankie walked through downtown Willow Bay heading toward his office. His mind kept returning to Amber Sloan. What had she done this time? Why had Peyton and Vanzinger been interrogating her?

Could they have found out about the thefts at the hospital?

Willow Bay General Hospital had recently become Frankie's latest and most lucrative client. Drugs had started to go missing from the dispensary at an alarming rate and the hospital's CEO knew someone on staff must be filching from the supply.

The hospital security team had tried and failed to uncover the suspected thief, but the CEO had decided not to contact the police. Hoping to avoid a PR disaster, he'd retained Barker and Dawson Investigations instead, and Frankie had spent much of the last few weeks running surveillance on the most likely culprits.

Having been spotted at the hospital on more than one occasion, Amber Sloan had automatically shot to the top of his list of suspects. Frankie had seen Amber a few times at his friend Little rays' trailer, back before Ray had gotten clean, and his friend had warned him then that she was trouble waiting to happen.

"She'd slit her own mother's throat if the price was right," Ray had told him without a hint of a smile. "Stay as far away from that crazy chick as you can. She's nothing but bad news."

The thought of Amber Sloan sitting only a few feet away from Peyton in the WBPD interview room made Frankie's skin crawl. He tried to remind himself that Peyton was a seasoned detective and that she could take care of herself, but his chest was tight with worry as he approached Barker and Dawson Investigations and opened the door.

"You back already, lover boy?" Barker boomed, as Frankie stepped inside. "I was just telling our new clients here that you had a lunch date. How'd it go?"

Stopping short beside Barker's desk, Frankie stared down at the couple sitting across from his partner. Veronica Lee and Hunter Hadley looked up at him, their smiles tense.

"It wasn't a date after all," he muttered, his forehead creasing into a frown. "Guess I got my wires crossed."

He walked over to his desk and dropped into his chair.

"You two hotshot investigative reporters need our services?" he asked, cocking his head and folding his arms over his skinny chest. "Or is my partner just pulling my chain again?"

"We want help finding out what happened to someone," Veronica explained, her voice strained. "Someone who went missing a long time ago. A woman who is most likely dead. The U.S. Marshals and the FBI haven't been able to figure out where she is and—"

Leaning forward, Frankie raised both eyebrows.

"Wait a minute. The FBI and the Marshals have been looking for this woman and can't find her, but you think we can?"

Barker cleared his throat and shot Frankie a dirty look.

"No need to sound so shocked," Barker griped. "I was a detective for a few decades, you know. A pretty damn good one, too, and I do know what I'm doing."

"It's a little more complicated than just a missing person," Hunter admitted, covering Veronica's hand with his own and squeezing. "The feds are looking for a body so that they can close out a case, but it's personal for us. We want to know the whole story."

Veronica held up a hand to stop Frankie's next words.

"Now, before we say more, I need you both to agree that whatever we tell you will be kept strictly confidential."

She lowered her voice as if someone might be listening in.

"Since there's an ongoing federal investigation related to the case, we have to be careful not to do anything that could be seen as interfering with or impeding their work."

"Of course," Barker responded. "We can do that. Right, Frankie?"

"Yeah, sure, my lips are sealed," Frankie agreed, curious about the FBI's involvement in the case. "So, who's this missing lady? What's her name?"

Hunter looked over at Veronica and nodded.

"Well, that's the problem," Veronica said slowly. "I don't know her name. I just know that she is, or she *was* my half-sister's mother and that my father claimed to have buried her on his ranch up in Montana."

Her words hung in the air as Frankie tried to absorb what she was saying. He had gotten to know Veronica while working on several cases in the past year, and he'd come to respect her. Not many reporters were as committed as she was to exposing the bad guys and uncovering the truth.

And like almost everyone else in town, he also knew that her father had been a fugitive from justice for decades before showing up in Willow Bay over the winter.

And if the stories in the paper are true, daddy dearest was a serial killer.

But Frankie hadn't heard anything about her having a sister. Of course, things seemed to happen pretty fast where Veronica Lee was concerned.

"So, you think *your father* killed this woman?"

40

"Yes, my father, Donovan Locke, said he'd buried her in the woods by his ranch," Veronica explained, her green eyes bright. "And the feds have found bodies up there. Six so far, I think. But none that match Skylar's DNA."

"And Skylar's your half-sister?" Barker asked, making notes on the pad in front of him. "Her mother was one of Locke's victims?"

Swallowing hard, Veronica gave a weak nod.

"We haven't told anyone about Skylar's past besides the doctors that have been helping her."

She looked at Barker and tried to smile.

"Dr. Horn...Reggie...well, she knows, but other than that..."

Hunter put an arm around Veronica's shoulders.

"Skylar deserves to know who her mother was, and what happened to her," he said softly. "The U.S. Marshals and the FBI have recovered the remains of six women, and they are still trying to track down the network of traffickers that worked with Locke. They have their hands full."

"And we can't just wait around," Veronica added. "We need to find out the truth so that Skylar can move on with her life."

Pulling a photo from her bag, Veronica slid it across the desk toward Barker. The older man looked at it, then handed it to Frankie.

A painfully thin girl stared out of the picture, her solemn green eyes dominated her pale face, and long silvery blonde hair fell over her shoulder in a thick braid.

"She's just a kid," Frankie murmured, handing the photo back to Veronica. "How old is she?"

"We...we aren't sure."

Veronica's voice tightened with pain.

"Skylar doesn't remember her mother, at least not clearly, and Locke never told her anything. He never even told her he was her father. The Marshals found out through a DNA match."

"Poor kid must be pretty confused," Frankie said, his voice grim. "And I'd love to help, of course. But you two are investigative reporters. Why bring us in?"

Glancing at Hunter, Veronica shook her head.

"He thinks I'm too *emotionally invested* to be able to handle the investigation objectively," she said with a grimace.

"We'll get the answers we need faster with more resources involved," Hunter countered. "Besides, Veronica and I have our commitments at the station. We're hoping you guys can stay focused on finding out what happened to Skylar's mother."

Thinking of their current caseload, Frankie sighed.

"Well, we do have another big case going on...."

"But we can handle both," Barker interrupted. "Now, we will need to get all the background information, and we'll need to know what you've done so far, and where you think we should start."

The image of Amber Sloan sitting in the interview room flitted through Frankie's mind. As much as he wanted to help the sad girl in the photo find her mother, he also wanted to make sure Amber Sloan wasn't up to anything that could put Peyton in harm's way.

"I think we should start at the beginning," Hunter said, his deep voice cutting through Frankie's worrisome thoughts. "I think we need to go to Montana and see where it all started."

Frankie's heart plummeted.

"You mean go up to where all those dead bodies are buried?"

He looked to Barker with pleading eyes.

"Aren't there wolves and shit up there?"

But his partner wasn't listening. Instead, Barker was watching Hunter tap a number into his phone.

"Deputy Santino, it's Hunter Hadley. I've got a favor to ask."

CHAPTER SIX

Hunter dropped his duffle bag next to the curb and checked to see that Gracie was still behind him. The Lab was a seasoned traveler, but they'd had a bumpy landing, and he wanted to make sure she was still holding up. As he bent to ruffle the dog's soft white fur, a Chevy Tahoe pulled up behind him.

"You been waiting long?"

Deputy Vic Santino jumped out of the big vehicle and circled around to stand in front of Hunter. The U.S. marshal appeared to be dressed for cool weather with his lean figure bundled in black jeans and a sweater and his dark hair curling over the collar of a thick jacket. He regarded Hunter with a smile, revealing a row of even white teeth.

"I never thought I'd see you up in these parts again."

Returning Santino's smile, Hunter shook his head.

"Never say never, my friend. You'll only tempt fate that way."

A groan behind him caused Hunter to turn around. Frankie Dawson had exited the terminal. He held one hand over his stomach while the other hand clutched at the handle of a battered suitcase.

"Now I remember why I don't like to fly," Frankie muttered as he parked the suitcase next to Gracie. "I get air sick."

Pete Barker appeared next to Frankie. He adjusted a lightweight backpack over his shoulder and caught sight of Santino, who nodded and removed his dark glasses.

"I'm Deputy Vic Santino with the U.S. Marshal Service."

Barker held out a big hand.

"I'm Pete Barker, good to meet you."

He rolled his eyes in Frankie's direction.

"And that's my partner Frankie Dawson. He and the airplane didn't get along very well."

"If that's everyone," Santino said, opening the back of the SUV for the luggage, "then let's get this show on the road."

Settling into the passenger seat of the Tahoe, Hunter gazed out the window at the scenery flashing by. He tried to picture the landscape as it had looked the last time he and Santino had driven through, but it had been the dead of winter then, and it was now alive with the colors of spring.

Local temperatures had been warming in the last few weeks and much of the snow had melted. As they sped through the foothills beneath snowcapped mountains, Hunter marveled at the new leaves sprouting from cottonwoods and willows.

Such a pretty place. Hard to imagine it hid such an ugly secret for so long.

The Tahoe made good time, and soon they were turning onto a narrow road leading through a dense cluster of trees. Hunter drew in his breath as they pulled up to a white gate draped with yellow crime scene tape.

Sitting upright in his seat, he felt his blood pulsing hard in his veins as he waited for Santino to jump out and push the gate open. His anxiety mounted as the Tahoe bumped along the drive, then stopped beside the big ranch house.

The compound looked different than Hunter had remembered. It was daylight for one thing, and the ground was almost clear of snow. Only a few icy patches remained on the hard-packed earth surrounding the hideout that Donovan Locke had used for more than two decades while he'd been on the run.

Looking past the fence toward the towering trees beyond, Hunter felt a chill ripple down his spine. Donovan Locke had died out there, as had the women Locke had chased down and killed.

If there really are such things as ghosts, surely they haunt that forest.

"We've had a few different teams out here," Santino said as they all climbed out of the SUV. "The house itself has been searched and practically torn apart by an FBI special response team, and we've scoured the surrounding forest."

Gracie jumped down and sniffed at the ground with interest, staying close to Hunter as Barker and Frankie joined them.

"We even brought in ground-penetrating radar." Santino's voice was grim. "So far, we've recovered the remains of six bodies."

"Where are the bodies now?"

Frankie's eyes were wary as he looked around the courtyard.

"They've already been moved to Quantico," Santino answered. "The FBI is leading the effort to identify the remains."

"So, if you include Astrid Peterson and Skylar's mother, Locke must have killed at least eight women here on his own property," Hunter said, shaking his head in disgust. "And no telling how many women he killed while he was driving that big truck of his around the country."

Looking toward the barn, Hunter frowned.

"What about Locke's semi?"

"It's been searched, photographed, tested, and dismantled," Santino assured him. "Nothing but a heap of parts now."

The sinking feeling that there was nothing left to do washed over Hunter. Everything had been searched and Skylar's mother hadn't been found. Had Locke lied about burying her on the grounds? Had they wasted a trip up to the ranch?

"Who owns this place now?" Barker asked, stretching his back and staring up at the house. "What'll happen to it?'

"The U.S. Marshal Service has seized the property," Santino said. "Standard practice with assets used for illegal purposes or acquired through illegal activity."

Frankie stepped forward with an indignant expression.

"If this place belonged to Veronica and Skylar's father, shouldn't it go to them?" he asked. "I mean, the guy caused them a lot of suffering, you know. It doesn't seem fair."

Santino didn't argue.

"All Locke's victims deserve compensation," he agreed. "Which is why proceeds from the sale could eventually be paid to those victims...or, at least to the victims we can identify."

"And you say the FBI is already working on identifying the remains?" Hunter asked. "How long will that take?"

A woman's voice sounded behind them before Santino had a chance to respond.

"We're working on it as fast as we can, Mr. Hadley."

Spinning around, Hunter saw Special Agent Charlie Day walking toward them. Her blonde, shoulder-length hair skimmed the shoulders of her navy-blue jacket, and her slim black jeans were tucked into the tops of sturdy work boots.

"Charlie?"

Hunter couldn't keep the surprise and pleasure out of his voice. He'd worked with the seasoned FBI agent the previous fall, and she'd proven to be a determined and resourceful ally.

"What are you doing here?" he asked. "Is this your scene?"

A smile lit up Charlie's light gray eyes as she nodded.

"Yes, I'm the lucky agent in charge."

Her smile faltered as she met Hunter's dark gaze.

"It's good to see you again, Hunter," she said softly. "I only wish it was under better circumstances."

Looking at the other men, Charlie adopted a professional tone.

"Well, gentlemen. Let's begin our tour."

* * *

Staring up through the hole in the floor, Hunter felt a wave of anxiety wash over him. The thought of being locked in the little room below ground for weeks or months on end was horrifying.

No wonder Skylar doesn't want to talk about what she's been through.

He climbed up the flimsy ladder on weak legs, suddenly feeling claustrophobic and desperate to get out. Charlie and the others waited for him at the top, and he struggled to hide the panic on his face as he emerged.

"Pretty scary down there, isn't it?" she murmured.

Hunter nodded, not trusting himself to speak.

"And that's not the worst of it," she said. "We believe Locke kept the women down there while he waited to ship them out. If they managed to escape, or if they made him mad, he would release them into the woods and hunt them down."

"Is that where you found the bodies?" Barker asked, moving closer to look down into the hole in the floor. "In the woods?"

Trying to regain his composure, Hunter bent to stroke Gracie's fur as Charlie responded. Her voice was crisp and professional, but Hunter detected a bitter edge to her words.

"All the women we found were shot to death and buried in the woods outside the fence," she confirmed. "The bullets we recovered matched guns found inside the house."

"And you don't know who any of these women were?" Frankie asked. "I mean, somebody had to have been looking for them, right?"

Charlie hesitated as she met Frankie's frustrated gaze.

"Actually, one of the women has been identified," she finally said. "That's why I was assigned to the case."

A spark of hope lit in Hunter's chest at the revelation. If they'd identified one of the women, a trail had been opened. There was no telling where it could lead.

"A girl I'd been looking for as part of another investigation was buried under a fir tree about twenty yards beyond the gate. She'd been shot in the head."

The room fell silent as Charlie looked out the window, her eyes focusing on the bright blue sky beyond as she paused, seemingly lost in thought.

"That girl's mother had been waiting for her daughter to come home for the last eight years," Charlie finally said, no longer trying to hide the bitterness. "And all that time she'd been out *there*."

Turning back to Frankie, she sighed.

"At least her mother finally knows what happened," she said stiffly. "But she'll be getting her daughter back in a box."

An urge to get outside the confines of the house filled Hunter's chest, and he led Gracie across the room.

"I'll take Gracie out and let her do her business," he said to the group, already moving toward the door.

The sun was just starting its descent toward the west when he stepped out into the courtyard and followed Gracie toward the back lawn. He turned his head at the sound of voices nearby.

Santino stood by the old barn talking in hushed tones to two men in standard-issue FBI jackets and heavy black work boots. As the men climbed into a dusty SUV and drove toward the gate, Santino turned to Hunter and waved him over.

"We'd better get on the road pretty soon," Santino said. "I don't like being out here after dark. Too many bad memories."

"I don't blame you," Hunter agreed, able to recall the night they'd confronted Donovan Locke in the forest nearby as if it'd been yesterday. "But I want to go out and see the dig site before..."

A sudden bark from Gracie stopped his words. Looking around, Hunter realized that the Lab had disappeared into the old barn. Another frantic bark led him through the old wooden doors.

The barn appeared to be empty. Only a few wooden planks, some oil stains, and a few bits of debris littered the floor.

"Gracie, what is it?" Hunter called out, following the dog to the far corner of the drafty barn.

Scratching the wooden floor under the old building's back wall, Gracie barked again, looking back at Hunter with desperate eyes.

"What have you found, girl?" he asked, crouching beside her. "There's nothing here."

"We took everything out and even scanned the floor," Santino said, coming up behind them. "I guarantee nothing's under there."

Hunter reached down to stroke Gracie's fur, trying to calm her, but she drew back and kept barking.

"Gracie was trained as a cadaver dog by the military," he told Santino. "And she's never been wrong before..."

Both men looked at the barn wall and then at each other. Hunter leaned forward and felt the rough wood, his eyes searching for gaps.

"You thinking what I'm thinking?" he asked, his voice grim.

"Yep. I'll get a crowbar." Santino turned on his heels and jogged out the door. "Wait here."

Minutes later he was back, and they were already prying a thick wooden board off the frame when Charlie appeared in the doorway.

"What's going on?" she asked. "We heard the dog barking and..."

The sound of splintering wood drown out her next words. Hunter's heart stopped as he saw that the board had been nailed over a narrow alcove in the wall. A patch of material was visible within.

Wrenching off another board, he blinked hard, not sure what he was seeing. The faded fabric of what appeared to be a woman's coat lay in a heap on the ground. A glint of metal caught Hunter's eye, and for a minute he couldn't catch his breath.

A silver class ring lay on the ground beside the coat. Littered around the ring was a scattering of small white bones.

Charlie came up behind Hunter to peer over his shoulder. With a sudden intake of breath, she dropped a hand on his arm and attempted to pull him back from the grisly sight.

"Get Gracie out of here," she instructed in a curt tone, gesturing toward the still-barking Lab. "Take her outside and calm her down."

Wrenching his eyes away from the remains of the woman inside the wall, Hunter saw Barker and Frankie gaping into the hidden compartment with wide eyes.

Santino held out an arm to keep them from stepping closer.

"All of you move back out of the barn so we don't contaminate the scene," Charlie ordered, pulling out her cell phone. "I need to get my team back here."

But Hunter didn't move. His eyes were glued to the board he'd pried off and thrown to the ground. A shiver ran through him as he whispered the word that had been scratched into the wood.

"Skylar."

CHAPTER SEVEN

The petunias had blossomed overnight, producing delicate pink buds that filled Skylar with delight as she knelt in front of the wide flower bed. She'd been amazed that spring had come so early to South Florida. Captivated by the tropical colors and intoxicating scents around her, she found herself wondering if the ranch still had patches of ice melting on the ground.

After she'd moved into the house on Marigold Lane, Skylar had started spending most of her time in Ling Lee's big backyard. It was the one place she felt completely safe, and she found that gardening kept her mind and hands busy.

Moving on to the vegetable patch, Skylar bent to pull a few weeds, then jumped back in surprise as a sleek black snake slithered past her hand. She watched the unwelcome intruder disappear under a hedge, then looked back to where Winston was sunning himself on the porch.

"Are you going to let him get away like that?" she called to the big tabby cat. "Don't you want to protect your territory...or me?"

But the cat was too comfortable to be lured away from his warm spot on the porch. Blinking his golden eyes in blatant disinterest, Winston opened his mouth in a wide yawn, then looked away.

Turning back to the vegetable patch with a smile, Skylar began to pull the weeds from the soil, already planning the fresh salad she'd make for Ling and Veronica that evening.

She knew how busy Ling had been lately as she prepared to take on her new role as mayor, but the older woman had never made Skylar feel like a burden. In fact, both she and Veronica had gone out of their way to make Skylar feel comfortable and welcomed.

For the first time in her life, Skylar felt as if she had a real home. She knew it may not last, that eventually Ling or Veronica might ask her to leave, but she couldn't let herself think about that now.

She'd lived in fear her whole life, much of which was spent underground in Donovan Locke's safe room, and now that she was free, she wasn't sure what lay ahead for her.

Everything in the world outside the ranch was still so new and so very different. So many new faces and new experiences. So many memories that still haunted her.

Maybe, for now, it was enough just to be away from the man she'd always known only as the Professor, and to have Veronica and Ling Lee as her new family.

"You really do have a green thumb, Skylar."

Twisting around in surprise, Skylar saw Hunter Hadley standing on the back porch. His light-hearted words conflicted with the tense expression on his handsome face.

"I thought you were away on a business trip until tomorrow."

Skylar stood and dusted off her hands.

"Is everything okay?"

Hunter dropped his eyes, and Skylar felt a ripple of unease roll through her as Veronica stepped through the back door to join him on the porch.

"Ronnie, what are you doing home from work already?"

The sight of Gracie trotting out behind her sister diverted Skylar's attention. She crossed to the porch and sunk onto the top step, careful not to crowd Winston.

Reaching out a hand to scratch the fur behind Gracie's ears, Skylar made room for Veronica next to her.

"We wanted to talk to you as soon as possible," Veronica said, her solemn tone adding to Skylar's unease.

Settling onto the step beside Veronica, Hunter leaned forward. Pain, or maybe it was pity, seemed to darken his eyes.

"I need to tell you what I found out on my trip," Hunter said softly. "I'm not sure if you knew where I was going..."

"You went to the ranch, didn't you?"

Skylar pulled Gracie's soft body closer. Something about the Lab's presence calmed her. She always felt safer when the dog was nearby.

"Yes, I went to the ranch to meet with Deputy Santino."

Hunter cleared his throat, and Skylar saw Veronica squeeze his hand in encouragement. She thought she knew what he was about to say, but his words still stabbed through her like a knife.

"We believe we've found your mother's remains."

His voice suddenly sounded very far away.

"The FBI is performing some tests now in their lab up in Quantico. We should know for sure in the next few days, but...well, we found some evidence that makes me think it's her."

Raising his phone toward her, Hunter pointed toward the display.

"And we found this," Hunter said. "It was near...near the body."

The photo on the screen showed a silver class ring. The words *Sky Lake High* were engraved around a small sapphire.

Transfixed by the image, Skylar stared at the ring. She'd seen it before in her dreams. Or was it a memory?

"It's time to go to sleep, Skylar."

Her mother's words were soft as she snuggled next to Skylar in the twin bed and grasped her little hand.

"But I'm not tired yet," Skylar complained, not wanting to admit she was scared by the noises the Professor was making overhead. "I can't sleep."

Her mother sighed and pulled her closer.

"Well, how about I tell you a bedtime story? Would that help?"

Skylar nodded, hoping the story would be about a princess, or maybe a magical kingdom far, far away from the safe room. She relaxed as her mother began to speak in a hushed voice.

"Once upon a time there was a little girl who lived with her mother and father next to a beautiful lake-"

"Was there a monster in the lake?" Skylar asked, pulling her mother's hand closer so she could twist the pretty ring on her finger.

"No, the lake was...perfect. In fact, it was so perfect that I named you after it," her mother said. "It was called Sky Lake, and it was the most magical place in the whole world."

Skylar looked up to see the shine of tears in her mother's light blue eyes. She thought hard for a minute, then lifted a small hand to tug on a long strand of her mother's silvery blonde hair.

"Were you that little girl in the story, Mommy?"

"Yes, baby, I was that little girl."

Her mother sniffed, then hugged her even tighter.

"I used to live by Sky Lake. One day we'll go there together."

"Skylar? Skylar?"

The persistent voice startled Skylar. She blinked and looked at Veronica, who was staring at her with worried green eyes.

"Are you okay?"

The vivid memory of her mother faded back into the past as Skylar realized she was still sitting in the sunny garden, and still staring down at Hunter's phone.

The silver ring with the bright blue stone was the same ring her mother had worn. The very ring her own small fingers had touched and twisted as a child.

"That's my mother's ring," Skylar whispered. "Sky Lake is where she wanted to go. The place where we'd live happily ever after."

CHAPTER EIGHT

Watching the emotions play across Skylar's face, Veronica sensed her sister pulling away again, slipping into the withdrawn, trance-like state that could last for a few seconds, several minutes, or even hours.

Veronica had been tempted to try to draw Skylar back into the real world the first few times she'd drifted away, but Dr. Reggie Horn had recommended that, as long as the girl was in a safe place, they should leave her in peace to process her thoughts and emotions at her own pace and in her own way.

"I'll go get her some cold water," Veronica murmured, heading into the kitchen. "I think I need something to drink as well."

Crossing to the refrigerator, Veronica lifted out the pitcher of water with a shaky hand. Unable to calm her nerves, she leaned against the counter and sucked in a deep breath, suddenly wishing her mother was home to offer Skylar comfort and advice.

Ling Lee had developed a special connection with Skylar after the girl had come to live with them. Veronica suspected the suffering and heartache they'd each experienced at the hands of Donovan Locke had helped them forge a bond that no one else could understand.

Her mother was the only one who truly knew Locke, and the only one who had also witnessed the level of depravity Skylar had been forced to live with all those years.

But Ling wasn't home, and Veronica would have to care for Skylar on her own. The town's new mayor-elect was busy interviewing candidates to join her growing staff, and her schedule would only grow busier once she'd been sworn into office.

"You okay in here?"

Hunter's broad shoulders filled the doorway. As he moved further into the kitchen, Veronica could see Skylar still sitting on the step with Gracie close beside her.

"I guess so," Veronica said with a shrug. "I just hate to see her like that. She looks so.... *lost.*"

"Reggie told you not to worry too much," Hunter reminded her. "She said it's just Skylar's way of coping with her PTSD."

Pulling Veronica toward him, he wrapped his strong arms around her, and she allowed herself to rest her head on his chest.

"Once Skylar has a chance to come to terms with what happened, and when she starts feeling safe, the episodes will stop."

His voice was soothing, but Veronica knew it wasn't that simple.

Leaning back, she looked up to meet his eyes.

"How can she come to terms with any of this until she finds out who she is and where she comes from?"

Veronica slipped out of his arms and stared down at a thick manila folder on the kitchen table. Hunter had brought it back with him from Montana, and she knew it held clues to Skylar's past.

She also knew any trail Locke had left behind would reveal further horrors that might cause Skylar more distress.

Veronica had already seen her sister's name carved into the wooden board in Locke's barn. Hunter had shown her a photo on his cell phone as soon as he'd arrived from the airport.

Gesturing toward the folder, Veronica tried to gather her courage. She shivered at the thought of the horrors it might hold.

"Is there any information about Sky Lake in that?"

Hunter hesitated, then nodded.

"Sky Lake, Kentucky is Donovan Locke's hometown."

Letting his words sink in, Hunter crossed to the table and opened the file. He scanned the printout on top, then flipped through a few pages until he found what he was looking for.

"Deputy Santino recognized the name right away," Hunter told her, pulling a map out of the file. "Sky Lake had been listed in Locke's record, but Santino never put two and two together to link the name of Locke's hometown with the name of his daughter."

Veronica's mind spun as she tried to process the information.

"So, Skylar's mother is from the same town as Locke?"

"We can't know for sure, but it seems likely."

Trying to think through the possible next steps, Veronica started at the most obvious option.

"Have you or Deputy Santino searched the database for any women that went missing from Sky Lake, yet?"

"Charlie searched the FBI database, as well as all local and state databases," Hunter confirmed. "Nothing looked promising."

Disappointment flooded through her at his words, then she frowned and cocked her head.

"Charlie? You mean Agent Day is involved with the case?"

"She's leading the effort to identify the remains found at Locke's ranch. She was at the ranch when we arrived."

He studied her with a thoughtful expression.

"You aren't still thinking there was something going on between me and Charlie Day, are you? Cause I already told you that-"

"Of course not."

Veronica felt her back stiffen in spite of her best efforts not to let the thought of the attractive FBI agent get to her.

"I'm just glad we've got people we can trust on the case," she assured him. "With Agent Day and Deputy Santino helping us we've got to be able to find out who Skylar's mother was, and how she ended up on Locke's ranch."

"I hope so," Hunter said, looking down at the folder. "But, no one reported a woman missing from the town in the last two decades, and there's no evidence that Locke had ever gone back to his hometown after going on the run."

Reluctantly dropping her eyes to the table, Veronica saw Hunter studying a list of names in the folder. Her eyes widened at the first two names on the list.

"Who are Harriet and Thomas Locke?" she asked, leaning closer to get a better look.

"Says here that Harriet is Donovan Locke's mother, and that Thomas is his brother," Hunter said, tapping a long finger on the two names. "Last known address for both is still in Sky Lake."

Veronica was momentarily speechless at the thought that she and Skylar had a grandmother and uncle living in Kentucky. Ling Lee was the only family Veronica had ever known up until her father had made his untimely appearance the previous winter.

"Could Locke have stayed in touch with his family?' she murmured, thinking out loud. "Could they know what Locke was up to, and who Skylar's mother was?"

Shaking his head, Hunter pointed at the handwritten notes beside the names. According to the investigator, both Harriet and Thomas Locke claimed they hadn't seen Donovan Locke since he'd been indicted on trafficking charges twenty-eight years before.

"They aren't likely to admit anything different now than what they told the U.S. Marshals when they were searching for Locke."

Veronica wasn't so sure.

"Now that Locke is dead, they may change their story," she suggested. "Maybe they were too scared to talk before."

Movement outside the kitchen window drew Veronica's attention. She watched Skylar cross to the vegetable patch and sink to her knees. As her sister began to pull weeds, Hunter came up behind Veronica and looked over her shoulder.

"I don't want to tell her she may have family up in Sky Lake," Veronica said, keeping her eyes on Skylar. "At least not yet."

"I agree." Hunter moved back to the table and picked up the file. "Which is why I've asked Frankie and Barker to go up to Kentucky ASAP and see what they can find out."

Tempted to offer to go along with them, Veronica held her tongue as Hunter went out the back door to check on Gracie and Skylar, reminding herself that her next special report on trafficking was due the following day. She couldn't afford to leave Willow Bay now.

If I'm late with another report, Spencer Nash might take the opportunity to cancel the rest of the series as he's been dying to do.

Her ongoing investigative series on organized crime had rankled the criminals she was trying to expose, and recently Channel Ten had received several anonymous threats against her and the station. The station manager was getting nervous and had been talking to Veronica about moving in other directions.

Veronica figured the threats must mean she was getting close to the top of the trafficking network, and she was determined that nothing would stop her from bringing down those responsible for causing so much pain and suffering.

The buzz of her phone on the kitchen counter pulled her eyes away from the window. She groaned as she saw the text message from Misty Bradshaw.

Still haven't heard back from WBPD. Any update on your end?

Thumbing in a quick response, she winced as she tapped *Send*, wishing she had a real update to offer.

Nothing yet. I'll call Chief Ainsley to get an update. Will stay in touch.

It had been several days since Misty had given her statement to Nessa, and Veronica had been too preoccupied to find out what the chief of police had done with the information since then.

She tapped on Nessa's name in her contact list and waited as the phone rang again and again. After five rings the call rolled to voicemail.

"Nessa, I'm calling to find out if you've followed up on the information Misty Bradshaw gave you. She's feeling a little nervous, as I'm sure you can imagine. Please call me back as soon as you can."

Disconnecting the call, Veronica wondered again if she'd done the right thing by convincing Misty Bradshaw to go to the police.

If Amber Sloan ever finds out what she's done, Misty's brand new start on life might be over before it's even begun.

CHAPTER NINE

Nessa had just gotten Charlie Day on the phone when she heard a ping in her ear and looked down to see a message pop up on her screen: *Incoming Call from Veronica Lee.* Tapping the icon to send the call to voicemail, she tried to concentrate on what Charlie Day was saying.

The FBI agent had agreed to give her an update on the Donovan Locke investigation, and Nessa was eager to hear what the Bureau had uncovered during the latest search of Locke's ranch up in the Bitterroot Valley.

Willow Bay had been subjected to Locke's wrath the previous winter when he'd come to town seeking revenge on his ex-wife, and the fugitive killer's deadly partnership with the leader of the local Diablo Syndicate had left the town shaken.

Nessa was eager to close the books on the case and put the whole ordeal behind her as soon as possible.

"Please tell me you haven't found any more bodies up there," she said, holding the phone close to her ear.

"We found another body," Charlie responded dryly. "But we think it might be the last one. If all goes well, we'll be wrapping up the crime scene in the next few days."

"Have you been able to identify any of the victims yet?"

Charlie hesitated, then cleared her throat.

"All the remains have been sent to a forensic anthropologist at the lab in Quantico," she said evasively. "They're working up DNA profiles to run through CODIS and then we'll know more."

Sensing the agent was holding back information, Nessa wondered what the feds had found that couldn't be shared with the local PD.

"There isn't anything else I should know, is there?" Nessa asked. "I mean, you didn't find anything up there that could bring more trouble to Willow Bay, did you?"

Another long pause on Charlie's end confirmed Nessa's suspicion. The FBI agent wasn't telling her everything, and whatever she was keeping from her may have something to do with Willow Bay.

"I've gotta go," Charlie said abruptly. "But I will let you know what we find out as soon as I can."

"But, Charlie, I need to know-"

Realizing the call had been disconnected, Nessa dropped the phone on her desk with a dissatisfied huff.

"Great, that's just *wonderful*," she muttered in frustration.

"Sorry to interrupt, Chief, but Agent Marlowe is getting ready to meet with the state prosecutor about the deal with Amber Sloan. I thought you might want to sit in on that."

Looking up to see Peyton standing in her doorway, Nessa felt a flush work its way up her neck.

Nothing like having a tantrum in front of your team to instill confidence.

She tucked a red curl behind her ear and straightened her jacket.

"Thanks, Detective Bell, I think I should," Nessa agreed, peeved that Marlowe hadn't invited her himself. "I'll be right there."

Before she could make it around her desk, Jankowski stuck his head into the office.

"Can I have a word, Nessa?"

He stepped inside and shut the door before she could respond.

"You never told me that Detective Ramirez was so...so *experienced* when you assigned me to be his new partner," the big detective murmured in a low voice. "The guy is what...like sixty?"

Nessa crossed her arms over her chest and glared at the big detective. She'd worked with Diego Ramirez before she'd moved from Atlanta to Willow Bay, and she knew the older man was a good detective as well as a decent human being.

"Ramirez's age has nothing to do with his ability to do the job," Nessa snapped back, not bothering to lower her voice. "He's one of the best detectives I've ever worked with, and this department is lucky to have him."

Holding up his hands in surrender, Jankowski shook his head.

"Okay, maybe you're right, but why'd *I* get saddled with him?"

Nessa shook her head in amazement. She'd managed to hire in one of Atlanta's finest detectives to replace Marc Ingram, who was currently fighting charges of corruption and aiding and abetting the Diablo Crime Syndicate, and here she was getting push back from the one person she'd counted on to help Ramirez settle in.

"You're the senior detective in the department, so I thought you'd be the best choice to partner with the new guy," Nessa admitted. "I figured I could count on you to show Ramirez the ropes and get him started out on the right foot. Maybe I was wrong."

Smoothing a strand of blonde hair back into place with a big hand, Jankowski sighed. His face softened as he read the disappointment in Nessa's eyes.

"Okay, okay, I'll give it a shot," he said, backing toward the door. "But you know better than anyone that I'm not an easy partner to deal with. Ramirez has his work cut out for him."

Nessa watched Jankowski's broad shoulders disappear down the hall with worried eyes. He wasn't going to be happy when he found out her ulterior motive for bringing in Ramirez.

Resting a hand on her stomach, Nessa looked down and sighed. Somebody would have to run the department when she went out on maternity leave. She thought Ramirez would make a fine acting chief.

I just hope Jankowski and the rest of the team will think so, too.

* * *

Nessa's appearance in the briefing room seemed to surprise Marlowe, but he quickly regained his composure.

"Chief Ainsley, I'm glad you're here," he called out. "I was just asking Ms. Odell to review the immunity agreement we plan to offer Amber Sloan in exchange for her help."

Taking a seat next to Riley Odell, Nessa frowned over at Marlowe.

"What exactly is this woman going to help us with?"

She stared pointedly at Peyton and Vanzinger, who flanked Marlowe on the other side of the table.

"What does she know...or should I say, who does she know?"

Peyton shot Marlowe an uncomfortable glance before answering.

"Amber claims she can deliver a key contact in the Syndicate. Someone who had been working directly with Diablo to arrange shipments."

Turning to Riley, Nessa noted the prosecutor's doubtful expression. It seemed like the only one in the room eager to sign the agreement was Agent Marlowe.

"I've examined Amber Sloan's record," Riley said. "And she's certainly racked up an impressive list of arrests. Funny thing is, she's never actually been convicted of any crime."

Vanzinger spoke up for the first time.

"Yeah, I noticed that myself," he said. "Either she has a good lawyer, or she's got connections in high places."

Throwing Vanzinger an annoyed glare, Nessa tried not to sound too defensive as she responded.

"That's the kind of statement that gives the department a bad name, Detective," she scolded, then exhaled loudly. "If Amber Sloan was exonerated of the crimes she was accused of committing in the past, it's not up to us to retry her now."

She avoided meeting Marlowe's eyes, knowing he was eager to proceed with the immunity arrangement regardless of her opinion.

"But that doesn't mean she should get a free pass in the future."

Marlowe dropped a heavy hand on the table, his pretense of objectivity evaporating.

"Amber Sloan is the only eye-witness we have willing to work with us at this time," he said, directing his words solely at Nessa. "It may be the only chance we have to infiltrate the core of the network."

"Well, we do have one other option."

Riley pushed a thick folder toward Marlowe.

"That's the file on Ivan Sokolov," she said, opening the folder to reveal a picture of a massive man with thick eyebrows arranged in an angry scowl. "He was Diablo's cousin and second-in-command, and he's looking at serious time, so if we're throwing around immunity offers, he may be willing to play."

Ignoring the skeptical expression on Marlowe's face, Nessa nodded in tentative agreement.

"Sokolov must have plenty of information to share," she added. "And he's looking at a life sentence, so I'd say he'll be interested."

Her voice faltered as she felt her phone begin to vibrate in her pocket. Most likely Veronica was calling again, and Nessa was sure the reporter would be asking about Misty Bradshaw's statement.

I don't want to be the one to tell her Amber Sloan was granted immunity.

But Marlowe wasn't ready to give up yet as he adopted a patronizing tone that set Nessa's teeth on edge.

65

"If there's a chance that Amber Sloan or Ivan Sokolov can get us close to the rotten core of this organization then we should work with them both," he insisted, slapping his hand on the table again. "We may be able to take out the whole damn network."

"But what about Misty Bradshaw?" Nessa asked, standing to face Marlowe. "Are we willing to sacrifice her after she put herself in danger by naming Amber Sloan?"

Leaning back in his chair to stare up at Nessa with dark, impenetrable eyes, Marlowe was unmoved.

"We aren't sacrificing anyone, Chief Ainsley. We're simply using every resource we have to achieve a higher goal."

He looked around the table.

"In the end, Misty Bradshaw and every other woman in South Florida will be safer once we take down this group," he stated. "Now, does anyone else have any objections, or can we move forward?"

CHAPTER TEN

Peyton swallowed back the words of protest that filled her throat. She couldn't let her worry for Misty Bradshaw override the task force's need to protect the community from a threat which had already destroyed so many lives. At the same time, she had an obligation to keep Misty safe, and she wouldn't let her down.

I'll just make sure Amber Sloan doesn't find out Misty was the informer.

Surveying the faces around the table, Peyton could see that Vanzinger and Riley weren't going to raise further objections, either. And based on the glum look on the chief's face, even Nessa seemed resigned to go along with the FBI agent's plan.

They had a chance to get to the heart of a major trafficking network, and they had to take it before it slipped away. Peyton only hoped that Amber Sloan and Ivan Sokolov would play fair.

If they give false information or double-cross us, we could end up wasting valuable time. Innocent lives could be ruined in the meantime.

After an uncomfortable pause, Marlowe cleared his throat.

"Okay, then if we're all in agreement, we can go ahead and finalize the immunity deal with Amber Sloan."

He rose from his chair as Riley closed Ivan Sokolov's file.

"And I'll approach Mr. Sokolov's lawyer to see if they want to discuss a possible deal," the state prosecutor said crisply.

Marlowe made it to the door before he turned back to address Peyton and Vanzinger.

"I want to sit in on the initial interview with Ms. Sloan," he said with a frown. "If she's going to try to bullshit us, I want to know it from the start."

Nodding stiffly, Peyton glanced at Vanzinger in time to see a flash of irritation cross his face. Her new partner looked as offended as she was that Marlowe expressed such little faith in their judgment.

They'd both been around long enough to know better than to trust Amber Sloan, and they didn't need him or his agents babysitting them. It went without saying that everything the informant divulged had to be treated with skepticism.

Once Marlowe had disappeared down the hall, Vanzinger turned to Peyton and Riley with a disgruntled frown.

"Amber Sloan's waiting in interview room three," Riley said, with an arched eyebrow. "And since she has dismissed her lawyer, I'm going to need a witness with me when we sign the agreement, so..."

Giving his wife a broad wink, Vanzinger grinned over at Peyton.

"So, it couldn't hurt to ask her a few questions since we'll already be in there," he finished, heading toward the door.

Peyton looked over at Nessa's chair, but the chief had already left the room. Following Vanzinger and Riley down the hall, Peyton hesitated in the doorway of the interview room, suddenly sure they were making a mistake.

"Wait..."

But Riley was sliding the file toward Amber Sloan, who sat at the little wooden table wearing the lightweight blue shirt and baggy pants given to every female inmate booked into the county jail.

"Sign here, and here," Riley murmured, pointing to the signature lines on the agreement as Peyton peered over her shoulder.

Snatching the offered pen from Riley's hand, Amber scribbled her name on the lines indicated then dropped the pen and leaned back in her chair with a huff.

"Okay, now when can I get out of here?"

"I'll get the paperwork started once I leave here," Riley said, her voice cold. "But I want to remind you of your obligations under the terms of the agreement. You are to make yourself available for questioning at the convenience of the WBPD and the FBI."

Amber glared up at Riley with an impatient nod.

"Okay, I got it," she muttered. "Now do whatever it is you have to do to get me out of here."

Sinking into the chair across from Amber, Vanzinger leaned forward and propped his elbows on the table, as if preparing for a long conversation.

"It'll take a while before they come to get you," he said with a pleased smile. "So, we might as well use the time wisely and hear what it is you have to say right now."

"I thought I was going to be talking to the FBI," Amber protested. "And I'm not talking before I'm out of these stupid clothes."

Peyton moved toward the table, knowing it was too late to turn back. They'd signed the agreement and now she had to make sure Amber Sloan gave them the information she'd promised.

"We'll start the release process as soon as you start talking," Peyton said, sitting down next to Vanzinger. "You get immunity if you provide information leading to organized crime in the area. If you lie to us or hold something back, your immunity gets revoked."

Shrugging her thin shoulders, Amber pushed her thick bangs back from her forehead and pinned Peyton with a bored stare.

"I know the guy who scheduled Diablo's drug shipments and arranged transportation for other *high-value* cargo."

"What high-value cargo?" Vanzinger asked, taking the bait. "Are you saying this guy is involved in human trafficking?'

The smirk on Amber's face told Peyton that she was playing with them and that she was starting to enjoy the game.

"What's the guy's name, and where can we find him?"

Peyton tried to keep the frustration out of her voice. She couldn't give Amber the reaction she wanted. She had to keep control of herself and of the interview.

"I don't know his real name," Amber admitted. "But his username is Mack, and he uses a message board on the dark web to arrange the shipments. If you give me some time, I can set up a meeting."

"Have you met him before?" Vanzinger asked. "I mean, have you met him in person?"

Producing a coy smile, Amber trained her gaze on Vanzinger.

"Well, we aren't dating, if that's what you mean, but, yes, I've met him a few times."

"Why'd you have to meet in person?" Peyton shot back.

Amber hesitated before answering, her eyes drifting down to her copy of the immunity agreement still resting on the table.

"I had to hand-deliver a special shipment," she finally said.

"So, this guy was actually down here in Willow Bay?"

The question seemed to fluster Amber, so Peyton asked again.

"Did you meet up with him in Willow Bay?"

"Close enough," Amber snapped, her eyes flashing.

Leaning forward in anticipation, Peyton worked to keep her voice steady. She didn't want to spook Amber now.

"Where's the guy from?" she asked. "Where does he live?"

"I don't know, and it doesn't matter."

Amber's mouth curled into a half-smile as she stared at Peyton.

"He can go anywhere he wants, whenever he wants. That's what makes him so dangerous."

Peyton exhaled and sat back. Amber wasn't going to give them what they wanted so easily.

"So, what, this guy has superpowers?" Vanzinger asked.

"Yeah, he can fly," Amber said with a smirk. "And he can appear and disappear when you least expect it."

Tired of Amber's attitude, Peyton played her only card.

"I think you're withholding vital information, which automatically violates the agreement," she said, pushing back her chair and standing up. "And that just may delay your release."

Narrowing her eyes, Amber studied Peyton's face, as if calculating how serious she was. Ignoring the warning voice inside her head, Peyton held Amber's gaze.

"I've only seen the guy a few times," Amber finally admitted. "But based on what I know, I'd say he's from Kentucky."

A hard knock sounded behind Peyton, and she jerked around to see that the corrections officers had arrived. They would escort Amber back to the jail where she would be processed for release.

As Peyton watched the uniformed officers lead Amber into the hall, she had the feeling that they'd just made a terrible mistake.

* * *

Barker and Dawson's Investigations was only a ten-minute walk away from the police station, and Peyton found herself standing in front of the unimpressive office building before she'd had a chance to clear her head or shake off her misgiving about Amber's release.

Checking her reflection in the window, she ran a hand through her short pixie cut and straightened her jacket over her slim shoulders, then pushed open the door and stepped into the little office. She hoped a few minutes with Frankie would help her forget about work for a while.

"Peyton, long time no see!" Pete Barker called out, his puppy dog eyes lighting up. "How's it going over there at the WBPD? I hear you guys have got some new blood in Major Crimes."

"Yep, Chief Ainsley's brought in a new detective to partner with Jankowski," Peyton agreed, catching sight of Frankie's empty desk.

"A guy named Diego Ramirez. He used to work up in Atlanta. You know him?"

The retired police detective furrowed his brow and shook his head.

"Name doesn't sound familiar, but if Nessa brought him in, I'd be willing to bet he's a damn good detective," Barker said with conviction. "She's a smart woman. The best partner I ever had."

Hearing the nostalgia in his voice, Peyton raised her eyebrows.

"Better not let Frankie hear you saying that," she teased. "He'd be pretty torn up to know he's not your favorite."

"You're probably right," Barker agreed. "But he's not here, and I'm sure you're not going to tell him, are you?"

Heart sinking at his words, Peyton shook her head.

"No, your secret is safe with me."

She stood awkwardly by Frankie's desk for a long beat, then cleared her throat.

"So, will he be back soon?" she asked, feeling vaguely pathetic. "I haven't gotten to see him since you guys got back from Montana."

"Oh, well...I guess he didn't tell you that he's leaving again first thing in the morning," Barker said. "He went home early. Wanted to pack a bag and help his mother with a few errands before we go."

A frown settled between his thick eyebrows.

"I know it's not my place, but is everything okay with you two?"

His fatherly tone brought a glimmer of tears to Peyton's eyes. It had been a long time since she'd had a father to count on, and for the first time in a long time, she felt the grief well up and threaten to spill over.

"Hey, I'm sorry, I didn't mean to say something wrong."

Barker jumped up and circled around the desk, grabbing a napkin from under his coffee cup and handing it to Peyton.

"It's okay," she sniffed, dabbing at her eyes. "I guess I'm a little stressed with work and...well, everything."

"Frankie told me you moved back to Willow Bay to take care of your mother," Barker said, his voice gentle. "Is she doing all right?"

Wadding the napkin into a ball, Peyton tossed it toward the trashcan by Barker's desk and shrugged.

"She's doing as well as can be expected," she said. "We're taking it one day at a time and all that, but it's...well, it's cancer so..."

A shadow fell over Barker's eyes, and he nodded.

"My wife Caroline died of cancer," he murmured, swallowing hard. "Watching her go through that...trying to be strong for her. It was the hardest thing I've ever done."

The raw pain in his eyes scared Peyton.

Is that how I'll feel once Mom is gone? Will that be me in a few months?

Panic began to brew in her stomach, and the need for a stiff drink surfaced as if on cue. Peyton had managed to drink herself through all kinds of trauma and pain over the years, but she was sober now, and she couldn't afford to lose herself in a bottle.

Her mother needed her. The trafficking victims she was trying to help needed her. She looked at Frankie's empty chair with a mixture of regret and relief.

At least Frankie doesn't need me. At least I won't be letting him down.

Giving Barker a sad smile, Peyton crossed to the door.

"Tell Frankie I stopped by," she said. "And tell him to stay safe."

"Oh, he'll be fine," Barker said, sinking back into his chair. "Sky Lake is a pretty small town, so I imagine we won't get into too much trouble."

"Sky Lake?" Peyton asked. "Where's that?"

Barker hesitated as if maybe he'd said too much.

"It's in Kentucky," he finally admitted. "We've got a lead in a missing person's case, but I shouldn't say anymore."

As Peyton stepped onto the sidewalk and headed back toward the station, she tried to convince herself that it was just a coincidence. Frankie going up to Kentucky on a case could have nothing to do with

Amber Sloan's claim that her darknet contact is from Kentucky. Could it?

Of course, I never did put much faith in coincidences.

CHAPTER ELEVEN

Frankie leaned forward in the passenger's seat of the rental car, eager to see the little Kentucky town that Donovan Locke had called home. The plane ride up had been nice and smooth, unlike the flight to Montana, and Frankie considered it a positive sign that the trip would go just as smoothly.

"Look, there's the Sky Lake Sheriff's Office."

He pointed out the window at a single-story brick building topped with a massive flagpole, and Barker put on his blinker and slowed to look for parking along the busy, two-way street.

Easing the compact car into an empty space by the curb, Barker shut off the engine and turned to Frankie.

"Let me do the talking," he said, putting a heavy hand on Frankie's arm before he could jump out of the car. "I know how these small-town departments work. They don't like smart-asses."

"Whatever you say, boss," Frankie replied with a mock salute. "If they prefer dumbasses, you're their man."

Frankie shook off Barker's hand and climbed out onto the sidewalk. His long, skinny legs had carried him halfway to the front door of the building when Barker caught up to him.

"I mean it, Frankie," Barker puffed. "Let me take the lead."

Pushing through the glass double-doors, Barker stepped into a small lobby. The young, uniformed officer behind the reception desk looked up as they approached. He gave a curt nod at Barker's greeting but didn't seem very happy to see them.

"I'm hoping to talk to Sheriff Holt." Barker's voice was gruff. "We're investigating a case and have a few questions for him."

The officer's eyes rested on Barker, then flicked to Frankie, who kept a straight face, deciding it was best not to smile. He didn't want to ruin Barker's tough-guy routine.

"The Sheriff's in a meeting right now," the officer said, sounding suspicious. "Which department are y'all with?"

"We're with Barker and Dawson Investigations."

Barker said the name of their two-man firm with a casual confidence that implied the officer should be familiar with it.

"And I'm a retired detective from the Willow Bay PD down in South Florida," he added. "I still consult with them on occasion."

Forcing himself not to react to Barker's misleading statement, Frankie reached into his pocket and felt around for a stick of gum. He wondered what Barker would do if the man in front of them decided to call and verify if they were in fact consulting for the WBPD.

But before the officer could react to Barker's claim, a deep voice spoke up from behind them.

"South Florida? What brings y'all to Sky Lake?"

Frankie spun around to face a man in a tan uniform and wide-brimmed hat. He was tall, about Frankie's height, but outweighed him by at least fifty pounds of what looked to be mostly muscle.

"We're looking for Sheriff Holt," Frankie blurted out, then shot Barker a guilty glance. "We have a few questions to ask."

Hitching up the belt around his sturdy waist, the man produced a wide smile. There was something oddly wolfish about the smile, and Frankie found himself taking a small step back.

"Well, I'm Archer Holt. What can I do for you boys?"

Stepping in front of Frankie, Barker stuck out a hand.

"It's good to meet you, Sheriff Holt. I'm Pete Barker, and this is my partner, Frankie Dawson."

Barker glanced over at the officer behind the desk, who was still staring at them with narrowed eyes and lowered his voice.

"We're working a case and were hoping to get a minute of your time," Barker said. "We just have a few questions."

"Sure," the sheriff replied without hesitation, "but I'm not sure how I'll be able to help with a case down in Florida."

Following Holt's broad back past the front desk and down a short hall, Frankie allowed himself to relax.

The guy may be big, but he's friendly. More like a big puppy than a wolf.

Frankie unwrapped the stick of gum in his hand and popped it in his mouth as they entered a small office.

The sheriff lowered his strapping frame into a leather desk chair and motioned for Frankie and Barker to take a seat across from him.

"We're working a missing person case," Barker said, getting right to the point. "I guess you could call it a cold case."

"You guys have a cold case unit up here?"

Frankie's question earned him a glare from Barker, as Holt threw back his head and laughed.

"If you saw the budget I'm working with you'd understand what's so funny," the sheriff finally said, displaying his big white teeth in an amused smile. "And fortunately, Sky Lake's a quiet town, so we don't have enough open cases to keep a cold case unit busy."

"This case involves a young woman that would have gone missing from Sky Lake about twenty years ago."

Sheriff Holt cocked his head and frowned as if contemplating Barker's statement. He leaned back and removed his hat, running a hand through a thick thatch of light brown hair.

"I've only been the sheriff for the last five years," he said slowly as if working out the math. "I took over after Sheriff Duffy retired. He'd been the sheriff for near about twenty years before that."

"Well, we'd also like to talk to Sheriff Duffy, then," Barker said, taking a small notebook and pen from his pocket. "But in the meantime, is there any chance you can search your missing persons records?"

Holt gave a reluctant shrug.

"I guess we could try, but I grew up here and know just about everyone in town. I've never heard of anyone going missing. At least, nobody that didn't turn up later."

Unzipping his backpack, Frankie pulled out a file folder and opened it on the desk. He flipped through a few pages inside, then pulled out a photo of Skylar and pushed it toward Holt.

Frankie ignored Barker's frown of confusion as the sheriff stared down at the girl in the picture.

"Does she look familiar?" he asked, holding his breath.

He knew it was a long shot, but if Skylar took after her mother, the man might pick up on a family resemblance.

After a long beat, Holt shook his head.

"She's a pretty girl...but, no, I've never seen her around here."

Plucking Skylar's photo off the desk, Barker stuck it back in Frankie's folder and cleared his throat.

"What do you know about Donovan Locke?"

The change of topic seemed to confuse Holt. He cocked his head and frowned as he leaned forward over the desk.

"Who'd you say you were working for?" he asked, the good old boy attitude slipping. "Cause Donovan Locke's old news, and we don't need anyone coming to Sky Lake to stir up new trouble."

Frankie's stomach dropped as he saw Holt's eyes narrow.

"Y'all aren't working for the press, are you?"

The image of Veronica Lee and Hunter Hadley floated through Frankie's mind. They were both investigative reporters, and Hunter was co-owner of Channel Ten. It would certainly seem like they were working for the press to Holt.

"No, we're not reporters, we're private investigators," Barker assured him, adopting a conspiratorial tone. "I'm just a retired police detective trying to make a living."

Holt didn't seem convinced as he met Barker's gaze.

"Look, we're not here to cause trouble," Frankie said, unable to keep quiet any longer. "But Locke's a hometown boy, and we think the woman we're looking for might be from here, too. Just seems like a hell of a coincidence."

The sheriff's frown deepened.

"Locke's like the boogeyman around here," he said, pushing back from the desk. "Every kid in town grows up hearing stories about Locke and what he did way back when. Anytime something bad happens around here there are whispers that Locke's come back."

Picking up his hat, Holt stuck it back on his head with a sigh.

"But that's all they are, just stories and whispers."

Holt stood and looked down at Frankie.

"The FBI and the Marshals have come here plenty of times over the years trying to track down Locke, and never found so much as a sniff of him. Now that they've killed him, I consider the case closed."

Frankie opened his mouth to protest, but Barker spoke up first.

"Thank you for your time, Sheriff. We'll show ourselves out."

* * *

Frankie was still sulking when they pushed through the door of the Frisky Colt Diner. He'd expected Barker to pressure the sheriff into letting them search through the files. They needed to find out if a woman had gone missing before Holt had become sheriff.

"Holt wasn't going to cooperate, so stop pouting," Barker said, shaking his head. "We need to find Sheriff Duffy. I bet the old-timer will appreciate a chance to tell us all about the good old days."

"Yeah, you're probably right," Frankie muttered. "You old-timers sure do like to hear yourselves talk."

Spotting two empty stools at the counter, Frankie pulled Barker after him. He climbed onto the nearest stool, resisting the temptation to spin around like he'd done as a boy in Memphis.

Barker stared at the other stool with a raised eyebrow, then settled his bulky frame in next to Frankie, murmuring an apology to an attractive woman on the stool next to him.

"Oh, you're all right, honey," the woman said, shooting Barker a smile. "Go on and make yourself at home."

Pushing a small hand through dark, bouncy curls, the woman waved to the waitress behind the counter. A glint of silver on her ring finger caught Frankie's attention.

"Be right with you, June," the waitress called out as she hurried by with a loaded tray.

Frankie shrugged off his backpack, trying not to stare as the woman named June turned back to the counter. Sneaking a peek at her hand, he felt his pulse quicken.

That can't be the same type of ring we found in Locke's barn, can it?

He forced himself not to get too excited.

Half the people in this town probably went to Sky Lake High, and knowing my luck, they could all be wearing the same class ring

Pulling out the picture of Skylar, he stared again at the girl's sad, green eyes and silvery blonde braid. She was a striking girl, and if her mother had looked anything like her, she would have stood out in any town.

Frankie had brought along the photo to show to as many people in Sky Lake as possible. He hoped that someone in the close-knit

80

town might see a resemblance to a woman they'd once known. Perhaps someone they still missed.

Leaning across Barker, Frankie dropped the photo on the counter in front of June and tapped on Skylar's face with a long finger.

"You wouldn't happen to know this girl, would you?" he asked.

June's smile froze in place as her eyes settled on the photo.

"Is that...*Summer?*"

Her voice morphed into a shocked whisper.

"How'd you get that picture?"

"You know this girl?"

Nodding slowly, June leaned closer.

"She used to be my best friend, but..."

Sliding the photo closer, June studied it, then exhaled sharply.

"Sorry, I must be going crazy," she said, shaking her head and swallowing hard. "That's not Summer, but it sure looks like her."

She pushed the picture back toward Frankie.

"It's just the resemblance...it's uncanny."

Frankie scooped up the photo and held it toward her.

"We're trying to find anyone who might be related to this girl," he said, leaning across Barker again. "You said she looks like your friend...like Summer. How can we get in touch with her?"

"I'm sorry, but that's impossible."

Turning her head to look nervously for the waitress, June again pushed dark curls back from her heart-shaped face. The ring flashed by, giving Frankie an idea.

"Listen, we're trying to help this girl find her mother," Frankie said, still holding up the photo. "Her mom went to Sky Lake High School, so maybe you know her."

Barker pulled on his arm and shot him a warning look, but Frankie shrugged him off as June turned back to face him.

"Well, it can't be Summer," she said in a strained voice. "Summer Fairfax left town a long time ago and no one's heard from her since."

CHAPTER TWELVE

Hunter paced outside the baggage claim at Sky Lake Regional Airport and checked his watch again. Special Agent Charlie Day was scheduled to arrive at any minute, and Hunter was anxious to get into town and find out if Frankie and Barker really had uncovered the truth about Skylar's mother.

Eager to follow up on Barker's call the day before, he had quickly contacted Charlie and convinced her to meet him in Sky Lake to talk to the local authorities and check out their findings.

If Frankie and Barker were right, Skylar's mother had been a young woman named Summer Fairfax, and they now had the chance to piece together her story and give Skylar the closure she deserved.

Catching sight of Charlie's willowy figure hurrying toward him, Hunter held up a hand to wave her over.

"Kentucky's a lot warmer than Montana," Charlie said, shrugging off her thick wool jacket and adjusting a sleek carryall over her shoulder. "And I didn't get a chance to go home first, so I guess the clothes I brought with me will have to do."

"Well, I'm glad you didn't stop to re-pack." Hunter was already moving toward the rental car lot. "I don't think I could have waited another day now that we may have found Skylar's mother."

He looked down at the tagged key fob the rental car agent had handed him and checked it against the numbers on the parking spaces in the little lot.

"A Chevy Tahoe," he muttered, double-checking the tag, which listed the vehicle as a *Standard White SUV*. "Why am I not surprised?"

Pushing away an uneasy feeling that the Tahoe was a sign of more trouble to come, Hunter loaded their bags into the back and climbed into the driver's seat.

"So how are things going at the ranch?" he asked, merging onto the highway and heading west. "You about done there?"

"Just about," Charlie agreed, pushing on a pair of dark sunglasses, and looking out at the passing scenery. "Although you never know. We may find out something here that'll open up a new line of investigation leading us back there."

Hunter nodded absently and checked the GPS to see how close they were to the exit for downtown Sky Lake. Charlie turned her head to study his profile, and when she spoke her voice was softer than usual.

"I understand Willow Bay's about to get a new mayor."

Surprised that the busy FBI agent had kept up with Willow Bay's local politics, Hunter nodded but kept his eyes on the road.

"How did your father take the loss?"

Hunter replayed the conversation they'd had about his father the first time they'd met. He'd shared personal details with the agent that few people knew, and apparently, she hadn't forgotten.

"He's still in denial," Hunter admitted, shaking his head. "I don't think he really believes he'll have to leave office."

A pang of empathy for his father tightened Hunter's chest. No matter how much he disapproved of his father's behavior, Hunter wasn't sure the older man could adjust to life as a regular citizen after so many years of being the town's mayor.

"It'll be good for him in the long run," he added, trying to sound upbeat. "A new start for him, and a break for the rest of the town."

Wanting to change the subject, Hunter looked over at Charlie, unable to see her eyes behind the dark glasses.

"So, what's the plan?" he asked, seeing the exit ahead.

Barker had already warned him that the town's sheriff wasn't likely to share anything useful with a reporter, but an FBI agent investigating a series of homicides would be a different story.

"I was able to pull up some background on Sky Lake last night in my hotel room," Charlie said, reaching into her bag and pulling out a small, lightweight laptop. "The state and national databases don't show any records of missing women from the town. At least not during the last two decades."

"That's what the sheriff told Barker," Hunter confirmed. "But a local woman said that her friend Summer Fairfax left town without a trace about twenty years ago. No one's heard from her since then."

Opening the laptop, Charlie studied the screen.

"The town's sheriff is a man named Archer Holt. I've arranged to meet him along with the previous sheriff, Lowell Duffy. Perhaps they can shed some light on what happened to Summer Fairfax, and why she wasn't reported as missing."

She snapped the laptop shut.

"Sometimes people don't want to be found, so maybe they know something her friend doesn't."

Hunter steered the Tahoe off the exit, following directions from the GPS to the Sky Lake Sheriff's Office. Wedging the big SUV between two cars along the curb, he turned toward Charlie.

"I'm guessing you want to do the talking?"

"I'd say that's a good idea," she agreed. "Although I doubt either of them like the FBI getting involved in their town any more than they like the press snooping around."

But the older man who greeted them in the lobby seemed happy to see them. He smiled and held out a calloused hand.

"Lowell Duffy," he announced in a hoarse voice. "And you must be Special Agent Charlie Day. Although from the name I wasn't expecting someone so easy on the eyes."

Brushing aside the comment, Charlie gripped his hand and returned the smile. She gestured toward Hunter.

"This is Hunter Hadley. He's working with me to investigate the case I'd mentioned to Sheriff Holt."

Lowell turned to study Hunter with curious eyes.

"Now I see why she let you tag along," the old man said to Hunter with a wink. "You two make a good-looking couple."

A protest rose in Hunter's throat, but the old man had already turned toward a narrow hall. Charlie raised her eyebrows at Lowell's retreating back, then followed him into a small office. Hunter stepped in behind her.

"Archie, you've got some visitors," Duffy called out.

The man behind the desk winced and waved for them to sit down.

"I'm Sheriff Archer Holt," he said, throwing Duffy an exasperated glare. "But our retired Sheriff still thinks of me as little Archie Holt."

"I appreciate you meeting with us so quickly, Sheriff Holt," Charlie said in a warm voice. "And I'm hoping you can help clear up a few questions regarding a young woman named Summer Fairfax."

Hunter saw Duffy's good-natured smile disappear.

"Have you been talking to Conrad Fairfax?" Duffy asked with a frown. "After all this time he just can't accept the truth."

"And what is the truth?"

Charlie's demeanor cooled at Duffy's blustering.

"The truth is that Summer Fairfax left town near about twenty years ago after an argument with her boyfriend," he said, crossing his arms over his chest defiantly. "She left her folks a letter saying she was running off to Hollywood or some such place, but they insisted there must have been foul play."

"What did you do?" Charlie asked. "Was there an investigation?"

The old man shrugged.

"We looked into it, but the girl was already eighteen and she had every right to go wherever she wanted."

"What about the boyfriend? You said they had a fight?" Charlie's smooth brow furrowed into a frown. "Did you interview him?"

A defensive edge entered Duffy's voice.

"Sure, I did, and he was as surprised as everybody else that Summer just up and left," he insisted. "Look, she was already eighteen, and there was no sign of foul play. There was nothing more for me to do."

"What was the boyfriend's name?" Charlie asked, opening her laptop and balancing it on her knee.

Duffy shot a look at Holt, as if asking for help, but the sheriff remained silent.

"Beau Sparks," Duffy finally said, "He was a nice kid from a good family. From what I remember he seemed pretty torn up that she skipped town."

Lifting her eyes from her laptop, Charlie cocked her head.

"You mentioned her father, Conrad Fairfax. He didn't agree with you that Summer left on her own volition?"

Lowell shook his head.

"Both her parents were in denial. Her father even hired a hotshot investigator from New York, but he came up with nothing."

Anger boiled over in Hunter's chest at the sheriff's words.

"You're telling me you think it's completely normal for an eighteen-year-old girl to leave town without a trace and never contact her parents or friends again?"

Sheriff Holt held up a big hand and cleared his throat.

"Look, Mr. Hadley. Our job isn't to decide what is *normal*, and Sheriff Duffy has already explained that there were no signs of foul play. So, if that's all..."

Pulling out his phone, Hunter scrolled to the photo he'd taken of the class ring found in Locke's barn. He zoomed in on the initials engraved in the silver and held it up to Holt.

"Based on where this ring was found, I'd say there was definitely foul play involved," Hunter gritted out, turning back to Duffy. "Apparently you weren't competent enough to figure that out."

"That's enough," Charlie said, her voice firm. "We are investigating a very serious crime."

She gave Hunter a warning look, then turned to Holt.

"Now, Sheriff Holt, can you help us find the missing person report filed by Summer Fairfax's parents? Oh, and I'd also like to see any files on the department's subsequent investigation."

But Holt's eyes were fixed on the phone in Hunter's hand.

"Are you saying Summer is...*dead?*"

"All we can say is that this ring has been recovered from a crime scene," Charlie answered before Hunter could open his mouth. "Now, about those files."

* * *

Hunter pulled the Tahoe into the lot outside Sparks Air Charter and shut off the engine as Charlie studied the scant information in the file Holt had reluctantly handed over.

"Says here that Summer's boyfriend was a local kid named Beau Sparks." She looked up to survey the big building in front of them. "Back then he worked for his father. Let's see if he still does."

Seeing the *We're Open* sign in the window, Hunter pushed through the front door and held it open for Charlie to follow him in.

No one seemed to be manning the long reception counter that separated the lobby from the spacious hangar, but two men could be seen loading boxes onto a small Cessna.

Eventually, one of the men looked up and jogged toward them. He smoothed down his short, spiky hair and nodded a greeting. The polite smile evaporated as Charlie Day held up her badge.

"Beau Sparks?"

The man shook his head, his eyes still on Charlie's badge.

"No, I'm Curtis Webb, Beau's partner."

"Partner?" Hunter pointed to the name over the door. "I thought Beau's father owned the company."

Pulling his gaze away from the badge, Curtis turned to Hunter.

"That was before my time," he said, his eyes curious. "Why? What's his daddy got to do with anything?"

"We need to speak to Beau as soon as possible. Is he here?"

Charlie looked past Curtis toward the Cessna, where a man with long, lanky hair and a baggy uniform was still loading boxes.

"What do y'all want with Beau?" Curtis stepped in front of Charlie, blocking her view of the hangar. "He's not in trouble, is he?"

"No, we just need to ask him a few questions about his ex-girlfriend, Summer Fairfax. We're investigating her disappearance."

She raised her eyebrows and asked again.

"So, is he here or not?"

"No, he's not here," Curtis said, moving back toward the hanger. "And I'd recommend y'all call first next time. Beau's in and out a lot. Kinda makes his own schedule."

Charlie dropped a card on the counter.

"How about you ask him to call me when he gets in," she asked, earning a worried nod from Curtis.

Turning to leave, Hunter noticed the other man had stopped working to listen in to the conversation. When he saw Hunter looking at him, he dropped his eyes and resumed loading the airplane.

Back in the Tahoe, Charlie flipped to the next page in the file Holt had given them. She studied the notes Sheriff Duffy had written twenty years before, then looked over at Hunter and sighed.

"You ready to meet Summer's parents?"

Dread settled into Hunter's chest at the thought of telling Conrad and Elaine Fairfax that their daughter had been the victim of a serial killer and that she'd had a daughter of her own before she died.

And what will they think about Skylar? She may be their granddaughter, but she's also the child of the man who abducted and murdered Summer. Would they be able to accept her?

Sky Lake Farm and Stables was about twenty minutes outside town. As Hunter turned the Tahoe onto the long drive, Charlie pointed further up the road. An older man was leading a horse toward a long, white stable. He stopped and stared at the Tahoe as they approached.

"Mr. Fairfax?" Charlie called out as she stepped out of the vehicle. "I'm from the FBI. Could I speak to you?"

"It's about Summer, isn't it?" the man said, his thin face deathly pale under the bright sun. "You've found her, haven't you? You've found my little girl."

Stepping closer, Charlie held out a photo of the class ring.

"Is this your daughter's ring, Mr. Fairfax?" she asked gently.

Conrad's eyes filled with tears as he saw the engraved initials.

"We bought that ring for Summer right before she graduated," he said, nodding weakly. "It was one of the only things missing from her room after she disappeared. Her mother always said if we found that ring..."

His voice broke on the words, and he turned away to wipe his eyes. When he turned back, he sounded stronger.

"Where was she?" he asked quietly. 'Where did you find her?"

"We found her remains while investigating a known fugitive. A man named Donovan Locke. He was killed during an attempt to capture him." Charlie's voice was gentle. "We believe your daughter had been kept on his ranch for some time before she died."

"I always knew Summer wouldn't have willingly left her mother or her horses. She loved her horses..."

89

Conrad looked back at the horse standing behind him with dazed eyes, before turning to Charlie.

"Her leaving like that....it killed Elaine. The coroner said she'd had a heart attack, but I knew it was a broken heart."

Pain twisted the older man's face, and Hunter steeled himself for what had to come next. They had to tell him all of it now. It wouldn't be fair to keep anything from him after he'd waited so many years to know the truth.

"Summer had a child while she was being held at the ranch." Hunter's throat tightened around the words as Charlie pulled out the photo of Skylar. "She had a daughter."

"Is she...is she still..."

Conrad's voice faltered as he saw the photo, and he swayed on his feet. Reaching out, Hunter put a strong hand on the older man's shoulder to steady him.

"Yes, your granddaughter is still alive," he said, his voice thick with emotion. "She's a very brave girl, and now she's in a safe place."

CHAPTER THIRTEEN

The white Chevy Tahoe drove past Mack and turned left onto Fullerton Road. He caught a glimpse of the FBI agent's blonde hair and dark glasses through the window as she stared out from the passenger's seat.

Mack knew that the U.S. Marshal Service had finally managed to chase down and kill Sky Lake's most infamous resident. He'd seen the breaking story on the news along with everyone else in town.

And he wasn't surprised that the feds had shown up in Sky Lake again. They would want to tie up any loose ends and ask the usual questions. He'd been ready for that.

But he hadn't been prepared for their interest in Summer Fairfax. Why would the feds suddenly be interested in a girl who had run off twenty years ago? Should he assume they knew Donovan Locke had been involved with Summer's disappearance, and that they may have even found her body?

But do they know Donnie hadn't acted alone? Do they suspect that someone else in Sky Lake was involved?

Thinking about the FBI's visit out to Sky Lake Farm and Stables, Mack tried to convince himself he had no reason to worry. Conrad Fairfax had remained clueless all these years and had no evidence or information to provide to anyone.

Even after the old man had hired a big-city investigator to poke around, he still hadn't been able to prove that his daughter hadn't left town of her own free will.

There's nothing to link me to Summer or to Donnie, is there?

A shiver of fear slipped down his back as he imagined the feds showing up at Silent Meadows Farm. A search of the old house and the cemetery behind it would likely earn him a cell in death row over at the Kentucky State Penitentiary.

While he'd been careful over the years to only work with people he knew, and that he could trust, Mack wondered if Locke had gotten messy at the end. Had the man who'd always protected him ended up betraying him?

And now that Donnie's gone, how can I know who to trust?

Taking out his phone, Mack signed into the darknet board that Locke had operated. All his messages from the Professor were still there. That had been Locke's username. He and Mack had exchanged encrypted messages on the board without much fear of discovery.

Now Mack wondered if their messages had been compromised. He scrolled through the recent history looking for anything that might reveal his real identity or his location but could see nothing out of order.

The man Mack still thought of as Donnie had been careful to use coded language, even within the encrypted messages, and over the years he had only communicated when there was a job to be done.

Locke had never revealed the location of his hideout after he'd gone on the run, but he'd kept in touch, and he'd expected Mack to be ready and waiting whenever he needed help transporting cargo or laundering money through the local bank.

All Locke had to do was post a message on the darknet board and Mack would take care of it. And while he'd been paid generously for his help, Mack knew he'd had no choice. Locke had known his secrets, and he wouldn't have hesitated to use them to destroy Mack if he hadn't been useful.

Donnie and my father were two of a kind. Selfish to the very end.

But Locke was dead now. He'd gone down in disgrace, leaving an ugly stain on the whole town, just as Mack's father had left a stain on their family.

I can't let their mistakes bring me down, too. If the feds find their way out to the old farm, my face will be the one plastered across the news.

But the feds were in town asking questions, and they wouldn't be wasting their time if they didn't suspect someone in town was involved with Summer's disappearance.

Could they know I'm responsible for what happened to Summer?

Staring blankly at the phone in his hand, Mack let his mind drift back to that long-ago night.

Mack threw the rock as hard as he could, using his pent-up anger to propel it out toward the middle of the dark lake. He watched as the water rippled and sparkled under the moonlight, then reached for another rock.

He hesitated as the trees rustled behind him, lowering his arm just as a slim figure slipped out of the shadows.

Stepping onto the grassy bank of the lake, Summer Fairfax stopped at the water's edge and dropped her head into her hands. Mack heard a muffled sob as the girl's shoulders began to shake.

"You okay, Summer?"

The girl spun around, her eyes wet and smudged with mascara.

"You scared me," she gasped. "What are you doing here?"

She wiped a pink-tipped finger under each eye and smoothed back her long, silvery blonde hair as Mack tried to come up with a response.

"You know what, it doesn't matter," she muttered. "Nothing matters."

"You don't mean that, Summer," Mack said, inching closer. "You're just mad now and need some cheering up."

Shaking her head, Summer turned away.

"What I need is to be left alone."

A hot flush spread up Mack's neck at the rebuke. Her rejection stung, even though he knew he was foolish to care. He'd been fixated on Summer for years, knowing she was out of his league, but unable to resist her pull.

There weren't many girls like Summer Fairfax in Sky Lake. The special ones always ended up leaving. Especially the rich girls that left for college before moving on to a better life in a bigger city.

"Aren't you supposed to be hosting a party back there?" he finally said, keeping the hurt out of his voice. "You'll be missed. Everyone will talk."

Summer rolled her eyes and shook her head.

"Let them talk, I'm not going back in there," she snapped, turning toward the lake. "I just want to get away. Go somewhere far, far away."

A strand of silky hair blew toward him, and he was tempted to reach out and touch it, but he feared she would recoil from his touch.

She was too stressed and too upset. He needed to get her alone. Somewhere they could talk. Then he could tell her how he really felt.

"I can take you over to Silent Meadows if you want," he said, holding his breath. "There's no one to bother you there, and you wouldn't have to go back to the party. You could stay there until everyone leaves."

Raising her face to his, Summer hesitated, as if considering her options. Finally, she lifted her narrow shoulders in a resigned shrug, and he felt his pulse quicken as the frown between her pretty eyes faded.

It wasn't until he was leading her up the porch steps to the old house that Mack began to worry his father might be waiting inside. The old man had been passed out drunk when he'd left, but that was no guarantee he hadn't woken up for another round.

A set of headlights turned onto the drive and moved closer, lighting up the porch as Mack stepped in front of Summer. He didn't recognize the car, and it wasn't until the driver stepped out and spoke that he realized who his visitor was.

"I need to see the old man."

Mack froze at the sight of the hard, familiar face.

"Donnie? What're you doing here?"

"Like I said, I need to see the old man."

Donovan Locke put a boot on the bottom step, but Mack blocked his way.

"He's out cold, Donnie," Mack protested. "He's not going to be able to see anyone or anything until the booze wears off."

Glancing over his shoulder, he saw Summer's shocked face. If he'd ever had a hope with her before, that was surely gone now. The daughter of a man like Conrad Fairfax was surely too good for the son of the town drunk.

"The old man still owes me money. A lot of money. I'm done waiting."

Summer was suddenly standing beside Mack. He put up a hand to stop her, but she shook it off.

"You leave Mack alone," she demanded. "Go on. Get out of here."

The scorn on her face was clear to see in the moonlight, as was her luxurious fall of long, blonde hair and her shapely young figure.

"You don't know who you're talking to, do you, girl?"

Not liking the look in Locke's eyes, Mack tried to shield Summer, but she pushed past him to stare down at Locke's leering face.

"I know who you are."

Mack's heart dropped at her words.

"You're Donovan Locke," she accused. "My father told me all about you and what you've done to disgrace this town. I've seen pictures of you in the paper, and I heard all about your hand."

She pointed down to his right hand in triumph, her gaze focused on the three remaining fingers. Her eyes widened as she saw the big gun appear in Locke's left hand

"You sure are smart," Locke muttered. "And you sure are pretty."

He held the gun up to Summer's smooth, pink cheek and ran the muzzle down the side of her face.

"Real pretty indeed."

He sounded almost amused.

"And I'd hate for that to change."

Mack wanted to protest, but he knew Donnie too well. The man wouldn't hesitate to eliminate anyone that got in his way.

"I need that money," Locke said, not taking his eyes off Summer, who seemed to be frozen in fear. "You gonna wake up the old man or should I?"

"He's not got two pennies to rub together, Donnie." Mack tried to keep his voice steady. "I'd give you anything we have, but we're broke."

Locke nodded slowly, apparently ready to take him at his word. He knew Mack wouldn't dare lie to him, not after he'd seen what Locke was capable of doing when he got mad.

"Okay, I'll go, but you tell the old man I'll be in touch. I expect him to keep up his part of the bargain. And if he won't, you'd better."

Mack nodded, knowing it was pointless to argue with Donnie when he was in one of his moods.

"And I'll take this one here as payment in the meantime."

Locke stuck his gun in his waistband and grabbed Summer's arm. She opened her mouth to protest, but Locke jerked her toward him and put his hand back on the butt of his gun.

"You make a sound and I'll shut you up permanently," Locke growled. "Looks like I'm gonna have to teach you how to behave."

Impotent rage flooded through Mack, but he knew there was nothing he could do as long as Locke held the big gun in his hand.

"She's mine."

Mack's voice cracked on the words as Summer turned to him in silent reproach. But Locke just shook his head and laughed. It was an ugly sound.

"You want to keep this lovely piece all to yourself, Mack? That's not very generous, is it? Especially for someone who owes me, big time."

Unable to meet Summer's pleading gaze, Mack turned to Locke, but the man's hard face was unmoved.

"She knows who I am, Mack, and she knows I've been here."

Locke shuffled backed toward the car, pulling Summer with him.

"Once she runs home and tells her daddy I was here, the place will be swarming with feds. You and the old man don't want that, do you?"

Watching as Summer slipped out of his grasp forever, Mack tried again. "But...she'll...she'll be missed. They'll be looking for her, and-"

"Then you'd better think of something fast," Locke advised, sounding impatient. "I'm pretty sure you inherited your old man's talent for lying."

Forcing Summer's hands behind her back, Locke pushed her toward the car as she began to struggle and scream.

"Help me, Mack! Please, help me!"

But Mack's feet wouldn't move. His dream girl was in the middle of a very real nightmare, and there was nothing he could do to stop it.

"Where...where are you taking her?"

He sounded weak, and he knew it, but the rage had shriveled into shame. Another man was claiming his prize while he could only stand and watch.

"Don't you...worry about...that."

Locke huffed out the words as he opened the trunk and shoved Summer inside. Once he'd slammed the lid, he turned back to Mack.

"Don't worry, you'll never see her again," Locke assured him. "It'll be like she never even existed."

The buzzing of his phone in his pocket startled Mack back into the present. He looked around, half expecting to see Locke walking toward him. But Locke was in the past now, and Mack needed to focus on the present and the future.

The feds knew something, and if they connected him to Donovan Locke, they'd find more than just his connection to Summer.

I've gotta make sure they never find my little secret in the cemetery.

CHAPTER FOURTEEN

Veronica walked to the front window again and peered out onto Marigold Lane, hoping to see Hunter's black Audi pulling onto the drive. She'd already checked to make sure his flight had arrived on schedule, and Hunter had promised to come to the house as soon as he landed, but the street was still empty.

Looking down, Veronica saw Winston nestled in his favorite spot on the windowsill. The big tabby seemed to be keeping an eye on the street as well. His soft purring was the only sound in the quiet room.

The whole house felt strangely empty as Veronica turned away. Skylar had been on the back porch most of the day, voraciously reading the stack of books she'd checked out at the library, still overwhelmed that there were so many books in the world and that she was allowed to checkout as many as she wanted.

And Ling Lee had driven off to attend the last of several going away parties organized by the teachers and staff at Willow Bay High School. After decades as a popular teacher and principal, Ling was finally passing the reins to assistant principal Jai Patel so that she could move on to her role as Willow Bay's new mayor.

The thought that it was Ling's last day sent an unexpected wave of nostalgia through Veronica. Her mother had been a fixture at the school for so long; it was hard to believe it was all coming to an end.

But after the last year of turmoil and all the big changes that had taken place in her life, Veronica knew it was time to accept the hard truth that nothing ever lasted forever.

A flash of movement outside the window caught her attention, and her heart leaped as she saw Hunter climbing out of his Audi. Her melancholy mood lifted as her eyes studied his tall figure.

While the world had been changing around her, there was one thing, one person, that had remained strong and stable. Through it all, Hunter had been there for her, the one constant in her tumultuous world. The only one besides her mother she could truly count on.

Catching sight of a blonde head emerging from the passenger's seat, Veronica's dreamy smile faded. Special Agent Charlie Day must have decided to come back with Hunter. Perhaps she felt it was her duty to give Skylar the news about her mother in person.

Veronica smothered the spark of jealousy that flickered inside her at the sight of the lovely agent climbing out of Hunter's car. She couldn't let herself fall into that trap again.

Hunter was doing everything humanly possible to find out what had happened to Skylar's mother, and Charlie had helped him get access to information he'd have had a hard time finding on his own.

Telling herself she should be grateful to have Charlie involved, Veronica hurried to the front door and swung it open.

"Agent Day, how nice to see you. I didn't know you were coming."

Hunter bent to give Veronica a distracted kiss, then followed her into the living room, his handsome face tense.

"I know you have important news to share," Veronica said, meeting Charlie's somber gray eyes. "Should I go get Skylar?"

"I'm here," a soft voice said from the doorway.

Veronica turned to see Skylar leaning against the doorframe, balancing a stack of books in her thin arms. Her green eyes were hopeful as they rested on Hunter, and her mouth lifted in a shy smile.

"I heard your car pull up. I was hoping Gracie might be with you."

"Sorry, she's with Finn," Hunter replied with a wince of regret. "But I did bring someone who wants to talk to you."

A glint of panic appeared in Skylar's eyes as she saw Charlie standing behind him, and Veronica stepped forward to lay a calming hand on her sister's shoulder.

"Skylar, this is Special Agent Charlie Day with the FBI."

Stiffening at the words, Skylar turned her eyes to Charlie.

"I already told Deputy Santino everything I know about my...my father," she said, her voice faltering on the word.

"Yes, Deputy Santino told me how brave you were, Skylar. He said you were a big help, but I'm not here to talk about your father."

Charlie hesitated as if gauging Skylar's reaction. When she continued, she spoke in the soft, soothing tone that Veronica associated with therapists and grief counselors.

"I want to tell you what we've discovered about your mother."

The words sent a shiver down Skylar's small frame, and Veronica felt her own heart begin to hammer in her chest.

"I think you've been told that remains found at Donovan Locke's ranch match your DNA, so you know they belong to your mother."

Skylar nodded gravely.

"Yes, I know that. Hunter and Veronica told me."

"That's good because we now know who your mother was."

Charlie produced a reassuring smile, but Skylar's expression didn't change. She just stared at her in stunned silence.

"Your mother's name was Summer Fairfax."

Pulling out a photo, Charlie held it toward Skylar, who stared at the young woman in the photo with wide eyes.

"Your mother was only eighteen years old when she went missing from a small town in Kentucky."

"Sky Lake," Skylar murmured. "She told me stories about it."

Nodding, Charlie stepped closer.

"That's right. After she left Sky Lake, she somehow ended up at Locke's ranch in the Bitterroot Valley."

Skylar looked up, her eyes suddenly bright with tears.

"My mother...did she have any family in Sky Lake?"

Veronica held her breath as Charlie nodded.

"Yes, her father still lives in the area."

Charlie's words hung in the air for a long beat. When Skylar spoke, her voice was hopeful.

"So, I have a grandfather?"

At Charlie's nod, Skylar turned eager eyes to Veronica.

"Can I meet him, Ronnie?" she pleaded. "Can I go to Sky Lake?"

* * *

Veronica followed Hunter out to his car, impatient to have a few minutes alone with him before he drove Charlie back to the airport.

But when they reached the Audi, she hesitated, suddenly scared to hear what he'd found out about Locke's mother and brother while he was in Kentucky.

Do I want to know the family who produced a monster like my father?

Of course, if Skylar went up to Sky Lake to meet her grandfather, she would undoubtedly find out about their father's connection to the town. She might even run into Harriet and Tom Locke. The possibility gave Veronica no choice.

"So, did you see Locke's mother and brother?" she asked Hunter in a low voice before he could unlock the car door.

"No, Charlie wanted to speak to Skylar as soon as we confirmed that Summer Fairfax was her mother."

He looked back to where the agent stood on the porch, animatedly talking into her phone, then turned back to Veronica.

"We notified Conrad Fairfax about his daughter, then came here."

Sensing her disappointment, Hunter moved closer, lifting a hand to brush a strand of dark, silky hair back from her face. Veronica inhaled the familiar scent of his cologne and sighed.

"It's just that Skylar doesn't know Locke was from Sky Lake, too," Veronica said, resisting the impulse to lean forward and rest her head against his broad chest. "She doesn't know she has other family up there. I'm not sure how she'll take it."

Reaching out to put a finger under her chin, he tilted her face up.

"They are your family, too, you know."

He raised his eyebrows and cocked his head.

"But if you don't want to meet them..."

The click of Charlie's heels on the driveway behind them saved Veronica from having to respond. Instead, she turned to ask Charlie the other question that had been eating away at her.

"Do you know how Summer Fairfax ended up on Locke's ranch?"

The agent dropped her phone into her pocket and shook her head.

"Not yet. Locke left town when Summer was just a little girl, so it's unlikely they knew each other before she went missing."

"But they could have had a mutual acquaintance," Veronica suggested. "Someone who'd kept in touch with Locke might have known Summer, or at least had access to her."

Charlie arched a delicate brow and smiled.

"That's exactly what I'm thinking," she said. "Which is why our cyber crime team is focusing on any of Locke's activities or connections linked to Kentucky. If there's someone in Sky Lake that Locke kept in touch with, we'll find them."

Satisfied that the FBI seemed to be making every effort to find out how and why Summer Fairfax had ended up with Locke, Veronica watched as Hunter and Charlie got back into the Audi.

But before they could drive away, Charlie rolled down the window and waved Veronica over.

"Chief Ainsley keeps asking for an update in the Locke case," she said as Veronica bent down. "I wasn't sure who you've told about Skylar's connection to Locke. I know how information can spread in a town like Willow Bay."

Veronica hesitated, her mind whirring through the possibilities.

"Skylar's been through so much already," she finally said. "If she decides to stay in Willow Bay and build a life here, she may not want to be thought of as the serial killer's kid."

Remembering all the attention she'd had to endure after the news about Locke got out, Veronica was terrified of Skylar facing the same media storm.

"And I'd hate for the press to get hold of the story," Veronica admitted. "I know that sounds hypocritical coming from a reporter, but I know better than most what can happen when someone's private trauma becomes big news. Skylar's not ready to handle that."

"Okay," Charlie agreed, putting on a pair of dark sunglasses and settling back into her seat. "I'll try to keep the connection between Locke and Skylar confidential for now. But eventually, these things have a way of coming out."

The words started an uneasy ache in Veronica's stomach.

"Oh, I know that better than most," Veronica agreed with a grimace. "But I hope Skylar has a little time to come to terms with the situation before the whole town knows. Or the whole country for that matter."

Watching the car pull away, Veronica tried not to worry. Skylar would be okay. Once things settled down, she could start a new life. Dr. Horn's words came back to her as she turned toward the house.

"A wise man once said that new beginnings are often disguised as painful endings. With time, you begin to see the difference."

The thought reminded Veronica of Misty Bradshaw, and the call she'd had to send to voicemail. She pictured the young woman's hopeful smile, and the flash of dimples on her pale, freckled face.

Misty was trying so hard to start a new beginning, but she needed help. Pulling out her phone, Veronica scrolled through the calls and texts she'd ignored during Hunter's and Charlie's visit. Tapping on the message from Misty, she listened with growing anger.

"Veronica? This is Misty. I haven't heard back from Detective Bell and I'm getting scared. Some guy tried to follow me back to my new place today. I think I lost him, but he…well, what if Amber sent him?"

The fear in Misty's voice was palpable even over the phone.

"Please, can you find out what's going on?"

After the message ended, Veronica quickly scrolled to Nessa's number. But the call rolled to voicemail. Walking back toward the house with angry strides, Veronica decided she'd have to pay the chief of police another visit.

No matter what else was going on in her life, she had a duty to protect her source.

I helped Misty get into this situation. Now, I have to help her get out.

CHAPTER FIFTEEN

It was well past lunchtime when Nessa realized her appetite had suddenly returned with a vengeance. The nausea that had plagued her for months had been miraculously replaced with hunger pains, and she was craving comfort food.

Leaving her office, she headed for the lobby, distracted by thoughts of the grilled cheese sandwich with extra pickles she was going to order at Bay Subs and Grub. She pushed through the front door and barreled straight into Jankowski, who was followed by his new partner, Diego Ramirez.

"Whoa there, Chief," the detective said, putting out a hand to steady her, his eyes falling to her stomach. "Is everything okay?"

"Yes, I'm fine," Nessa snapped, pulling her jacket over her mid-section. "I'm just in a hurry."

Holding the door open with one thick arm, Jankowski moved to the side, giving her plenty of room to pass. As she stepped through the door, he cleared his throat.

"Did you know Agent Day was in town?" he asked. "Ramirez and I just saw her drive by with Hunter Hadley."

"Charlie Day is in Willow Bay?"

Nessa stood awkwardly on the sidewalk with both Jankowski and Ramirez staring at her. The older detective raised his eyebrows.

"You sure everything's okay, Nessa?"

Diego Ramirez had a round, weathered face and kind, brown eyes. She suddenly felt foolish for her childish behavior.

I blame my hormones. That, and being hungry.

"I'm fine, guys," she said, forcing a smile. "And I'll call Charlie now and find out what she's doing in town."

Once the detectives were gone, Nessa pulled out her phone and tapped on Charlie's name. The agent answered on the second ring.

"If you're still in town, let's grab lunch," Nessa said, foregoing a greeting. "Unless you prefer to be alone with Hunter Hadley."

"How'd you know I was in Willow Bay?"

Nessa heard a loud announcement in the background as Charlie spoke.

"I have spies everywhere," she teased. "You didn't think you could come to my town without me knowing, did you?"

"I'm impressed," Charlie said with a laugh. "But it was really just a drop-in visit to take care of some loose ends on the Locke case. I'm already back at the airport."

Frowning at the vague answer, Nessa wondered what the agent was really up to. And why was Hunter Hadley involved?

"You'd tell me if there was something I needed to know, right?"

"Of course," Charlie assured her. "And I'll give you an update soon. But right now, I have to catch my flight and-."

Another announcement drowned out Charlie's voice.

"Where are you headed?" Nessa asked once the announcement was finished. "You on your way back to Montana?"

"No, I'm off to Kentucky. One of Locke's victims was from a little town called Sky Lake, so that's my next stop."

Charlie sounded tired. Nessa wondered if the stress was finally getting to the normally calm and collected FBI agent.

"We're still trying to identify the victims and notify next of kin when possible," Charlie added. "Donovan Locke created a lot of heartache for a lot of people, and it's...it's hard to witness."

Wincing at the raw pain in Charlie's voice, Nessa felt a new burst of anger and outrage toward Locke and every animal like him.

How dare these bastards hurt so many good people?

Just then she heard a voice calling her name and turned to see Veronica Lee storming toward her on the sidewalk. The reporter's eyes were blazing, and her face was set in an unhappy scowl.

"I'll let you go, Charlie," Nessa said, keeping her eyes on Veronica. "But when you have more time to talk, call me back."

Ending the call, Nessa stuck her phone back in her pocket and braced herself for whatever Veronica was about to throw at her.

"I need to talk to you, Chief Ainsley."

"I was just heading out to lunch," Nessa said, feeling another pang in her stomach. "But you're welcome to walk with me to Bay Subs and Grub if you'd like."

Veronica fell into step beside Nessa as she headed west toward the Riverwalk. The sun was directly in front of them, still high in the sky, and Nessa squinted against the glare, thinking wistfully of the sunglasses she'd left back on her desk.

"I just got a message from Misty Bradshaw. She thinks someone's been following her, and she's pretty sure the guy must be one of Amber Sloan's goons."

Bristling at the reporter's accusatory tone, Nessa was tempted to shoot back a defensive reply, but when she looked over at Veronica, the strain on the young woman's face stopped her.

"I know you're worried, but we've got Amber Sloan under surveillance, and we're doing everything we can to make sure she won't be able to bother Misty or anyone else."

The crosswalk in front of them turned red, and Veronica stopped and spun toward Nessa.

"I'd say Amber did a lot more than just *bother* Misty," Veronica said, her indignant outburst causing the pedestrians around them to look over in surprise.

"Keep it down, Veronica," Nessa muttered. "I shouldn't even be talking to you about an open investigation."

As the crosswalk light turned green, the people beside them streamed across the street, but Veronica stood still on the sidewalk.

"So, there is an active investigation?" she asked. "You are going to hold Amber Sloan accountable for what she's done?"

Dropping her eyes, Nessa realized she was no longer hungry.

"Yes, we have opened an investigation, and we're still looking into the claims," Nessa said slowly, fighting back a wave of guilt. "But I can't guarantee Amber Sloan will be charged with any crime."

A tense silence fell over them as they faced each other. Veronica studied Nessa with wounded eyes as if she'd been betrayed.

"I brought my source to you, assuring her that you were trustworthy," she said in a raw voice. "Now she's being followed and threatened, and you won't tell me what's happening? And Amber Sloan is still on the street, free to continue preying on the young women in this community?"

Nessa lifted a hand in protest, but Veronica wasn't finished

"Maybe you can sleep at night knowing Amber's out there, but I can't." Veronica swallowed hard. "Not when Misty Bradshaw's out there, too, scared for her life."

Turning away, Veronica began to walk back the way they'd come, her head down, her stride no longer full of energetic anger. Nessa watched her go, feeling as if she'd just failed an important test.

She'd never felt good about offering Amber Sloan immunity, but now she was starting to think they'd made a terrible mistake.

* * *

The cheese and pickle sandwich had been abandoned, half-eaten on Nessa's desk when Peyton knocked on the doorframe and stuck her head into the office. Vanzinger's red crew cut was visible in the hall behind her.

"You wanted to see us, Chief?"

Sliding the remains of her lunch into the trash, Nessa wiped her mouth with the last clean napkin and waved Peyton and Vanzinger toward the chairs across from her.

"I received a complaint about Amber Sloan."

Peyton frowned, but she didn't look particularly surprised.

"Okay, what is it this time?"

"Misty Bradshaw thinks Amber has someone following her."

It was Vanzinger's turn to frown. He leaned forward, propping his elbows on the desk.

"Has Misty been threatened? Did the guy do anything to imply Amber was the one who'd sent him?"

"I'm not sure," Nessa admitted, "which is why I need you two to go talk to Misty and Amber. Find out what's going on."

Opening a file on her desk, Nessa scanned the agreement Amber had signed, hoping to find a loophole or a way out. But the immunity deal was fairly straightforward. Unless they proved Amber wasn't fulfilling her part of the bargain, she would remain a free woman.

"Has Amber been able to provide us with any useful information about her supposed contact?" Nessa asked. "Anything actionable?"

"She's given us some details about a user on the darknet message board that Diablo used to set up some of his shipments," Vanzinger said. "She doesn't know it, but the task force has infiltrated the board and has been monitoring the activity. So far, her information has been corroborated by what we've found."

Nessa raised her eyebrows.

"So, you think she really can deliver one of the key players in the trafficking network?"

The detectives in front of her looked at each other, then nodded.

"She said this guy goes by the username Mack, and that he's from Kentucky," Vanzinger said. "The cybercrime guys have verified there is in fact a user on the message board who goes by the username Mack, and they've been able to trace him back to an ISP in Kentucky."

Surprised that Amber's intel seemed to be legitimate, Nessa felt her interest rising.

"And Amber's setting up a meeting with this guy?"

Peyton nodded.

"Amber claims she's going to schedule a pick-up that will allow the task force to catch this guy Mack in the act."

"But why does Amber need to be involved?"

Distrust surged through Nessa at the thought of her team's safety resting in Amber Sloan's hands.

"Why can't we just use the ISP to track down the guy?

Vanzinger shrugged his thick shoulders.'

"Riley doubts we'll get a judge to force the ISP in Kentucky to provide details," he explained, looking as unhappy as Nessa was feeling. "Not on the word of one informant and not without direct evidence of a specific crime."

Something in his words triggered her memory. Charlie said she was going to a little town in Kentucky.

"You said the ISP was in Kentucky. Did they say which town?"

"Yep, they said the guy was probably connecting from some little town in the middle of nowhere," Peyton said, checking her notes. "I'd never heard of it."

Cocking her head, Nessa tried to recall Charlie's words.

"This little town, is it called Sky Lake?"

CHAPTER SIXTEEN

The chief spoke just as Peyton found the name of the town listed in her folder. One of the ISPs that the task force was tracking was located in Sky Lake, Kentucky. She looked up at Nessa, her amber eyes wide, then looked back at the folder.

"Yes, that's it. How did you know?"

"Operation Stolen Angels isn't the only federal task force investigating the town," Nessa said, shaking her head. "Special Agent Charlie Day is heading there now as part of the Donovan Locke investigation."

Unfamiliar with the specifics of the Locke investigation, Peyton stared at Nessa, trying to imagine the possible connections.

"Did Agent Day say what she was looking for?" Vanzinger asked, his face revealing his surprise. "Did she say how the town is connected to Locke?"

"No, but I was able to see in the files that it's Donovan Locke's hometown. He grew up there, so maybe it's just a routine trip."

The police chief's tone suggested she doubted that was the case.

"But, I'm thinking you'd better update Agent Marlowe and the rest of the task force. We don't want the two investigations to be stepping on each other's toes."

As Peyton and Vanzinger stood to leave, Nessa raised a hand to stop them.

"Make sure you talk to Misty and Amber today. That's a priority."

"You got it, Chief," Peyton agreed. "We'll take care of it."

But as she followed Vanzinger's broad back down the hall toward the briefing room, Peyton continued to stew on the connection between the serial killer Donovan Locke and the man Amber Sloan knew only as Mack.

If they were from the same town, and they were involved in the same dirty business, they might be cut from the same cloth.

This guy Mack may be more dangerous than Amber's led us to believe.

Marlowe was sitting with one of his agents going through a pile of paperwork when they entered the briefing room. He didn't look up until Vanzinger pulled out a chair and lowered his big frame right next to him.

"Yes, Detective Vanzinger? Do you have something for me?"

"Not sure if you're aware, but it seems that the special response team investigating Donovan Locke's ranch in Montana has taken a sudden interest in his hometown."

Vanzinger paused to let his words sink in.

"We just found out that the agent in charge, Special Agent Charlie Day, is heading to Sky Lake, Kentucky as we speak. What we don't know yet, is why."

The detective had Marlowe's full attention. He pushed back his chair and faced Vanzinger, a frown creasing his stony brow.

"I suspected the investigations would overlap," Marlowe said slowly, "after all, Locke had been dealing with the Diablo Syndicate. But I didn't realize Agent Day had been assigned to the case."

He turned to Peyton, his eyes suddenly keen and bright with interest. She had the fleeting thought that it was the first time the senior FBI agent had reacted to the case with any visible emotion, other than impatience.

"I think it's time I talked to Agent Day. If she's tracked Locke's connections back to Sky Lake, we may be on to the same perp."

* * *

Peyton and Vanzinger left Marlowe to follow up with Charlie Day as they drove out to Amber Sloan's apartment. Their Dodge Charger had just turned into Fox Hollow Apartments when they saw a teenage girl jump out of a sleek SUV and scurry across the lot.

"She's not going where I think she's going, is she?" Peyton asked Vanzinger as they watched the SUV pull away, its driver hidden behind the darkly tinted windows.

But the girl headed straight for Apartment 124. By the time she knocked on Amber's door, Peyton and Vanzinger had gotten out of their car and were charging up behind her.

Amber opened the door, her face filling first with shock, and then with anger, as she saw the detectives standing behind her guest.

"Are you guys checking up on me?" she hissed, ignoring the panicked girl in front of her. "Are you spying on me?"

"Just what is going on here?" Peyton demanded.

She recognized the girl. It was one of the girls she'd seen at the park with Amber. The one who still had braces.

"Who was in that SUV?" Peyton demanded.

Recoiling at the question, the girl hesitated, then darted past her, running along the edge of the building before slipping around the corner.

"Nice job," Amber muttered. "You always this good with kids?"

"You've been warned about dealing drugs or recruiting girls to work for you," Peyton said, incensed by the woman's flippant response. "If you violate those terms, the immunity deal will automatically be canceled, and you'll be prosecuted."

Amber pushed her frizzy bangs off her forehead and rolled her eyes as if Peyton was being overly dramatic.

"The poor girl lives in the neighborhood. She was just trying to sell some girl scout cookies."

"You think it's funny?" Vanzinger asked, his hands balling into big fists at his side. "Does it amuse you to screw up some kid's life?"

Crossing skinny arms over her chest, Amber sighed.

"You both need to take a chill pill. I'm doing nothing wrong."

"That's not what I've heard," Peyton said, then stopped herself from saying anything more.

But Amber's bored expression had turned into a suspicious frown.

"What have you heard?" she asked, her eyes narrowing with anger. "Who's been talking about me? I have a right to know."

A chill settled over Peyton at the thought of Amber finding out that Misty had been the one who had turned her in, and who had even filed a written report.

"It doesn't matter," Vanzinger said before Peyton could reply. "All you need to remember is to stay away from any minors, any drugs, and anyone associated with your past lifestyle."

"If I see young girls hanging around here again, I'll tear up that agreement myself," Peyton added. "You've been warned."

Walking back to the Charger, Peyton looked around to see if the girl with braces was anywhere in sight, but she was gone.

They pulled back into traffic and headed for Hope House, determined to see Misty and to make sure she was okay. If their visit to Amber had proven anything, it was that Misty's fears were justified and that she needed to stay well away from Amber Sloan.

But when Peyton asked for Misty at Hope House, the receptionist told her the girl was no longer a resident.

"She left a few days ago," the receptionist said. "I believe our staff was able to find her a place nearby."

"Can you give us her new address?" Peyton asked, her concern growing. "We really need to talk to her."

The receptionist shook her head.

"Sorry, I don't have that information."

Turning toward Vanzinger in dismay, Peyton felt a surge of panic, but her partner wasn't ready to give up. He leaned forward and flashed a wide smile at the woman behind the counter.

"I bet a pretty lady like you could find that address if you wanted to." He used a deep, smooth voice that earned a cringe from Peyton. "You'd be doing us a really big favor."

To Peyton's surprise, the woman returned Vanzinger's smile, then lowered her voice.

"I really don't know her address," the woman said. "But Misty's scheduled to attend an NA meeting here tomorrow morning. If you want to see her, you could try back then."

Deciding that was their best and only option, Peyton followed Vanzinger outside, suddenly tired and discouraged.

She checked her messages and felt her spirits lift when she saw Frankie's missed call. But listening to his voicemail, a growing sense of unease took over.

"Hey, Peyton, call me when you get a chance. I'm headed back to Kentucky tomorrow, and it'd be nice to see you before I go."

CHAPTER SEVENTEEN

Barker hesitated by the door, then turned back to Frankie. His anxious expression revealed his misgivings about the plan they'd agreed to with Hunter and Veronica. Frankie would travel back with them to Sky Lake when Skylar went to meet her grandfather, then stay on for a few days to investigate. Barker would stay in town to continue working on the case for Willow Bay General Hospital.

It had all been settled, but Barker's big, puppy dog eyes still seemed unsure as he paused, one hand on the doorknob.

"Stop stressing about it, man. I'll be on my best behavior," Frankie groaned, drawing an imaginary X over his thin chest. "Cross my heart and hope to die, stick a-"

"Okay, I get the idea, I'm going," Barker said, shaking his head. "There's just something about that town I don't like."

Frankie wasn't sure if he should be insulted or touched that Barker was always worrying about him.

"Go on, get out of here." Frankie kicked his feet up onto his desk. "Reggie's going to be pissed if you're late again."

Relieved to see the door finally close behind his partner, Frankie pulled out his phone, determined to try Peyton's number one more time. Although Frankie didn't share Barker's dislike for Sky Lake, he didn't want to go back to the little town without seeing Peyton first.

The door swung open again before he could tap on Peyton's number. Thinking Barker had returned, Frankie screwed his face into a scowl, ready to give the older man a piece of his mind.

I'm not some dumb amateur, I'm the senior partner in this firm, and...

The angry words died on his lips as he saw Peyton's dark cap of hair and big amber eyes appear in the doorway.

"Good, you're still here," she said, stepping into the room. "I was worried you'd leave town again before I had a chance to see you."

Dropping his phone on the desk, Frankie swung his feet to the ground and stood, trying to play it cool. But he couldn't keep a goofy grin from spreading over his face.

"I was just going to call you. Thought we could grab some dinner."

"Sounds good," Peyton agreed, circling the desk to stand beside him. "I haven't eaten all day, I'm starving."

But the happy gleam in her eyes dimmed when she saw the print-out on Frankie's desk. Following her gaze, he scooped up the travel itinerary, folded it, and stuck it into his back pocket.

"Sky Lake Regional?" Peyton asked, biting her lip. "What's taking you up there again?"

"Just a missing person's case," Frankie murmured, hating that he had to keep secrets from her. It felt almost like lying.

But he and Barker had agreed not to tell anyone about Skylar, or her connection to Veronica Lee and Donovan Locke. Of course, Peyton wasn't just anyone. She had helped save Veronica's life and had been part of the team that had rescued Ling Lee.

Veronica won't mind if I tell Peyton that she has a half-sister, will she?

Deciding it was best to keep his mouth closed, at least for the time being, Frankie found himself asking the question that had been bugging him for days.

"By the way, what's up with Amber Sloan? Why were you questioning her the other day?"

Peyton blinked in surprise.

"We were checking into a complaint, but she's been released already," she replied. "Why? How do you know her?"

"Amber's been involved in the drug scene for years."

At Peyton's raised eyebrows, Frankie clarified.

"I mean, I don't know her personally, but I have friends who say she's bad news. From what I hear that chick is into some seriously messed up stuff."

Before he could elaborate, Peyton's phone buzzed in her pocket. Her face fell as she saw the incoming number.

"Sorry, I've got to take this."

Sinking back into his chair, Frankie tried to look busy on his computer while Peyton answered the call.

"Mrs. Epstein, is everything okay? Is the fever back?"

Frankie looked up at the fear he heard in her voice. She held the phone against her ear in a tight grip as she listened to the caller.

"No, you did the right thing," Peyton said into the phone, her voice grim. "I'll be there as soon as I can. I won't tell her you called."

She tapped to end the call, then turned to Frankie.

"My mother's not well."

Shoving the phone back in her pocket, Peyton sighed.

"I'm really sorry, but I'm going to have to go check on her," she murmured. "She didn't want to bother me, but her neighbor, Mrs. Epstein, says her fever's back and well..."

"Yeah, of course, you better go check on your mom." Frankie jumped up from his chair. "We'll see each other when I get back."

He tried to mask the disappointment that flooded through him. He knew the main reason Peyton had moved back to Willow Bay in the first place was to take care of her mother.

She didn't come back here just to date my sorry ass, that's for sure.

Forcing his feet to move, Frankie followed her to the door. When she stopped and turned back to him, he managed a weak smile.

"What did I do to deserve a boyfriend like you?" she whispered, lifting her face to his, and depositing a soft kiss on his lips. "I don't know what I'd do without you."

Her words replayed in his head as she stepped through the door, but they didn't have the effect he'd expected. He knew he should be ecstatic. The woman he loved had just called him her boyfriend. She'd pretty much said she couldn't live without him.

But as he watched Peyton walk down the street and disappear around the corner, Frankie couldn't shake a terrible feeling that he would never see her again.

* * *

The light was on in the living room when Frankie walked up the narrow path and felt around in his pocket for his keys. Raised voices could be heard inside, even though he knew his mother was alone.

Overdressed housewives in some town or another were at it again, and his mother would be settled into her usual spot on the couch, transfixed by the drama.

Sometimes Frankie thought his mother was as addicted to her television as he was to his bottle.

She uses the noise to drown out the memories, and I use the booze.

Instead of turning to each other after Franny had died, they'd turned away, preferring the numbness and forgetfulness to the guilt and blame. And now, so many years later, that numbness had become an addiction. It felt so much better not to feel anything at all.

Pulling out his keyring, Frankie looked down at his hand, but he couldn't make himself stick the key in the lock. His nerves were on edge and he wasn't in the mood to pack and go to sleep.

Although his flight would be leaving just after dawn, there was no way he'd be able to sleep while he was still worrying about Peyton.

She'd come running when her mother had needed her just as she should have. After all, Peyton had left a good job in Memphis to come home and take care of her.

A sliver of envy pierced Frankie as he imagined Peyton sitting quietly by her mother's bedside, her conscience clear as she did what any good daughter would do.

So, what is a good son supposed to do? Let his sister die on the floor? Become a drunk and hide so he doesn't have to face the truth?

He'd been hiding from it for so long, Frankie wasn't sure what the truth was anymore. Too many years, too much booze, too many what-ifs, and regrets. Was he to blame for Franny's death, or was it his mother's fault? Did they blame each other or themselves?

Maybe it didn't even matter who had caused the hurt and the pain. It was too late anyway. Scar tissue had hardened between them, and they could never fully heal. Never return to the way they'd once been.

Knowing he should go in and get some sleep, he shoved the keys back in his pocket and retraced his steps down the front path. Heading toward the corner, he pulled out his phone. Tapping on a number in his contact list, he held the phone to his ear and pushed back the craving for a drink.

Just one damn sip is all I need. Just a little taste.

He heard a click, then a grumpy voice sounded in his ear.

"What do you want, Frankie?"

"Hey, Little Ray, what's up, man?"

* * *

Approaching the corner of Citrus Drive and Huntington Street on foot, Frankie saw the sign for Fox Hollow Apartments just ahead. He'd tried to talk Little Ray into picking him up and driving him over, but the big man had flatly refused.

"I'll give you Amber's address," Ray had finally conceded, "but I'm not going anywhere near her. I hear she's in trouble with the feds, and I don't need any new trouble."

The parking lot was dark and quiet as Frankie searched for Unit 124. He wasn't sure what he was going to say. All he knew was he didn't trust Amber, and he wanted to make sure she wasn't a threat to Peyton before he left town.

As long as she doesn't find out I'm messing with her case, it's all good.

Of course, Amber was a suspect in the case he and Barker were working on for Willow Bay General as well, and confronting Amber would likely compromise his undercover work for the hospital.

Already regretting his rash actions, Frankie knocked on the door. He heard a scuffling sound inside, then the deadbolt clicked.

"Yeah?" Amber's narrowed eyes and frizzy bangs appeared from behind a thick chain. "What do you want?"

Leaning forward to peer inside, Frankie tried to remember which kind of pills had gone missing from the hospital dispensary.

"Percs or benzos. Whatever you got."

She studied him through the crack, then shut the door. He heard the chain rattle, then the door swung open.

"I know you. You're Frankie, Little Ray's friend."

She produced a knowing smirk.

"An ex-con, right?"

"I did some time, but my conviction was overturned," Frankie said, not sure why he was explaining himself. "You got something for me, or not?"

Moving back, Amber gestured for him to follow her inside, keeping her eyes on him as he stepped into the dim apartment.

"I thought Little Ray had gone clean."

"He did, that's why I'm coming to you," Frankie muttered.

Amber laughed, as if he were joking, and stared at him.

"Sorry, I've gotta be careful who I do business with, you know."

She stepped close enough to put a hand on his chest. Frankie tried not to recoil as she grinned up at him, her breath stale with cigarette smoke, her eyes slightly bloodshot.

"I'm having a little trouble with my supply chain, so I don't have any benzos right now," she said, leaning closer. "But if you're looking for some fun, I may have just what you need."

Lifting her hand off his chest, Frankie inched backward.

"I'm all good in that area, thanks anyway."

Amber's grin faded, and she shrugged.

"Suit yourself," she said, suddenly bored. "Give me your number and I'll give you a call once I can get more benzos."

"Get 'em from where?"

A suspicious frown settled over her face.

"Why the fuck do you care?"

"No reason," Frankie said, holding up his hands. "Just making conversation."

The frown deepened.

"You working for the cops? Or the feds? Did Detective Bell send you here to try to trap me into fucking up my immunity deal?"

"Immunity? For what?"

The surprised look on Frankie's face seemed to convince Amber that he had no idea what she was talking about.

"It doesn't matter. Forget it," Amber muttered, her anger disappearing as swiftly as it had come. "Some bitch of a detective is trying to railroad me. She thinks she's smart, but she doesn't know who she's messing with."

Resisting the urge to defend his girlfriend's honor, Frankie decided it was best not to give Amber any reason to suspect he even knew Peyton.

"I wouldn't mess with the WBPD if I were you," he said, trying to sound casual. "They threw my ass in the state pen for no reason, so you never know what they might do if you piss them off."

"Not me. I'm no pushover like you."

Amber didn't bother hiding her disdain.

"I haven't gone to jail yet, and I don't plan to start now."

He nodded as if impressed, then cocked his head.

"You actually got them to offer you immunity?"

"Yep, all I gotta do is give them some info about a supplier I know, and they'll let me off with a slap on the hand."

Frankie widened his eyes.

"You aren't scared to snitch out your supplier?"

"I don't call it snitching," she said in a smug voice. "I'm just selling information, and the payment is my freedom. Besides Mack is just a nobody. A middleman. There's nothing he can do."

Amber seemed pleased with herself, and Frankie decided he was pleased as well. From what he could tell, Amber posed no immediate threat to Peyton, and she was under an immunity agreement which would limit her ability to do more harm in the community.

Although Amber hadn't admitted she was getting her pills from someone at the hospital, Frankie was beginning to feel that it had been a productive visit.

As he closed Amber's door behind him and headed back toward Citrus Drive, he decided the only thing that could go wrong would be Peyton finding out he'd butted into her case.

Unless Amber mentions to Peyton that I came by looking for drugs.

The thought killed his good mood. Now he had another secret to keep from Peyton. Unless he admitted to what he'd done.

But he'd jeopardized her case, maybe even her job. If he told her, would she ever trust him again? No, better to keep it a secret.

After all, it's just a secret, and secrets aren't technically lies, are they?

CHAPTER EIGHTEEN

Amber slid the chain back into place and turned the deadbolt. She leaned against the door and stared into the quiet room, suddenly wishing she had talked Frankie into staying. He seemed like an okay guy, and she could have used a little company. The place had begun to feel very empty without the steady stream of buyers and sellers that usually filled her apartment.

Crossing the room, she stared down at her open laptop, wondering if Mack had responded to her message. She'd have to deliver on her promise soon, or the snobby state prosecutor may decide to tear up her immunity agreement.

A sharp knock stopped her before she could sit down. Wondering if Frankie might have come back to take her up on her offer, she hurried to the door, pulled back the chain, and turned the deadbolt.

The man outside wasn't Frankie. He pushed past Amber and scanned the room with hard, wary eyes.

"What was Frankie Dawson doing in here?"

"None of your business," she snapped, flustered by his sudden appearance. "Now, what do you want?"

The man grabbed her arm, his fingers digging in hard.

"Don't get smart with me," he said, his voice cold. "You think your deal with the feds protects you from the Syndicate?"

Wrenching her arm away, Amber stepped back.

"What do you care about Frankie, anyway?" she muttered. "He's just some ex-con who wanted to get high."

The man shook his head.

"No, he's a private investigator who thinks he's some kind of glorified detective," the man sneered. "And he has a habit of sticking his nose in other people's business."

Amber frowned, replaying her conversation with Frankie. She hadn't said anything incriminating, had she?

"It doesn't matter," she said. "He's not a problem."

"No, but his new girlfriend might be."

Rubbing at her bruised arm, she met the man's cold stare.

"Yeah? Who's his girlfriend?"

"Detective Peyton Bell."

A flush of humiliation flooded through Amber at his words. She cringed at the thought of how easily she'd fallen for Frankie's little routine.

The rotten creep played me, and I fell for it like an idiot.

At least she hadn't told Frankie anything Peyton hadn't already known. There was nothing he could do with the information.

"Like I said, it doesn't matter," Amber insisted. "I didn't tell him shit, so don't worry."

"I am worried, as are my friends in the Syndicate," he said, moving closer. "They asked me to remind you to keep your mouth shut. They think you might say too much."

Amber lifted her chin and tensed her body, preparing to put up a hell of a fight. She didn't care how many connections he had at the WBPD or how high up he was in the Syndicate. He wasn't going to lay a finger on her.

"I know what to do," Amber muttered between clenched teeth. "And you can tell your buddies to back the fuck off."

Studying Amber's flushed face, the man seemed to be contemplating his next words carefully.

"You know a girl named Misty Bradshaw?"

The question took her by surprise, and she hesitated, then nodded. Misty had run out on her after only a few months. The girl still owed her a considerable amount of money.

"She's the one who ratted you out" he stated bluntly. "Filed an official statement and everything. I thought you should know."

The man moved toward the door, as Amber struggled to hide the rage building inside her at the revelation of Misty's betrayal.

With one hand on the door, the man looked back.

"You wouldn't happen to have any new girls in the pipeline, would you?" he asked. "Anyone who might be *available* soon?"

"I thought you were too high and mighty to go with my girls," she replied stiffly. "Ready to go slumming after all?"

"It's not for me," he snapped in disgust. "I've got a buyer on the hook, so let me know. I could use the money."

Amber watched the door slam shut behind him, then hurried to her laptop. She felt a grim surge of satisfaction at the sight of Mack's reply on the darknet message board, suddenly glad she had waited to schedule the pickup.

She had a job for him to do first. Once Mack had taken care of her latest problem, she could decide if she would turn him in to the cops, or if she'd just keep jerking them along.

Perhaps the warning from the Syndicate should scare her into keeping her mouth shut, but she doubted they'd be too concern about a low-level middleman like Mack.

In the animal kingdom, he'd be a worker bee or an ant. Just a body used to move things from one place to another. The Syndicate might not even notice he'd gotten snagged. Or if they did, they wouldn't know she'd been the one who'd set him up.

Of course, they'd found out about Misty going to the cops, so maybe they would know if she worked with the feds.

Maybe next time they pay me a visit, I'll be the one who goes missing.

Typing out a message on the darknet board, Amber decided she'd have to worry about that later. Right now, she needed Mack to help her out, and she couldn't afford to wait.

This isn't the time to start losing my nerve.

The man with the Kentucky accent didn't seem any more dangerous than the other men she'd had to deal with in her life. All she had to do was offer him enough money, and he'd been on his way.

She clicked *Submit* on the message and closed out the browser. Refusing to think of Mack, or Frankie, or Detective Bell, Amber shuffled toward the bedroom.

It was time to get some sleep. She would find out in the morning if Mack had accepted her offer, and if so, she would need all her wits about her. Tomorrow might be a very busy day.

CHAPTER NINETEEN

The sunlight filtered into the crowded meeting room, drawing Misty Bradshaw's eyes to the gorgeous spring day outside. The Narcotics Anonymous meeting was scheduled to last another twenty minutes, but Misty had already told Dr. Horn that she had a job interview and would need to leave early.

Slipping past the rows of metal folding chairs, Misty tiptoed to the back of the room and pushed through the door, trying not to make a sound. The Hope House lobby was empty as she crossed to the big glass doors and stepped out into the sunshine.

If she hurried, she would have just enough time to stop by the room she was renting and change clothes. She was planning to wear the navy-blue skirt suit she'd found at the tiny thrift store behind the Willow Bay Methodist Church. It made her feel like a grown-up for the first time in her life.

She walked toward the street, too nervous and excited about the interview ahead to notice the dirty white Camry parked by the curb.

"Misty!"

Pausing at the sound of her name, she looked over to see a thin woman in skinny jeans and a baggy black sweatshirt leaning against the Camry. Thick bangs cast a shadow over the woman's sharp features, but Misty recognized Amber Sloan right away.

"Hey, Misty, can I talk to you?"

Bile rose in Misty's throat as she quickened her step, keeping her eyes fixed to the pavement ahead of her.

"Come on, Misty, I just want to say I'm sorry."

Footsteps sounded behind her on the pavement, and a soft hand fell on her shoulder. Misty spun around, her eyes wide with fear and anger as she faced the woman who still haunted her dreams.

"Go away, Amber."

Misty's voice shook with emotion as she looked around, hoping to see someone who might help her, but the sidewalk was empty.

"I don't want to...to see you, or to talk to you," she stammered. "I'm sober now. I'm finally thinking straight, and I know what you did to me, and to the other girls, is wrong."

"That's why I want to apologize," Amber said, her voice softer than Misty remembered, her eyes not as hard. "I've gotten sober, too. Or at least I'm trying."

Frowning in confusion, Misty shook her head.

"You told me you never used your own supply."

"I lied," Amber admitted. "How else could I have done all those terrible things? That wasn't me, not the real me."

Misty squinted into the sun, unable to see the expression on Amber's face. Was she telling the truth? Had she really been an addict all along? Did it even matter?

"Look, I've been going to NA meetings, too." Amber lowered her voice and moved closer. "I saw you in there, and I thought...well, I thought I should at least try to apologize. I know it might be too late..."

"It is too late," Misty agreed, stepping back. "I hope you *have* gotten help. Anyone who could do what you've done *needs help*."

Fighting back the anger that threatened to take over, Misty drew in a deep breath, then exhaled slowly.

"But that doesn't mean I can ever forget what you've done, and I'm sure as hell not ready to forgive you."

Just then two teens on bikes raced past them, causing Misty to take another step back. But she was too close to the curb. Her foot found only air, and she began to totter backward toward the street.

Grabbing Misty's arm, Amber steadied her, pulling her back onto the sidewalk just as a pick-up truck sped past behind her, causing her shoulder-length hair to fly around her face.

"I'm trying to make amends," Amber repeated as if nothing had happened. "I've even been helping the cops."

Still shaking from her near miss, Misty stared at Amber, her big, brown eyes blinking against the sun.

"You're helping the cops? How?"

"We're gonna take down one of the guys responsible for setting up the syndicate in the first place," Amber said, looking over her shoulder, then back at Misty. "That way he won't be able to hurt anyone else."

"Who?" Misty asked, her tone hardening. "Which guy?

Amber's hesitation confirmed Misty's fear. The woman was lying. Spinning on her heel, Misty started down the sidewalk again.

"Mack," Amber called after her. "We're gonna set up Mack."

Misty stopped and looked back. She'd heard the name before. Amber had picked up a shipment of pills from him the same day two of Amber's girls had gone missing. Misty had always suspected it had been an even exchange.

"Really? You're turning him in?"

"I told you, I'm trying to make amends."

Glancing at her watch, Misty nodded.

"Good, I'm glad. But I've gotta go. I'm late for an appointment."

"I can give you a ride if you want," Amber said, pointing back to her Camry. "I owe you that much."

A shiver rolled through Misty at the thought of getting into Amber's car. She never wanted to be anywhere near the woman again, no matter how late she'd be, or how far she'd have to walk.

"I don't need anything from you," Misty said, her voice firm. "I'm just fine on my own."

With a sense of relief, she turned and walked away.

She didn't look back.

* * *

Misty approached the house on Gladstone Drive with hurried steps. Climbing the stairs to the little room over the garage, she unlocked the door, then looked over her shoulder toward the street.

She was suddenly sure she would see Amber's Camry parked by the curb. But the residential street was empty, and she scolded herself for being paranoid.

After my interview, I'll call Veronica Lee back and tell her what Amber said. Maybe I'll even call Detective Bell. They'll make sure she stays away.

Entering the little studio apartment, Misty closed the door behind her and locked it, making sure both the deadbolt and chain were securely in place.

Then she turned to see that the navy-blue suit was still on the hangar just as she'd left it. Throwing her purse on the foldaway sofa, she opened the tiny refrigerator and pulled out a bottle of water.

The encounter with Amber Sloan had left her dry-mouthed and a little shaky. She'd need to regain her composure before her interview.

Unscrewing the lid, Misty took a long sip from the bottle, then turned to the closet. She didn't have shoes that matched the blue suit, so her black pumps would have to do. She opened the door and reached in for the pumps.

An iron hand gripped her wrist, and a sharp pain shot up her arm. Wrenching her arm back, she saw a syringe fall to the floor just as a man's face appeared in the shadows above her.

Before she could scream, the man looped a strong arm around her neck and clamped a hand over her mouth.

"Amber Sloan asked me...to pay you...a little visit."

The man dragged her toward the sofa, knocking the blue suit to the floor, and crushing it under his boot.

She brought her knee up with a sudden thrust, but the man took his hand off her mouth to counter the blow.

"Are you Mack?" she gasped in a weak voice, starting to feel the effect of whatever was in the syringe. "Are you..."

"What did you say?"

Giving her a sharp shake, he lowered his angry face to hers.

"What did you call me?"

"Mack," she choked out. "Amber's setting you up..."

Panic filled the man's face, and he looked toward the door as if he expected a SWAT team to burst in at any minute.

"What did she tell you?" he demanded, yanking her toward him.

But his voice was fading, along with the room, and the rest of the world. Her eyes were too heavy to hold open, and she closed them, blocking out the rage in the man's eyes, sinking into darkness.

CHAPTER TWENTY

Veronica looked over at Skylar, who was staring out the car window at the changing landscape of green fields and fenced-in horse pastures. The girl had been quiet on the flight up from Willow Bay, and she now sat silently in the backseat of the rental car, her hand resting on Gracie's soft head.

"You okay?" Veronica asked, wishing she knew what was in her sister's mind. "You still want to go through with this?"

Turning her big green eyes to Veronica, Skylar nodded.

"I want to meet my grandfather," she said, sounding sure. "And I know my mother wanted to take me to Sky Lake. I feel like I owe it to her to go. Like she'll be watching over me."

The blue Nissan slowed, and Hunter glanced in the rearview mirror, meeting Veronica's anxious eyes.

"We're almost there," he called back from the driver's seat. "Just down this road and you'll be able to see the farm."

Frankie turned around to offer Skylar a wide smile.

"Maybe you and me can learn to ride horses," he said with a wink.

A nervous smile lifted the corners of Skylar's mouth, and she leaned forward to look through the front windshield just as a long white barn came into view.

"There it is," Skylar whispered, pulling Gracie closer in her excitement. "It's just like I thought it would be."

Passing the sign for Sky Lake Farm and Stables, Veronica felt her own excitement building. As the car rolled to a stop, Hunter pointed toward an older man with snow-white hair who was waiting by the stable. Holding a wide-brimmed hat in one hand, the man lifted his other hand in greeting as they all climbed out.

"Mr. Fairfax, it's good to see you."

Hunter strode forward to shake the older man's hand, then gestured back toward the car.

"This is Veronica Lee and Frankie Dawson," he said, "but I'm sure we're not the ones you've been waiting to see."

He turned to Skylar, who was holding tightly to Veronica's hand.

"Skylar, this is your grandfather, Conrad Fairfax."

Moving forward, Conrad studied Skylar's face, his eyes bright with unshed tears as he approached.

"My goodness, you sure do take after your mother."

His voice was thick with pain, but he managed a smile.

"I have something of hers I'd like to show you."

He motioned for Skylar to follow him into the stable, but she hesitated, looking to Veronica for help.

"Go see what it is," Veronica prompted, feeling her sister's hand trembling in hers. "It's okay, Gracie and I will go with you."

They walked into the stable together, and Skylar gasped in pleasure as she saw Conrad standing beside a horse with a snow-white coat that perfectly matched the older man's hair.

"How beautiful," Skylar whispered, lifting a small hand to tentatively stroke the horse's neck. "It's so soft."

"Her name's Sunshine." A sad smile accompanied his words. "And this saddle belonged to your mother."

Running his hand along the soft chestnut brown leather, Conrad looked down into Skylar's face. His smile faltered as he studied his granddaughter's delicate features.

"I'll teach you how to ride if you like," he said, turning away to adjust the saddle. "Summer had a horse a lot like Sunshine when she was about your age. She loved that horse so very much."

The older man dropped his head, trying to hide his tears as Skylar continued to stroke the horse's neck and withers.

"She told me about this place."

Skylar spoke to Conrad's bowed head.

"She wanted to come back here more than anything."

Pulling a wrinkled handkerchief out of his back pocket, Conrad wiped at his eyes and lifted his head.

"Your mother talked about Sky Lake? What else did she say?"

A shadow passed over Skylar's eyes at the question, and Veronica felt the girl's hand tighten around her own.

"Skylar was too young to remember very much," Veronica explained, wanting to spare Skylar the pain of admitting how little she could remember about her mother. "Her mother was...was taken from her when she was just a little girl."

Conrad winced, his red-rimmed eyes turning to Veronica.

"Yes, of course," he said, trying to hide his disappointment. "I understand. I was just hoping...well, we never knew what happened."

Reaching into his shirt pocket, he pulled out a folded piece of paper. He carefully unfolded the paper and held it out to Veronica.

"This is the letter we found in Summer's room," he said. "My wife never believed it was Summer's handwriting, although it was written by someone who did a good job mimicking it."

Skylar stared down at the paper, her eyes scanning the words scrawled across the page.

"No, that's not my mother's writing. I would know it anywhere."

She frowned and shook her head as if it hurt to remember.

"She wrote stories for me and I kept them after she was...gone. I had them until *he* found them. I had them until the Professor took them all away."

"The Professor?"

"That's what she called Donovan Locke," Veronica explained, seeing in dismay that Skylar had retreated behind a blank expression and glazed eyes. "Apparently he often pretended to be a professor in order to lure young women into trusting him."

Conrad's face tightened with anger.

"Donovan Locke grew up around here," he said stiffly. "He was always bad news. But he'd left town years before Summer went missing, so I never...well, no one ever suspected..."

His next words came out before Veronica could stop him.

"That brother of his is a strange character, too. Never did seem to grow up," Conrad said. "Last I heard Tom Locke still lives with his mother. Still works with Beau Sparks over at his charter service, too."

Feeling Skylar stiffen next to her, Veronica wished she'd told her sister that their father's family was still alive and that they still lived in Sky Lake. She'd been too scared, fearing that Skylar would want to meet them, and Veronica wasn't sure she was ready for that.

But as they followed Conrad up toward the house, Skylar pulled on Veronica's arm, holding her back as the others walked ahead.

"Why didn't you tell me?" she whispered, her eyes filled with hurt. "I'm tired of being kept in the dark. I want to know who I am and where I come from. I want to meet my family."

* * *

The rehabilitation center was located just over the county line in Jefferson County. Harriet Locke's neighbor had given them directions, along with a detailed account of how Harriet had broken her hip several weeks before.

"Poor Harriet will be there for another month at least," the neighbor had assured them in a conspiratorial tone. "Of course, most old folks don't ever come back after such a fall."

Veronica stared at the brown, single-story building with dread. The woman who had given birth to a sociopath waited behind the concrete walls and narrow windows, and she was about to meet her, whether she wanted to or not.

"It'll be okay," Skylar said, slipping her small hand into Veronica's. "I have a good feeling about this."

Her sister's words brought a reluctant smile to Veronica's face as she realized they'd suddenly switched roles. The frightened girl who had needed to be protected was suddenly the one offering comfort.

Opening the big glass doors, Frankie waved them through. Hunter followed them into the lobby, accompanied by Gracie on a leash. They all stood awkwardly by the reception desk, waiting for a compact woman in a stark white uniform to finish a phone call. The woman's name badge identified her as Dee Wiggins.

"We're here to see Harriet Locke," Veronica finally said, when the woman put down the phone. "We're not on the visitor's list, but..."

"That's all right, honey," the woman said with a smile. "We're always glad to have visitors around here. We don't get enough of them if you ask me."

She slid a clipboard toward Veronica.

"Just sign in here and I'll need to see an ID from one of you."

Lowering her voice, she muttered in Veronica's direction.

"Seems a waste of time to me, but ever since the U.S. Marshals came here a few weeks back my supervisor's been on my case to follow all the rules. Even the dumb ones."

Frankie pulled out his wallet and presented his driver's license.

"Looks like I got this just in time," Frankie said, handing it to Dee with a flourish. "Although the picture doesn't do me justice."

"Florida, huh?"

137

Dee studied the license with interest as Veronica wrote her name on the clipboard, then added Skylar's name under her own.

She looked down at Gracie and smiled, writing in the dog's name on the line below.

"No pets are allowed inside," Dee said, peering over the counter at the white Lab. "But I'm guessing that's one of those service dogs, so that's okay."

She slid the clipboard toward Hunter and her smile widened.

"The old girl will be glad to see you," she said, watching with interest as he picked up the pen and added his name and Frankie's to the list. "She doesn't get many gentlemen callers, other than that son of hers."

Leading the group down a brightly lit corridor, Dee stopped outside a closed door and knocked.

A woman's frail voice called out, although Veronica couldn't make out the words. Pushing open the door, Dee walked inside.

"Mrs. Locke, you've got a load of visitors to see you."

The elderly woman in the bed fumbled on the bedside table for her glasses, then stared over at Veronica, who stood still in the doorway.

"Come on in, dear," she said, adjusting the covers around her and smoothing down her wispy white curls. "I won't bite."

Moving into the room, Veronica pulled Skylar along with her, until they stood only a few feet from the hospital bed.

"You two can go on in," Dee told Hunter and Frankie, slipping past them into the corridor. "And let me know if you need anything."

Harriet looked past Veronica and Skylar, her eyes widening as she saw Hunter and Frankie's tall figures filling up the room.

"I'm sorry to come here without calling first, Mrs. Locke," Veronica said, inching closer. "But we have news about your son."

Worry flooded the older woman's face.

"What's happened? Is Tom all right?"

Shaking her head, Veronica hurried to explain.

"I meant your other son...Donovan."

Harriet's look of concern was replaced by a flash of suspicion. "Who are you?" she asked. "What do you know about Donnie?"

Feeling her throat constrict, Veronica looked back to Hunter and Frankie for help, but Skylar spoke up first.

"My name's Skylar," she said softly. "Donovan Locke was my father, and I...I wanted to meet his family."

The shock on Harriet's face told Veronica the older woman hadn't known about Skylar. Perhaps she hadn't even known Donovan Locke had been killed.

"I'm sorry if you didn't know your son was dead," Veronica said, swallowing hard. "I thought the Marshals would have told you."

"Yes, a deputy marshal told me that Donnie had been killed. They've come back to question me a few times since."

Harriet studied Veronica's face.

"The deputy said Donnie had been involved in more bad stuff, but he hadn't mentioned anything about his having another daughter."

She kept her eyes on Veronica.

"He had a wife and a little girl, you know, back before he'd gotten arrested. I was told they were killed in a car accident."

Veronica reached for Harriet's thin hand, cursing the terrible web of deceit, lies, and pain Donovan Locke had created for everyone who'd gotten near him.

"I'm that little girl," Veronica said through numb lips. "My mother and I weren't killed in a car accident. We went into hiding after the trial. He's my father, too."

She felt Skylar come up beside her to take Harriet's other hand, and they stood by the bed in silence for a long moment, as if in mourning, although Veronica knew she could never grieve for the man who'd ruined so many lives.

"I'm sorry for what Donnie has done," Harriet finally said, sounding tired and fragile. "I tried so hard to be a good mother to that boy. I tried to do right by his real mother."

It took a minute for Veronica to absorb what she was saying.

"Real mother?" she asked. "So, Donovan wasn't your son?"

Harriet shook her head.

"Of course, he was. We adopted Donnie early in our marriage. Treated him the same as we'd treat any biological child," she insisted. "He was just a teenager when my husband passed. That's when he started getting into trouble."

Her voice turned grim at the memory.

"And then after the trial, and everything in the papers, he was gone. Just like that, it was over."

"So, he didn't keep in touch?" Veronica asked, dazed by Harriet's revelation. "You never heard from him at all?"

Sinking lower in her bed, Harriet's energy seemed to fade.

"No, he just...disappeared. I knew it was for the best, but it broke Tom's heart just the same."

Harriet looked to a photo on the bedside that showed a man with long, disheveled hair and an uncomfortable smile. Veronica felt Hunter step up behind her to get a better look at the photo, just as a knock sounded on the door.

A woman in blue scrubs appeared in the doorway holding a tray. She seemed surprised to see the group of people filling up the room.

"Oh, I didn't know you were having a party in here," she said, navigating toward Harriet's bedside. "She's due for her medication."

Veronica stepped back from the bed, but Skylar stood still, clinging to Harriet's hand.

"So, you aren't my grandmother?" she asked in a small voice, ignoring the woman with the tray.

"I'd be tickled to have two pretty granddaughters like you girls," Harriet said, producing a faint smile. "But I imagine you don't want anything to do with me after everything Donnie has done."

Letting Veronica pull her away, Skylar seemed reluctant to go.

"We don't blame you, do we, Ronnie?"

Veronica shook her head, knowing the woman in the bed was no more responsible for Donovan Locke's crimes than she was. But the guilt could be hard to shake. He'd left them all wounded.

"Of course not, and we can keep in touch if you'd like," she said, guiding Skylar toward the door. "But we'll let you rest now."

As they made their way back to the rental car, Hunter got Skylar and Gracie settled into the backseat, then pulled Veronica and Frankie to the side.

"Tom Locke was at Beau Spark's charter company the day Charlie and I stopped by. I recognized him from the photo."

Frankie nodded at Hunter's words.

"Yeah, Conrad Fairfax said he's worked there for years."

"Are you thinking Tom may be the link between Locke and Summer?" Veronica asked. "That maybe Locke stayed in touch with his little brother after he left Sky Lake?"

Shrugging his shoulders, Hunter looked back toward the rehabilitation center, his eyes thoughtful.

"If Tom worked with Summer's boyfriend around the time she went missing, it's possible he could have been involved somehow."

"I think it's time we talked to Tom Locke," Frankie added. "The dude has some explaining to do. Now we just have to find him."

But as they drove back toward Sky Lake, Veronica wasn't sure she wanted them to find Tom Locke.

If he's anything like his brother, I don't want Skylar anywhere near him.

Looking at her watch, Veronica was suddenly glad they were scheduled to fly back to Willow Bay on the last flight out that afternoon.

She pulled out her phone to check her messages, then hesitated and scrolled through her missed calls. A sense of foreboding tightened her chest as she realized Misty Bradshaw had never returned her call.

CHAPTER TWENTY-ONE

The waiting room was packed with expectant women and nervous fathers-to-be as Nessa tried not to stare at the various sizes of bumps on display. Waiting for her name to be called, she pulled her jacket around her own expanding waistline and shifted on an uncomfortably narrow chair.

Lifting her eyes to the little television mounted on the wall, she saw that Tenley Frost was anchoring Channel Ten's noon broadcast. The anchor's sleek auburn hair, perfectly applied make-up, and smooth delivery revealed nothing of the trauma she'd endured at the hands of Donovan Locke only months before.

If rumors around the station were true, Tenley had recently been seen at a local restaurant having dinner with Special Agent Clint Marlowe. Although Nessa hadn't decided yet if the big, stony-faced agent was a good match for the elegant news woman, she was glad that Tenley had moved on from slimy Garth Bixby.

Her ruminations on Tenley's love life were cut short by a buzzing in her pocket. The phone's display announced an incoming call from Deputy Marshal Vic Santino.

Answering the call using her quietest library voice, Nessa stood and walked to the far end of the waiting room.

"Santino, what's up?"

"I just got an update from an investigator who's been following Locke's money trail," Santino said, not bothering to ask if she had time to talk. "Looks like Locke had sources in several small towns laundering money for him."

Nessa looked around, making sure she wasn't close enough for the other expectant parents to overhear her side of the conversation.

"I'm guessing one of the sources must be in Willow Bay," she said. "Otherwise you wouldn't be calling to tell me about it."

"You guessed right," Santino confirmed. "Cashier checks issued at the Willow Bay Federal Credit Union were deposited into accounts that Locke managed."

Holding the phone closer to her ear, Nessa paced to the window, looking out toward the parking lot and the Willow River beyond.

"Who bought the checks?" she asked. "Do we have a suspect?"

"Not yet," Santino admitted. "The checks were purchased with cash, and none exceeded an amount that required the bank to file a report with the federal government."

A nurse stepped out of the back and called a name. Nessa turned around, unsure if she'd been summoned, but another woman with an impressive bump was already struggling to heft herself out of a chair. She watched as the woman waddled into the back, then returned her attention to the call.

"Okay, so someone in Willow Bay has been paying Locke for services rendered or helping him launder money from his trafficking activities."

"Right, that's what we have to assume," Santino agreed. "And I thought your team could look into it."

Nessa thought of Agent Marlowe and the joint task force. They'd been looking into the Diablo Syndicate's financial dealings, and she knew Locke had worked with the syndicate in the past. Maybe Operation Stolen Angels would be able to help.

Recalling her earlier conversation with Charlie Day, Nessa wondered if the FBI agent might also have useful information.

"You mentioned that sources in several small towns had been helping Locke launder money," Nessa said. "Was Sky Lake, Kentucky one of those towns?"

Santino hesitated.

"What do you know about Sky Lake?"

"I know it's Locke's hometown, and I know that Agent Day was following up on a lead there just this week."

She lowered her voice even further.

"I also know that a suspected trafficker we're after has been traced back to an ISP in Sky Lake."

Hearing someone call her name, Nessa turned to see the nurse looking around the room, chart in hand.

"A bank in Sky Lake also issued cashier's checks which ended up in Locke's accounts," Santino confirmed. "We don't know who purchased the checks yet."

"Sorry, Deputy Santino, I've got to go," Nessa said, heading toward the nurse. "But I'll be in touch soon to figure out a plan of action. If Locke had an accomplice in Willow Bay, we'll find him."

* * *

Nessa stepped off the scale, trying to see the numbers the nurse was noting on her chart. She always closed her eyes when they were weighing her, then spent the rest of the visit trying to peek at the results.

"Let's get your blood pressure," the nurse said, directing Nessa to a plastic chair that looked even smaller than the one out in the lobby.

Strapping the cuff around Nessa's arm, the nurse adjusted her stethoscope and began to pump. The nurse frowned as she listened, then bent to write more numbers on the chart.

"You don't seem happy," Nessa said, trying to coax a smile out of the no-nonsense woman. "Is everything okay?"

"The doctor will go over everything with you during your exam," the nurse said, leading Nessa into a small, cold room.

She handed Nessa a paper gown and gestured toward a long examination table covered in stiff white paper.

"Take off everything and put this on," the nurse instructed briskly, before walking to the door. "Dr. Proctor will be in momentarily."

Taking off her clothes, Nessa folded them, stacked them on a chair in the corner, then balanced her purse on top.

She pulled on the paper gown and hopped up on the table, feeling anxious and vulnerable. Thinking of the nurse's cold demeanor, she rehearsed the complaints she would make to the doctor when she arrived.

But when the door opened to reveal Dr. Proctor's kind, familiar face, Nessa could think of only one thing to say.

"Is everything okay with the baby?"

"Let's listen and find out, shall we?"

The doctor held the fetal Doppler to Nessa's stomach and smiled as a reassuring *thump, thump, thump* filled the room.

"Sounds pretty good to me," Dr. Proctor said, as Nessa heaved a sigh of relief. "But I see in your chart that your blood pressure is elevated. Have you been under extra strain lately?"

Resisting the urge to roll her eyes at the understatement, Nessa shrugged and tried to look innocent.

"Well, work can be kind of stressful at times, but I'm managing."

"Looking at your chart, I'd say we'll need to put you on bed rest if your blood pressure remains elevated or gets any higher."

Nessa blinked in shock. She'd never even considered she wouldn't be able to work up until the very end. That's what she'd done with both Cole and Cooper. Of course, she'd been a bit younger back then, and she hadn't been trying to run a whole police department.

"I can't...do that," she stammered. "The department needs me."

"Well, your baby needs you, too, I imagine," the doctor said, her voice kind. "And I'm sure if you do need to go on bed rest, the department will manage to survive without you."

Nessa sat through the rest of the appointment in a worried daze, even though she knew worrying would only make things worse.

Once she was back in her clothes and out on the street, Nessa tried to tell herself that the high blood pressure reading had been a fluke. She'd let the stress of the job get to her lately, but she would take it easy going forward.

Hurrying toward the parking lot, Nessa promised herself there would be nothing to worry about as long as she put her health and that of the baby first.

And as long as Jerry doesn't know what the doctor just said.

She would never hear the end of it if her husband knew her position as chief of police might be causing her to develop high blood pressure. And if he knew the doctor was considering putting her on bedrest, there would be no way of getting around it.

No, she didn't dare tell Jerry. At least not before she'd decided who would be taking over as the acting chief of police when she went out on maternity leave.

Diego Ramirez was an ideal candidate, but she feared Jankowski would have a hard time accepting his new partner as his new boss. Besides, Jankowski had seniority, and he knew the town better than anyone else on the force.

If only he wasn't so impulsive and hot-headed.

Pulling her Charger onto the highway, Nessa headed back toward the station, pushing away her concerns about her health and her future plans. She needed to speak to Peyton and Vanzinger.

Locke's accomplice may still be operating in Willow Bay, and they needed to find him and stop him before he could do any more harm.

CHAPTER TWENTY-TWO

Peyton had arrived at Hope House just as the Narcotics Anonymous meeting was ending, but she didn't see Misty Bradshaw in the stream of people leaving the meeting room. Disappointed not to have a chance to talk to the young woman, and determined to make sure she was safe, Peyton had asked to see Dr. Reggie Horn.

After pacing the lobby for twenty minutes, she finally heard the click of high heels on the floor and turned as a petite black woman outfitted in a tailored jacket, slim black pants, and knee-high boots approached.

"Peyton, good to see you," Reggie said with a wide smile. "Is this a personal or an official visit?"

It was a fair question. The director of Hope House often ran the AA meetings Peyton attended, and they'd come to know each other fairly well over the last few months.

"Official, I guess," Peyton said. "Although I'm really just trying to check on Misty Bradshaw and make sure she's okay. I wanted to catch her after the NA meeting, but it doesn't look like she attended. Now I'm hoping you can give me her address."

The director of Hope House hesitated, perhaps weighing the young woman's right to privacy over concern for her safety.

"Misty left the meeting early for an appointment," Reggie said, a frown creasing the smooth ebony skin of her forehead, "and I'm not so sure she'll want a police detective showing up at her new place."

"It's important," Peyton insisted, thinking of the orders Nessa had given. "Misty thinks someone's been following her, and Chief Ainsley asked me to check it out."

With a reluctant sigh, Reggie crossed to the reception desk and wrote the address on a slip of paper.

"It's an easy walk from here," she said, handing Peyton the paper. "Might be better not to pull up outside in a police cruiser."

Peyton had driven over in her unmarked Dodge Charger, but she decided to take Reggie's advice. A quick walk in the mild spring weather might be the only exercise she'd get all day.

She approached the house on Gladstone Drive on foot, following a footpath around to the side, where a wooden staircase led up to the little studio apartment over the garage.

Taking the stairs two at a time, Peyton reached down to confirm her holster and Glock were safely in place. She adjusted her jacket and smoothed down her dark hair, then knocked on the door.

There was no response. She could detect no sound or movement behind the door. Knocking again, she waited, then called out.

"Misty, are you in there?"

"She's not home."

The voice startled Peyton, and she swung around, nearly losing her footing on the landing. A woman with a baby balanced on her hip stood at the foot of the stairs.

"You know Misty Bradshaw?" Peyton asked, trying to catch her breath. "Do you know when she'll be back?"

Shaking her head, the woman shielded her eyes from the sun and looked up at Peyton.

"You aren't one of those porch pirates, are you?"

Confused, Peyton shook her head.

"No, I'm with the Willow Bay Police Department," she said. "Just performing a wellness check."

The woman's shoulders relaxed.

"Oh, well I saw Misty leave this morning, but then she had a delivery, so I wanted to make sure you weren't snatching her package. We've had trouble with porch pirates lately."

Peyton looked around the small landing, but it was empty.

"I don't see a package," she said, looking down at the neighbor.

But the baby had started to fuss, drowning out her voice

"If I see Misty, I'll tell her you stopped by," the woman called out, turning to carry the shrieking baby back down the path.

Looking back at the door, Peyton knew it was useless to knock again. She impulsively reached down and tried the handle, but the door was locked.

Frustrated, she jogged back down the staircase, deciding there was nothing else she could do for now, and trying to assure herself that the young woman would be fine.

After all, If I can't find Misty, Amber won't be able to find her either.

* * *

Nessa was waiting for Peyton when she walked into the task force briefing room. The chief had assembled the team for a special meeting, and she stood at the front of the room wearing a stern expression, like a teacher presiding over a class of delinquents.

Pointing at an empty chair between Agent Marlowe and Vanzinger, Nessa waited for Peyton to take a seat.

"I got a call from Deputy Marshal Vic Santino today," she said, pacing in front of the whiteboard. "He told me that Donovan Locke had been laundering money through a source in Willow Bay, and he's hoping our task force can find out who it was."

Peyton felt Marlowe shift beside her, but before he could respond, a female agent from the Tampa field office spoke up from the back of the room.

"We've been investigating the money trail to and from the Diablo Syndicate for months," she said, as all eyes turned to her. "As far as I know, Donovan Locke hasn't shown up on our radar."

Nessa faced the agent with a curious frown.

"How about Sky Lake, Kentucky? Did the money trail lead you to Locke's hometown? Is that on your radar?"

The agent paused, then looked to Marlowe for help.

"You know Sky Lake is on our radar, Chief Ainsley," Marlowe said dryly, shifting again in his chair. "A user on the darknet board we're tracking was using an ISP in Sky Lake to connect. We think it's the same guy Amber Sloan has agreed to set up."

Turning to the whiteboard behind her, Nessa wrote the words *Sky Lake* at the top. She added notes below the words as she spoke.

"Okay, so we have someone in Sky Lake using the darknet message board to communicate with the Syndicate," she said. "And someone in Sky Lake was laundering money for Donovan Locke."

"And we know Special Agent Day was working on a lead there," Vanzinger added. "Agent Marlowe, did you ever talk to Agent Day?'

Vanzinger looked to Marlowe and raised his eyebrows expectantly.

"I did talk to Charlie Day," Marlowe admitted, his voice softening as he said the agent's name. "She's identified one of Locke's victims. The poor woman was from Sky Lake, so Charlie went there to investigate the circumstances around her disappearance."

"Did *Charlie* say who the woman was?" Nessa asked, looking a bit peeved. "Did she give you a name?"

Shaking his head, Marlowe dropped his eyes and leaned back in his chair, giving Peyton the distinct impression he wasn't telling them everything he knew.

But then, I haven't told them everything I know either. Like how Veronica Lee hired Frankie and Barker to work on a case in Sky Lake.

Peyton looked at her watch, figuring Frankie would already be in Sky Lake. He hadn't said how long he would be gone, and she hadn't had a chance to speak to him after she'd run out to check on her mother the night before.

"Seems Sky Lake might be a dangerous place to visit," Vanzinger said, looking at the list Nessa had written on the whiteboard.

Jumping to her feet, Peyton moved to the back of the room, avoiding Nessa's questioning gaze as she slipped out into the hall. Taking out her phone, she tapped on Frankie's number.

"Peyton, what's up?" Frankie said, answering on the second ring. "Is everything okay?"

"Yes, I just wanted to...to check on you."

She suddenly felt foolish. Noises in the background made her think Frankie must be outdoors, somewhere near traffic.

"I'm all good," he assured her, sounding distracted.

"What's Sky Lake like?" she asked, unable to resist.

A car honked somewhere nearby as he hesitated.

"It's a nice town," he finally said. "Now, what's going on?"

"Look, I probably shouldn't say anything, but our task force has tracked several leads back to Sky Lake."

Peyton looked over her shoulder, making sure the door to the briefing room was still closed.

"We think someone in Sky Lake had been working with both Donovan Locke and Diablo before they were taken down," she said, wondering if she was doing the right thing. "If this guy is anything like the scum he was working with, he's a very dangerous man."

"Sorry, Peyton, a bus just drove by so I couldn't hear you," Frankie said, his voice raised over the traffic around him. "How about I call you back once I'm in a quieter place?"

"No, Frankie, I need to tell you something."

153

"What is it, Peyton? I've got to go."

Peyton's throat constricted as she tried to speak.

"Peyton? You still there?"

"I'm here, Frankie," she managed to say. "Just...be careful."

CHAPTER TWENTY-THREE

Frankie stuck his phone back in his pocket and tugged on Hunter's sleeve, pointing across the street to a small white office building. Elegant script lettering across the wide front window spelled out *Taggert Realty* above a colorful flowerbox bursting with petunias, geraniums, and begonias.

"That's June Taggert's office," Frankie said, pulling Hunter after him. "Let's see if she's in there. We can ask her what she remembers about Summer's last day in Sky Lake."

Hunter looked toward the town square where Veronica and Skylar had taken Gracie to stretch her legs before lunch. Dark clouds were gathering in the east, and it looked like they may be in for spring showers before the afternoon was through.

"Come on, it'll just take a minute," Frankie insisted, cutting across traffic as a car honked and squealed on its brakes.

Pushing through the door of the realty office, Frankie immediately recognized the dark-haired woman he'd met at the lunch counter during his previous visit.

June Taggert sat at a mahogany desk, head bent over a ledger. She looked up at the tinkling of a bell over the door, her eyes narrowing as she saw Frankie's lanky figure step inside.

"Nice place you got here," he said, plucking a brochure out of a rack by the door and flipping through it. "Too bad I'm not looking for a new house."

"What are you looking for, then?" June asked coolly, standing up behind the desk. "Because I'm kind of busy today."

Crossing the little room, Frankie nodded solemnly.

"I understand. I guess that's why you never looked for your best friend after she went missing?" He clenched the brochure in his hand. "You were kind of busy?"

The door opened again before she could reply, and Hunter appeared in the doorway. June's eyes rested on Hunter's tall, lean frame with an appreciative gleam as she swept past Frankie.

"Welcome to Taggert Realty," she said, her icy glare replaced with a flirtatious smile. "How can I help you? Are you looking to rent or buy in the area?"

"His name is Hunter Hadley, and he's with me."

Frankie felt a surge of satisfaction as June's smile faltered.

"We're in town to find out what happened to Summer Fairfax," Frankie added. "You remember her, right? Your best friend?"

"All of a sudden everyone's asking about Summer," June snapped, turning back to the desk. "And I already told the FBI everything I remember."

Shooting Frankie a warning look, Hunter moved in front of June, blocking him out.

"I know it's upsetting to talk about, Mrs. Taggert, but we're trying to help Summer's family find out what happened to her."

Hunter's words seemed to soften June.

"Oh, I'm not married," she protested with a rueful smile, arching an eyebrow. "At least not anymore. And you can call me June."

Hunter returned her smile.

"What can you tell us about the day Summer disappeared, June?"

"Like I just told that FBI agent, Summer left town after she got in an argument with Beau," she said, her voice tightening. "She left her parents a note saying she was going to California."

156

June crossed her arms over her chest in a defensive gesture as Hunter moved closer and cocked his head.

"Beau? You mean Beau Sparks, Summer's boyfriend?"

"Yes, back then Beau and Summer dated."

She dropped her eyes and circled back around her desk, just as Frankie recalled something he'd seen in the brochure. He smoothed the crumpled paper and turned to the back cover.

"Says here Taggert Realty was formerly Sparks Realty." He handed the paper to Hunter, his eyes on June. "Why would that be?"

June snatched the brochure and threw it on her desk.

"Beau and I got married after Summer left town." Her words were bitter. "It didn't last long. I now use my maiden name. Not that it's any business of yours."

Resting a restraining hand on Frankie's arm, Hunter showed no outward sign of surprise.

"Okay, and Summer didn't tell you she was leaving?" Hunter asked, his voice still gentle. "Or contact you after she left?"

"No, she didn't tell me anything."

Frankie studied June's impassive face, sure the woman was hiding something. He couldn't stop himself from voicing the one thought that kept running through his head.

"Doesn't sound like you were best friends after all."

A red flush rose in June's cheeks, and she sucked in a deep breath.

"I think we're done here. I'd like you to leave."

Glaring at Frankie, Hunter shrugged and backed toward the door.

"We need to get going, anyway," he said, gesturing for Frankie to follow. "Thank you for your time, Ms. Taggert."

"I'll meet you in a minute, boss." Frankie kept his eyes on June. "I just want to ask this nice lady about a deal on some swamp land I might want to purchase."

But Hunter had already pushed through the door. As it swung shut behind him, Frankie turned to face June.

"Come on now, *June*. It's just me and you. Tell me the truth. What happened the day Summer disappeared?"

When June didn't respond, he continued.

"Maybe you were glad she left," he suggested, thinking through the possibilities. "I mean, that way you were free to chase Beau."

"You don't know what you're talking about," June snapped, her voice cracking. "I was devastated when Summer left."

Hearing the lie in her voice, Frankie shook his head.

"You weren't devastated, were you?"

He was suddenly sure the words were true.

"Someone who's devastated doesn't just go on with life as if nothing happened. Not when a person they loved disappears off the face of the earth."

Tears sprang to June's eyes, but to Frankie, they looked like crocodile tears. He bet they usually helped June get her way.

"Why are you saying these awful things?" she asked. "What have I done that's so terrible?"

Skylar's small, serious face appeared in Frankie's mind, and a white-hot burst of anger filled him at the thought of all the poor girl had been through.

"*Nothing*, that's what," Frankie said between clenched teeth. "You didn't do a damn thing. Not when Summer went missing. Not after she never showed up again."

Shaking her head, June backed away.

"Summer just *left*...it was her choice. What was I supposed to do?"

"She didn't just *leave*," Frankie protested. "She was abducted and murdered by a serial predator. While you and everyone else in this town did *nothing*."

June stared at Frankie in shock.

"That's not true," she forced out in a raw whisper. "That's not possible. Now get out of my office."

Frankie knew he'd crossed the line.

He wasn't supposed to tell anyone about Summer, not yet. Only her father knew the truth about what had happened.

I think I better get out of here before I make things worse.

Turning on his heel, Frankie froze, surprised to see an older woman with grey curls standing in the doorway holding two coffees.

From the expression on her face, he imagined the woman had heard some of their conversation. Maybe all of it.

"Excuse me, ma'am."

Frankie scooted past the woman with an awkward nod, leaving both women staring after him with open mouths.

Raindrops started to patter down around him as Frankie walked back toward the town square. He knew he'd made a terrible blunder, and it wouldn't take long for everyone in Sky Lake to hear the news that Summer Fairfax was dead.

CHAPTER TWENTY-FOUR

June took the coffee cup from Pearl Abbott and turned away, still in shock over Frankie Dawson's claim that Summer had been abducted and murdered. She knew it couldn't be true. She'd been with Summer that last night, and she knew what had happened. She'd lived with the guilt all these years.

"Would you mind handling the open house at the Granger's this afternoon, Pearl?" she asked, trying to keep her voice steady. "I've got a migraine coming on. I think I'll wrap up here and go on home."

"Sure, just as long as you'll be okay." The older woman watched her with worried eyes. "I'll get the signs and flyers from the back."

Crossing to the door after Pearl had gone, June turned the deadbolt and slid the barrel lock into place. Pulling down the blinds, she leaned against the wall, drawing in a deep breath and allowing herself to remember what she'd tried so hard to forget for the last twenty years.

June surveyed the crowded room without feeling the satisfaction she'd expected. The small gathering Summer had arranged while her parents were out of town had turned into a full-fledged party. Half the graduating class at Sky Lake High School had shown up after the flurry of calls June had made earlier that day.

But her plan to get Summer in trouble with her parents hadn't worked out as June had hoped. Her best friend hadn't gotten mad or ordered everyone to leave.

Instead, Summer was flitting around the room like a silver butterfly, while Beau followed every graceful movement with his adoring blue eyes. Of course, Beau wasn't the only one besotted by Summer. Most men's eyes lingered on Summer when she was near.

June hated the way men would stop on the street and stare when Summer walked by, and it irked her that Summer seemed totally unaware of the effect she had on them.

But it wasn't until Summer started dating Beau that June had begun to truly resent her best friend. As long as Summer was around, June knew she would remain invisible to the one person she desperately wanted to notice her.

Now, watching Summer once again light up the room, June decided she might as well make a last attempt to lure Beau away. She'd already done her best to convince Summer that Beau wasn't good enough for her, hoping she'd have a chance if Summer broke things off.

But Summer had fallen hard for Beau and refused to be swayed. It was going to take more than words to come between the lovebirds. Perhaps alcohol would be a good start.

Picking up the half-empty bottle of gin she'd been sipping from all night, June crossed to the sofa by the window. Beau sat alone, waiting for Summer to finish a giggling conversation with a trio of girls just arriving.

"Ready for a refill?"

June held up the bottle, and Beau lifted his glass. He kept his eyes on Summer as he down the contents in one gulp.

"What the hell was that?" he asked, coughing into his hand. "I was drinking water. I'm in training, you know."

Laughing at his stunned expression, June refilled his glass.

"Come on, you've got to start acting like a college boy if you want to keep Summer," she teased. "Real men drink gin, not water."

161

Beau frowned and ran a hand through his tousled blonde hair. He took another drink from his glass just as a flash of blue lights lit up the window behind them.

Looking out onto the wide drive, June saw a black and white cruiser. The flashing lights on top illuminated the words *Sky Lake Sheriff's Department* on the side of the vehicle.

"Shit, the cops," Beau said, setting his glass on a side table and jumping up. "I better let Summer know."

"Wait here," June protested, grabbing Beau's hand and pulling him back down. "If they take you in, you could lose your scholarship."

Beau's eyes widened at the thought of being arrested.

"I'll tell Summer to handle it," June said, her voice firm. "It's her house, after all, and she's the one who invited all these people."

Within minutes Summer was standing by the police car. But she didn't appear to be upset. Instead, she was laughing it up with Sheriff Duffy and his new recruit, Archer Holt.

Summer had brought out cold bottles of soda for the men, offering them an apologetic smile as she explained she didn't know why so many people had shown up, but that they'd all be leaving soon.

June watched through the window in irritation as the Sheriff's car drove away with Summer waving after them. She could imagine the lecherous sheriff eyeing Summer's captivating image in his rearview mirror as he left.

Turning back to Beau, who was still sitting on the sofa watching Summer through the window with puppy dog eyes, June felt a sharp pang of jealousy. There had to be some way to erase the lovesick look in his eyes.

"She's got them all panting after her," she said, forcing out a knowing laugh. "And Summer loves all the attention."

Beau ignored the comment as he tried to stand up.

"She doesn't appreciate you, Beau."

Arranging her features in a sympathetic frown, she pushed him back onto the sofa and sat down next to him.

"It's only fair that you know," she murmured. "You deserve that much."

"Know what?" he asked, suddenly suspicious.

June sighed and dropped her eyes.

"Summer's gonna go off to college and leave you behind," she said softly. "I figure she won't think twice about you once she's gone."

Draining the liquid at the bottom of his glass, Beau shook his head.

"Summer told me nothing will change between us when she goes to college," he said, slurring his words. "She promised we'll still be together."

"That's not what she told me."

June did her best to look sad.

"Summer would kill me if she knew I was telling you this, but you have a right to know. Once she's at college, the guys will be all over her, and she's looking forward to...well, to trying new things."

Beau rubbed his eyes as June took a long swig from the bottle before pouring more gin into his glass.

Looking up to see Summer making her way toward them, June felt the room spin around her as she turned to Beau. This might be her last chance to make her move. She couldn't lose her nerve now.

June lowered her lips to Beau's, meeting his in a long, lingering kiss. She felt him stiffen in surprise, but he didn't pull away.

She deepened the kiss, suspecting he was too drunk to resist, and that he was unaware Summer was standing only yards away.

Finally pulling back, June looked over Beau's thick shoulder to see Summer standing still in shock, her face a mask of hurt and disbelief. Spinning around, Summer pushed her way through the crowd to the door and disappeared into the night.

Beau turned his head too late to see Summer's frantic exit, and June quickly hid the satisfied smile that appeared as he sank deeper into the sofa. Seconds later his eyes closed as June snuggled in beside him.

The next thing she was aware of was the cramping pain in her neck. Sitting up, she stretched and looked around, realizing she was alone in the room. The empty gin bottle rolled under her feet as she tried to stand.

Gaining her balance, June shuffled through the rooms, first upstairs, then downstairs. The house appeared to be deserted.

Wishing the pounding in her head would go away, she opened the front door and stepped out into the mild night. All the cars were gone, except for Beau's little pick-up truck.

June's heart raced as she crossed to look in the window and saw Beau slumped in the cab of the pick-up, his arm slung over his face.

She pulled on the doorhandle, but it was locked. Suddenly scared, she rapped sharply on the window. Beau flinched, then sat up straight, looking around in a panic.

"Where's Summer?" he asked, opening the door and sliding out of the truck. "Someone said she'd run past, heading toward the lake, but I couldn't find her."

June cringed as she remembered what she'd done. The alcohol and her jealousy had taken over. She looked at Beau, knowing she'd have to come clean. If she didn't tell him, Summer would.

"Summer saw us kissing," she said. "She ran out of the house, and she hasn't come back. She probably doesn't want to be found."

Staggering toward the lake, Beau called out into the dark sky.

"Summer? Summer are you out there?"

June followed him down a well-worn path, past the boat house. Dark water lapped at the shore as they looked around.

"Are you sure she came down here?" June asked.

"Yes, I remember someone saying she'd run past them toward the lake," Beau insisted. "And if she isn't at the house..."

His voice faded away as he looked across the water. A rowboat bobbed gently up and down about twenty yards from shore.

"Summer!" he yelled.

There was no responding cry as Beau began to undress, removing first his shirt and then his jeans.

"She wouldn't have done anything stupid," June said, but Beau was already splashing into the water, his muscles as smooth and hard as a Greek statue, his blonde hair shimmering in the moonlight.

Soon the water had reached his chest, and then he was swimming. Reaching the boat, he struggled to get up and over the side. Finally, he gave up and pulled the boat behind him as he made his way back to the shore.

June ran out to help him drag the boat out of the water. Looking inside, she saw Beau's letter jacket. The one he'd given Summer only a week before. The one that June had hated to see her friend wearing.

The jacket was there, but Summer was not.

Turning to Beau, she saw that he was staring back toward the water, his eyes wide with shock.

"She's out there," he moaned. "I've got to find her."

"You've been drinking. You'll drown if you go out there, again," June cried, grabbing his hand before he could dash back into the lake. "Besides, it's too late. She's...gone. Summer is gone."

Beau gripped June's hand, his panic mounting.

"This is our fault. She's dead out there because she saw what we did. She saw us betraying her, and...she...she..."

"Stop it," June yelled, her own fear and guilt starting to build.

"But they'll all blame us. They all saw us kissing in there, and they'll know what happened to Summer is our fault."

Fear blossomed in June's chest as she thought of facing Summer's mother and father. They would be home the next day. What would they say? What would the whole town say about her when they found out what she'd done?

"I'll take care of this."

June inhaled deeply, forcing herself to think.

"No one ever has to know," she said, forming the plan in her mind as she spoke. "All they'll know is Summer's gone."

Beau's face was pale with shock as he stared at her.

"What are you talking about?"

165

"I'll write a letter," she said, sounding more confident than she felt. "I'll make it seem like Summer wrote it. I'll leave it for her parents telling them she was running off to...to Hollywood. I'll tell them not to go after her."

Beau shook his head.

"It'll never work. They'll search for her. They'll -"

"We've got to try." June took both his hands in hers and squeezed. "As long as we stick together, and stick to our story, it'll work. No one ever has to know the truth."

Now, more than twenty years later, June wondered if she and Beau had gotten it wrong. What if Summer hadn't drowned in Sky Lake that night? What if she had been abducted by a serial killer as Frankie claimed?

A sick ache filled June's stomach as she remembered how she'd gone up to Summer's bedroom and left the forged note for her friend's parents to find. That note had prevented Sheriff Duffy from performing a true search. It had left Summer's parents in agonizing limbo for decades.

I was just trying to protect Beau. I thought it was the right thing to do.

Of course, it had also ensured that she and Beau would form a bond over their terrible secret. A bond that had eventually led to marriage. But their secret had festered between them, and deep-down June knew that Beau had never gotten over Summer.

She'd finally had enough, and they'd been divorced for over five years. June had moved on. She'd found a new man, and things had been looking up. She'd even started thinking that she and Archer Holt might tie the knot one day.

I guess that'll never happen now. Not if Archer and the whole town find out I wrote the letter to Summer's parents, and that I've been lying about everything all these years.

But if Summer had been abducted and killed, June knew she would have to come clean. Whatever information she had, no matter how small, might help the FBI stop the killer before he could kill again.

Crossing to her desk, she opened the top drawer and looked in at the little card inside. Special Agent Charlie Day had left her number, telling her to call if she remembered anything else.

June figured it was time to make that call.

Picking up the phone on her desk, June dialed the number on the card and held the phone to her ear as it began to ring. She turned at a soft sound coming from the back room.

Could Pearl have come in the back door?

A voice sounded on the other end of the connection.

"This is Special Agent Charlie Day."

Resisting the urge to hang up, June cleared her throat.

"Agent Day, this is June Taggert."

She swallowed hard, hoping she was doing the right thing.

"There's something I need to tell you."

CHAPTER TWENTY-FIVE

Mack couldn't believe what he was hearing. The stupid woman was actually calling the FBI. After twenty years of hiding her deceitfulness and lies, it appeared that she was finally going to tell the truth. Or at least, her version of the truth.

Opening the back door, he stepped up behind June, furious, but relieved that he'd arrived in time to prevent her from opening a can of worms that had been closed for decades.

"Who do you think you're calling?"

June jumped out of her chair and spun around to face him.

"Mack? What are you doing sneaking up behind me?"

His eyes were fixed on the phone in her hand. Before she could move, he grabbed the phone, jabbing his thumb on the display and ending the call.

Seeing June's face fill first with shock, and then with fear, Mack threw the phone onto the floor.

"Summer died because of you."

He spat the words at her, finally able to tell her what he'd really been thinking all these years.

June recoiled, shaking her head in denial.

"You always wanted what she had."

Mack's voice was flat as he took a step closer.

"You were always jealous of her. You wanted her gone."

The mask of normalcy he usually wore fell away. June was the one who had started the series of events leading to Summer's abduction and death. It was time she paid.

"If you hadn't been such a whore, Summer would never have been out on that lake," Mack hissed. "Everything that happened to Summer after that was all your fault."

"That's not true," June protested. "She was my...my *best friend*."

"Real friends don't make a play for their best friend's guy," he muttered. "They don't try to sabotage their friend's relationship."

Mack slipped the long syringe out of the pocket of his jacket with one smooth movement. Before June knew what was happening, he had stabbed the needle into the soft flesh of her upper arm.

Letting out a gasp of pain, June dropped shocked eyes to the syringe Mack still wielded in his hand. A thick drop of clear liquid oozed from the tip of the needle.

"Why did you...do..."

But June's voice was already fading. Fear filled her eyes as she tried to keep them open, but within seconds her body had crumpled to the floor at his feet.

Mack looked down at her motionless body with cold eyes.

You had it coming. I should have done this years ago. Decades ago.

A sound at the front door caused Mack to look up. A shadowy figure was visible through the blinds just as a key slipped into the lock with a metallic click.

Someone was coming through the front door.

* * *

Mack struggled to catch his breath after his mad dash out the back door and down the alley. He'd managed to make it out onto Fullerton

Road without encountering anyone else and had ducked under the bus stop shelter to escape the light rain that had started to fall.

Only the barrel lock June had slid into place had prevented Pearl Abbott from catching him standing over June's body.

I guess it was the old biddy's lucky day.

Feeling his pocket buzz, Mack sank onto a bench and pulled out his phone. An alert had popped up notifying him that someone had replied to a message thread on the darknet board.

Amber Sloan was asking him to handle an expedited shipment. She was willing to pay extra. So much extra that Mack was instantly suspicious.

He thought back to his previous trip, replaying Misty's words before he'd silenced her.

"Amber's setting you up..."

Her words hadn't surprised him. Mack had known from their very first meeting that Amber was the lowest sort of criminal, so he didn't doubt Misty's claim. Amber would set him up in a heartbeat if the feds made it worth her while.

And there were other considerations as well.

Frequent trips to the same place too often could draw unwanted attention. Border patrol and customs used systems to track flight activity. They were constantly trying to identify suspicious aircraft.

So far, after all these years, Mack had managed to avoid detection by keeping his illicit flights to a minimum, making sure to blend in with the legitimate flights coming in and going out of Sky Lake.

Mack was trying to calculate his next move when a young woman holding a bright red umbrella walked past the bus stop. He stared after her, not sure he could believe what he was seeing.

That's Summer. But it can't be her. Can it?

Studying the girl's long silvery blonde hair and slim figure, Mack decided his eyes had been playing tricks on him.

She's younger than Summer but just as lovely. Maybe even more so.

Heart racing, he watched the girl stop and call to her companions. Mack quickly dropped his head when he saw the skinny PI with the big mouth and the sharp-eyed reporter.

They hurried toward the girl, followed by an attractive young woman with long dark hair and a big, white Labrador retriever.

The dog stared over at Mack as if it sensed his heightened emotions, and Mack wondered what the animal was thinking.

Maybe it can sense I'm a killer. Maybe it can smell death on me.

Then the crosswalk light changed, and the girl and her companions walked on toward the Frisky Colt Diner, while Mack followed the group with his eyes.

He'd just seen an angel, and he couldn't let her get away.

CHAPTER TWENTY-SIX

Veronica shook the rain off her jacket and hung it on an old wooden coat rack by the door. Taking the soggy red umbrella from Skylar, she dropped it into the umbrella stand and looked around for the hostess, suddenly famished.

The lunch rush at the Frisky Colt Diner appeared to be over, and there were several empty tables available. Veronica spotted a table by the window with plenty of room next to it for Gracie to relax while they had their lunch.

"Sit anywhere you like," a waitress said, passing by with a friendly smile. "Just gotta run this check and I'll be right with you."

Making a beeline for the table by the window, Veronica slid into a booth, gesturing for Skylar to sit next to her.

"I'm hungry enough to eat a horse," Frankie said, as he and Hunter settled in across from them.

He caught Skylar's eye and winked.

"But not Sunshine, of course. I'd never eat Sunshine."

Skylar rolled her eyes and laughed, already comfortable around Frankie, and Veronica couldn't help but join in.

She was glad to see a happy smile replace her sister's usual pensive expression. She wondered if Skylar could finally start to heal.

Now that Skylar's met her grandfather, and seen her mother's hometown, maybe she can find some closure and move on with her life.

"Y'all ready to order?"

The waitress stood by Veronica wearing an ill-fitting brown polyester uniform and a wide smile, seemingly unconcerned by Gracie's presence beside their table.

Veronica asked for the soup of the day and a large, iced tea. As she waited for the others to order, a man pushed through the front door and hovered by the counter. His eyes searched the room, stopping at their table.

"Be right with you, Beau," the waitress called out.

Twisting his head toward the door, Frankie peered past the thin frame of the waitress, staring at the man with blatant interest, taking in his thick blonde hair and broad shoulders.

After she'd confirmed their order, the waitress crossed to the front. Veronica saw Hunter staring after her, his body tense.

"Sorry about the wait, Beau," the waitress said with a tired sigh. "I've been as busy as a one-armed paper hangar today."

"Y'all still short of staff around here?" the man asked, his deep voice carrying easily across the dining room to their table.

"Oh yeah, I've been pulling double shifts ever since Darla went AWOL," the waitress said with a good-natured laugh. "But I've also taken home double tips, so I guess I shouldn't really complain."

She gestured toward an empty stool.

"If you're eating on your own there's a spot at the counter."

Shaking his head, the man pointed to an empty table in the corner.

"Curtis and Tom will be here any minute, so I'll grab a table."

"Suit yourself," the waitress said. "I'll send the boys over when they get here."

Veronica waited until the man had walked past, then raised her eyebrows, waiting for an explanation from Hunter and Frankie.

"That's Beau Sparks," Hunter murmured in a low voice, giving Skylar an uncomfortable glance. "I mentioned him to you before, remember?"

173

"He's Summer's old boyfriend," Frankie blurted, oblivious of Hunter's attempt at discretion. "And we just found out he married Summer's best friend after she went missing."

Noting the stricken look on Skylar's face, Veronica took her hand and squeezed it, lifting her boot to kick Frankie under the table.

Frankie didn't seem to notice the kick. He was again looking toward the door, which had opened to reveal a slim man in dark jeans and a white flannel shirt.

Pulling off a Kentucky Wildcats baseball cap, the man ran a hand through his spiky brown hair and crossed to the corner table.

"That's Beau's business partner, Curtis Webb," Hunter said, his eyes now alert with interest. "Charlie and I met him over at their charter company."

The door hadn't quite closed when a tall, gangly man pushed through, trudging in after Curtis. Veronica felt a spark of recognition.

"And that's Tom Locke," Hunter added before Veronica could ask. "We saw him over at the charter company, too. Only at that point, I didn't know who he was."

"That's the man in Harriet's photo," Skylar said, her green eyes wide. "In the frame by her bed."

Veronica nodded at her sister's words, suddenly realizing where she'd seen Tom before. She surreptitiously studied his long, unkept hair, nervous eyes, and slumped shoulders, thinking the man wasn't what she'd expected.

He doesn't look anything like Donovan Locke. But then, why should he? They hadn't been related by blood.

Glancing over her shoulder to the table in the corner, Veronica saw Beau Sparks staring in their direction. He dropped his eyes when he realized Veronica was watching him, but not before she saw the stricken look on his handsome face. She felt a surge of sympathy.

Seeing Skylar must be like seeing a ghost from the past. It can't be easy.

The handsome man had been Summer's boyfriend, and her sudden disappearance would surely have been traumatic.

How horrible to never know what had happened to your girlfriend all these years. It must have been unbearable for Beau.

Veronica's pity was overshadowed by the familiar pang of guilt that usually followed thoughts of her father's victims and the loved ones they'd left behind.

Locke hurt so many people. And part of him lives on in me, and in Skylar, whether we like it or not. His legacy lives on as long as we do.

The disturbing thoughts were interrupted by the entrance of a big man in a tan Sheriff's uniform and a wide-brimmed hat. Taking off his jacket, the man dripped rainwater on the floor and stomped his big boots on the mat by the door.

Waving a greeting at the waitress, he slid his sturdy body onto an empty stool at the counter just as Frankie turned to Hunter.

"Look who the cat dragged in," he said, clearly unimpressed. "I'm gonna go over there and-"

"This isn't the time or place," Hunter protested, putting a restraining hand on Frankie's arm. "We need to eat and get Skylar and Veronica back to the airport. Then we can talk to Sheriff Holt."

The crackling of a police radio drew Veronica's eyes back to the lunch counter. She watched the sheriff slip a handheld radio out of his belt just as a dispatcher's high-pitched voice filled the little diner.

"Unit one we've got a Code 3 on a possible 10-54 south of your location at 201 Fullerton. Deputies are en route now and requesting back-up."

Rising from his seat, the Sheriff headed to the door without a backward glance. The dispatcher's voice cut off as the door closed behind him.

Veronica stared through the window as Sheriff Holt charged down the sidewalk. Anxious murmurs rose from the tables around them.

"Code 3 is an emergency," one elderly man said, loud enough for everyone in the diner to hear.

The wide-eyed woman next to him nodded.

"I think Taggert Realty's at 201 Fullerton," she added. "But what's a 10-54 supposed to mean?"

The old man shrugged as Frankie muttered under his breath.

"By the way, Sheriff Holt ran out of here, I'd say it means the shit's just hit the fan."

Ignoring his remark, Veronica turned to see Beau Sparks open the door and hurry after Holt. The blonde man jogged toward the crosswalk as an ambulance raced past the diner with its siren blaring.

Several people in the diner got up from their tables and crowded around the window to get a better view. Hunter stood up, looking down at Veronica and Skylar.

"You all stay here while I go see what's going on."

Veronica shook her head. The reporter in her wasn't about to sit there and have lunch while Hunter chased down a story only a few blocks away. There was no way she would let him go on his own.

"Frankie, you stay here with Skylar, we'll be right back."

As she followed Hunter to the door, she noticed that Beau's two companions were no longer sitting at the corner table.

I guess everyone in town will want to see what's happened.

Once on the street, she and Hunter joined a stream of other onlookers moving toward the ambulance, which had come to a stop in front of a building a few blocks down.

Sheriff Holt was yelling for everyone to stay back as two uniformed deputies tried to set up a perimeter. Veronica and Hunter arrived just in time to see the ambulance crew unload a gurney and race inside.

A small hand gripped Veronica's arm, and she turned to see Skylar standing next to her. Frankie gave an apologetic shrug.

"Gracie ran after you guys and Skylar followed," he explained, panting slightly. "They're younger and faster than I am."

The white Lab suddenly barked, and Hunter grabbed at her leash as she began to charge toward the office door.

"Whoa there, girl," Hunter soothed, pulling the frantic dog back toward the street. "Come on, Gracie, it's okay."

But the dog seemed intent on getting in the office, and as Hunter pulled her back, he bumped into a bystander, losing hold of the leash.

Gracie darted forward just as the door opened again, and Skylar lunged after her, reaching out to grip the leash at the last minute.

Stepping up to take the leash from Skylar's hand, Frankie passed it to Hunter, and together they managed to lead the distressed dog away from the scene.

But Skylar had frozen in place. The girl was standing motionless, staring into the realty office with a stricken expression. As Veronica approached, she heard a woman's hysterical cries from inside.

"June's dead, Beau," the woman sobbed. "She's dead!"

Following Skylar's gaze past the paramedic hovering by the door, Veronica recoiled and gasped in horror.

A woman's body was sprawled awkwardly on the floor, her dark curls splayed around her ashen face. Her mouth was open in a silent scream as she stared in their direction with wide, unseeing eyes.

* * *

Skylar remained silent during the drive to Sky Lake Regional Airport. After seeing June Taggert's dead body, the girl had reverted into the quiet, unresponsive state Veronica had come to dread.

A wave of helpless anger washed over Veronica. She stared out the passenger's side window of the rental car, too distracted to appreciate the deep shades of orange and red that flooded the sky as the rain clouds dispersed and the sun began to set.

Only hours ago, she'd been hopeful that her sister was finally on the road to a new beginning. Now she was wondering if Skylar would ever get that chance.

How can she forget the lifetime of trauma Locke put her through? Could anyone endure that and just go on to live a normal life?

She sighed, overwhelmed by her dark thoughts, prompting Hunter to reach over and take her hand in his.

"Are you sure you two will be okay on your own?" His voice was somber. "I can try to switch my flight and go back with you if you'd feel better having me there."

"No, we'll be fine once we get home," Veronica insisted. "And Gracie will look after us."

Looking back at the white Lab sitting next to Skylar, Veronica had to admit Gracie's frantic reaction to June Taggert's dead body was hardly reassuring.

The dog had been through considerable trauma of her own after training in the Middle East as a cadaver dog with the U.S. military, and she could be unpredictable in stressful situations.

But her quiet presence helped calm Skylar's nerves, and Veronica was grateful that Reggie Horn had given her sister an ESA prescription. It allowed Skylar to take an emotional support animal with her in public places and when flying.

"Besides, you and Frankie need to find out what really happened to June Taggert," she added, keeping her voice low. "Summer's best friend died just after you guys were in there asking her what she knew about Summer's disappearance. That is quite a coincidence."

"I'm definitely eager to hear her cause of death," Hunter agreed. "Charlie Day is trying to find a flight now, so she should be here fairly soon. Once she talks to Holt we'll know more."

Veronica refrained from rolling her eyes. She knew they were lucky the FBI agent was rushing down to the little town. Especially if the local Sheriff's behavior at the scene was any indication of how cooperative he'd be.

"Sheriff Holt certainly seemed rattled by the whole situation," she said, recalling the big man's flushed face. "I'm guessing they haven't had many homicides in Sky Lake."

"He did seem pretty shocked," Hunter agreed. "And it didn't help that half the town came to watch the show."

Thinking back to the scene, Veronica frowned.

"Did you see Tom Locke there? He left the diner, but I didn't see him in the crowd outside Taggert Realty."

"No, I didn't see Tom, come to think of it," Hunter said. "Although Beau Sparks sure looked upset."

He steered the car off the exit ramp leading to the airport, as Veronica tried to stifle a pang of regret that she couldn't stay and help Hunter and Frankie investigate.

She wanted to know what had really happened all those years ago.

Somehow Summer Fairfax disappeared from her idyllic life in Sky Lake and turned up on Locke's ranch in Montana. Her life had tragically ended in Locke's barn, but her story didn't end there. It lived on in Skylar.

Veronica felt as if Summer Fairfax and the other women buried on Locke's ranch were calling out for their stories to be told. She wanted Skylar and the other families to know what had happened to their loved ones. She wanted them to find closure.

But for now, Skylar's safety and well-being had to be Veronica's top priority. She couldn't risk her sister suffering any more trauma.

She needed to get Skylar home where she would be safe.

After she'd said good-bye to Hunter at the gate, and guided Skylar and Gracie onto the small airplane, Veronica allowed herself to take a long, deep breath.

"We'll be back in Willow Bay, soon," Veronica whispered to Skylar. "We'll be safe there."

Hearing the flight attendant's announcement that they were ready for takeoff, Veronica dug in her purse for her phone and switched it to airplane mode.

As she scrolled through her missed calls and text messages, she noted with dismay that Misty Bradshaw still hadn't returned her call.

Tomorrow I'll check on Misty and make sure she's okay. No matter what else happens, I've got to see her tomorrow.

She dropped her phone in her purse and settled back in her seat, then picked up Skylar's small hand and held it as the plane taxied down the runway and lifted smoothly into the sky.

Looking out the window, Veronica watched as the lights of the small town below receded into the dark.

CHAPTER TWENTY-SEVEN

Nessa waited until Cole and Cooper had stepped onto the school bus before closing the front door and heading back to the kitchen. She filled her thermos with water, grabbed a banana out of the fruit bowl, and slung her work bag over her shoulder.

"You weren't planning on leaving without saying good-bye, were you?" Jerry asked from the doorway. "I feel like we haven't seen each other all week."

"Of course not."

Nessa crossed the room and lifted her face for a kiss, but Jerry just stared down at her without moving.

"Okay, what's going on?" he asked, putting both hands on her shoulders. "You're not telling me something. What is it?"

Shrugging out of his grip, Nessa stepped back.

"I'm just worried about going out on maternity leave," she said, deciding a half-truth would have to do for now. "I'm not sure if Jankowski is up for the challenge of taking over as acting chief, or if I should ask Ramirez. And I don't even know if he's willing to take on the responsibility."

"Sounds like you have two good options," Jerry said. "You should consider yourself lucky. Either one will do a good job."

Jerry's tone had lightened, and Nessa felt a guilty surge of relief that he hadn't pried further. She wasn't ready to worry him over her high blood pressure reading. Not yet.

It was probably just a fluke anyway. I'm sure it's fine.

Once she was in her Charger and on the road, Nessa realized she had never gotten that kiss from Jerry.

We'll make up for it tonight. I'll add it to the top of my to-do list.

The thought of all the things she needed to do prompted a grimace, and she began running through the plan of her busy day as she navigated the Dodge through the early morning traffic.

Her phone began to buzz as she approached the East Willow Bridge, and she activated her hands-free headset.

"Agent Day, I was wondering when you'd get around to calling me back," Nessa said, mentally checking an item off her list. "Where are you calling from today?"

"I just landed in Sky Lake," Charlie said, her normally crisp voice sounding a little wilted. "I'm investigating a homicide with a possible connection to Locke."

Nessa was instantly alert.

"Is it another cold case?"

"No, it's actually a very hot case. The victim was killed yesterday."

The agent's words sent a shock through Nessa, and it took her a minute to formulate her next question.

"How the heck is the homicide connected to Locke, then?"

It was Charlie's turn to hesitate.

"We believe Locke had an accomplice in Sky Lake who might be trying to silence any remaining witnesses."

Nessa had a sinking suspicion she knew why Charlie had called.

"You weren't just returning my call, were you?" she fumed, suddenly angry. "You're calling to tell me that someone in Willow Bay is involved, or is in danger, aren't you? You've kept me in the dark, and now you're calling to tell me people are getting killed."

Charlie sighed, but she didn't argue.

"The investigation into Locke's activities is still ongoing," she said, unruffled by Nessa's outburst. "We're still unraveling Locke's web of crimes and contacts."

Shaking her head in frustration, Nessa forced herself to take a deep breath. Getting overly upset wouldn't help her blood pressure.

"So, who is this accomplice?" she asked in a calmer voice. "And who in Willow Bay may be his next target?"

"We're not sure who the accomplice is, yet" Charlie admitted. "And we don't know for sure he will go after anyone in Willow Bay."

Nessa waited for the blow to fall.

"But Veronica Lee and her...her family have a connection to Locke, so any accomplice of his might pose a threat to them."

"Okay, that makes sense," Nessa said. "But what aren't you telling me? What else is going on?"

Clearing her throat, Charlie hesitated. When she spoke, she chose her words carefully.

"There's something else you need to know about Veronica and her connection to Locke, but it isn't my place to tell you."

Before Nessa could protest, Charlie continued.

"Talk to Veronica, let her know she can trust you," she advised. "She and certain members of her family could be in danger."

Nessa started to ask another question, but Charlie stopped her.

"I've got to get to a meeting with the Sky Lake sheriff now," she said. "Then I'll interview Hunter Hadley and Frankie Dawson to-"

Startled to hear the two men were in Sky Lake, Nessa interrupted.

"Hunter and Frankie are up in Sky Lake?"

"Yes," Charlie confirmed. "And they were near the scene when the homicide victim was discovered."

Head spinning, Nessa tried to make sense of what she was hearing.

"What were they doing up there in the first place?" she sputtered.

"They're investigating a missing person's case," Charlie replied, sounding rushed. "Look, I've got to go, but please, speak with Veronica Lee as soon as possible. She can explain more."

The connection dropped, and Nessa found herself steering the Dodge left onto Bay Street. She would stop by Channel Ten News before going into the station.

She needed to talk to Veronica. It was time she found out what exactly was going on.

* * *

Nessa spotted Veronica Lee's slim figure and long dark hair beside a white Channel Ten News van before she'd even turned into the station's parking lot.

The reporter was talking to a young black man Nessa recognized as Finn Jordan, cameraman and co-owner of the news station.

As Nessa pulled the Dodge into the space next to the van, she saw Finn's white Labrador retriever staring out from the van's passenger's side window, as if waiting to go out on assignment.

"Looks like I got here just in time," Nessa called, climbing out of the Charger. "I need to speak to you, Veronica. This can't wait."

"I need to speak to you, too, Chief Ainsley."

Veronica's tone was just as impatient as Nessa's had been.

"How about I give you two a few minutes to speak in private," Finn said, backing toward the van with raised eyebrows. "Gracie and I will wait in the van and make sure the equipment's ready."

Once Finn had disappeared into the van, Veronica turned to Nessa.

"Misty Bradshaw isn't responding to my calls anymore, and I'm getting really worried about her."

Veronica's words sounded like an accusation, but Nessa didn't take offense. She was also worried, and she feared Amber Sloan may have had something to do with Misty's lack of communication.

Nessa had never fully trusted Amber, and she suspected the immunity agreement had been a terrible mistake. But it was too late for second-guessing now. She'd just have to try and fix it somehow.

"I've assigned Detective Bell and Detective Vanzinger to check in with Misty, but they haven't been able to make contact yet," she admitted. "But they'll keep trying until they confirm she's okay."

Giving Nessa a miserable nod, Veronica didn't appear optimistic.

"Now I need to know what's going on with you," Nessa said, pulling her jacket over her bump. "Agent Charlie Day called me this morning from Sky Lake."

She studied Veronica's expression, hoping for a reaction, but Veronica didn't seem surprised.

"She says there's been a suspected homicide up there that may be connected to Donovan Locke."

Holding Veronica's gaze, Nessa saw a flash of anxiety in the reporter's green eyes as she continued.

"Agent Day thinks whoever killed the victim up there, may pose some kind of threat to you and your family down here."

"Sounds like Agent Day had a lot to say," Veronica replied, crossing her arms over her chest.

Nessa nodded.

"Yep, and she also said I needed to talk to you to find out more."

The words hung in the air for a long beat as the two women stared at each other. Without warning, Veronica dropped her head into her hands and let out a long, ragged sigh.

When she lifted her face to Nessa, it was tight with emotion.

"You know that Donovan Locke was my father," she said. "But he also had another daughter. A girl they found at his ranch."

Nessa kept her face still, masking her surprise.

"Once Deputy Santino confirmed through DNA that Locke was her father, he told us, and...well, she's been living with me and my mother ever since."

"Okay," Nessa said slowly. "So, this girl..."

"Her name's Skylar," Veronica said. "And for now, she's using our last name, since she didn't want to use Locke."

The anxiety in Veronica's voice had faded, and she looked almost relieved as Nessa tried to absorb the information.

"So, Skylar's your half-sister?"

"She's my *sister*," Veronica said defensively. "Half or whole isn't important. She has no one else, and she's been staying with me and my mother."

Nessa held up her hands in surrender.

"I didn't mean to minimize your connection," she said. "And I'm sure she's glad to have a family. But why keep it a secret?"

Veronica's face hardened.

"Skylar's a victim and a survivor. She has a right to privacy. She also has the right to tell her own story if and when she feels ready."

"Okay, I get it, but why'd you hire Barker and Dawson Investigations? What are they looking for up in Sky Lake?"

"Hunter and I asked them to help us find out who Skylar's mother was," Veronica said. "We knew she was one of Locke's victims, and he'd already admitted to killing her. We wanted Skylar to know who her mother was."

Veronica looked over at the van where Gracie sat in the window.

"Gracie went up with them to Locke's ranch in Montana. She found remains in Locke's barn."

Turning back to Nessa, Veronica gave a resigned sigh.

"A class ring was found with the remains. It led us back to Sky Lake. The rest was pure detective work," she said. "Frankie and Barker found the trail back to Skylar's mother, and Charlie Day was able to confirm their findings."

Nessa felt as if she'd missed something.

"So, Skylar's mother was..."

"A woman named Summer Fairfax," Veronica finished. "She disappeared from Sky Lake when she was just eighteen years old. No one there ever knew what happened to her."

A shadow fell over Veronica's face.

"Well, *someone* knew," she corrected herself. "Someone must have helped Locke abduct Summer and cover his tracks."

"That must be the person Agent Day is worried about," Nessa said. "She thinks Locke had an accomplice over the years. Someone who helped him launder money and traffic women and drugs."

The door to the van opened and Finn stuck out his head.

"Sorry, Ronnie, but if we're gonna be able to set up in time for a live feed, we need to get going."

Veronica gave him a thumbs-up, and Finn retreated into the van.

"Agent Day thinks Locke's accomplice may have killed the woman in Sky Lake yesterday," Nessa said, speaking quickly. "She believes he's trying to erase his tracks and eliminate possible witnesses."

Knowing she didn't have much time, Nessa decided to be blunt.

"Charlie Day warned me Locke's accomplice might try coming after you and your family. I guess she was talking about Skylar."

Veronica's face grew pale at the thought, then she shook her head.

"Whoever killed June Taggert is up in Sky Lake," she insisted. "And Skylar and I are down here. Besides, no one even knows Skylar is in Willow Bay, or that she's Locke's daughter."

Crossing to the van, Veronica put her hand on the door.

"As long as it stays that way, we'll be fine."

CHAPTER TWENTY-EIGHT

Peyton was huddled around a desk with Marlowe and several of his agents when Nessa opened the door and stuck her head into the briefing room. The police chief spotted her next to Vanzinger and slipped inside.

"Amber Sloan has set up the meeting with Mack," Vanzinger announced as soon as he saw Nessa. "He's agreed to make a pick-up from Windy Harbor Airpark the day after tomorrow."

Vanzinger's blue eyes were bright with excitement as he delivered the news, but Nessa didn't seem impressed.

"We need to keep this operation strictly confidential," Marlowe cautioned behind Vanzinger, his voice stern. "That means no one talks about the operation outside of this room."

"Agent Marlowe, are you sure Amber's not playing us?"

Peyton heard the doubt in Nessa's voice, and winced, expecting Marlowe to snap back at her, but the FBI agent just shrugged.

"You never can be sure with someone like Amber Sloan, but everything she's given us so far has checked out. I think it makes sense to take a chance."

The skeptical look on Nessa's face remained.

"And you think the task force can take this guy down?" she asked. "Do you even know who Mack really is, or what he's capable of?"

"No, we don't know his real identity yet, which is why this operation is so important," Marlowe replied. "What we do know is that Mack has been a key player in the trafficking syndicate for years and that he's handled shipments for Diablo and other users on the darknet board Donovan Locke was using."

Challenging Marlowe with a hard stare, Nessa moved closer.

"If this guy really was working with Locke and Diablo, he could be just as dangerous," she said. "So, you need to be real sure you know what you're doing."

Peyton saw Marlowe's back stiffen, but he just nodded.

"Rest assured we'll take every precaution, Chief Ainsley."

He turned back to the table and continued to review the plans, as Nessa motioned for Peyton and Vanzinger to join her in the hall.

When they were alone, the hard expression fell away, and her shoulders slumped.

"We need to find Misty Bradshaw," Nessa said. "If you can't find Misty, I think you'll need to pay Amber Sloan another visit."

* * *

Fox Hollow Apartments looked even more worn and shabby than Peyton had remembered. She and Vanzinger had banged on Misty's door and tried to look through the windows, but no one was home in the apartment over the garage or in the main house.

Deciding they'd better follow Nessa's instructions without delay, they were once again standing outside Amber's door, and they had a plan to persuade Amber to let them inside.

Peyton doubted Misty was being held inside the little apartment, but there could be clues, or maybe Amber would let something slip.

"What do you want now?"

Amber stood in the doorway wearing a pink tracksuit and a scowl.

"We want to go over the plans again," Vanzinger said, pushing his way into the room. "Just to make sure everything's in order."

Following Vanzinger inside, Peyton kept one hand on her Glock as she looked around the apartment as if making sure they were alone.

"I've already gone over everything with Agent Marlowe," Amber said, immediately suspicious. "It's all set for the day after tomorrow at the Windy Harbor Airpark. I'll make the drop and leave. Your team will be waiting to move in. What more do you want to talk about?"

Peyton cocked her head.

"We need to know if you're willing to wear a wire, for one thing," she said. "That way we can make sure you're safe during the drop and can record anything Mack might say to incriminate himself."

"I'm not worried," Amber scoffed. "I can take care of myself. And Mack doesn't talk much, so we don't need to bother with a wire."

Catching Peyton's dubious expression, Amber frowned.

"What's wrong, Detective Bell?" she asked, her eyes hostile under her frizzy bangs. "If you have something you want to say, don't hold back, just spit it out."

An angry flush washed over Peyton's cheeks at the woman's disrespect. She didn't want to put Misty in jeopardy, but something was telling her Amber Sloan would never just let Misty walk away.

If anyone had done something to harm Misty Bradshaw or to scare her out of town, it had to be Amber Sloan.

"Do you know a woman named Misty Bradshaw?" Peyton asked, ignoring Vanzinger's startled stare. "We need to speak to her."

"Never heard of her," Amber said with a sarcastic smile. "What's she supposed to have done?"

Putting a restraining hand on Peyton's arm, Vanzinger spoke up.

"She's not done anything that we know of," Vanzinger said. "We just need to talk to her. Her family's looking for her."

"Well, if I ever meet her, I'll let her know you two are looking for her," Amber sneered. "Now, I got stuff to do."

"Listen, we have witnesses that have seen you and Misty together," Peyton said, not willing to give up. "So, just tell us where she is, and we'll leave you alone."

A crazed gleam lit up Amber's eyes, and she moved closer, sticking a small finger in Peyton's face.

"Are you calling me a liar, Detective Bell?"

Spittle flew from the woman's lips along with her bitter words, and Peyton stepped back, startled by her outburst.

"Cause if you're calling me a liar, then our deal is off," she threatened. "I'll tell Mack the shipment is canceled."

"Let's all calm down," Vanzinger said, using his thick body to shield Peyton from Amber's wrath. "There's no need to get upset. We're only asking a few questions."

Storming to the door, Amber wrenched it open.

"Just go, cause I don't need this shit," she muttered. "I've done my part and kept my word and you still treat me like trash."

Vanzinger took Peyton's arm and steered her out the door.

As she stepped out onto the corridor, Peyton saw a shadow slip around the corner. She tried to pull loose from Vanzinger's hand, but he kept hold of her arm as he turned back to Amber.

"You go ahead and cancel the plan," Vanzinger said, his voice cold. "As long as you don't mind doing some serious time. Just make sure you don't go anywhere near Misty Bradshaw."

The sound of a car starting somewhere close by drew Peyton's attention. She was suddenly sure someone had been listening outside the door. Had they overheard their whole conversation?

Amber slammed the door shut just as Peyton twisted out of Vanzinger's grip. She jogged down to the edge of the corridor, but the parking lot was empty.

Whoever had been listening was gone.

* * *

191

Peyton was still rattled when she and Vanzinger arrived back at the police station. She sank into her chair and stayed slumped at her desk while Vanzinger went to get a cup of coffee in the break room.

Her phone vibrated in her pocket, and Peyton was tempted to ignore it, then reminded herself that her mother may be calling.

Breathing a sigh of relief as she saw Frankie's name appear on the display, she tapped *Accept Call* and held the phone to her ear, a smile spreading across her face despite her previous bad mood.

"I was hoping you'd call," she said. "It's been a rough day."

"Tell me about it," Frankie replied, his voice hoarse. "It's not been a day in the park here, either."

Peyton's smile faded.

"Have you been drinking, Frankie?"

The phone went quiet, then she heard him sigh.

"I had just one last night," he finally said.

"Just one drink made you feel this bad?"

"Just one bottle."

Peyton didn't laugh. She knew it wasn't a joke. When Frankie fell off the wagon, he fell hard.

"Why, Frankie?" she asked. "What happened?"

"It's this case," he muttered. "It's just, well, I've been working this case, and I got a little too emotionally invested and..."

"And what?"

Peyton wasn't sure she wanted to hear his answer.

"And so yesterday I kind of...*went off* on a woman I was interviewing," he admitted. "And she turned up dead an hour later."

She waited for the punchline, then realized he was serious.

"Say that again?"

"I went to question a woman. An old friend of the missing person Veronica hired us to find."

Frankie's voice faltered.

"Let's just say the discussion got a little heated, and an hour later the woman turned up dead. Her assistant heard us arguing and now the Sheriff thinks I'm a *person of interest*."

Peyton stared at the phone, momentarily speechless.

"And you'd been drinking?" she finally managed to get out.

"What are you trying to say?"

She winced at the hurt and frustration in Frankie's voice.

"Don't tell me you actually think I could have killed her?"

"Of course not," Peyton protested, realizing how her question had sounded. "I know you better than that."

She sucked in a deep breath.

"I know you couldn't hurt a fly, but the police up there don't know you. And if you were drinking, they may try to use that against you."

"I wasn't drinking...not then," he said. "But after that, I just freaked out. I mean, what if they try to pin this on me? I can't go back to prison. I can't go through that again."

Guilt tore through Peyton at the thought of her role in Frankie's past wrongful conviction. But she couldn't waste energy on regrets. The best way to make it up to Frankie was to help him now.

"Okay, so who is this missing person you've been looking for?"

"I'm not supposed to tell you."

He sounded like a petulant child, and Peyton fought the urge to scold him like one. Taking a deep breath, she tried again.

"Frankie, I can't help you if you keep secrets."

Her words prompted a stab of doubt at the thought of the secrets she'd been keeping from him. But that was different, wasn't it?

"I won't tell anyone what you tell me," she assured him. "But I need to know what's going on."

There was a long silence on the other end of the connection.

"The U.S. Marshals found a girl at Donovan Locke's ranch when he was taken down," Frankie finally said. "Turns out she was Locke's daughter. The FBI and the Marshals matched their DNA to prove it."

Peyton raised her eyebrows, surprised to hear he'd been working with the feds on his secret case.

"Veronica hired me and Barker to find out what happened to the girl's mother," he added. "We were with Deputy Santino and Agent Day when they found her mother's remains in Montana."

"I'm confused," Peyton interrupted. "Why would Veronica hire you and Barker to investigate?"

"Locke is Veronica's father, remember? So, the girl is her sister."

Peyton nodded, starting to put the pieces into place.

"We were able to figure out the mother was from Sky Lake, but we still don't know how she ended up at Locke's ranch in Montana," Frankie said, sounding increasingly glum. "So, we're here trying to find out about the mother, and then the shit hits the fan."

A growing sense of dread filled Peyton as she tried to follow all the incriminating threads that tied back to Sky Lake.

She was starting to think the little town had hidden its connection to a predatory network of corruption and death for decades, and that it had now caught Frankie in its dangerous web.

CHAPTER TWENTY-NINE

Frankie held the phone to his ear with a shaky hand. There was nothing Peyton could do to fix the mess he'd gotten himself into, but he couldn't bear to hang up. The sound of her voice eased the anxiety that had consumed him ever since June Taggert's body had been discovered the day before.

"I'll ask Agent Marlowe to talk to the sheriff in Sky Lake."

Frankie could tell Peyton was trying to sound optimistic.

"The joint task force has been looking into connections in the town," she confided. "And Agent Marlowe has already reached out to Agent Day to collaborate, so together we've got to be able to come up with a real suspect."

A roster of suspects rolled through Frankie's mind, but he had a feeling the sheriff wouldn't want to hear his ideas.

"Sheriff Holt is going apeshit," Frankie said, picturing Holt's red, sweaty face. "He claims there had never been a homicide in Sky Lake until we came along and started asking questions."

Frankie reached into his pocket for a stick of gum, but his pocket was empty. In fact, even his wallet was gone.

"I'd bet my last buck that Sheriff Holt's looking to pin this on an outsider," Frankie insisted. "And I'm an easy mark."

Feeling around in his other pocket, Frankie started to panic. His brand-new driver's license was in his wallet, along with his cash and credit cards, and now it was all gone.

195

"I'm going to try to find Agent Marlowe now," Peyton said. "We have a big operation planned for tomorrow, so I need to talk to him now, while I can still get his attention."

His heart plummeted at her words.

"Just be careful and stay sober," she added. "And call me later."

"Sure, I'll call you later," he muttered. "Even if Sheriff Holt arrests me, I should still get at least one phone call."

After he'd dropped the phone on the bedside table, Frankie paced the small hotel room, holding his aching head and trying to think.

He replayed Peyton's comment that the task force had a big operation planned for the next day. He didn't like being up in Sky Lake while she was doing dangerous work down in Willow Bay.

Giving in to impulse, Frankie scooped up his phone and tapped on Barker's name. He'd updated his partner earlier, admitting to the mess he was in, and Barker hadn't been happy.

But now Frankie wanted to ask a favor.

"I'm following a subject," Barker said, not bothering with a greeting. "And I think I've hit gold."

The excitement in Barker's voice made Frankie forget about the favor. It wasn't easy to get his partner worked up. The older man had been a police detective for years before retiring, and he'd seen a lot.

"You know Becky Morgan, right? The young nurse who leaves right at three o'clock every day?"

"Yeah, I've seen her come and go. Is that who you're tailing?"

Frankie pictured the young woman's blonde ponytail.

"She left work early, and seemed jumpy," Barker said. "So, I decided to follow her. You'll never guess where she went."

Barker continued before Frankie could even try.

"Bayside Municipal Park, right down the road from Amber Sloan's house," Barker said. "You know, the woman with the white Camry that's always hanging around the hospital."

"Oh yeah, I know Amber Sloan," Frankie replied, feeling a queasy ache in his stomach. "I wish I didn't."

Ignoring Frankie's sarcastic remark, Barker continued.

"Well, I got some photos, so I think we're going to be able to wrap up this case sooner than we thought."

His partner's good news didn't manage to cheer Frankie up. It only confirmed that Amber Sloan was a drug dealer and low-life who could put Peyton in danger.

"I need you to do me a favor," Frankie blurted, rubbing at his red-rimmed eyes. "I want you to keep an eye on Peyton for me. I may be stuck up here for a while, and I'm worried about her."

* * *

Archer Holt took off his hat and ran a hand through his matted hair. Frankie figured the sheriff had to be pushing forty, but he still had a thick head of brown hair with no signs of gray.

"Let's go through this one more time," Holt said, leaning back in his chair. "Why'd you go into Taggert Realty, and what we're you and June arguing about when Pearl Abbott arrived?"

"He's already gone through all this," Hunter protested. "We came to Sky Lake to find out what happened to Summer Fairfax, and whoever killed June Taggart must think she knew too much."

Holt ignored Hunter's remark, keeping his eyes on Frankie.

"It's quite a coincidence that you show up in town and start an argument with June Taggert. How do you explain that?"

Clearing her throat, Charlie Day put up a hand to halt Holt's rant.

"Did your crime scene team find any fingerprints or trace evidence from the scene?" she asked. "Has your medical examiner completed the autopsy yet? Do we know what was in the syringe, or what was found in Ms. Taggert's system?"

The FBI agent's questions deepened Holt's scowl.

"We're working on it, Agent Day, but this is a small force, and we don't have the kind of resources you're used to."

"I'd be happy to call a special response team in to help you out," Charlie said. "They could probably be here by the end of the day or tomorrow morning at the latest."

Holt gave a firm shake of his head.

"We may be small, but we don't need the feds to do our work for us," he said, turning hard eyes on Frankie. "Mr. Dawson, I'm not ready to charge you with anything yet, but I suggest you stay in town until we complete our investigation."

A cold sweat broke out across Frankie's forehead at the sheriff's words. The nightmare was starting all over again. He could be charged with a crime he hadn't committed, and like last time, he could end up in prison.

"And I suggest you think twice about trying to pin June Taggert's death on me, Sheriff."

Jumping out of his seat, Frankie crossed to the door.

"My lawyer is Leo Steele, and if you haven't heard of him, you might want to look him up, cause he'll eat you and your little department here for lunch if you try to railroad me."

Wrenching open the door to the interview room, Frankie stalked out into the lobby and through the front door. He turned left and started walking, hoping he was heading in the right direction.

He paused outside a liquor store, consumed by the growing need for a drink, then put his hand to his empty pocket.

Where the hell is my wallet? With no money and no ID, I'm screwed.

The realization that he couldn't even get on a plane and fly home without his ID caused another surge of anxiety to roll through him.

Looks like I'm staying in Sky Lake, whether I like it or not.

CHAPTER THIRTY

The door slammed behind Frankie, causing the metal table they were sitting around to rattle. Hunter resisted the urge to follow Frankie out the door; it would be best to let him cool off and calm down. Besides, he wanted to make sure the sheriff didn't do anything rash. It was obvious that Holt was in over his head, and that he was grasping at straws.

"You're on the wrong track with Frankie," Hunter said. "And trying to use him as a scapegoat isn't going to work.'

Taking out his press credentials, he dropped them on the table in front of Holt. The sheriff's eyes narrowed as Hunter continued.

"It's clear that the incompetency of the Sky Lake Sheriff's office allowed Donovan Locke or one of his buddies to get away with abducting and murdering a young woman in your town."

Hunter held Holt's hostile gaze as he spoke, but he sensed Charlie's unease as she watched the exchange.

"The people of this town may be interested to know it took private investigators and federal agents to find out what really happened to Summer Fairfax."

He ignored the flush of anger that filled Holt's face.

"And why was that? Because you and Sheriff Duffy couldn't be bothered to run a proper investigation. I'd say it all makes for a very compelling story."

Standing and crossing to the door, Holt flung it open.

"I don't talk to reporters about ongoing investigations," he said, motioning toward the hall. "Now you need to leave."

Hunter headed toward the door, giving Charlie a nod as he passed. He'd expected the sheriff to throw him out after finding out he was a reporter. But the man had given him no choice.

Sheriff Holt needed to know he would be held accountable in the press and by the townspeople. Otherwise, Frankie might end up as Holt's fall guy for the town's first official homicide in decades.

Deciding to look for Frankie back at the hotel, Hunter climbed in the blue Nissan and headed east. He'd only gotten a few blocks when he spotted Frankie's lanky figure leaning against the brick wall outside Sky Lake Wine and Spirits.

"Come on, Frankie," he yelled through the window. "Let's go."

Frankie shuffled to the sedan and got in without a word. He slumped back in the seat and clicked on his seatbelt, staring out the window with listless eyes as Hunter sped away.

Only when they pulled up outside Sparks Air Charter did Frankie sit up and take notice.

"Beau Sparks was Summer's boyfriend," Hunter said, opening his door. "I want to know why he never looked for his girlfriend."

Striding up to the front door, Hunter heard Frankie's footsteps crunching in the gravel behind him. He held the door open for Frankie to pass through, then stared past the counter toward the big hangar and the airstrip beyond.

Beau's blonde hair and broad back were visible next to a small turboprop Cessna. Tom Locke's less impressive figure appeared beside Beau's. He strained to push a white cardboard box through the open loading doors, then crawled in after it.

"Mr. Sparks?" Hunter called out.

He slipped around the counter and waved for Frankie to follow him into the big hangar.

"I'd like to ask you a few questions if you have a few minutes."

Approaching Beau with an apologetic smile, Hunter held up his press credentials and stuck out a hand. Beau automatically shook the offered hand, but his eyes were wary.

"I'm an investigative reporter and I'm looking into the disappearance of Summer Fairfax."

Hunter kept his eyes on Beau's face, watching for a reaction.

"If you have a minute, I'd like to ask you a few questions, but let me first offer my condolences."

Beau frowned and shook his head as if he didn't understand.

"I know you and June Taggert were divorced, but I'm sure her death has been a shock. So, I'm sorry for your loss."

A shadow of grief passed over Beau's handsome face.

"Thanks. June was a good woman. She'll be missed around here."

Taking out his notepad and pen, Hunter met Beau's eyes.

"Now, I understand you and Summer were an item before she disappeared. What can you tell me about the last night you saw her?"

A crash sounded from inside the Cessna, and Beau called out.

"Tom, you okay?"

A puffy face surrounded by long, disheveled hair appeared in the open cargo door. Tom Locke lifted a hand in Beau's direction.

"All's good, boss," he said. "We're almost ready to go."

"Are you Tom Locke?" Hunter called out. "I'd like to ask you some questions as well if you don't mind."

Tom's eyes darted toward Beau, then back to Hunter.

"Questions about what?"

"About the night Summer Fairfax disappeared," Hunter said, keeping his voice crisp and matter of fact. "It won't take long."

Stepping down from the little plane, Tom stood next to Beau. He avoided Hunter's eyes, shifting restlessly from foot to foot.

"Beau, you told Sheriff Duffy that you'd been drinking and ended up kissing June Taggert that night."

Hunter looked down at his notepad and scanned the page on top, reading through his notes from the sheriff's files.

"Summer got mad, left the party, and you passed out," Hunter said as if reciting a shopping list. "That sound about right?"

Beau nodded, but his face tightened, and his eyes darkened.

"Yeah, that's what I told the sheriff," Beau agreed. "And I never saw Summer again. She'd been planning to go to some fancy college, so I pretty much figured she'd left me behind."

"Is that why you were mad at her, Beau?" Hunter asked, cocking his head. "Were you mad at Summer because she was going to leave you behind and go on to better things?"

The accusation flustered Beau just as Hunter had expected.

"I didn't say I was mad at her," he protested.

"Then why'd you kiss her friend? And why didn't you look for her once she went missing?" Hunter prodded. "I mean, come on, you must have been mad at her, right?"

Tom cleared his throat, and Hunter turned to him, sensing he was agitated by the questions.

"What about you, Tom? Were you at Sky Lake Farms that night?" Hunter asked. "Did you see Summer?"

"Summer wasn't about to hang around with me," Tom said, keeping his eyes on the ground. "She was Beau's girl."

Watching Tom's hands clench and unclench at his side, Hunter decided to keep pressing. The questions about Summer were obviously bothering the man, and he wanted to know why.

"I see that Sheriff Duffy questioned you a few times, Tom," Hunter said, referring again to his folder. "Why was that? Why did he suspect you might know where Summer had gone?"

A flash of anger lit up Tom's eyes.

"Sheriff Duffy and Deputy Holt accused me of having something to do with her leaving, but I didn't know anything," he said, shaking his head. "They even threatened to arrest me."

Frankie spoke up behind Hunter.

"Why'd they pick you?" he asked. "I mean, if you weren't even there that night, why would Duffy suspect you?"

Lifting his chin in a defiant gesture, Tom met Frankie's gaze.

"Everyone around here thinks I'm cut from the same cloth as my big brother," he said. "They knew what Donnie had done, and they judged me guilty by association."

He looked at Beau, his eyes bright.

"You and your daddy were the only ones who ever gave me a chance," Tom said. "You hired me when no one else would."

Beau gave Tom an awkward nod, then turned to Hunter.

"We've answered your questions," he said, checking his watch. "Now we've got a flight scheduled and we need to get moving."

As they walked back to the car, Frankie looked at Hunter.

"Is it just me, or is Beau Sparks hiding something?"

"That's just what I was thinking," Hunter said, opening the door. "But he's stuck to his story for twenty years, so I don't think he's going to change it now."

Settling into the passenger's seat, Frankie looked over.

"You really thinking of doing a story on Summer's disappearance?" he asked, sounding worried. "And Skylar?"

"Not without Veronica's and Skylar's approval," Hunter assured him. "First we need to find out what really happened. Then, when they're ready, it'll be their story to tell."

Frankie nodded as if satisfied by Hunter's answer, and turned his tired eyes back to the window.

But the question had turned Hunter's thoughts to Veronica and Skylar. Seeing June Taggert's dead body had shaken them both, and as he drove back toward the hotel, he breathed a sigh of relief that they were safely back in Willow Bay.

CHAPTER THIRTY-ONE

T he sun was just starting to set over Fox Hollow Apartments as Amber Sloan shoved the bag full of pills into her backpack and zipped it up. She noted the lightweight of the backpack as she slung it over her thin shoulders and grimaced, knowing the man waiting for her at the park wasn't going to be happy.

The steady supply of fentanyl Amber had been getting from Becky Morgan during the last few months was drying up. The nurse had recently been transferred from the oncology ward to the coronary care unit, and her access to the highly potent opioid would be minimal going forward.

Amber had managed to bully and blackmail the young woman into scraping together another delivery, but it hadn't been easy. The nurse had become paranoid lately, sure she was being watched.

"This is the last time," Becky had insisted. "People at the hospital are starting to ask a lot of questions."

Her blonde ponytail had practically quivered with indignation.

"I'm not willing to risk my job and my license to get you more of *this!*" She shoved a plastic shopping bag toward Amber. "I'm done."

"Oh, I doubt it," Amber had sneered. "I think you'll find a way if you don't want my new buddies at the FBI to find out what you've been up to. I don't think you'd like prison."

Snatching the bag, Amber had seen panic building in Becky's eyes.

"You wouldn't," the nurse had gasped. "You'd get arrested, too."

"Oh no," Amber had replied with a smirk. "I have this wonderful little thing called immunity."

But as she crossed to the door, Amber knew no matter how much she pressured Becky, the nurse was no longer a viable source of the fentanyl she'd been supplying to her contact at the Syndicate.

Amber would have to tell the man she was meeting that the gold mine had dried up.

Opening the door just a crack, Amber peered out, worried that nosy Detective Bell and her muscle-bound partner might be standing guard outside.

But the corridor and parking lot appeared to be empty.

Amber pulled out her phone and tapped in a message.

You there?

The response came back within seconds.

Yes, ready for delivery.

She scanned the path to the white Camry. All seemed clear.

On my way.

She tapped *Send*, but before sticking the phone back in her pocket, Amber checked the darknet message board, hoping to see a reply from Mack about the pick-up the next day.

But there was no reply.

Mack's silence was worrisome. If the set-up had to be called off, Amber knew the feds would like nothing more than to tear up the immunity agreement.

If they do, I'll be the one facing prison time instead of Becky Morgan.

Pulling open the door, Amber pushed all distracting thoughts from her mind and slipped outside. She made it across the parking lot and into her car without seeing any signs of the two detectives, or anyone else.

She switched on her headlights and steered the Camry out of the lot, turning right onto Huntington Street. She kept under the speed limit as she drove the short distance to Bayside Municipal Park.

The park had officially closed at sunset, and the playground and grassy playing fields were already abandoned and cloaked in thick shadows. A sliver of moon cast a soft glow on the one vehicle parked in the lot.

A sleek, black SUV with dark tinted windows sat idling by the curb next to the picnic area. The big vehicle's lights were off, but Amber could hear the engine's steady purr as she brought the Camry to a stop beside it.

Shutting off the car's engine, she rolled down her window, listening for any sounds from the dark park beyond, but even the cicadas and birds had gone quiet.

"You got something for me?"

The man's voice sounded beside her open window, and Amber jumped, her nerves immediately racing in response to the burst of adrenaline caused by the man's sudden appearance.

"You scared the crap out of me," she hissed. "Why are you always sneaking up like that?"

"I told you I was here," the man muttered, sounding bored. "Do you have the package?"

Unzipping her backpack, she reached in for the bag of pills just as headlights lit up the lot around them. The man turned his face away, and Amber froze in place, sure that Detective Bell must have followed her after all.

But the car belonging to the headlights stopped just inside the entrance, made a U-turn, then headed back the way it had come.

"Let's do this in my car," the man muttered, walking back toward the SUV before she could reply.

Amber stared after him as he retreated into the dark vehicle, her heart still thumping from the two scares she'd suffered in the last sixty seconds.

She glanced back in her rearview mirror, then surveyed the surrounding area again, still feeling the hair on the back of her neck standing on end.

Opening the Camry's door, she winced as the overhead light lit up the interior, illuminating the fast-food wrappers, cigarette butts, and discarded debris that littered the passenger seat and floor.

She jabbed at the light, managing to turn it off, then lifted the backpack up and slung it over her shoulder. Climbing out of the car, she immediately stepped into a deep pothole, twisted her ankle, and grabbed for the car door.

The simple drop-off was going wrong at every turn, and Amber felt the urge to get back in the Camry and drive home. Something about the whole night seemed off.

But the man in the SUV wasn't a patient person, and he wouldn't take kindly to her leaving with the package. She knew there would be another man waiting somewhere for it, and another man after that.

The Syndicate was full of impatient, angry men who wouldn't leave her alone until they'd gotten what they considered to be theirs.

I better just get it over with. Besides, it's time to break the news that the Willow Bay General gravy train is coming to the end of the line.

Tottering around the SUV, Amber pulled on the handle of the passenger's side door, then hoisted herself up onto the smooth, leather seat.

The musky scent of the man's cologne was overpowering, and she held her breath as she looked over at his thin, stony face.

"Okay, so what do you have for me?"

He sounded unimpressed as if he didn't expect much, and Amber decided she'd better just go ahead and tell him the truth.

"It's not the usual amount," she admitted. "My source is drying up, so this might be the last package for a while."

The man's face didn't change. He just held out his hand.

Amber dug in her backpack and pulled out the bag. She dropped it onto his open palm, and he held it up as if considering its weight.

"So, what do you have for me?" Amber asked, expecting the man to try to negotiate the price down since the package was lighter than usual. "You can take ten percent off what we agreed."

Preparing to go all the way up to twenty percent, she was surprised to see him shrug his shoulders.

"That's fine with me," he said, a strange smile lifting the corners of his mouth. "But before we get to the money, there's someone I want you to meet."

A hand reached out from the darkness of the backseat and wrapped around Amber's throat. She grabbed at the hand, clawing at it with all her strength, but it only squeezed harder.

A scream of pain and fear hovered in her throat, but Amber produced only a wet gurgle as the hand held fast.

"You may remember him," the man in the driver's seat was saying. "He wanted to be the one to give you what you deserve."

A deep voice sounded in Amber's ear, and she felt hot, labored breathing on her neck as the man behind her leaned closer.

"You remember me, don't you Amber?"

Amber's eyes widened in terror as she recognized Mack's voice.

"I'm the guy you've been planning to turn into the FBI so you can try and save your own sorry ass."

Mack raised a syringe in front of her face, showing her the long needle before bringing it down with a sharp jab to her arm.

Feeling the drug's deadly effect instantly take hold, Amber knew the game was over. She'd played hard, and she'd lost, and now only darkness remained.

CHAPTER THIRTY-TWO

Mack waited until Amber had stopped struggling, then moved his hand from her throat to her chest, feeling around for any telltale wires that would let him know the feds were listening. But there was nothing out of order, and he dropped his hands, letting Amber's body slump against the door.

"No wire," Mack said, grabbing the strap of her backpack and pulling it toward him, "unless there's something in here."

He stuck a hand in the old backpack and felt around, before pulling it out empty and throwing the bag back on Amber's lap.

"Nothing," he muttered. "I'll check her car when I dump her in the trunk. Then I can ditch it somewhere before I fly out."

"Not so fast."

The man in the driver's seat caught Mack's eyes in the rearview mirror, and Mack paused, his forehead creasing into a frown as he returned the stare.

"I did you a favor, right?"

Mack nodded, recalling the man's message alerting him to Amber's betrayal. He hadn't been surprised to hear she'd ratted him out to the feds, or that the shipment she'd scheduled for pick-up the next day was just a ruse to get him to fly down to Willow Bay.

The man had explained that once Mack arrived, the feds would take him into custody, and Amber would get off scot-free thanks to an immunity agreement she'd negotiated with the state prosecutor.

The information had confirmed Misty Bradshaw's warning that Amber was setting him up, and Mack had acted quickly to prevent her from doing any further damage.

But apparently, the Syndicate's favors weren't free.

"What do you want?" Mack asked. "I don't have much time."

Mack hadn't had a chance to properly dispose of June Taggert's body before it could be discovered, and now Sky Lake was in the middle of its first official homicide investigation in years.

It wasn't a good time to start raising suspicions. He needed to get home before anyone noticed he'd left town.

"This won't take long."

The man's voice was as cold as his eyes.

"I want you to take care of someone who's become a problem for the Syndicate," he said. "I'd consider it a personal favor."

* * *

Mack stood above the Camry's trunk and peered inside. He'd injected Amber with enough Fentanyl to kill a man twice her size, but he wanted to be sure the opioid had done its job.

Pushing a tangle of frizzy brown hair to the side, he rested two fingers on Amber's discolored neck and waited. Detecting no pulse, he studied her slack face and the pallor of her skin, then allowed himself to relax. The woman in front of him posed no further threat.

He slammed the trunk shut and looked around the empty lot. The black SUV had already driven away, leaving Mack alone to clean up the mess and take care of the Syndicate's little problem.

But as he climbed into the Camry's driver's seat, Mack pictured the girl with the silvery hair, the one that looked like Summer and had the momentary impulse to take the car on a different mission.

My angel is here in Willow Bay. She could be waiting for me nearby.

He knew they would be together eventually; it was only a matter of time. But he had to have a plan. He couldn't afford to alert the local authorities or the feds to his intentions before he was ready to make his move.

And he couldn't risk the Syndicate coming after him if he failed to deliver on his promise now.

First, I need to finish what I started. Then I can come back for my angel.

Forcing all thoughts of the girl out of his mind, Mack followed the instructions the man had given him. Within minutes the Camry was turning into the Fox Hollow Apartments.

He pulled into an empty parking space at the edge of the lot, climbed out of the car, and headed for Unit 124, Amber's key ring at the ready in his hand.

Once he'd made it safely inside the small apartment, Mack pulled out Amber's phone and tapped in the text, just as he and the man in the SUV had planned.

I know where Misty is, but need to hurry. Will wait at my place for you.

Pressing *Send*, he dropped the phone on a cluttered table, then quickly searched the little apartment, looking for anything that might incriminate him or the Syndicate.

The lights were off in the apartment's single bedroom, but a weak glow of moonlight shown through a small window. Mack crossed over to see that the window faced out onto a scruffy patch of grass.

He opened the window and loosened the screen. He might need an alternative escape route if his target didn't show up alone, or if she proved to be more resourceful than he anticipated.

Once the apartment was secured, Mack prepared the syringe, attaching the long hypodermic needle and filling it with the deadly mixture of fentanyl and oxycodone that would solve the Syndicate's little problem once and for all.

Checking his watch, Mack assumed a position behind the front door. But as the seconds ticked by, his nerves began to jump, and he put a hand on the concealed holster that held his Ruger.

He knew the gun might be needed, although he considered it to be a last resort. Not only would a gunshot attract unwanted attention, but the bullet might be traced back to him or his weapon.

The fentanyl would be much quieter, and practically untraceable.

Holding the syringe at the ready, he peeked through the window and checked his watch again. Finally, a black Dodge Charger pulled into the lot and parked next to the white Camry.

As a single figure emerged and headed toward him, Mack unlocked the deadbolt and opened the door a crack. Moments later he heard a soft knock.

"Amber? It's Detective Bell. I got your message."

Mack held his breath as he saw the door swing inward.

"Amber? Are you in there?"

The detective moved closer and looked into the room, while Mack remained still, waiting for her to take another step forward. When she did, he stepped out from behind the door and hooked an arm around her neck, pulling her all the way into the room.

Gripping the syringe in his free hand, he thrust it down toward the woman's thrashing legs, sticking the tip of the needle into one lean thigh and pushing down hard on the plunger with his thumb.

The detective's head reared back and connected with Mack's chin just as the heel of her boot slammed into his shin. He grunted and staggered backward but managed to maintain his grip.

"You're...even stronger...than Misty," he grunted out, struggling to pull the woman back from the doorway. "She fought back, too."

Feeling the woman start to sag in his arms, Mack allowed himself to take a deep breath. The drugs were doing their job; it was only a matter of time until Detective Peyton Bell stopped moving altogether.

Suddenly the door burst open without warning and a man's burly figure filled the doorway.

"Put your hands up!"

Mack saw the glint of a weapon in the shadowy figure's hand, but he doubted the man would use it with the woman between them. Shoving Peyton forward, he reached down to pull his Ruger out of its holster.

"Barker...he's got a gun," Peyton gasped.

Surprised that she was still conscious, Mack glanced down, glimpsing stark fear in the detective's wide amber eyes as he lifted his gun and fired.

But the big man had responded to Peyton's warning by lunging to the side, and the bullet whizzed harmlessly past his head as he lifted his own gun in Mack's direction.

Bolting into the bedroom, Mack raced to the window and pushed out the screen as he climbed through.

He jumped to the ground and sprinted toward the street, shoving his Ruger back in its holster as he reached the road, knowing he had to get away from the area before the man called Barker could raise the alarm.

Once the police responded and found an officer down, a massive manhunt would surely begin. And it wouldn't take long for them to discover Amber's body in the trunk of her car.

But if Mack could make it back to the airfield, he would be out of town before anyone figured out what had happened.

And with Amber out of the way, there would be no evidence left behind linking him to the scene; he would be home free. He could still get back to Sky Lake before anyone knew he'd ever been gone.

CHAPTER THIRTY-THREE

Veronica rinsed off the last plate and stacked it in the dishwasher, then turned back to her mother. Ling Lee was already yawning and checking her watch now that they'd finished their dinner of pasta, fresh bread, and salad.

"I think I'll go up to bed early," Ling said, rubbing her eyes. "I couldn't fall asleep after you and Skylar got back last night, and then I was up early for my meeting with Mayor Hadley."

Scooping Winston off the counter, Veronica hugged the cat's warm body against her chest and followed Ling into the hall.

"Listening to Mayor Hadley would tire anyone out," Veronica said, rolling her eyes at the thought of the outgoing mayor. "Why'd you have to meet with him?"

"Be kind, Ronnie," Ling scolded gently. "The poor man has had quite a shock. I almost feel bad for him."

Veronica raised her eyebrows.

"Well, I feel even worse for the people in this town," Veronica replied, shaking her head. "He's put himself and his friends first for decades. At least now we'll have a mayor who puts the people first."

"Right now, I'm going to put myself first." Ling stifled another yawn. "I'm going to take a shower and then go straight to bed."

Veronica's phone vibrated in her pocket as she watched her mother disappear up the stairs.

She'd been expecting Hunter to call from Sky Lake to say good-night and was surprised to see Finn Jordan's name on the display.

"Hey Ronnie, there have been shots fired at a local apartment and an officer is down at the scene."

The cameraman's rapidly spoken words betrayed his impatience.

"Are you available to report live?"

Veronica didn't hesitate before responding.

"When will you be here?"

"I'm already in the van and on the way," Finn answered. "I'll swing by your house in five minutes."

Still carrying Winston, Veronica hurried up to her room, taking the stairs two at a time. She exchanged her jeans and white t-shirt for a navy-blue pants suit and high-heeled pumps, ran a brush through her long, dark hair, and swiped on a classic red lipstick.

Forgoing a look in the mirror, she rushed back into the hall where Ling Lee was coming out of the bathroom wrapped in a thick bathrobe. She stared at Veronica's pantsuit and heels in surprise.

"Ronnie, where are you going?"

"There's been a shooting. A police officer's down," Veronica said, hoping Finn wasn't already waiting outside. "I'm going to report live at the scene. The news van should be here any minute."

Ling stepped forward to take Veronica's arm.

"Are you sure you're up for this, Ronnie?" she asked, studying her daughter's face. "You've been through so much already this week."

Shrugging off Ling's hand, Veronica moved toward the stairs.

"It's my job, Ma," she said with a sigh. "If I'm not up for this, I might as well find a different career."

"Now you're making sense," Ling replied. "You can get a nice safe job that doesn't involve traffickers, dead bodies, or serial killers."

Veronica rolled her eyes again and raised a finger to her lips, gesturing to the closed door beside them.

"Sounds kind of boring, Ma," Veronica murmured. "Now, let's not wake up Skylar. She doesn't need anything else to worry about."

Hearing the news van pull up outside, Veronica hurried down the stairs, her mind already focused on the job ahead of her.

She approached the big van and opened the door, surprised to see Gracie in the passenger's seat. The Lab jumped down, wagging her tail in excitement as she greeted Veronica.

"I was thinking maybe Gracie could stay with Skylar while we're on the scene," Finn said. "I didn't have time to take her home."

"Skylar's asleep already," Veronica said, looking back toward the dark house. "And if I go back inside, I'll have to listen to another lecture from my mother."

Finn looked down at Gracie and shrugged.

"Looks like you're coming with us, girl."

Waving Veronica and Gracie back into the van, Finn ran around to the driver's side and jumped in.

"All right, let's get this show on the road."

* * *

Veronica leaned forward in her seat as the Channel Ten News van approached Fox Hollow Apartments. An ambulance with flashing lights sat in the parking lot as several uniformed policemen guarded the perimeter, waving cars past the entrance.

Bumping the big van up onto the curb, Finn steered over a rutted patch of grass and parked at the edge of the lot, just past the perimeter. He grabbed his bulky camera case and turned to Veronica.

"You ready for this?"

She nodded, already opening the door and stepping down onto the uneven ground, eager to find out what had happened. Gracie jumped out after her, sticking close to her heels.

"Everyone, move back," an officer called out, motioning to the small crowd of onlookers as the ambulance siren began to wail.

Veronica recognized the officer as Dave Eddings. She circled around to his right, keeping her eyes on the ambulance as Finn settled Gracie next to the van.

"Officer Eddings, can you tell us what's going on?" Veronica called. "Can you confirm that there's been a shooting?"

But Eddings turned away, his eyes trained to the door of Unit 124 as it opened. A team of paramedics swiftly rolled a gurney out of the apartment toward the waiting vehicle.

As the paramedics prepared to lift the heavy gurney into the ambulance, the pause allowed Veronica to get a good look at the woman strapped on top. Shock flooded through her as the gurney slid into the back of the ambulance and the doors slammed shut.

Staring after the flashing lights of the departing vehicle, Veronica pictured the dark pixie cut and fine features of the woman on the gurney. Something terrible had happened to Peyton Bell.

Veronica turned back to the apartment in time to see a familiar face emerge. Pete Barker stepped out into the corridor, his salt and pepper hair disheveled. A deep crease settled between his baggy, puppy-dog eyes as he looked around.

"Mr. Barker, what happened to Detective Bell?" Veronica called across the lot. "Was she shot? Is she going to be okay?"

Just then Alma Garcia stepped up to Barker, blocking Veronica's view. Willow Bay's senior crime scene technician held a syringe in a plastic bag as she asked Barker a question. They both turned as the officers waved a black Dodge Charger into the lot.

Veronica's heart jumped when she saw Chief Ainsley and Detective Vanzinger exit the unmarked vehicle and walk toward Unit 124. They nodded to Barker and Alma, then disappeared inside.

"Okay, let's get some initial footage," Finn said from behind her. "Spencer wants us to shoot a segment and then go live at eleven."

Holding the microphone toward her, Finn glanced down at his iPad and scanned the display.

"According to Google a twenty-eight-year-old woman named Amber Sloan lives in Unit 124," Finn said. "But we shouldn't use her name just yet. We'll need to find out what's going on first."

He looked up when Veronica didn't take the microphone.

"Ronnie, what's wrong?"

"Amber Sloan," Veronica murmured, her throat suddenly dry. "That's...that's the woman Misty Bradshaw reported to the WBPD."

Before Finn could respond, a flurry of sharp barks burst through the air. Spinning around, Veronica saw Gracie scratching at the ground beside a dirty white Toyota Camry.

"Come here, Gracie," Finn called, shifting the big camera and moving toward the frantic Lab. "Get over here."

Veronica grabbed the leash from inside the van and scurried toward Gracie. The dog's barks conjured memories of the scene outside Taggert Realty, and a burst of adrenaline sent her pulse racing as she approached.

A deep voice sounded beside her, and Veronica was relieved to see Pete Barker take hold of Gracie's collar and tug her backward, but the dog's barks only grew more frantic.

Finally managing to pull the Lab away from the Camry, Barker called over to Alma in a hoarse voice.

"Your team needs to check the car." He nodded down at Gracie. "She's been trained as a cadaver dog, and I'm pretty sure this is her way of letting us know she's caught the scent of a dead body."

Alma stared at Barker, and then at the Camry, before nodding to an officer beside the building. The officer stepped into Unit 124, and moments later Nessa and Vanzinger exited the apartment.

They headed toward the Camry while the crime scene techs and uniformed officers began herding the crowd away from the Camry.

Nessa's face was drawn and pale as she met Veronica's eyes, but she didn't speak. She just walked past the news van to where the white car sat in its lonely parking space.

Vanzinger followed Nessa to the car, leaning to look into the windows. He frowned over at Barker, who still held Gracie's leash.

"You sure about this?" The big detective sounded skeptical. "I don't see anything inside the car."

"I was with this dog less than a week ago when she found a body that both the FBI and the U.S. Marshals had overlooked," Barker replied, his voice grim. "I'd say you better look in that trunk."

Nessa turned to Alma and nodded.

"Let's open the trunk," she said. "I've seen Gracie do her thing before, and from what I've heard, she's never been wrong."

Moving toward the car door, Alma used a gloved hand to try the handle. The door was unlocked. She then moved back to the trunk and looked over at Nessa.

"You ready?" she asked, swallowing hard.

At Nessa's thumbs-up, Alma opened the trunk.

Veronica held her breath, unable to tear her eyes away from the car. She felt Finn's tense body next to her as he also strained to see.

Alma looked in the trunk, then moved aside to let Nessa peer in. After a long pause, Nessa turned to Vanzinger.

"Looks like Gracie was right. We've got ourselves a homicide."

* * *

"This is Veronica Lee with Channel Ten News and I'm reporting live at the scene of a homicide outside the Fox Hollow Apartments."

Veronica spoke into the microphone as Finn operated the camera.

"Emergency crews responded to reports of shots fired around nine o'clock this evening, and we arrived just as paramedics were transporting a woman from the scene. So far we've received no update as to the woman's identity or condition."

Gesturing to the lot behind her, Veronica moved to the side so that Finn could get a clear shot of the crime scene tent that had quickly been erected over the white Camry.

"The WBPD crime scene unit also discovered a body in the trunk of a car in the parking lot, and a full investigation is in progress."

Stepping back into the shot, Veronica kept her voice steady.

"Police have yet to confirm the victim's identity, or to release any information about a possible suspect, but we'll continue to bring you updates from the scene as the night progresses."

Finn wrapped the segment and lowered the camera as Veronica let out a sigh of relief. She turned to see the medical examiner's van pull into the lot, and watched as a petite woman and a tall, stocky man in matching protective coveralls climbed out.

"That's Iris Nguyen, the chief medical examiner," Veronica said, following Finn back to the van to check on Gracie. "It'll be a while before they transport the body back to her office for autopsy, so if you want to go drop Gracie at home, I can wait here."

Rubbing Gracie behind the ears, Finn shook his head.

"She'll be okay in here," he said, then pointed over Veronica's shoulder. "Besides, we need to ask Chief Ainsley if they know who did this. If a suspect is on the loose, we need to put out a bulletin to our viewers ASAP."

Veronica turned to see Nessa and Barker in a huddle beside the chief's black Dodge Charger. Motioning for Finn to wait, Veronica hurried toward them.

"Was Amber Sloan in the trunk?"

Her question made Nessa jump, and the police chief turned with a wary expression as Barker dropped his eyes.

"I can't confirm the victim's identity until we notify next of kin," Nessa said, but the look in her eyes answered Veronica's question.

"How did she die?" Veronica asked. "Any suspects yet? Do you have a description we can pass on to our viewers?"

"Iris needs to do an autopsy before we'll know cause of death," Nessa snapped, pushing past Veronica. "And right now, I'm more worried about the victim who's still alive."

Veronica stared after the chief, then turned to Barker. The grief in his big brown eyes stopped her next question.

"Peyton was attacked," Barker said, keeping his voice low. "She was injected with something in a...a syringe. The guy had a gun, and he got off a shot, but..."

Lifting a big hand to smooth back his hair, Barker cleared his throat and tried to regain his composure.

"Well...I managed to run the perp off, but Peyton passed out. She was still unresponsive when the paramedics took her away."

Barker's voice was heavy as he met her eyes.

"They took her to Willow Bay General, but they didn't seem hopeful she would pull through."

Veronica put a hand on the older man's solid shoulder, knowing what must be going through his mind.

"I gotta tell Frankie," he murmured softly, confirming her fear. "I gotta let him know what's happened to his girl."

CHAPTER THIRTY-FOUR

The small lounge at the Fairfax Inn was practically empty as Frankie stared down into his glass of mineral water. Hunter had refused to order him anything stronger, and since he was currently without funds, Frankie knew he couldn't complain.

"According to sources in town, June Taggert had been seeing Sheriff Holt for the last few months," Hunter said, ignoring the beer he'd ordered for himself. "I talked to at least three different women who were happy to give me all the gory details."

Charlie raised her perfectly arched eyebrows but didn't reply.

"I'd say that's a pretty big conflict of interest," Hunter added, clearly hoping to get a reaction from the FBI agent.

As he took an unenthusiastic sip of the bubbly water, Frankie heard his phone begin to vibrate beside him on the wooden bar.

Seeing Barker's name on the display, he was tempted to send the call to voicemail, not ready for another one of Barker's lectures on staying sober. But the timing of the call piqued his interest.

Ten o'clock was pretty late to be getting a call from the older man. *Isn't it already past Barker's bedtime?*

Frankie tapped *Accept Call* and held the phone to his ear, suddenly scared to hear what Barker had to say.

"What's up, partner?"

The hesitation on the other end confirmed Frankie's suspicion.

"Okay, let me guess, then," he added. "You've got bad news."

"Yeah, Frankie," Barker choked out. "It's bad."

A shiver ran down Frankie's spine at Barker's words. He looked up to see Hunter and Charlie watching him, their eyes instantly concerned by the fear written across his face.

"Peyton's in the hospital," Barker said. "She was attacked at Amber Sloan's apartment. I tried to stop the guy but...I didn't get there in time to...to..."

"How bad is it?"

Frankie's hand tightened around the phone.

"Tell me the truth, Barker," he demanded, closing his eyes. "Peyton's going to be okay, isn't she?"

"It doesn't look good," Barker admitted. "The perp stuck her with a hypodermic needle. The doctors think he used a mix of opioids. Probably fentanyl...maybe other drugs."

Barker's voice suddenly sounded far away, and Frankie lifted the phone from his ear and stared at it.

"What is it, Frankie?" Hunter asked. "Are you okay?"

Shaking his head, Frankie dropped the phone on the bar and ran to the men's room. He bent over the sink just in time to retch up the few sips of water he'd taken.

Cold sweat dripped from his forehead, sliding down the drain as he tried to stop the spinning in his head. The bathroom door opened, and Frankie saw Hunter's expensive leather shoes stop beside him on the tiled floor.

Disjointed thoughts drifted through his head, and for a minute he wasn't sure who was in the hospital. Was it Franny, or Peyton?

Franny died on tiles that looked a lot like these.

The memory of Franny's small body on the dirty tiles sent another wave of nausea through him, and he retched again, although this time nothing came out.

"Barker said to call him back when you feel better."

Frankie didn't move. He wasn't sure if his stomach was finished.

"I know you're worried about Peyton," Hunter added. "But you can't give up hope. She's a strong woman, and she's-"

"Yeah, I know, she's a *fighter*," Frankie muttered bitterly, not looking up. "That's what they'll say at her funeral. She *was a fighter*."

Pushing himself upright, he caught his reflection in the mirror and winced. His skin was as white as June Taggert's had been.

As white as Franny had been when I found her.

He turned around to face Hunter, still dizzy.

"I've got to find my driver's license."

He grimaced at the acidic aftertaste of bile in his mouth.

"I can't get a flight home without it."

Hunter gripped Frankie's arm to steady him.

"Where did you last have it?" he asked.

Shrugging his shoulders, Frankie pulled away. He couldn't think. His head ached with the effort as he tried to concentrate.

"You gave your ID to the woman at the rehab center when we went to see Harriet Locke, didn't you?" Hunter asked.

Frankie nodded, picturing Dee Wiggins at the rehab center's reception desk. The last time he'd seen his driver's license, she'd been holding it.

"Yeah, I bet that's where I left it," he said, wiping his mouth with the back of his hand. "Let's go. It's probably still there."

"Hold on." Hunter reached out to stop Frankie from bolting toward the door. "They won't let us in this late, and we can't get a flight now anyway. We'll go to the rehab center first thing in the morning to get your license. Then we'll go to the airport."

Knowing Hunter was right, Frankie reluctantly followed him back to the table, where Charlie waited with a pained expression.

"I'm going up to my room."

Frankie picked up his glass of mineral water and drained it, then set it back on the bar with a shaky hand.

"I'll see you two first thing in the morning."

As he walked toward the elevator, Frankie refused to listen to the little voice that kept whispering in his head. The voice that told him his license wouldn't be at the rehab center, and that there wouldn't be any available flights out of Sky Lake.

I don't care if I have to hitchhike or walk the whole damn way. I'm getting back to Willow Bay even if it kills me, and I'm going to see Peyton before it's too late.

* * *

It was still dark outside when Frankie crossed to the blue Nissan sedan in the Fairfax Inn parking lot the next morning. His hands settled over the key fob in his pocket, and he looked back over his shoulder as he thumbed the *Unlock* button.

Expecting Hunter to come charging out after him, Frankie was relieved to see that he was the only one in the dark, empty lot.

I'll get out to the rehab center and be back here before Hunter even knows I've taken the car.

Frankie had been up all night, unable to sleep or stop the tortured thoughts of Peyton alone in a hospital bed hundreds of miles away. He'd snagged the key fob off the bar before going to his room the night before, thinking he might drive down to Willow Bay on his own.

But without a license or any money, he figured he'd only end up stranded by the side of the road or stopped by the highway patrol for driving without a license.

Finally, just before 6:00 AM, he'd come up with the plan to take the rental car to the rehab center and demand his wallet back. That way he and Hunter would have a chance to catch the first flight out.

The sun was just rising over the rehabilitation center when Frankie turned the Nissan into the parking lot. A soft orange glow lit up the modest building and brightened the dull, brown exterior.

Stepping out of the car, Frankie looked toward the front entrance, glad to see bright lights streaming through the windows. But when he pushed on the glass door, it was locked.

"They don't let visitors inside until seven."

Frankie stared into the shadow cast by the awning over the door. He could just make out a tall figure leaning against the wall. As he moved closer, the man's puffy face and long, disheveled hair came into view.

"Tom Locke? What are you doing here?"

"I should ask you that," Tom replied, but he didn't sound offended. "Sometimes I visit my ma before going to work. She gets lonely, you know."

The dark circles under Tom's eyes reminded Frankie of his own haggard face. He suspected the man had gone without sleep, as well.

"I left my wallet and license here," Frankie found himself saying. "I need them to get back home. My girlfriend's in the hospital."

Tom's face creased with concern.

"That's terrible," he said, scratching at the stubble on his chin. "I hope she's going to be all right."

"You and me, both," Frankie said, looking through the glass door anxiously. "How long until they open up?"

Looking at his watch, Tom frowned.

"It'll be a while more, but maybe we can get their attention."

He lifted a big fist and rapped on the glass door, leaning forward to stare into the well-lit lobby. Seeing no movement inside, he rapped even harder.

A startled face appeared behind the glass, and Frankie recognized Dee Wiggins. The small woman stared at them for a long beat, then unlocked the door.

"Visiting hours don't start until seven," she said, giving Tom a stern look. "You should know that by now, Mr. Locke."

"I left my wallet here the other day," Frankie burst out, desperate to prevent the woman from locking them out again. "It has my driver's license in it and I need to catch my flight."

Dee studied Frankie's face, then nodded.

"Oh yes, I remember you," she said. "You're from Florida."

"Right, and I gave you my license, but you never handed it back."

The woman frowned.

"I certainly did," she protested. "You stuck it back in your wallet."

Frankie's heart sank at her words.

"But then you left your wallet on the reception desk."

A glimmer of hope kindled in his chest.

"Great, can you get it for me? I need to get to the airport."

Pursing her lips, Dee shook her head.

"We don't run a lost and found operation," she informed him. "But we did you the favor of mailing your wallet back to the address on your license. You should receive it in the next few days."

"But I need my wallet to get home, or I won't be there to receive it," he sputtered, knowing it was pointless to argue.

Dee shrugged her small shoulders and moved to shut the door. Then she hesitated and looked over Frankie's shoulder to where Tom was standing.

"Your ma has her physical therapy first thing this morning, Tom, so she won't be ready for visitors until later this afternoon."

Closing the door, she turned away and disappeared from view.

"Looks like we're both out of luck," Tom said, darting a glance at Frankie. "What're you gonna do?"

"I don't know," Frankie admitted in a hollow voice. "I guess I'll ask Hunter to drive me back. It's only about a thousand miles."

Tom scratched his chin again.

"Is Hunter that guy you were with yesterday? The reporter?"

Frankie nodded, too depressed to speak.

"Ma told me y'all came here to see her," Tom said, meeting Frankie's tired eyes with his own. "She said you were nice."

It seemed to Frankie that months had passed instead of days since he and Hunter brought Veronica and Skylar to meet Harriet Locke.

He hadn't been a suspect in a homicide then, and he'd been sober. And more importantly, Peyton had been well. The world had been a different place. Now it was dark and uncertain.

"I guess I could take you to Florida on one of the charter planes if you wanted." Tom sounded tentative. "Where'd you say you live?"

"Willow Bay," Frankie stammered. "You can fly me down there...just like that? Won't it cost a fortune?"

Hope again ignited in his chest.

"I can use the Cessna that came back late last night," Tom said, sounding surer. "I'll figure out something to tell Beau and Curtis."

Frankie hesitated, wondering what he would tell Hunter. Would the reporter disapprove of him taking Tom up on his offer?

He might consider it a conflict of interest and try to stop me. After all, Tom Locke is still technically a subject in our investigation.

Pushing the worry to the back of his mind, Frankie focused on the only thing that mattered at the moment.

I have to get back to Peyton. I can't fail her like I failed Franny. I can't get back to Willow Bay too late to say goodbye.

CHAPTER THIRTY-FIVE

Hunter called Frankie's room again, but there was still no answer. He stuck his phone in his pocket and felt around for the key fob for the rental car. Realizing the key wasn't in his pocket, he looked around on the little table by the window where he'd dropped his receipt and change from the night before, but the fob wasn't there.

Crossing to the window, Hunter looked down into the parking lot, already suspecting the blue Nissan would be gone. The empty space confirmed his fears.

He hurried downstairs to the lobby, calling Frankie's phone again as he went, but this time the call went straight to voicemail.

"Call me back, Frankie," Hunter said, trying to decide what to do next. "I promise we'll think of a way to get you home."

Ending the call, Hunter stepped off the elevator, wondering if he should take an Uber to the airport. Maybe Frankie was trying to get on an early flight.

"Mr. Hadley, I need to speak to you."

Hunter turned to see Sheriff Holt standing by the front desk. The man's hat was askew, and his face was suffused with anger.

"It seems your friend has checked out already," Holt fumed, as Hunter approached. "They tell me he left first thing this morning."

The desk clerk spoke up behind the sheriff.

"Mr. Dawson checked out just before seven this morning," she confirmed. "He said something about getting a *flight out of Dodge.*"

The sheriff glared at the clerk, causing the young woman to recoil.

"Did he say where he was going? Was anyone with him?"

Assuming a disapproving frown, the clerk nodded.

"He was with *Tom Locke.*" Her voice was heavy with disdain. "You know, *Donovan Locke's* brother."

She lowered her voice to a whisper as she said the name as if she was saying a dirty word.

"They were in a hurry and were talking about flying somewhere."

Holt's eyes widened, and he swung to face Hunter.

"So, Dawson's skipping town, is he? Why am I not surprised? I ran a background check on him and saw he's served time and–"

"Then you'll also know he was falsely convicted and subsequently exonerated," Hunter snapped back. "And he has no obligation to stay in Sky Lake if he hasn't been charged with a crime."

Hunter's phone buzzed in his pocket, and Holt watched him with suspicious eyes as he read Frankie's text message.

I'm getting a charter flight home. Sorry for taking the rental.

Avoiding Holt's gaze, Hunter tapped in a reply.

Call me now. We need to talk.

But the phone remained silent as Hunter stared down at it, and when he looked up, the sheriff was striding toward the door.

Fearing what Holt might do if he caught up with Frankie, Hunter hurried after him, catching up to the sheriff just as he was getting into his big SUV.

The black Ford Interceptor was parked in the loading zone, and Hunter stepped in front of it and held up his hands.

"Wait, Sheriff Holt," he said, meeting the man's narrowed eyes through the windshield. "Where are you going?"

The sheriff opened his window and leaned his head out.

"I'm going out to Sparks Air Charter," he called. "I'm going to stop your friend before he leaves town. Now get out of my way."

"Frankie hasn't done anything wrong, Sheriff Holt," Hunter said, inching toward the driver's window. "He got some bad news last night and he wants to get home. Just give me a minute to explain."

Keeping his eyes on Hunter, Holt shook his head.

"I don't have a minute to spare," he said. "But if you want to ride along, you can fill me in on the way."

* * *

Holt's stony face didn't soften as Hunter explained why Frankie was desperate to get home. The sheriff just kept his eyes on the road ahead as Hunter waited for a response.

"Sounds like Willow Bay has some serious criminal activity going on," he finally said. "And I don't need you and your friends bringing those kinds of problems up here."

"We didn't bring any problems here," Hunter responded, unable to hide his frustration. "We came here because someone in your town abducted Summer Fairfax and she ended up dead. That same person may be involved in other crimes as well."

Ignoring Hunter's words, Holt continued to drive in silence.

"You can't just pretend that nothing ever happened," Hunter insisted. "The FBI isn't going to just go away."

"I can do what I want in my town," Holt muttered. "The FBI doesn't run things around here."

Hunter stared over at the sheriff in dismay, realizing nothing he'd said had gotten through. The man was in serious denial, and he wasn't willing to listen to reason.

The sign for Sparks Air Charter appeared just past a sprawling maple tree, and Holt slowed the big SUV to turn into the lot.

Hunter caught a flash of blonde hair by the front door. Beau Sparks was waiting for them as they climbed out of the SUV and approached the building.

"I got your message, Sheriff Holt," Beau called out. "But Tom's already gone. He took a Cessna. Didn't tell me or Curtis where he's going or when he'll be back."

Waving the two men into the building, Beau led them back to the hangar and pointed to an empty space past two small planes.

"The Cessna was there late last night when I left, but it was gone when I got in this morning."

"Did Tom file a flight plan?" Holt asked, taking off his hat and wiping his brow. "Can you check that to see where he's headed?"

Beau hesitated, then led them to a computer on the reception desk.

"We aren't required to file flight plans for domestic VFR flights in good weather," he said. "But I am able to track the plane using GPS."

He tapped on the keyboard and pointed to a map on the screen.

"He's heading south. He'll likely avoid controlled airspace," Beau said. "I'd say he's going somewhere in Florida."

"Where could he land around Willow Bay?" Holt asked, shooting Hunter an I-told-you-so look. "That's where he's likely heading."

After more tapping on the keyboard, Beau pointed to a small dot on the map.

"Windy Harbor Airfield is just outside Willow Bay, Florida."

"Okay, we'll let's get going."

Beau raised his eyebrows in confusion.

"What are you talking about, Archer?"

"It's Sheriff Holt to you, Beau," the sheriff muttered. "And one of your employees has helped a suspect in June's death get away."

He held a big finger up to Beau's face.

"Now you're going to fly down there and help me bring him back."

"You want me to fly you down to Willow Bay?"

Banging a big fist on the reception counter, Holt sent a stack of papers fluttering to the floor.

"Hell, yes," Holt growled. "Either that or you can let me fly the plane myself. You know I'm a decent pilot."

Beau looked alarmed at the suggestion.

"You're in no shape to be flying," he said, looking to Hunter for help. "You're upset about June...we all are...but you need to calm down so we can talk this through."

"That's bullshit," Holt responded. "I'm trying to catch the man who killed June and you're going to help me."

The side door to the hangar swung open as Holt was speaking, and a slim man in a Kentucky Wildcats baseball hat stepped inside. His eyes widened as he took in the scene in front of him.

"Curtis, you better talk some sense into your partner," Holt called out. "I need to get down to Willow Bay, Florida as soon as possible, and I need one of your planes to take me there."

Holding up his hands in surrender, Curtis turned to Beau.

"I don't know what's going on here, but if Deputy Holt needs to get down to Florida, I say we take him."

"It's *Sheriff* Holt, not *Deputy*," Holt gritted out. "And now that someone here is talking sense, let's get going."

Beau and Hunter wore matching frowns as Curtis readied one of the planes. Holt climbed on board and settled into a seat in the back.

"I better go with him," Beau said, nodding toward Curtis. "I don't think he should be flying alone with Archer...I mean Sheriff Holt...when he's this upset."

"I'll go, too," Hunter added impulsively, moving toward the plane. "We can fly back up once this is all settled."

Rising from his seat, Holt blocked Hunter from boarding.

"Your free ride stops here, Mr. Hadley," Holt said. "I don't need you interfering in my investigation any further. And if you speak to your buddy, tell him I'm coming for him."

CHAPTER THIRTY-SIX

The mild spring day was picture perfect, and Nessa would have enjoyed the short walk from the police station to the medical examiner's office under different circumstances. But the late night at the crime scene had taken its toll. Everything from her head to her feet ached as she approached the bulky concrete building.

"I thought you'd decided to sleep in," Jankowski teased as she walked into the lobby. "I was about to tell Iris we'd have to start without you."

Jankowski seemed to be in a good mood for once, and Nessa impulsively reached out to him, suddenly glad to have him with her.

"I'm a little tired today," she admitted, resting her hand on his thick arm. "And not in the best frame of mind to view an autopsy."

"Is there such a thing as being in a good frame of mind to watch someone cutting up a dead body?" he asked, raising one eyebrow.

The door to the back opened to reveal Iris Nguyen's petite figure.

"I thought I heard someone talking out here," the medical examiner said, standing back so they could walk through. "Maddie Simpson called in sick today, so Wesley and I are on our own at the moment."

Following Iris back to the autopsy suite, Nessa hoped her stomach would hold up to whatever the medical examiner had planned. She pulled on the protective wear Iris handed her, glad that the voluminous coveralls camouflaged her growing bump.

As she was adjusting her face mask, Nessa felt her phone buzz in her pocket. She wiggled an arm out of the coveralls and slipped her phone out of her pocket.

"Hunter Hadley's calling," she murmured to Jankowski.

"He can wait," the big detective said, his voice clipped and his good mood dimming at the mention of Hunter.

Nessa shot Jankowski a sympathetic look. He was still grieving Gabby's death. And knowing that his ex-wife had been dating Hunter Hadley before she'd been killed hadn't made it any easier for him.

Can't really blame Jankowski for holding a grudge, can I?

Sticking the phone back in her pocket, Nessa forced her eyes and her mind back to the metal table in front of her.

Wesley Knox stood beside Iris, his brawny frame twice her size as he helped her fold the sheet back. Wincing at the sight of Amber Sloan's frizzy brown bangs above her discolored face and bruised swollen neck, Nessa found it hard to believe she was looking at the same woman she'd interviewed only a week before.

Amber hadn't been easy to like. But she'd been sharp, and cunning, and alive.

Now whatever force had animated her was gone. All the anger, and the energy, and the life inside her had drained away, leaving behind only the small, cold figure on the table.

"You can see the bruising around her neck," Iris pointed out. "But the damage wasn't life-threatening."

Using a gloved hand, Wesley lifted Amber's arm.

"Although we observed no external indicators of chronic drug abuse, we did find a needle puncture mark in her upper, left bicep."

Iris gestured toward a small, red wound.

"A hypodermic needle was used to inject drugs into her muscle."

"Do you know what kind of drugs?" Nessa asked, still staring at the puncture mark. "Or do you need to wait for toxicology?"

The medical examiner shook her head.

"I've requested a full blood panel so that we'll know the exact mix of drugs and toxins in her system, but the initial tests reveal a fatally high concentration of fentanyl, along with traces of other opiates."

"So, cause and manner of death are what?" Jankowski asked.

Iris considered the question before responding.

"I'd say manner of death is homicide, based on the neck wounds, location of the body, and absence of the syringe at the scene."

She looked down at Amber and sighed.

"Cause of death will be listed as toxic effects of fentanyl and whatever other drugs or toxins come back on the screening."

Glancing up at Nessa, Iris seemed to hesitate.

"I hate to share bad news, but I have a friend over at Willow Bay General." Iris chose her words carefully. "She told me the WBPD detective they're treating also had fentanyl in her system."

The look of sympathy in the medical examiner's kind brown eyes scared Nessa. She wasn't sure she wanted to hear the rest of whatever Iris was trying to tell her.

"What else did your friend say?" Jankowski asked in a grim voice.

"She said I'd likely have another body on my table very soon," Iris answered reluctantly. "I'm sorry...I just thought you'd want to be prepared."

Nessa dropped her eyes back to the table. This time, instead of seeing Amber's frizzy bangs, she pictured Peyton's dark pixie cut and pale, lifeless face laid out before her.

The disturbing image vanished in a wave of dizziness, and Nessa reached out to grip Jankowski's forearm for support.

"Nessa, you okay?"

Jankowski was instantly alert. He put out a strong hand to steady her and studied her suddenly pallid complexion.

"What's wrong?" he asked in a low, worried voice. "If you're not well you need to tell someone. You can't just try to hide it."

"I'm fine," she insisted, willing her dizziness to pass. "I just need some fresh air and a drink of water. It was a late night."

Looking to Iris and Wesley, Jankowski reverted to his usual brusque tone.

"I think we're done here. We've got what we need for now."

He kept a hand under Nessa's arm as they walked to the outer room and removed their protective gear. He was quiet until they'd made their way back into the lobby.

"I don't know what's going on," he said, stopping to meet her eyes. "But whatever it is, you need to put your health, and the baby's health first."

Nessa shook his hand off and turned away.

"The department will survive without you for a little while," Jankowski said, not ready to let the matter go. "Don't make the mistake I made. Don't put the job over the people you love."

Hearing the pain in his voice, Nessa turned to stare into his tortured eyes, then nodded slowly.

He was right. She needed to put her family first.

But the Syndicate was still operating in her community, and they'd most likely sent the man calling himself Mack to kill Amber Sloan and attack Peyton.

The man might have gotten to Misty Bradshaw as well. If he wasn't stopped, he might strike again.

* * *

The fresh air on the walk back to the station seemed to clear Nessa's head, and she decided to give Hunter Hadley a call back before going inside.

She watched Jankowski's broad back disappear into the building as she settled onto a bench and pulled out her phone.

"We've got a major problem," Hunter said, after answering on the first ring. "There's been a homicide in Sky Lake, and-"

"Yes, Agent Day already told me," Nessa interrupted. "She thinks someone connected to Locke might be involved."

"Well, the local sheriff disagrees."

Hunter's usually calm voice was strained.

"Sheriff Holt has decided Frankie Dawson makes a good suspect."

Frowning in surprise, Nessa listened with growing concern as Hunter described the situation up in Sky Lake.

"Once Frankie heard about Peyton being in the hospital, he was determined to leave no matter what Sheriff Holt wanted," Hunter explained. "He talked a local charter company into flying him back to Willow Bay. Now Sheriff Holt is flying down after him in pursuit."

Nessa tried to calm Hunter's concerns.

"Sheriff Holt has no authority here, so there's not really anything he can do to Frankie if he does find him."

Hunter hesitated.

"I'm not so sure Holt will agree with you on that. He seems set on dragging Frankie back to Sky Lake to face further questioning."

"Well, I'll be happy to tell Sheriff Holt that's not the way it works," Nessa replied, already preparing herself for the potential confrontation. "He'll need to work through the proper channels."

Checking her watch, Nessa saw she was already late for her next meeting. She stood and headed toward the station.

"I've gotta go, Hunter. If you hear from Frankie, let me know."

"I'm pretty sure Frankie will go straight to the hospital."

Hunter's words sent a sudden bolt of panic through Nessa, and she stopped and looked down at the phone, remembering what Iris had told her.

What if Peyton dies? What if she's gone before Frankie gets there?

She shuddered at the possibility of having to tell Peyton's family and friends that the detective hadn't made it.

But she couldn't let herself think that way. Not yet. There was still hope, and she still had a job to do.

"Detective Vanzinger is guarding Peyton's hospital room," Nessa said, trying to keep her voice steady. "I'll let him know Frankie might be coming. And I'll make sure he knows Sheriff Holt might show up and try to cause problems."

Her worries about Peyton had darkened Nessa's mood as she stepped into the building, but she didn't have time to sulk as Detective Ramirez called her into the briefing room.

The older man's round face was animated with excitement.

"The state prosecutor says Ivan Sokolov is ready to talk," Ramirez said. "Sokolov says he's got serious dirt to share on Marc Ingram."

"Let me guess, Riley Odell wants to cut time off his sentence to convince him to cooperate?"

The idea of another deal going south after the fiasco with Amber Sloan wasn't appealing, but Ramirez was enthusiastic.

"Come listen to the interview," he coaxed. "Sokolov is no Amber Sloan. He's a professional. If he talks, it'll be legit."

Nessa allowed the detective to lead her down the hall and into the viewing room next to Room 3.

Through the one-way glass, they could see Riley Odell's trim figure sitting across the table from Ivan Sokolov's massive frame. The big man overshadowed his lawyer, Eugene Wexler, who sat beside him, writing notes on a legal pad.

"Tell Riley to ask him about Sky Lake," Nessa murmured.

She was suddenly sure the man who'd worked so closely with Diablo and the Syndicate must know about Locke and his dealings in Sky Lake. It was highly likely he knew Mack, as well.

And now that Amber was no longer in play, Sokolov may be their only link to the man they needed to find before he struck again.

Ramirez turned to leave the room, but Nessa stopped him.

"Scratch that," she said. "I think I'll ask him myself."

Knocking on the interview room door, Nessa opened it and stepped inside. She nodded at Riley, who immediately played along, acting as if she'd been expecting the chief of police to stop by.

"Mr. Sokolov, you're looking well," Nessa said, sliding into the chair beside Riley. "I just wanted to ask you a few questions."

"Chief Ainsley, I have to say you're looking tired," Sokolov replied. "I guess the Syndicate is keeping you busy."

Nessa dropped the smile.

"What do you know about Sky Lake, Kentucky?"

Sokolov's eyes brightened, and he inclined his head.

"Good work, Chief Ainsley. I'm surprised you were able to track down Mack without my help."

"You don't have to answer her questions," Eugene Wexler said. "I advise you not to say anything further. They'll use it against you."

The lawyer pursed his lips in disapproval as if he already knew his client wasn't going to listen to his advice.

"You must have gotten someone else to talk," Sokolov said as if Wexler hadn't spoken. "Maybe someone who ended up on last night's news. Am I right?"

Keeping her face blank, Nessa felt her heart sink. Somehow Ivan Sokolov knew what was going on outside the jail. He knew that Mack was working with the Syndicate and that he was a dangerous man.

The question is, will Sokolov be willing to turn on him.

Nessa looked at Riley, who'd managed to keep her expression neutral, then sighed, and sat back in her chair.

"Okay, so you've got my attention."

Not wanting to waste time playing games, she decided to be blunt.

"You know Mack, and we want to find him. You want to get out of prison before hell freezes over, and Ms. Odell can make that happen."

Riley stiffened beside her as Sokolov laughed.

"It's very simple then."

He raised a big hand to stop Wexler's protest.

"You drop the trafficking charges against me, and I tell your little task force who Mack really is, and where you can find him."

Reaching out to put a warning hand on Nessa's arm, Riley stood and looked down into the big man's amused face.

"I'm sure you're getting hungry, Mr. Sokolov," she said. "We'll take a break and I'll have someone bring you some lunch."

She turned and left the room, pulling Nessa along with her. When the door shut behind them, Riley spun to face Nessa.

"Are you crazy? We can't make that kind of deal with him."

Ramirez emerged from the viewing room as Nessa held up a placating hand. Both the older detective and the state prosecutor stared at Nessa with wide eyes.

"We have a predator who's attacked one of our own," Nessa replied, pushing away her doubts. "Our first priority has to be finding the man who attacked Peyton and bringing him to justice."

"Dropping charges against Sokolov will mean the release of another predator into our community," Riley countered.

A hesitant voice sounded behind Nessa. Andy Ford stood in the hall, his freckled face was flushed, and he seemed agitated.

"There's a Sheriff Archer Holt from Sky Lake, Kentucky in the lobby," the young officer said. "I told him you weren't available, but he's raising quite a fuss."

* * *

"Sheriff Holt? I'm Chief Ainsley, how may I help you?"

Nessa stared at the big man in front of her. Dressed in a tan uniform and thick leather holster, he stood over six-feet tall and looked to be built of solid muscle.

Removing his wide-brimmed hat, Holt lowered his head in greeting. When he spoke, his southern accent was even more pronounced than her own.

"I'm sorry to barge in here, Chief Ainsley, but I need your assistance." He glared at Andy Ford, then looked back to Nessa. "If we could talk in private?"

"I'm in the middle of a homicide investigation, and one of my detectives is fighting for her life in the hospital," Nessa replied, her voice cold. "So, at this particular moment, I don't have the bandwidth to assist any other department. Especially one in another state."

Holt's face hardened.

"There's a man in this town named Frankie Dawson that's a person of interest in a homicide in Sky Lake. All I'm asking is for you to bring him in for questioning. I'll take it from there."

The door to the back opened, and Jankowski stepped out. He crossed to Nessa and cocked his head.

"Everything okay here, Chief?"

"I was just getting ready to explain to Sheriff Holt that Willow Bay is not part of his jurisdiction," Nessa said, keeping her eyes on Holt. "And if he'd like to question someone in the area, he'll need to work through the proper channels."

Moving closer, Jankowski nodded.

"That sounds reasonable to me, Sheriff Holt," the big detective said. "So, if you'll excuse us, we've-"

"I've flown all the way down here to talk to Frankie Dawson," Holt erupted, his voice booming through the lobby. "And I've got a charter flight waiting for us at the Windy Harbor Airfield north of town."

Nessa put out a hand to stop Jankowski from moving any closer to Sheriff Holt. She wasn't about to let a brawl start in her station.

"Unless you've got a warrant for arrest issued by a judge, you have no right to detain Frankie Dawson, or to take him anywhere."

She pointed to the door.

"Now, I suggest you get back on your plane and fly home and let us get on with our investigation."

"I'm leaving," Holt said, backing toward the door. "But you haven't heard the last of me."

As the door closed behind him, Nessa turned to Jankowski.

"We need to find Frankie Dawson."

"Why?" Jankowski asked. "You aren't really going to listen to Holt and bring him in for questioning, are you?"

Nessa sighed and shook her head.

"No, but I want to make sure he gets over to Willow Bay General without any trouble," she said. "I want him to get to Peyton before it's too late."

CHAPTER THIRTY-SEVEN

Peyton drifted in the heavy darkness, listening to the faint voice calling to her. The voice sounded familiar, and she wanted to know where it was coming from, but it seemed so far away, and she was so very tired. It would be so easy to sink back into the cocoon of darkness. So easy to just let go.

But the voice wouldn't let her. It wouldn't go away. Struggling to focus on the deep, soothing sound, she began to make out the words.

"I'm here, Peyton," the voice said, now close to her ear. "It's me, Frankie. You know, the guy that flew a thousand miles to see you."

The image of a man's thin face formed in the darkness, and Peyton strained to reach him, but her limbs were too heavy to move.

Frankie, where are you...where am I?

The words swirled in her head, trapped inside the darkness with her, echoing through her.

"Of course, I'd have come even if it had been a million miles," Frankie murmured. "I'd go around the whole damn world for you."

Peyton willed her eyes to open, but they were glued shut. The effort was too much, and she began to melt into the nothingness around her. Then he spoke again, calling her back.

Concentrating on Frankie's voice, she became aware of heat on her skin. It was his hand on hers. His touch was solid and real; an anchor keeping her from drifting away again.

"I think she can hear me, Barker," Frankie said. "I know she can."

A deeper voice answered Frankie. Pete Barker's frightened eyes floated through her mind, and Peyton saw him aiming a gun at the man behind her. A jolt of fear passed through her, then another voice sounded above her, and the image flickered out.

"I'm sorry, but it's time for her medication."

The heat from Frankie's hand fell away, and Peyton sent out a silent cry, begging him not to go.

"I'll be back soon," Frankie whispered in her ear. "I promise."

Pushing back against the dark, Peyton struggled to open her eyes. She was startled to see a flash of light, and the blur of a white figure bustling around her.

She blinked and tried to focus on the woman's face. It was a nurse. The woman didn't seem to notice she was awake as she held an IV bag up and hung it on a pole next to the bed.

Peyton could see a long tube hanging down, and she followed it with her eyes, seeing that it was attached to her hand. The nurse checked a machine by the bed, then made a few notes on the chart.

Her eyes grew heavy, and Peyton had to close them as the nurse picked up her hand and checked the taping that held the tube in place.

The *squeak, squeak, squeak* of rubber-soled shoes on the tiled floor, and the soft *click* of the door shutting, let Peyton know the nurse had left the room.

But whatever medicine the nurse had administered was dragging Peyton back into the dark, and she'd almost drifted away again when she heard the metallic scrape of the doorknob turning.

Once again forcing her eyes open, Peyton stared toward the door, hoping Frankie and Barker had returned. Instead, she saw a man peer into the room. The man took a furtive look over his shoulder before letting his eyes dart toward her bed.

Memories of the night before came crashing back. The same cold eyes had stared down at her as she'd fallen to the floor at her attacker's feet. He'd wanted her to die, and now he was here in the hospital looking at her with those same hateful eyes.

The surge of fear and adrenaline sent Peyton's heart racing; the machine by her bed began emitting a high-pitched *ping, ping, ping*.

Footsteps sounded in the corridor, and then the nurse was back, followed by Frankie and Barker.

They all stared down at her with eager eyes as she fought to keep her eyes open, desperate to tell them that her attacker was in the hospital. That he'd been outside her room.

But the inexorable pull of the medicine was too strong, and Peyton felt herself sinking back into the darkness.

* * *

"Peyton? Can you hear me?"

A nurse stood over her bed, looking down with an inquisitive smile. The woman's blonde ponytail and blue eyes reminded Peyton of a Barbie doll.

"Hello, I'm Becky," the nurse said, moving closer when she saw that Peyton's eyes were open. "You don't have to talk. It's probably best if you save your strength."

Nodding her head slightly, Peyton saw a flash of movement by the door and looked across the room with frightened eyes.

"You have a visitor if you feel up to it."

Becky gestured toward Veronica Lee, who stood in the corridor.

Peyton nodded again, and Becky waved Veronica inside.

"She needs her rest, so I have to ask that you keep the visit short."

Making sure the call button was close by, the nurse left, and Veronica pulled up a chair by the bed.

"I'm glad you're on the mend," Veronica said, taking a deep breath. "And I just wanted to thank you for trying to find Misty

Bradshaw. I know you went to Amber's place to look for her, and that's where you were attacked."

Peyton stared up at Veronica, suddenly remembering what her attacker had said as she'd tried to fight him off.

"You're even stronger than Misty...she fought back, too."

She closed her eyes against the memory.

That's why Misty Bradshaw disappeared. She was one of his victims.

The thought sent a sharp stab of regret through Peyton.

"You almost lost your life trying to save her," Veronica said as Peyton's mind spun with the realization that Misty was dead.

"He killed...her."

The words came out as a raw whisper, and Veronica stared down at Peyton in surprise.

"Did you say..."

"The man who attacked me...he said he...killed Misty."

Angry tears stung Peyton's eyes as she watched Veronica trying to absorb the fact that Misty was gone. The anger gave her energy. Or maybe the drugs were starting to wear off.

Whatever it was, Peyton was starting to feel stronger, and she lifted a hand and pointed toward the door.

"He was here in the hospital," she said, straining to be heard.

"Who was here?" Veronica asked.

But Peyton's throat tightened, and she began to cough.

Picking up a cup of water, Veronica held it to Peyton's mouth, allowing her to take small sips that felt like heaven on her dry throat.

"Frankie's downstairs," Veronica said, as Peyton drank. "He flew all the way from Sky Lake as soon as he could. And Detective Vanzinger's been guarding your door most of the day."

"No, the man who attacked me," Peyton finally managed to say. "He was here in the hospital. He was right outside my door."

CHAPTER THIRTY-EIGHT

Mack slipped off the elevator and headed straight for the hospital exit. After Frankie Dawson and Pete Barker had come dangerously close to finding him outside Peyton Bell's room earlier, he'd spent the next hour hiding in the empty patient room across the hall.

Expecting to be discovered at any minute by the big red-headed detective standing guard outside, Mack had hovered behind the door of the darkened room, peeking out into the corridor, and waiting for an opportunity to sneak away.

When the elevator doors had opened to reveal a slender woman with long dark hair, Mack had immediately recognized her as the woman he'd seen in Sky Lake. She'd been walking with the girl who looked like Summer. The angel that had come back to Sky Lake after all these years.

He'd listened with rapt attention as the woman checked into the visitor's desk. She'd given her name as Veronica Lee and said she'd come to visit Peyton Bell.

Seeing that the detective on guard was nowhere in sight, Mack had taken the chance to slip away.

He now walked quickly to the white van and climbed inside, trying to piece together what he'd seen. The dark-haired woman must be working with the two private investigators, the local police, and maybe even the FBI.

Taking out his phone, Mack opened his web browser and tapped *Veronica Lee* into the search field. As the results loaded, he scanned the listings.

The woman was a reporter with Channel Ten News. She worked with Hunter Hadley, the pushy male reporter who had been nosing around Sky Lake.

Mack clicked on Veronica's latest report and waited for the video to load. He saw her standing outside Amber Sloan's apartment as police officers and crime scene techs scurried around behind her.

"This is Veronica Lee with Channel Ten News and I'm reporting from the scene of a homicide outside the Fox Hollow Apartments."

Tapping on the screen to stop the video, Mack tried to think.

Why was Veronica Lee visiting Peyton Bell? Had the detective woken up? Is she providing a description of me right now?

Mack imagined a composite drawing of his face displayed on Veronica Lee's next Channel Ten report, and a cold voice spoke in his head, causing his hands to tighten around the steering wheel.

You're not going to be able to get yourself out of this one, are you Mack? But maybe that's for the best. Maybe fate is giving you a sign.

He pictured Veronica Lee walking next to the lovely girl who looked so much like Summer. Maybe the girl could finally be his, the way Summer never had been. She could be his muse, his angel.

Suddenly the voice was back, and it was louder this time.

All you have to do is find her and take her. It's what you were raised to do. It's what your daddy and Donnie would do if they were still alive. It's what fate is telling you to do.

Starting the engine of the white van, Mack looked again at the search results on his phone, scrolling until he saw the address.

It was time to find his angel and fly away.

* * *

The house on Marigold Lane basked in the warm spring sun as Mack drove past. The only movement came from a plump, orange tabby cat curled up in the front window.

Circling around the neighborhood, Mack parked the cargo van a block away and skirted behind the row of houses. He stopped outside the fence that enclosed the backyard and listened.

Someone was humming softly on the other side. The voice was light and feminine, and Mack was suddenly sure the girl was in there, waiting for him. Following the fence around to the gate, he pulled down on the latch and inched it open.

The girl's small figure knelt beside a colorful bed of flowers, as a thick braid of silvery hair hung down her back. Mack's heart began to gallop in his chest at the sight. She was so lovely, and she was right in front of him, waiting to be his.

Lifting a big fist, he knocked on the gate.

"Excuse me, Miss?"

The girl turned to him with wide green eyes.

"Sorry to bother you, but do you own an orange tabby cat?"

Instant concern filled the girl's lovely face, and she nodded.

"Yes, we do. I thought he was inside, but..."

"Well, a cat's been hurt one street over. The neighbor said it might live here, and I thought you'd want to know."

The girl pulled off the gardening gloves she'd been wearing and started toward the house.

"You'd better come quickly, Miss..."

Mack raised his eyebrows as if searching for her name.

"Skylar," she said. "I'm Skylar Lee."

"Okay, Skylar, I can show you where your cat is if you want, but we'd better get going. It's in some pain and..."

Dropping the gloves on the ground, Skylar crossed the yard toward him, and Mack turned and headed back toward the van, adrenaline coursing through his veins as she followed him.

The van sat by the curb, and Mack waved Skylar around to the other side as he slid the cargo door open.

"I put him in here so he wouldn't get run over," he said, leaning into the van's interior and reaching for the syringe.

Skylar looked in after him, a frown creasing the smooth skin of her brow as she saw the empty cargo hold.

"I'm sorry," Mack said, as he put a hand over her mouth and plunged the needle into the soft flesh of her arm. "This will let you sleep. When you wake up, it'll all be over, and we'll be together."

Bundling her small figure into the back of the van, Mack climbed in after her and closed the door behind them.

He held her tightly against him, staring into her disbelieving green eyes until they'd closed. Once her struggles had stopped, he checked to make sure she was still breathing, then climbed into the driver's seat and headed toward Windy Harbor Airfield.

He wouldn't have long before they'd figure out Skylar was gone. He needed to get back to the plane fast. He needed to be up in the air before they tried to stop him.

* * *

Mack waved at the security guard outside the Windy Harbor Airfield, steering the white cargo van past the little security booth without stopping.

The guard was accustomed to seeing Mack come and go from the airfield several times a month. He knew the white van belonged to an anonymous LLC that paid a considerable annual fee for the private use of two hangars, and that the men coming in and out didn't take kindly to questions or interest in their activities.

Pulling the van into one of the hangars, Mack was relieved to see the Cessna parked just where he'd left it. At first glance, there didn't appear to be anyone around.

But as Mack stepped out of the van, he saw Beau Sparks smoking a cigarette outside the hangar. The man's blonde head was turned toward the west, where a small plane had just taken off into the crystal blue sky.

Mack hadn't thought his plan through, and he suddenly panicked, unsure how to get Skylar past the big blonde man unseen.

Moving silently to the rear of the van, Mack put a hand on the hidden holster around his waist, assuring himself that his Ruger was loaded and ready for use if needed.

He still hadn't come up with a plan when Beau threw down his cigarette butt and turned toward the van. Mack ducked down and waited as Beau walked over and looked in the front window.

After a pause, he moved back to the side door and slid it open. Knowing he only had moments to act, Mack pulled out his Ruger and stepped up behind Beau, who was gaping into the back at Skylar's unconscious body.

"Don't make a sound or I'll put a bullet in your gut."

Mack's words startled Beau, and he twisted around with wide eyes, instinctively raising his hands.

"What are you-"

"Shut up," Mack growled, sliding the door closed again, and waving the gun toward the hangar. "Get in the plane."

Beau darted his eyes behind Mack, but there was no one nearby. No one who could get to him in time to stop a bullet.

"Go on," Mack ordered. "And don't try to run. I'd have no problem ending this right here. I should have ended this years ago. Maybe decades."

Urging Beau toward the hangar, Mack checked his watch, knowing he didn't have long. Someone was bound to show up soon, and he needed to be gone before they arrived.

Mack followed Beau onto the Cessna and motioned for him to move toward the rear. He knew what he had to do. He'd been looking forward to this moment for a long time.

"You still don't understand, do you?" he asked, shaking his head in disgust. "You still don't know Summer didn't drown that night. You don't know she left with me."

Confusion mixed with the fear in Beau's face.

"But...why did she leave?"

"She wanted to get away from you," Mack sneered. "She saw you kissing that whore and she wanted to get as far away from you as possible."

Beau shook his head.

"And you...killed her?"

Lifting his arm, Mack pointed the Ruger straight at Beau.

"I would never have hurt Summer," he spit out, fury causing his hand to shake as it gripped the gun. "I took her to Silent Meadows to tell her how I felt, but Donnie was there, and he...he wanted her."

"You mean *Donovan Locke* took Summer, and you didn't stop him?"

Mack nodded, his eyes bitter.

"Donnie always got what he wanted."

"And what about June?" Beau asked, his eyes widening at the sudden suspicion. "Did you ..."

Again, Mack nodded.

"She was gonna tell the FBI agent everything she knew," Mack said., then scoffed. "Even though she didn't know the truth."

Stepping closer to Beau, Mack lifted his chin in defiance.

"June only saw what I wanted her to see," he taunted. "She only saw you on the dock passed out drunk."

"You were there? You saw me?"

Beau's eyes stayed on the Ruger as he spoke.

"I wanted to make it look like Summer drowned, so I put your letter jacket in the boat," Mack admitted. "I knew it would take a few days for them to figure out she wasn't in the lake. It'd give me time to come up with a story."

Mack's voice suddenly sounded amused.

"Then you and June showed up and assumed she'd jumped in."

He shook his head and uttered an ugly laugh.

"As if Summer Fairfax would have killed herself over *you*. Of course, June's idea to write a note saved me a lot of trouble."

Inching even closer, Mack's voice lowered to a deep growl.

"But then she had to go and try to involve the feds. Once they started tearing apart her story, they'd have questioned everyone at the party. Everyone in the area."

Mack's eyes were bright with rage.

"They might even have started snooping around the old house. If they started poking around Silent Meadows, it would be all over."

Looking up from the gun, Beau cleared his throat.

"I thought that old place had been torn down," he said. "I thought your old man lost it along with everything else."

"Don't you talk about my father," Mack hissed.

"You're just like him," Beau insisted. "He was a loser and a crook, and no matter how much you've tried to distance yourself from him, you've always been covered in his disgrace."

With those words Beau charged, lunging toward Mack with sudden speed. He barreled into Mack's outstretched hand just as the gun went off, and his body slumped to the floor with a soft grunt, pulling Mack down with him.

Mack pushed Beau off of him and struggled to his feet. He looked down at the man he'd known since childhood with a pitiless stare, then began to drag the heavy body back to the rear of the cargo hold.

He needed to hurry if he wanted to get Skylar onto the plane before anyone else arrived.

The girl had been injected with just enough of his magic mixture to make her sleep for a few hours, and he wanted to be in the sky and headed home before she woke up.

CHAPTER THIRTY-NINE

Veronica sat next to Detective Vanzinger in the cramped hospital security office staring at the little black and white screen, while Frankie hovered behind them. They were all waiting to view security footage from the camera mounted in the corridor outside Peyton's hospital room.

After Peyton's startling claim that she'd seen her attacker at her door, it had taken a while for Frankie and Vanzinger to track down the proper security personnel, but they'd quickly convinced them to pull the video recorded during the hour before Veronica had arrived.

Just as the video began to play, Veronica's phone buzzed in her pocket. Knowing that Hunter might be trying to call her from Sky Lake, Veronica pulled out her phone.

Ling Li's photo appeared on the display above her number. Veronica was tempted to send the call to voicemail. She could call her mother back once she'd viewed the video and they'd identified Peyton's attacker.

"Don't keep your mom waiting," Frankie said over her shoulder. "It's not a good habit to get into, I should know."

Glancing back at the PI and rolling her eyes, Veronica thumbed *Accept Call* and held the phone to her ear.

"Skylar's gone," Ling cried into the phone. "She's not in the house or the garden, and the back gate's been left open."

"Slow down, Ma," Veronica said, feeling her stomach drop at the thought of her young sister out on her own. "She's probably just gone for a walk or something."

Pushing back the irrational fear that Skylar had been abducted, Veronica forced herself to take a deep breath and keep her tone calm. She didn't want to add to her mother's alarm.

"Hold on and I'll check her location, Ma," she said, pulling out her phone. "She's been wearing my old Apple watch lately, so I should be able to track her on the Find My Phone app."

Veronica tapped on the app and waited for it to load. As she stared at the dots on the map, her eyes widened in disbelief.

"Skylar's at the Windy Harbor Airfield."

Looking back at Frankie, she stared at him with stunned eyes, as her mother's voice erupted on the other end of the line.

"Stay at the house, Ma, in case Skylar comes back," Veronica ordered, talking over her mother. "I'm with Detective Vanzinger now, and we'll figure out what's going on."

She stared over at Vanzinger's grim face as she spoke.

"We'll find her, Ma. Just lock up the house and sit tight. I'll call you back as soon as I know anything."

Vanzinger spoke up as she ended the call.

"Windy Harbor Airfield is where the joint task force was planning an operation to take down a trafficker named Mack," he said. "We think he's based in Sky Lake."

He pulled out his phone as he continued.

"Amber Sloan had become an informant before she was killed, and she was going to set him up. Only we think he got to her first."

"So, you think this guy was the one who attacked Peyton?" Veronica asked with growing dread. "You think he could still be in Willow Bay, and that he could have abducted Skylar?"

Frankie answered before Vanzinger could.

"He's in Willow Bay, and from what we know, he's capable of almost anything." Frankie crossed to the door. "But if Skylar's with him, I bet he's trying to leave town. Trying to get back to Sky Lake."

"Where are you going, Frankie?" Vanzinger asked.

"I'm going to stop him," Frankie called over his shoulder. "Stay here and watch out for Peyton. And let Nessa know what's going on."

Holding up the phone in his hand, Vanzinger nodded.

"I'm calling her now, but..."

The door closed behind Frankie as Veronica turned to Vanzinger.

"Watch the video and find out who was here," she pleaded, backing toward the door. "Whoever he is, he may have Skylar."

Vanzinger held up his hands.

"Now where are you going?" he asked.

"I'm going to drive Frankie to Windy Harbor," she said. "From what I remember, he doesn't have a car."

✳ ✳ ✳

The big red Jeep sped northbound on Old Shepard Highway as Frankie stared down at Veronica's phone with desperate eyes. The app was no longer picking up the signal for the Apple Watch, and the dot on the map was gone.

"Can't you go any faster?' he asked, leaning forward in his seat.

Ignoring his question, Veronica kept her eyes on the road.

"So, you flew into Windy Harbor Airfield this morning?" she asked. "How did you manage that?"

"Tom Locke flew me down here," he admitted. "I guess I should have told you that earlier. He's actually a really nice guy."

Veronica wasn't sure she'd heard him correctly.

"You're telling me you let Donovan Locke's adopted brother fly you from Sky Lake to Willow Bay?"

"He works at an Air Charter company and I needed a way home," Frankie explained, pulling out his phone. "He might still be at the airfield. Maybe he could help us look for Skylar."

Staring over at Frankie, a terrible possibility occurred to her.

"Could Tom Locke be the man who attacked Peyton?" she asked. "Could he be this Mack guy the fed and WBPD are trying to find?"

Frankie shook his head.

"No way," he said in a firm voice. "I mean, Tom's a bit strange, but he's a good guy. He's not the killer type."

Shifting in his seat, he looked down at his phone again.

"Besides, Peyton was attacked last night," he added. "And Tom was in Sky Lake."

Veronica wasn't convinced.

"He flew you down here pretty fast this morning. Who's to say he didn't fly down to Willow Bay yesterday as well."

Digging out his phone, Frankie scrolled to recent calls.

"The guy even gave me his number in case I wanted to keep in touch," he said, tapping on the screen. "Would a killer do that?"

Veronica listened as Frankie waited for Tom to answer. Just as he was pulling his phone away from his ear, a voice sounded on the other end of the connection.

"You back in Sky Lake, already?" Frankie asked.

He darted a look at Veronica as he lifted the phone back to his ear. Whatever Tom said caused Frankie to sit up straight in his seat.

"Sheriff Holt's one crazy dude," Frankie finally responded. "But I need a favor. A girl I know is missing, and we think whoever took her is heading your way. We should be there any minute."

Disconnecting the call, Frankie shook his head and whistled.

"Sheriff Holt from Sky Lake flew down here after me," Frankie said. "The guy thinks I killed some lady up there and he's raising hell down here looking for me. Even threatened to arrest Tom if he took the plane without permission again."

"So, Tom *stole* the plane you guys flew down here?"

Veronica was growing more suspicious by the minute.

"Is he still at the airfield?"

"Yep, and we're about to be there, too," Frankie said. "The turnoff is just up there on the right."

Pulling the red Jeep up to the security booth, Veronica rolled down her window. The security guard put down his copy of the Willow Bay Gazette and looked over at Veronica with a scowl.

"You two know where you're going?"

"We're trying to find my younger sister," Veronica said, pulling out a photo of Skylar. "Have you seen her?"

The guard adjusted his glasses and studied the photo.

"No, I haven't seen her."

He handed the photo back and picked up his paper.

"Do you keep records of who's going in and out of here?' she asked, frustrated by the man's indifferent attitude.

"No, we don't," he said. "We're a private airfield. We don't bother our customers with paperwork. They pay us so they can land and park their planes without the hassles of a commercial airport."

Waving a hand at the guard, Frankie urged Veronica to drive on.

"I think I know where we're going."

He squinted through the windshield, pointing ahead to a row of big, white buildings.

"The hangar where Tom parked the plane is up ahead. He said Sparks Air Charter delivers shipments down here on a regular basis, so they rent out space."

A tall, lanky figure stepped out from one of the hangars as they approached. Veronica recognized him as one of the men she'd seen in the diner the day June Taggert had been killed.

Steering the Jeep toward the hangar, she looked past Tom to see a small plane parked inside, but there was no sign of Skylar.

"Beau left a message saying he brought Sheriff Holt down here in one of the planes," Tom said, as Frankie stepped out of the Jeep. "But now he's not answering my call."

Veronica studied Tom's earnest face as he spoke. He seemed tired, and a little confused. She couldn't imagine him having the energy to abduct anyone.

Catching Veronica's assessing gaze, Tom dropped his eyes.

"I think Beau must have flown back already," he said, directing the words at Frankie. "He probably needed to get home."

"Could Beau have taken Skylar with him?" Veronica asked.

She pictured the men in the Frisky Colt Diner and remembered how the handsome blonde man had stared at Skylar.

"Is that why we can't find her on the app?"

Tom frowned in confusion.

"Who's Skylar?" he asked, looking at Frankie.

Frankie pulled out the photo of Skylar and handed it to Tom.

"Oh, yeah. She's the one who went and visited my Ma," Tom said. "Ma told me she looked a lot like Summer Fairfax."

"She's Summer's daughter." Veronica's words caught in her throat. "And my sister."

Giving a sad nod, Tom handed the photo back to Frankie.

"Ma said both of those poor girls were born too pretty for their own good," he added. "You say Skylar's missing?"

"Yes, she is," Veronica said, feeling the panic starting to rise inside her as the seconds ticked by. "Can you take us to find her? Can you fly us up to Sky Lake?"

CHAPTER FORTY

Nessa stood up and stretched her back, sore from sitting in the little viewing room for the last hour. She and Agent Marlowe had been watching Jankowski and Ramirez question Ivan Sokolov about his connection to Mack, and it had been slow going.

Even Eugene Wexler had finally gotten fed up with Sokolov's games and had slipped out, claiming he was late for court.

"We've been lurking on one of the darknet message boards Locke was using," Jankowski said, turning a laptop toward the big man. "But we know there must be another way for Mack to communicate with the Syndicate."

Sokolov eyed the screen and smiled.

"You need to find the message boards used by the Southern Circuit," Sokolov said. "Mack's a very active member."

"What's the Southern Circuit?" Nessa asked Marlowe.

Leaning back to look up at her, Marlowe shrugged.

"A circuit is just a network of traffickers and suppliers that ship victims from city to city," he said, turning his dark eyes back to the viewing window. "Different circuits operate all over the country. The Southern Circuit operates throughout the southern US."

The casual tone Marlowe used to describe the organized abuse of women around the country turned Nessa's stomach.

"I need some air," she said, opening the viewing room door and stepping out into the hall.

She closed the door behind her and then leaned against the wall with a deep sigh. Her earlier bout with dizziness was gone, but she was still bone tired.

Letting her eyes close, Nessa tried to block the disturbing images that wouldn't leave her alone. Images like Amber Sloan's dead body in the trunk of the Camry, or Misty Bradshaw's scared face as she gave her statement.

When Vanzinger had called Nessa to tell her Peyton had woken up, and that she'd seen her attacker in the hospital. He'd also mentioned that Peyton claimed Misty Bradshaw was another of the man's victims.

"The scumbag confessed to killing Misty while he was attacking Peyton," Vanzinger had told her. "She's pretty torn up about it."

Nessa imagined Veronica Lee would be devastated by Misty's death as well. The reporter had tried so hard to help the young woman, and the WBPD had failed her miserably.

Hearing footsteps approaching, Nessa forced herself to stand tall. No matter how bad things had gotten, she couldn't let her team see her as anything less than strong and capable.

"Chief Ainsley, I've been looking for you," Dave Eddings said, sounding relieved. "Detective Vanzinger has been trying to reach you on your phone. He says it's urgent."

The young officer stared at her expectantly, and she nodded, reaching into her pocket.

"Looks like I left my phone on my desk," she said, suddenly flustered. "Can I borrow yours, Officer Eddings?"

Moments later Nessa was listening with stunned incredulity as Vanzinger told her Skylar had been taken.

"We think Mack must have taken her," Vanzinger said. "And Veronica Lee and Frankie Dawson have tracked her Apple Watch to the Windy Harbor Airfield outside town. They're headed there now."

"The same airfield Amber Sloan told us about?" Nessa asked. "The one Mack had been using to pick up shipments?"

Feeling Dave Eddings' curious eyes on her, Nessa turned her back on him and lowered her voice.

"So, they think he's headed back to Sky Lake with her?"

"That's what they're thinking, but I'm not so sure," Vanzinger said. "If Mack found out Amber Sloan was an informant, he's bound to know she's told us about him. He'll know we'll be watching every airfield or airport near Sky Lake."

Nessa clenched her hand around Eddings' phone. How were they supposed to find a man who had access to an airplane, and who was willing to kill anyone who got in his way?

"I've got to go have a talk with someone, Vanzinger," Nessa said, staring at the door to the interview room. "I'll call you back."

Thrusting the phone back at Eddings, Nessa stepped to the door and flung it open. Both Jankowski and Ramirez turned in surprise.

"I need to talk to Mr. Sokolov," Nessa said. "I think he's trying to sell us a load of crap about Mack, and I'm not buying it."

Sokolov turned to Nessa with a frown.

"You think I'm lying, Chief Ainsley?"

"I think you don't know as much as you pretend to."

She walked to the table and put both hands in front of the big man, leaning forward to stare down into his craggy face, and ignoring the warning looks Jankowski was giving her.

"I think you want a deal, but you don't have much to bargain with," she scoffed. "I think we might as well forget the whole thing."

Shifting in his chair, Sokolov was no longer smiling.

"You want me to prove I can get to Mack?"

"How would you do that?" she asked, trying to sound bored.

Sokolov nodded toward the laptop open on the table.

"Give me access to the laptop, and I'll get you access to the Southern Circuit," he said. "It'll give you a taste of what I can offer."

She looked at Jankowski. The detective hesitated, then he shrugged his broad shoulders and pushed the laptop toward Sokolov.

Moving his thick fingers over the keyboard with surprising speed, Sokolov quickly pulled up the site he'd been looking for and typed in a username and password.

He clicked on several messages, then turned the computer back toward Nessa with a sarcastic smile.

"This is the latest message from Mack on the Southern Circuit's message board," Sokolov said. "He offered fresh prime for top dollar and got a quick buyer. The pick-up happens tonight."

"Say that again in plain English," Nessa snapped. "What does all that mean?"

The door to the interview room opened again, and this time Agent Marlowe walked in, his face creased in a deep frown as he studied the computer screen.

"It means Mack's going to sell a young woman for a lot of money. The exchange is scheduled for tonight, but it doesn't say where."

The words made Nessa's chest tighten.

"Skylar," she said. "He's going to sell Skylar."

✳ ✳ ✳

Nessa let Jankowski drive her Black Dodge Charger on the way out to the Windy Harbor Airfield. She hadn't told him why she wanted him to drive, but her recent dizzy spells had made her hesitant to get behind the wheel.

The security booth appeared to be empty when they finally sped up to the airfield's entrance, and Jankowski rolled the Dodge through the gate without stopping.

Nessa surveyed the collection of white buildings ahead, surprised to see Sheriff Holt disappear into a hangar near the end of the row.

"That's Sheriff Holt from Sky Lake," Nessa said, her tone reflecting her distaste. "He was on a mission to find Frankie earlier. I guess he heard Frankie was headed back here."

Jankowski pointed to his left, where a vehicle was parked at an angle as if the driver had stopped suddenly.

"Is that Veronica Lee's Jeep?"

"It sure looks like it," Nessa said, as Jankowski steered the Charger toward the Jeep. "But I don't see anyone inside."

Peering past the abandoned vehicle, she saw an empty hangar.

"There's nothing in there," she said, looking back to where Holt had disappeared. "Let's see what Sheriff Holt is up to."

Jankowski threw the Charger in reverse and backed up, coming to a stop outside the hangar at the end of the row. Nessa saw that it housed a small Cessna.

As she got out of the car, she saw Holt circling the plane.

"Sheriff Holt!" she called.

Walking toward the hangar, she put her hand on her holster, double-checking to make sure it was still there.

"I'm looking for Frankie Dawson," Holt said, his tone aggressive.

He approached the loading door to the Cessna and wrenched it open before Nessa could protest.

"Who's in here?" he bellowed as he boarded the plane.

A slim man in a baseball cap peered out of the cockpit. He looked sleepy, and he yawned as he regarded Holt.

"Where have you been, Sheriff?" the man asked, not seeming to notice Nessa and Jankowski. "We better get going. Where's Beau?"

"I've been looking for Frankie Dawson and Tom Locke," the Sheriff said. "But it looks like they've flown off again. The other Cessna's gone, and they're nowhere to be found."

Nessa stepped closer to the Cessna and called up to Holt.

"Sheriff Holt, we're looking for a young woman who's gone missing. We have reason to believe she was brought here."

The man in the baseball cap turned to Nessa in surprise.

"There's no one in here but me," he said.

"And who are you?" Jankowski asked, his eyes narrowed.

Holt stepped in front of the man and scowled down at Jankowski.

"This is my pilot, Curtis Webb. He's co-owner of this plane."

"Pleased to meet you," the man called from behind Holt. "I'm Beau Sparks' partner. The only problem is, I can't find Beau."

Looking back at Curtis, Holt seemed to hear him for the first time.

"When's the last time you saw Beau?"

"He got out to smoke a cigarette about an hour ago I guess."

Curtis took off his baseball cap and ran a hand through his hair.

"When he didn't come back, I got out to look for him, but he was gone. I thought maybe Tom had come and taken him out to get some food, but the van's still here, so..."

Nessa turned to see a white van parked just inside the hangar.

"When I find Tom Locke, I'm going to wring his scrawny neck," Holt muttered.

The name vibrated through Nessa as she stared at the van.

"Tom Locke?" she said. "Is he any relation to Donovan Locke?"

The sheriff rolled his eyes.

"He's his brother," Holt said. "Why?"

Meeting Jankowski's eyes, Nessa could see he was thinking the same thing she was.

"Could Tom Locke have taken Skylar in the van and brought her back to the plane?" she asked, trying to think through the possibilities. "Could they be heading back to Sky Lake right now?"

Jankowski shrugged, but Holt seized on her words.

"That must be it," he said. "I never trusted that freak. He and Frankie Dawson must be working together."

Holt spun around to face Curtis.

"We need to get back to Sky Lake now."

"But what about Beau?" Curtis asked, looking out toward the van. "We can't just leave him here."

Waving away his protests, Holt prodded Curtis toward the cockpit.

"We need to go now," he insisted. "They already have a head start. Beau will get a flight back later this afternoon."

Curtis started to open his mouth again, then shrugged.

"I'll go with them," Nessa said, moving toward the plane. "If Skylar is in Sky Lake, I want to be there when they find her."

A big hand settled on Nessa's shoulder.

"You're staying right here," Jankowski said. "There's no way in hell I'm letting you on that plane in your condition."

The stubborn set to Jankowski's jaw convinced Nessa he wasn't going to budge, and she knew he was right. She couldn't put herself and her child in any more danger.

But as she watched the Cessna taxi down the runway, Nessa had a terrible feeling that she'd failed Skylar, and that she'd let a killer slip out of her hands.

CHAPTER FORTY-ONE

Frankie sat as still as possible in the leather seat, listening to the sound of the engine and tensing at each bump or sway of the Cessna. His usual motion sickness had kicked in just after take-off, and it was only getting worse as they flew north toward Kentucky.

Moving his head slowly to look over at Veronica, he saw that her face had also taken on a sickly pallor. Although the jostling of the plane didn't seem to bother her, she was sick with worry for Skylar.

"It's going to be all right," Frankie said, raising his voice to be heard over the sound of the engine and the air outside. "Right now Charlie Day is probably handcuffing Beau or Mack or whatever he's calling himself. Skylar will be waiting for us at Sparks Air Charter when we arrive."

He took a stick of gum from his pocket, unwrapped the foil, and stuck the gum in his mouth, hoping the chewing would help with the pain in his ears.

At least I don't feel like drinking anymore.

The idea of alcohol made his stomach clench, and he concentrated hard on keeping the meager contents inside.

"I don't feel good about this," Veronica said, looking up toward the cockpit to where Tom Locke sat behind the controls. "What if Beau doesn't take her back to Sky Lake? How will we ever find her?"

Twisting her hands nervously on her lap, Veronica glanced again at Tom, her face tight with anxiety.

"Can you ask him how much longer it'll be?"

Frankie hesitated, then nodded, trying to project an air of confidence as he unbuckled his seatbelt and willed himself to stand.

The plane rocked slightly as he got to his feet, and he staggered forward to the cockpit and maneuvered his long frame onto the seat beside Tom. He was careful not to look out the window.

Glancing over at Frankie, Tom smiled and handed him a headset that matched his own. He gestured for Frankie to put it on and showed him how to adjust the microphone.

"You don't like flying, do you?" Tom asked as Frankie perched stiffly in the seat next to him. "No need to worry, though. I've been flying these little planes for years. Just like driving a car for me now, only not as much traffic up here."

Frankie thought ruefully of his newly obtained driver's license, wondering if it was in a mail truck somewhere on its way to his mother's house. He pictured his mother sitting alone on her couch as the carrier dropped the envelope in the mailbox.

If this plane goes down, I'll never even get to use the damn license.

Dismissing the depressing thought, Frankie looked at Tom.

"How long until we get to Sky Lake?"

"We're almost there," Tom assured him. "I just hope Sheriff Holt isn't there to meet us. I've never been arrested before. I don't think I'd like prison."

Although Frankie didn't want to encounter Holt's rage either, the possibility that the irate sheriff would be waiting for them wasn't his biggest concern. Now that he felt confident Peyton was going to pull through, his biggest worry was for Skylar.

"You think Beau would hurt Skylar?" he asked.

Tom cocked his head, then shrugged.

"I can't really say for sure."

Tom paused, then looked over at Frankie.

"Between you and me, I've suspected something fishy has been going on for a while. I mean, Beau and Curtis are pretty cagey about some of the shipments. But they don't tell me much."

Studying Tom's worn face, Frankie wondered if the man was really as simple and naïve as he seemed.

"You've worked for Beau a long time, huh?"

Tom nodded.

"Yeah, after Donnie had all that trouble, Beau and Curtis were the only ones who were willing to give me a shot," he said. "My ma didn't want me working with 'em, but I didn't have much choice."

Before Frankie could ask what his mother had against Beau and Curtis, Tom motioned ahead.

"We're getting close. We'll be landing in a few minutes."

Frankie staggered back to his seat and leaned toward Veronica.

"He says we'll be landing soon."

Leaning toward the window beside them, Veronica bit her lip.

"I just hope he's taken us to the right place," she said, her voice vibrating along with the plane. "And I hope someone is waiting for us when we get there."

The plane began to descend, and Frankie buckled on his seatbelt and gripped the hand rest, suddenly sure they were going to crash. He closed his eyes and braced for impact, but felt only a hard thump, and then the sound of wheels on the ground.

Minutes later the plane went still, and Frankie opened his eyes.

"Uh, Frankie?"

It was Tom calling back from the cockpit.

"Yeah, Tom?"

"There are some people here to meet us," Tom said, his voice strained. "And it looks like they have guns."

* * *

Special Agent Charlie Day came into the reception area where Frankie Dawson and Tom Locke were being held. The team of FBI agents that had stormed the plane were in the hangar questioning Veronica, who refused to let Hunter Hadley leave her side.

"So, you guys gonna go find out who really took Skylar and stop wasting time with us?" Frankie asked. "We told you that Beau Sparks was in a different plane and that he's the one who has Skylar."

"There's only one problem with that theory, Mr. Dawson," Charlie said. "There's no sign of another plane anywhere. Not in the air, and not on the ground here or in Willow Bay."

Charlie didn't wait for Frankie's reaction. Instead, she approached Tom and stared down at him, taking in his rumpled clothes and tangled hair with an impassive gaze.

"Sheriff Holt and Chief Ainsley both called me and said they believe you may have abducted a young woman from her home in Willow Bay," Charlie said. "But we haven't found anything that would lead us to believe anyone else was on the plane."

"I never took *any* woman," Tom insisted, his eyes wide with shock. "After everything Donnie did, I know better than that."

Footsteps sounded behind Charlie, and Frankie looked up to see Veronica and Hunter approaching.

"Detective Vanzinger called," Veronica said, her voice shaking. "They've reviewed the footage from the hospital security camera, and Peyton was able to identify the man who attacked her."

She held the phone out to Frankie. Squinting down at the grainy image on the little screen, Frankie focused on the man's face.

His heart began to thump in his chest as he realized who had been standing outside Peyton's hospital room.

"It's Curtis Webb," Hunter said, his voice hard.

Jumping out of his chair, Tom leaned over Frankie's shoulder and stared down at the phone, then nodded.

"Yep, that's Mack all right," he said. "I'd know him anywhere."

CHAPTER FORTY-TWO

Hunter blinked in surprise at Tom, then looked over at Charlie. The FBI agent had told him all about the mysterious man named Mack who she and Agent Marlowe's task force were tracking down.

The man had been an accomplice of Locke's and he was believed to be a key player in the trafficking organization known as the Syndicate.

"Why call him Mack?" Charlie asked. "Is that his username?"

"Username?" Tom seemed confused. "Mack's just the nickname Curtis had when he was little. He got it from his daddy."

Seeing all eyes on him, Tom dropped his eyes and tried to explain.

"Mr. Webb always bragged that his boy was as tough as a Mack truck," Tom said. "I guess the name kind of stuck. At least until his daddy went to prison. That made Mack...I mean Curtis...real mad."

Charlie considered Tom's words, then cocked her head.

"Do you know of any connection between Curtis Webb and your brother Donovan Locke?" she asked. "Did they know each other?"

Shifting uncomfortably in front of Charlie, Tom nodded.

"Sure, when I was a kid, Mr. Webb and Donnie were in business together. Donnie was over at their place all the time."

Hunter felt Veronica shiver next to him, and he put an arm around her shoulders, pulling her closer.

"And did Curtis also know Summer Fairfax?" Charlie asked.

273

"Oh yeah," Tom said. "He had a crush on Summer like we all did. Only she would never give anyone but Beau the time of day."

The familiar way Tom spoke about Curtis made Hunter uneasy.

"Tom, do you know if Curtis and Donovan Locke worked together to abduct Summer Fairfax?" he asked. "Or did you ever suspect it?"

"I knew Donnie was a bad apple," Tom said, sounding sad. "But I always felt kinda bad for Curtis after Ma told me Mr. Webb had gone to jail. She said he died in disgrace."

Hunter tried again.

"So, you didn't suspect he had hurt Summer?"

"Oh, no. I would've told Sheriff Duffy if I thought that."

Studying Tom's red-rimmed, tired eyes, Hunter decided he was telling the truth.

As much as he wished Tom could tell them what Mack had done, and where he could be, it was clear that Curtis Webb had hidden his illicit activities from his employee.

Curtis had likely known Tom long enough to feel confident he wasn't the type to question the charter company's activities or to raise any suspicions to the authorities.

Hunter met Charlie's disappointed eyes. He had the feeling she was thinking along the same line he was.

We're wasting our time. Tom Locke doesn't have any useful information to help us track down Curtis Webb and Skylar.

Moving past Tom with a resigned sigh, Hunter crossed to the reception counter and studied the screen.

"Beau was able to track the airplane Tom was in using GPS."

He looked back at Charlie with hopeful eyes.

"So, there must be a way to track the plane Curtis is on as well."

Charlie called over to one of the FBI agents in the hangar, and within minutes the man had pulled up a GPS tracking system and map on the computer.

Two dots flashed on the map as Hunter and Veronica crowded in beside Charlie to see the screen.

Hunter's hopeful gaze dimmed as he saw that both dots were flashing over Sparks Air Charter. He turned to the two planes parked in the hangar. A third space at the end was empty.

The agent clicked on the program settings and checked the configuration. Finally, he turned to Charlie.

"Looks like the system they are using is configured to track three planes," he said. "Specially designed GPS devices have been installed on each of the planes, but it looks like one of the devices has been disabled."

"What do you mean by disabled?" Charlie asked. "Is it something you can fix?"

Stepping back from the computer, the agent shook his head.

"Most likely the device has been physically damaged or removed from the plane altogether," he said. "There's nothing I can do."

"There's got to be another way to track the plane."

Hunter wasn't ready to just give up.

"Doesn't the FBI have a tracking system, or is that the military?"

Charlie raised an eyebrow.

"Slow down, Mr. Hadley," she cautioned. "It's not that simple."

For once Charlie seemed flustered.

"There is an extensive radar network used to track planes that may be carrying drugs," she admitted. "But it's operated by Border Patrol and Customs, not the FBI, and that would take time."

Feeling Veronica step away, Hunter turned to see her approach Tom. She lifted a hand and rested it on his arm.

"Tom, I really need your help."

She stared up at the man's startled face, her eyes bright with pain.

"If you have any idea where Curtis could have taken Skylar, I need you to tell me," she pleaded. "You know him better than anyone. There's got to be somewhere he would go if he were in trouble."

Tom looked into Veronica's sad eyes and nodded.

"I guess he might go back home," he said with a shrug. "That's what I'd do if I was in trouble."

"You mean Curtis would take Skylar to his house?" Charlie asked, coming up behind Veronica. "Where does he live?"

Scratching at his chin, Tom frowned at the question.

"He lives in a house in town, but he won't go there."

He shook his head firmly.

"No, he'll go to the old farm. He'll take her to Silent Meadows."

CHAPTER FORTY-THREE

The ground shifted beneath Skylar, and she heard the sound of rushing wind all around her. She strained to open her eyes, but they were too heavy, so she kept still and tried to remember where she was and what had happened to her.

Winston!

She suddenly remembered that the tabby cat had been hurt. At least that's what the man had said before she'd looked in his van. But Skylar couldn't remember what had happened after that.

A sudden jolt sent her stomach lurching, and she forced her eyes open, unable to accept what her other senses were telling her.

Could I really be on an airplane? Am I flying?

Squinting into a beam of sunlight, she tried to lift a hand to shield her eyes, but her arm wouldn't move.

She looked down and saw both wrists had been strapped to an armrest with some type of packing tape.

Wondering if she was in the middle of a terrible dream, Skylar raised her eyes to the window beside her, blinking against the light of the sun as it continued to sink toward the horizon.

No, this isn't a nightmare. This is real.

She was definitely on a plane, and from the position of the sun to her west, she guessed they were flying north.

A sickening flipflop in her stomach let her know the plane was starting to descend, and she raised her head, ignoring the sharp cramp in her neck as she looked around the cabin.

The seat next to her was empty, but she couldn't be sure what or who was behind her. Looking toward the cockpit, she saw the back of a man's head. He wore a headset over his spiky brown hair, and she recognized the white collared shirt he was wearing.

It's the man I followed back to his van. How could I have been so dumb?

Skylar resisted the urge to call out to the man and ask where he was taking her. Her mouth was cottony dry, and she doubted she'd be able to make a sound in any case, much less get his attention over the sound of the wind and engine.

Looking back to the window, she strained to see the ground below as she felt the plane sink lower and lower in the sky.

Finally, the plane bumped to the ground, and Skylar felt it skip along uneven earth as it sped past a green field and what looked to be a forest of trees in the distance.

Her heart thudded against her ribcage as the plane jerked to a stop, and the man removed his headset and stood up. She was tempted to close her eyes and pretend she was still unconscious, but she found her eyes glued to him in horror as he approached.

"I'm Curtis," he said, sitting in the seat beside her. "Your mother used to call me Mack, but that was just a nickname."

When she just stared at him with wide eyes, he smiled.

"I'm glad you woke up," he said, lifting a hand to caress her braid. "Now you can see the old place before we have to leave."

Skylar tried to speak, but her throat was too dry, and she began to cough. Curtis jumped up and hurried back to the cockpit, returning quickly with a bottle of water.

"I bet you're real thirsty," he said, holding the bottle to her mouth. "Go on, take a sip."

He tipped a few drops into her mouth, then lifted a hand to point out through the window.

"This is the last place I ever saw your mother," he said, his voice quiet. "This is where it all started."

Reaching down to untie her wrists, Curtis didn't seem to notice the way Skylar recoiled at his touch.

"I've never forgotten how she looked that night," he said. "So sad, and so beautiful. I hated to give her to Donnie. It hurt to let her go."

His eyes stayed on Skylar as the sun set outside the window, the last splashes of orange and gold washing over her.

"You're even more beautiful than she was, you know? Or maybe my memory of her has faded."

Fury filled Skylar at the casual way he spoke about her mother.

"My mother suffered because of you," Skylar said, her lips stiff and dry. "She suffered and died because of you and my...my *father.'*

Angry tears filled her eyes and dripped onto her cheeks.

"You don't deserve to have memories of her that I'll never have."

Acting as if he hadn't heard her, he finished unstrapping her wrists and helped her stand up. He waited for her to find her balance, then pulled her after him, leading her off the little plane.

When she was outside on solid ground, Curtis pointed to a two-story farmhouse in the lot ahead. Even at a distance, Skylar could see that it was old and run down.

The house looked forlorn standing alone in the dusk, its weathered walls abandoned and unloved. Skylar could tell it had been a long time since anyone had cared for it, and the thought made her hate the man beside her even more.

Surveying the scraggly forest that lined the property around the old house, Skylar tried to calculate how far she'd have to run to get to the trees if she could somehow break free.

I could hide in there until someone comes to rescue me.

The thought made her wonder if anyone knew she'd been taken.

Does Veronica and Ling Lee know I'm gone yet? Will they come and look for me? Will they know where to find me?'

Taking her by the wrist, Curtis began to walk briskly toward the house. Skylar stumbled after him, trying to stay on her feet as she looked around desperately for a means of escape.

He stopped next to a black wrought iron fence next to a small cemetery. She saw that a weathered sign hung from one rusty nail.

Webb Family Cemetery – Sky Lake, Kentucky.

"This is where my ma is buried, along with my daddy and a whole lot of other relatives I never knew," Curtis announced.

He pulled her behind him, plowing through a clump of overgrown weeds until he stood in the middle of the little graveyard.

"This is where all my demons are buried," he said, then pointed to a headstone engraved with the name Susannah.

"Along with a few angels I couldn't let fly away."

Panic rose in Skylar's chest at the thought of the death that surrounded her, and she yanked against his hand, struggling to break free. But he held on tight as he surveyed the headstones around them.

"But there's one Webb that won't end up in this god-forsaken place," Curtis said in a bitter voice. "I vowed I'd never end up where my waste of a father did."

His grip tightened around her wrist as he spoke.

"I've worked hard to make sure that when the day came for me to leave this place, I could leave in style."

He grinned over at Skylar, and the shadows from the trees overhead deepened his eye sockets, turning him into a leering skeleton. Turning away in horror, Skylar's eyes fell on a long lock of dark hair visible beneath a patch of freshly turned dirt.

These aren't just old graves. This is where he brings his victims.

Swallowing back a terrified scream, Skylar retreated into the safe room inside her mind, leaving the horror of the crumbling headstones behind.

CHAPTER FORTY-FOUR

M ack felt Skylar's arm sag in his grip, and he knew he'd have to get her back on the plane soon. The drugs had worn off, but they'd leave her feeling weak. And although Sheriff Holt would no longer be able to arrest him, the FBI was now on his trail. They'd find him soon enough if he didn't make his escape.

"I just need to collect my little nest egg, and we can be on our way," he muttered, dragging Skylar toward the house. "We'll be free to start a new life together. Just you and me."

Settling Skylar on the porch steps, he noticed that her eyes were vacant. The fear that had lit them up earlier was gone. In fact, there was no emotion in them at all as she stared straight ahead.

He lifted her arm and then let it drop onto her lap. She offered no resistance and remained sitting just as he'd positioned her.

"My magic potion really did a number on you, didn't it?"

He ran a thumb along the smooth curve of her cheekbone as he spoke, happy when she didn't pull away.

"But maybe that's for the best. I've got work to do and it'll make it easier if you just stay put right here."

Circling around to the side of the house, Mack opened the door leading down to the old basement and pulled out a battered wheelbarrow that had seen better days.

He rolled it back toward the Cessna, wincing at the *squeak, squeak, squeak* of its rusty wheel, hoping that it would bear the weight he had planned for it.

The loading door to the plane was still open, and Curtis climbed in and made his way to the cargo hold in the back.

Picking up a thick blue tarp, he stared down at the big bodies he'd dumped on the floor earlier, trying to prepare himself for the hard work that lay ahead.

Both Beau Sparks and Sheriff Holt had been big men. Much bigger than Curtis. And it would be hard to get them unloaded and over to the cemetery for burial.

But there was no way he could take the two dead bodies on the run with him. He didn't want to carry around dead weight on the little plane, and besides, he would need the extra room to store more precious cargo.

Dragging Beau to the side of the plane, he positioned the wheelbarrow under the loading door and tipped him off. Grunting with the effort, he wheeled Beau to the cemetery and dumped him in the weeds, then returned to the plane for Holt.

Holt was bigger and heavier, and by the time he'd made it back to the house, Curtis was trembling and dripping with sweat.

Determined to get the job over with, he grabbed the shovel he'd recently used to bury Darla Griggs and began to dig in a spot where the soil was thin.

He worked steadily until he'd made a shallow grave, then hauled both bodies to the side and shoved them in. Covering the bodies with a thin layer of topsoil, Curtis patted the earth and admired his work.

They won't stay buried like that for long, but it should be long enough for me to get far away from here.

Sitting down on the porch step next to Skylar, Curtis sucked in air, trying to catch his breath. He looked over at the quiet girl, glad to see that the vacant look was still in her eyes.

"I figured this cemetery would be able to handle a few more bodies," he said, stretching the muscles in his back. "Although you must think I'm pretty crazy for doing this."

When Skylar didn't answer, Curtis just shrugged, figuring she could still hear him, even if she didn't respond.

"But all this is not my fault really."

He felt the old resentment building up in his chest again, the way it always did when he thought of his father. William Webb had been the guiding force in his life until the old man had ended up in jail.

After that Curtis had figured out the truth. His father had been a criminal and a loser. But it had been too late.

He'd already learned the family trade, and he'd had to accept that he'd inherited the Webb genes. There had been no going back.

"My father and Donnie were the ones who ruined me. They pretty much forced me into a life of crime."

He clenched his hands into fists, but the men he wanted to punch were already dead and gone.

"Their way of getting by was the only way I ever knew."

Turning to Skylar, Curtis tried to make her understand. If she understood why he did the things he did, she might forgive him. She might even learn to love him.

"After Ma died, not a single woman ever cared about me again," he said, his voice cracking. "I'd hoped Summer might be the one."

He took Skylar's limp hand and caressed it.

"But it wasn't meant to be," he murmured. "I was meant for you."

As the first glow of moonlight fell on Skylar's silvery blonde hair, Mack gazed at her in awe, sure that fate had brought her to him.

"You're my angel," he whispered. "You were sent to save me."

A thud from somewhere nearby jerked him back into reality. His heart started thumping with fear.

I've waited too long. The feds are here. They've finally found me.

Then he remembered they weren't alone on the property. Exhaling deeply, he turned to Skylar.

"I need to go get my nest egg," he said, getting to his feet. "It'll tide us over until I can set up shop somewhere else."

He heard another thud from inside the house, and then a crash.

I need to work on my magic formula. I'm not getting the amounts right.

He looked around the yard, seeing nothing out of place, and turned back to Skylar.

"You wait here," he instructed. "And don't try to run off. The drugs I gave you are potent. You wouldn't get far."

Skylar remained quiet, and he smiled down at her.

"Just a few more chores and we'll be out of here," he promised. "Then we'll be together, forever."

CHAPTER FORTY-FIVE

Veronica sat at the edge of her seat, watching through the front windshield with anxious eyes as the blue Nissan sped down Sky Lake Trail. The darkened road was lit only by the light of the full moon, but Hunter kept his foot dangerously close to the floor.

"Turn left right there," Tom called from his seat in the back next to Charlie Day. "See that little dirt road?"

Hunter made a sharp left turn onto the rutted road. Minutes later the Nissan skidded to a stop in front of a sagging gate. A dented sign reading *Silent Meadows Farm* had been screwed onto the fence post.

Opening his door, Hunter jumped out and pushed the gate back, prompting the old hinges to scream in rusty protest. Climbing back into the Nissan, Hunter drove up to the front of the old farmhouse and shut off the engine.

"This is Curtis Webb's family home?" Veronica asked, her voice betraying her doubt. "It looks abandoned."

"Ma told me it used to be a grand old place," Tom said. "But Mr. Webb kinda let things go after his wife passed."

Charlie leaned forward between the seats.

"Let's wait until my team gets here to go in," she said, checking her phone. "You were going pretty fast, Mr. Hadley. Looks like you lost them back there."

Tom rolled down his window and leaned his head out, letting in a heavy scent of magnolia and decay. A thud sounded somewhere nearby, followed by a muffled scream.

Forgetting Charlie's words of warning, Veronica jumped out of the rental car. Hunter and Tom chased after her, leaving Charlie no choice but to follow behind.

Veronica ducked under the flowering branches of a locust tree and followed the overgrown path leading to the front porch.

"Did that come from inside, or around back?" Hunter whispered.

"I'm not sure," Veronica whispered back. "But I think it came from somewhere upstairs."

Charlie pushed past them to put a hand on the doorknob. To Veronica's surprise, the knob turned smoothly in her hand.

"You all stay outside," the agent ordered, her voice stern. "I'll see if anyone's in here..."

Hunter raised a hand to protest, but Charlie had already stepped into the dark room beyond the rickety door. He turned back to say something to Veronica, then hesitated and put up a finger, as if listening to the sounds of the night around them.

"What was that?"

Turning her head to look toward the side of the house, Veronica heard the faint but unmistakable sound of Skylar humming.

Veronica's heart squeezed in her chest, and she hurried around the side of the house with Hunter close on her heels.

As she rounded the corner, Veronica gasped at the sight of Skylar's hair shining like a beacon in the moonlight.

Her sister knelt over a thicket of wildflowers growing along a black wrought iron fence. She was humming as she picked the wilted flowers and laid them in her lap.

Rushing forward, Veronica tripped over a shattered piece of wood and dropped to her knees. Her eyes fell on a small metal sign.

Webb Family Cemetery.

Hunter bent to help her up as Tom pushed through the gate and headed toward Skylar. But before he could reach her, he suddenly stopped still.

A slim man had stepped out of the shadows and lifted a gun toward Tom's temple. Veronica recognized Curtis Webb.

"This is private property, and y'all are trespassing," Curtis said.

The icy tone of the man's voice sent a chill up Veronica's spine.

"And now that you're here," he said, "I can't let you just leave."

Veronica moved back toward Hunter, who was slowly pulling his cell phone out of his pocket. She assumed he was alerting Charlie Day, and she used her body to block the glow of the phone's display.

"But me and Skylar have gotta go," Curtis said, his voice hard. "We have a whole new life ahead of us."

"You don't want to do this, Mack," Tom said, inching forward. "Now put that down and we can-"

Curtis rammed the muzzle against Tom's head.

"Don't call me that!" he yelled. "I'm Curtis now, and once I fly away from here, there will be no more Mack. I'm leaving that name and everything else my daddy gave me behind."

Tom lifted his hands in supplication.

"Okay, okay, I get it," he said. "But you've got to listen to reason."

"No, what I've got to do is get the hell out of here," Curtis snapped. "And you're going to help me by tying them up."

Nodding to Veronica and Hunter, Curtis nudged Tom with the gun.

"There's some rope in that wheelbarrow," he said. "Now tie 'em up nice and tight or I'll put a bullet in your brain. It'd be a pleasure after putting up with you all these years."

Tom donned a hurt expression, earning a nasty laugh from Curtis.

"Don't tell me you didn't know Donnie made me hire you," he sneered. "Why else would I hire a simpleton?"

Veronica saw Tom lunge toward Curtis just as a shot rang out. Hunter grabbed her and pulled her behind a thick Maple tree.

"Come on out!" Curtis yelled. "Unless you want her to die, too!"

Peering through the bushes, Veronica caught a glimpse of Tom's limp body sprawled on the ground.

Her heart dropped when she saw that Curtis had a thick arm wrapped around Skylar's neck as he rested the gun against the silvery wisps at her temple.

"Skylar!" Veronica couldn't hold back the desperate scream that tore from her lips. "Please, don't hurt her."

"Come out *now*, both of you," Curtis snarled. "Or I'm gonna blow this girl's head off right here and now."

Hunter put a restraining arm on Veronica's shoulder as she made a move to rise. Then a weak voice stopped her.

"You stay right where you are, Ms. Lee."

She saw Tom struggling to sit up.

"He's not gonna hurt Summer's daughter," Tom said, sounding breathless. "He wouldn't hurt his own kin."

Curtis frowned down at Tom, who was now sitting upright as blood streamed from his broken nose.

"You must have broken that stupid head of yours as well as your nose, Tom," Curtis said through clenched teeth. "This girl is no kin of mine."

Tom shook his head, ignoring the drops of blood that splattered onto the ground beside him.

"Your daddy never told you, did he?"

Pity shone in Tom's eyes.

"Your old man was Donnie's real father."

Tom staggered to his feet.

"His *biological* father."

Curtis tightened his arm around Skylar's throat, and he shook his head in denial.

"That's impossible."

"No, it's true," Tom said, his voice firm. "Ma told Donnie he was adopted. Told him on his eighteenth birthday. Said he was old enough to know the truth, and that his real daddy still lived in town."

"You're lying."

"That's the God's honest truth, Mack," Tom said, finally pressing his hand to his nose to stop the blood that had now soaked his shirt.

"Your daddy was Donnie's dad, too."

Veronica could feel Hunter's body tense up beside her in the dark, and she steeled herself, prepared to charge forward as soon as Curtis gave them an opening.

But Tom was still talking, his voice seeming to transfix Curtis.

"Donnie was your half-brother," Tom said. "And that girl there...well, she's Donnie's little girl. She's your kin."

Curtis cocked the gun and stuck it straight out toward Tom.

"You're a liar," he muttered, but doubt had crept into his voice.

Swallowing hard, Curtis took a step back, dragging Skylar with him, his gun trained on Tom's sad face.

"I'm sorry," Tom said. "But you gotta let her go."

Curtis didn't move as Tom stepped forward and took Skylar's hand, pulling her gently toward him. Curtis released Skylar, but her legs gave way and she sank to the ground between the men.

Ignoring the girl at his feet, Curtis raised the gun with both hands, pointing it squarely at Tom's head.

"I won't give her up again," he muttered, his voice flat as his finger tightened on the trigger. "I'll die first and take you with me."

Veronica felt Hunter spring forward just as a shot rang out. She screamed as Hunter tackled Curtis, sending his gun skittering away as they both slammed to the ground.

Racing forward, Veronica kicked the gun into the bushes and turned to Hunter, weak with relief as she saw him lifting himself up and off the ground.

They both looked down at the man sprawled in front of them. Curtis Webb had a nasty red hole in his chest. Blood gurgled out of the wound, staining his white shirt, and dripping into the dirt beneath him.

Footsteps sounded behind them, and Veronica looked up to see Charlie Day holding her Glock toward the ground with a dazed expression on her face.

"Thank you," Veronica said, meeting Charlie's eyes as she hugged Hunter to her. "You showed up just in time."

Charlie looked over Veronica's shoulder at Skylar, who had picked up a shovel and was digging into the dirt with stiff, jerky movements.

"No, honey, don't," Veronica urged, but Skylar just stared down at the dirt, where a pale hand now lay exposed.

"Oh God, no," Veronica cried, stepping back in horror.

Hunter stepped forward, and Tom staggered to his feet and helped him uncover the remains as Veronica stared down into the grave.

"Could that be...Misty Bradshaw?" Veronica asked, feeling sick to her stomach. "Could this be where he brought her?"

But as they wiped the dirt away Veronica saw that the poor woman wore a waitress uniform, along with a Frisky Colt Diner nametag that identified her as Darla Griggs.

"So that's where she went," Tom said quietly. "We all thought she just left town like all the others had done."

Veronica looked around the graveyard with wide eyes, wondering how many other women were buried under the dark soil. But Charlie was calling her and the others to join her on the porch.

"I found a woman upstairs," she said, her voice dry and shaky.

Veronica put her hand to her mouth, not sure she would be able to see another dead body without breaking down.

But then Charlie stepped aside to reveal a young woman huddled in a chair on the porch. Veronica made out big brown eyes and delicate features. She stepped closer and saw the slim hand clutching at a thin blanket. She recognized the tattoo on the girl's wrist. *PS* 23:4.

"It's Misty Bradshaw," Veronica whispered. "She's alive."

"She says he was planning to sell her," Charlie said in a low voice. "He told her she was going to be his last big payday before he left town for good."

Looking around at the house of horrors Curtis Webb and his father had created, Veronica suspected she would be forced to revisit Silent Meadows often in her nightmares.

As she moved toward Skylar, she saw Tom remove his jacket and arrange it over the unearthed remains of Darla Griggs.

Veronica pulled Skylar into her arms and hugged her, expecting her sister to be stiff and unresponsive. Instead, she felt Skylar's soft arms reach up to return the hug.

Veronica leaned back and looked down into Skylar's green eyes, which were so like her own.

"I knew you'd come for me," she said softly. "I didn't know how you'd do it, but I knew you'd find a way."

CHAPTER FORTY-SIX

The crowd outside City Hall was building as it neared noon, and the bright Florida sun had already prompted several men to remove their jackets. Nessa watched Ling Lee mount the steps to the makeshift stage, then looked down in surprise when she felt a fluttering sensation under her jacket.

"The baby's moving," she whispered to Jerry. "I think this little girl is as excited as I am to see things changing around here."

Taking Jerry's hand, she rested it lightly on her stomach, glad he was beside her to witness the swearing-in ceremony for Willow Bay's first woman mayor and relieved that her doctor had given her the all-clear to keep working for the time being.

An elbow jabbed into her other side, and she looked over to see Simon Jankowski struggling to get his jacket off. Although it was still officially spring, the weather was acting as if summer had already started, and the brawny detective was beginning to feel the heat.

She rolled her eyes as he bumped her again, but she was happy to have him with her as well. After everything that had happened in the last month, she was confident Jankowski would be ready to take the helm as acting chief of police when she went out on maternity leave.

Her old partner had mellowed in the last year, and while he still was hot-headed at times, she knew she could trust him with her life, and with her town.

A microphone crackled on the stage, and all eyes turned forward as Judge Eldredge stood at the podium.

"Thank you all for joining us today. As Willow Bay's City Council president, it is a great honor to be asked to perform the swearing-in of our newly elected mayor, Ms. Ling Lee."

The older man's dour expression conflicted with his words, but the crowd erupted into enthusiastic applause, and Nessa couldn't stop smiling as Ling Lee took her place next to the judge.

As Ling Lee raised her right hand and began to repeat the oath that Judge Eldredge recited in a dull, flat voice, Nessa recognized a young woman standing just off-stage.

Misty Bradshaw stood with the rest of Ling's new staff. As an intern in the new mayor's office, the young woman was well on her way to starting a new life.

Thinking of how close the woman had been to a much darker future, Nessa couldn't help but feel profound relief. Despite her mistake of trusting Amber Sloan, Misty had survived, and Nessa knew she had learned a valuable lesson about setting priorities.

And that's a lesson I'm going to have to teach Agent Marlowe as well.

She didn't see the FBI agent in the crowd, although Tenley Frost was sitting on her own near the back.

Perhaps the rumor about those two is just more idle gossip.

As the ceremony came to an end, the Channel Ten camera crew moved forward to capture the moment.

Ling Lee turned to receive congratulations from her daughter, and Veronica Lee looked overjoyed as she gave her mother a hug and posed for the cameras.

Noting that Skylar wasn't on the stage with them, Nessa looked around, wondering if the crowd and festivities had been too much for the girl to handle. She'd been through a terrible ordeal, and Nessa knew it may take a long time for her to heal.

Then she caught a flash of movement on the steps just past the stage and saw Skylar sitting with Finn's big white dog.

The girl's silvery-white hair blended in with the dog's silky coat, and Nessa marveled at the unusual color. She thought of the photo that she'd seen of Summer Fairfax, amazed at the resemblance between the mother and daughter.

Another flutter in her stomach made her look down with a smile and pat her small bump.

I wonder if this little girl will be a redhead like her mother.

Standing and filing out of the row behind Jerry, Nessa saw that Agent Marlowe had watched the swearing-in ceremony from the back of the crowd.

His tall, lean frame towered over a willowy blonde woman in an immaculate suit and heels.

Charlie Day smiled up at Marlowe as he leaned down to whisper something in her ear. Nessa watched them with raised eyebrows.

The intimate way they were talking made Nessa suspect their relationship wasn't strictly professional, and she couldn't deny they made an attractive couple.

Deciding not to interrupt their cozy conversation, Nessa moved past them without a greeting, only to hear Charlie call out to her.

"Chief Ainsley? Could I talk to you for just a minute?"

Jerry looked back, and Nessa hesitated.

"Go on," he said, with a resigned smile. "I'll wait by the car."

Waving for Jankowski to follow her, Nessa crossed to where Charlie and Marlowe were standing.

"We've gotten results from a phone found on Curtis Webb," she said in a low voice, getting straight to the point. "The phone belonged to Amber Sloan. I think you'll be very interested to know whose prints we found on it."

Nessa leaned in, as did Jankowski.

"The prints belong to Marc Ingram. I believe he was a former detective in your force."

Trying to digest the information, Nessa just nodded.

"Well, we have a federal warrant for his arrest," Charlie added. "Just wanted you to know we plan to bring him in later today."

She looked at her watch and smiled.

"The agents should be picking him up right about now."

A matching smile spread across Nessa's face as she walked back to her car. The town had a new mayor, and Marc Ingram was no longer her problem.

Things were looking up in Willow Bay, and even though Nessa knew she was getting heavier by the day, everything else suddenly felt much lighter.

CHAPTER FORTY-SEVEN

Peyton paced the hospital waiting room, wondering if the swearing-in ceremony had gone well. She would have loved to have been at City Hall to support Veronica Lee's mother, but her own mother had been scheduled for surgery, and she'd had to spend the morning in the hospital, waiting to hear the results.

Running a hand through her dark hair, Peyton tried to stay positive, but the feeling that she hadn't done enough to take care of her mother ate away at her.

If only she'd been home more, maybe she would have noticed her mother's deteriorating condition. Maybe they would have detected the new tumors sooner.

Once again, she'd put her job over her family. Remorse rose up in her chest, and the fact that she'd almost gotten herself killed made it all seem even worse.

She winced at the thought of leaving her mother to die on her own.

Leave it up to me to be selfish even in death.

Pushing away a sudden craving for a drink, Peyton wondered where Frankie had gotten to. He'd said he was going to the cafeteria to get them some coffee, and she needed it badly.

Peyton crossed to the door and looked out into the corridor, too scared to leave in case the doctor came out with news about her mother.

Finally, she saw Frankie's lanky frame appear at the end of the corridor. Tucker Vanzinger's red crew cut could be seen bobbing along behind him.

The look on Vanzinger's face was grim, and Peyton hoped he wasn't about to deliver bad news. She had enough to deal with.

"Has the doc come out, yet?" Frankie asked, handing her a steaming cup of coffee. "Any word on how she's doing?"

"No, nothing, yet," Peyton said, looking past Frankie to where Vanzinger stood. "What's going on?"

Vanzinger looked around the waiting room and pointed to an empty row of chairs.

"Let's sit down for a minute," he said. "I know this is terrible timing, but I wanted to tell you before you heard it on the news."

Raising her amber eyes to Frankie, she searched his face, trying to see if he knew what was going on, but he only shook his head and shrugged.

"Nessa just called and told me that Marc Ingram has been taken into federal custody," Vanzinger said. "Agent Day told her they found his prints on Amber Sloan's phone."

He paused, as if unsure how much to say, then took a deep breath.

"Based on what they've found so far, the feds believe Ingram arranged for Curtis Webb to carry out a hit."

"A hit?" she asked, confused. "A hit on who?"

Vanzinger lowered his voice and took a deep breath.

"On you," he said. "Ingram ordered a hit on you."

Shock settled over Peyton at his words. She'd thought the attack at Amber Sloan's apartment had been a terrible accident. She'd assumed she had stumbled in on the killer as he was trying to dispose of Amber's body.

The knowledge that Ingram had wanted her dead, and that he had come very close to getting his wish, crashed over her like a wave.

Feeling Frankie come up beside her, Peyton allowed herself to sink into him for support. Vanzinger remained standing there, staring at her with worried eyes, but she didn't know what to say.

"Ms. Bell?"

A doctor stood behind Frankie. The woman still wore surgical scrubs and a hair cap, but she'd pulled down her mask to speak.

"Yes, that's me. How'd my mother do? Is she okay?"

"Your mother pulled through the surgery without any complications," the doctor confirmed. "She's in recovery now."

Sagging with relief, Peyton managed a weak smile.

"And were you able to get everything out?"

The doctor nodded.

"It looks like we got everything," she assured Peyton. "Now, try to relax, and someone will come to take you back to her shortly."

Frankie waited until the doctor had left, then turned to Peyton and gave her a tight hug. She looked up into his face, seeing his relief, and realized he'd been almost as worried as she had been.

Looking around for Vanzinger, Peyton saw him standing awkwardly by the door. She crossed to him, grateful she finally had a partner she could count on.

"I think I traded up when I swapped Ingram for you," she said, trying to laugh. "At least you haven't tried to kill me."

Relief flooded Vanzinger's face, and he broke into a grin.

"Not that I haven't been tempted on occasion," he teased. "But I think I'll keep you around for a while."

A nurse opened the door and gestured to Peyton, and she started after her, then stopped and turned back to Frankie.

"Come on," she said. "Come with me."

"I think only family is allowed in the back."

Frankie motioned for her to go without him.

"But I'll wait right here for you."

Walking back to take him by the hand, Peyton put a hand on Frankie's stubbly cheek and lifted her face to his.

Holding his gaze, she shook her head and sighed.

"Don't you know, Frankie?" she said softly. "You are family now."

CHAPTER FORTY-EIGHT

Frankie was feeling restless when he left the hospital. Peyton's mother had seemed in good spirits, and she'd been happy to have Frankie in the room with her. But he'd wanted to give the mother and daughter some time alone, so he'd made his excuses and headed back to Barker and Dawson's Investigations

"You missed a great ceremony," Barker said, as Frankie pushed through the front door. "The look on old Eldredge's face was priceless when he was giving Ling Lee the oath."

The image of the grumpy old judge having to swear in Ling Lee as mayor brought a wide smile to Frankie's face.

"I guess he'll miss his old crony," Frankie said. "He and Mayor Hadley had been running things in this town for too long."

"Yeah, it's about time we all move on," Barker agreed.

As Frankie sat down at his desk, Barker cleared his throat.

"And speaking of moving on, my contact at Willow Bay General called and said they're sending over our final payment."

He raised his eyebrows and held out his hands as if expecting a big reaction from Frankie. When Frankie just nodded, Barker shrugged and continued.

"Well, they were very pleased with the way we handled the case," he said. "They think they'll be able to deal with the employees who were involved without creating a scandal."

Frankie thought about Becky Morgan, wondering what would happen to the young woman with the blonde ponytail.

He figured she'd been a victim of Amber Sloan as much as Misty Bradshaw or any other woman she'd preyed upon.

"Aren't you happy?" Barker asked, then a frown creased his forehead. "You didn't get bad news at the hospital, did you? I mean, Peyton's mother is okay, isn't she?"

"Yeah, actually that went really well," Frankie said. "Her mom made it through the surgery without problems."

Barker continued to frown.

"So, what's the problem then?"

Scratching at his chin, Frankie had to admit he wasn't sure.

As happy as he was to be part of Peyton's family, he still felt as if something was missing in his own. Seeing Peyton and her mother together had stirred up feelings he tried to keep buried.

"It's nothing," Frankie said, suddenly standing up. "But I think I need to get going."

"But, you just got here," Barker protested.

"And you just said we've closed out our only open case," Frankie replied. "So, I'm taking the rest of the day off."

Pushing through the door, Frankie strode along the sidewalk, stopping beside the shiny black Mustang he'd recently purchased.

It was the kind of car he'd always wanted as a teenager. The type of car he and Franny would always stare at open-mouthed anytime one drove past their house.

He climbed in the driver's seat and looked in the rearview mirror, wondering if he'd ever be satisfied with the man he saw looking back.

Now that he had the girl, and the job, and the car he'd always wanted, it should be enough.

But somehow, it still doesn't feel right.

Starting the car, Frankie revved the engine, trying to drown out the noise in his head.

Finally, he pulled away from the curb and drove home. He needed to see his mother. It was time to clear the air.

He parked the Mustang in the driveway and stepped out, hearing the blare of the television before he'd made it to the front porch.

Opening the living room door, he saw his mother on the couch, her slippered feet propped on the coffee table as she watched two women arguing in front of a swimming pool.

She didn't look at him until he sank down next to her on the couch and took the remote out of her hands.

He clicked off the television, throwing a blanket of silence over the room, then turned to his mother.

"I'm sorry I failed you, Ma."

He forced himself to look her in the eyes, and was surprised to see how frail she looked, and how tired. When was the last time he'd really looked at her? When had she gotten so old?

"I tried to save Franny, but I couldn't, and...and I'm sorry."

The creases in her forehead deepened at his words.

"All this time, you've been thinking Franny's death was *your* fault?" she asked, blinking back sudden tears.

Frankie nodded, not trusting himself to speak.

"It wasn't your fault, Frankie."

She sat up straight and turned to face him.

"I was Franny's mother, and I should have done something," she said, taking his hand. "If anyone's to blame, it's me."

They locked eyes for the first time in a long time, and Frankie recognized the guilt and the pain written across her face.

He'd seen that same guilt in the rearview mirror earlier, and it was that same pain that kept him reaching for the bottle.

Taking a deep breath, he produced a weary smile.

"I guess Franny wouldn't want us to ruin the rest of our lives feeling like shit, would she?"

"Watch your mouth," his mother scolded. "You may be a grown man, but I can still take a switch to you."

This time when they looked at each other they laughed.

"Do you remember what Franny used to say whenever you gave her a hard time?' Frankie asked, picturing Franny's impish grin.

His mother nodded and rolled her eyes.

"She'd say, give me a break, Ma...God's not finished with me yet."

They both sat there in silence for a long beat, and Frankie felt something hard and bitter between them melting away.

"Well, I think Franny was right," Frankie said, squeezing his mother's hand. "I don't think God hasn't finished with her yet."

He swallowed hard and tried to explain.

"I mean, I sometimes get the feeling that maybe she's up there working to keep us safe," he said. "You know, like a guardian angel watching over us."

His mother nodded and blinked hard a few times.

"You're a real good boy, Frankie. You always have been"

She squeezed his hand and wiped at her eyes.

"Now, give me back my remote."

CHAPTER FORTY-NINE

Hunter Hadley left the crowd behind, walking quickly toward the parking garage while checking his phone messages. He didn't see his father until he bumped into him; he skidded to a stop as his father glared up at him with an angry smile.

"I see you attended the swearing-in with your girlfriend," the ex-mayor said. "I guess you'll be spending more time in City Hall now that there's someone there you actually like."

"I hope you'll enjoy your retirement, Father," Hunter said, knowing his father wouldn't believe him. "It'll give you a chance to relax and focus on new things. Maybe have some fun."

His father scoffed and shook his head.

"Don't pack me off to the retirement home just yet," he said. "Once Ling Lee makes a mess of things, I'll be back."

Pursing his lips, the older man raised his chin defiantly, looking more like a petulant child than a retired politician.

"In the meantime, I have plenty of things to keep me busy."

As his father stalked away, Hunter almost felt sorry for him. It couldn't be easy letting go of your whole identity.

He heard footsteps coming up behind him and turned to see Charlie Day walking along the sidewalk next to Agent Marlowe.

"You interested in some breaking news?" Charlie asked, lifting one perfectly arched brow. "It's bound to come out soon, and I think you and Veronica Lee will be especially interested."

"You've got my attention," Hunter said, forgetting for the moment about the mission he was on. "What's happened?"

Charlie looked over at Agent Marlowe, but he motioned for her to do the honors.

"Federal agents just picked up Marc Ingram," she said in a crisp voice. "A federal warrant for his arrest had been issued based on his suspected role in Amber Sloan's death and Detective Peyton Bell's assault. The evidence is compelling."

"Thanks for the tip," Hunter said, his mind whirring with the news. "Where are you off to now?"

Charlie's smile faded.

"My team's still working on identifying all the women at Locke's ranch," she said. "And now we've also been assigned to the Silent Meadows scene. It's a lot of work."

The thought of having to dig up dead bodies and notify grieving families was sobering. Hunter didn't know how Charlie managed to do it day in and day out and still keep her cool.

"You know I'd love to do a story on your work," Hunter said impulsively. "Or maybe even a series of reports on the cases you've handled, and how you've managed to stay sane through it all."

Marlowe chuckled at the look of alarm that appeared on Charlie's face at Hunter's suggestion.

"Doesn't look like she'd be up for that, Mr. Hadley," he said. "Although I bet she'd look great on camera."

"Well, think about it," Hunter said, taking out his phone. "You've got my number, Agent Day."

As the two agents walked away, Hunter tapped in a text to Finn Jordan and Jack Carson, giving them the information about Marc Ingram and asking them to follow up.

He didn't want to bother Veronica while she was still celebrating with her mother, besides, he had another surprise planned for her and Skylar.

Looking at his watch, Hunter hurried into the garage.

He needed to get to Reggie's office to pick up the surprise before he went to Veronica's house.

After all the terrible surprises the family had endured in the last few months, Hunter had a feeling they were going to love this one.

CHAPTER FIFTY

Veronica was in the kitchen with Ling Lee and Skylar when she heard the doorbell. Setting down the cup she was holding, she dragged Skylar along behind her and threw open the front door, eager to see the surprise Hunter had been promising to deliver.

Looking at Hunter's empty hands, Veronica's face fell with disappointment. She looked past him to where his black Audi sat in the driveway but could see nothing unusual.

"Okay, where is it?" she asked. "You've been bragging about this great surprise all week, and now you show up empty-handed?"

"You've got to guess what it is first," Hunter said with a teasing smile. "I'll give you a hint. It's small and gold and it'll be a constant reminder of my affection."

A nervous ache started up in Veronica's stomach. She couldn't believe Hunter would actually propose to her in the hallway of her house while she was wearing jeans and a t-shirt.

But what if that is exactly what he's doing? What will I say?

"Ronnie! There's something you need to see in the backyard."

Suddenly glad for the reprieve, Veronica raced back down the hall and out to the yard.

Gracie sat on the porch next to Winston. Both animals were watching a small golden retriever trotting around the yard, sniffing at the flowers and exploring the bushes.

"Who is that?" Veronica asked, turning to see that Hunter had followed her outside and that he'd pulled Skylar along with him.

"Her name's Goldie," he said, obviously proud of himself. "Dr. Horn trained her as an ESA, and she wants Skylar to have her."

Skylar watched the little dog prance around the yard, then turned pleading eyes to Veronica.

"Can I keep her, Ronnie?" she asked, then turned to Ling. "Please, can I keep her?"

Ling Lee smiled and nodded.

"Hunter let me in on the secret already," she admitted. "And I think it's a great idea."

Stepping down into the yard, Skylar knelt beside her flower bed and called to Goldie in a sweet, high-pitched voice.

"Come here, Goldie!" she called. "Come here, girl."

"You were right," Veronica said, coming up to put a hand on Hunter's arm. "This was a great surprise."

Hunter pulled her close.

"Well, the credit goes to Dr. Horn," he said.

Ling Lee spoke up behind them, sounding subdued.

"Dr. Horn may be thinking ahead," she said. "She told me that Skylar's been talking about Sky Lake a lot. Dr. Horn thinks it may be cathartic for her to go back for a visit. I'm guessing she wanted her to have Goldie with her for support."

Veronica stared over at her sister. She wasn't sure the girl was up to facing the little town again so soon, and she wasn't so sure she was ready either. But as she watched Skylar smiling down at Goldie, she heard Dr. Horn's voice in her head and thought she may be right.

Sometimes facing your fears is the only way to conquer them.

* * *

Sky Lake Farms and Stables was in bloom as they arrived. Flowering bushes lined the long drive, and several horses were grazing in the pasture beyond the long white barn.

Veronica saw Conrad Fairfax standing in the same spot they'd left him the last time they had visited. He strained to see Skylar as she jumped out of the car, and his face broke into a pleased smile when she rushed toward him, Goldie trotting at her heels.

"I hope you don't mind, but I took the liberty of inviting some other guests to join us today," Conrad said, leading them around the barn toward a patio. "I thought we could all get to know each other a little better."

Walking toward the patio, Veronica was shocked to see Tom Locke and his mother seated at a wide, round table.

"Ms. Lee, it's good to see you," Tom said, standing as they approached. "And I know y'all have already met my Ma."

Veronica greeted Harriet, then turned to see Skylar approaching, her green eyes shy but friendly.

"Come sit next to me, Skylar," Harriet called out. "And introduce me to that puppy of yours."

As Skylar talked with Harriet, Conrad led Veronica and Hunter toward the edge of the patio.

"When I heard that Tom Locke had helped find and save my granddaughter, I decided I'd better meet him and thank him."

Conrad looked over at Tom, who was watching his mother and Skylar with a happy smile.

"He's a nice man," Conrad said. "And he and I have a lot in common. Donavan Locke cast a shadow over both our lives for decades, and we're both trying to start fresh. I've even invested in his new charter company. I think he has a good future."

"I'm glad you and Tom have found each other," Veronica said. "I know Skylar likes him, and she's so eager to have as much family as she can, after all the years she was alone."

Laughing as he watched Goldie take a snack from Skylar's hand, Conrad sighed and shook his head.

"It sure is good to have her here. I was hoping she might come to stay for the summer," he said, turning hopeful eyes to Veronica. "She could learn to ride Sunshine, and Goldie could come, too."

"I think that sounds nice," Veronica said, looking around. "I know her mother wanted her to love this place as much as she did."

Conrad wiped at his eyes and nodded.

"I've been waiting to do something until Skylar was here," he said. "I received Summer's ashes from the FBI, and I wanted to spread them in the lake. It would mean a lot if Skylar was there."

Taking a deep breath, Veronica nodded, knowing it would be hard, but thinking that might give Skylar the closure she needed.

Later, as the sun set over Sky Lake, Conrad and Skylar held up a small, porcelain urn and tipped Summer Fairfax's ashes into the clear, cool water.

"We made it home, Mom," Skylar whispered as she stared into the lake. "We finally made it home."

Turning away, Skylar called to Goldie, who chased a butterfly toward the water's edge, then shook her coat, splashing Skylar with water and prompting a surprised laugh.

The sweet sound hung in the warm air, and Veronica leaned back against Hunter's strong chest, feeling safe and content for the first time in a long time.

If you enjoyed ***Her Silent Spring***,
You won't want to miss the next book in the series:
Her Day to Die: A Veronica Lee Thriller, Book Five

And sign up for the Melinda Woodhall Newsletter to receive upcoming bonus scenes and exclusive insider details at www.melindawoodhall.com/newsletter

ACKNOWLEDGEMENTS

THE TIME AND EFFORT NEEDED TO WRITE A BOOK is always greater than expected, as is the support, patience, and encouragement I get during the process from the loved ones in my life. While writing to schedule can be a challenge, it's always easier when I know my family will be there to support me no matter what.

As I wrote *Her Silent Spring*, I was incredibly lucky to have my loving husband, Giles, and my five fantastic children, Michael, Joey, Linda, Owen, and Juliet to lean on.

I'm also truly grateful to be able to rely on my extended family, including Melissa Romero, Leopoldo Romero, Melanie Arvin, David Woodhall, and Tessa Woodhall.

The positive feedback and support from the readers of my series motivates me every day to keep writing, as do the fond memories I have of my mother sitting in her chair enjoying a good book.

ABOUT THE AUTHOR

Melinda Woodhall is the author of the new *Veronica Lee Thriller* series, as well as the page-turning *Mercy Harbor Thriller* series. In addition to writing romantic thrillers and police procedurals, Melinda also writes women's contemporary fiction as M.M. Arvin.

When she's not writing, Melinda can be found reading, gardening, chauffeuring her children around town, and updating her vegetarian lifestyle website.

Melinda is a native Floridian and the proud mother of five children. She lives with her family in Orlando.

Visit Melinda's website at www.melindawoodhall.com

Other Books by Melinda Woodhall
Her Last Summer
Her Final Fall
Her Winter of Darkness
Her Day to Die
The River Girls
Girl Eight
Catch the Girl

Made in the USA
Columbia, SC
26 September 2024

43153358R00190